March Comes In Like a Lion

Volume 2

Translator:	Jocelyne Allen
Proofreading:	Varrick Robinson
Production:	Glen Isip
	Nicole Dochych
	Risa Cho

SANGATSU NO LION by CHICA UMINO
© Chica Umino 2008
All rights reserved.
First published in Japan in 2008 by HAKUSENSHA, INC., Tokyo.
English language translation rights arranged with HAKUSENSHA, INC., Tokyo
through Tuttle-Mori Agency, Inc., Tokyo.
Published in English by Denpa, LLC., Portland, Oregon, 2023

Originally published in Japanese as *Sangatsu no Lion* by HAKUSENSHA, Inc., 2008
March Comes in Like a Lion, Vol. 2 serialized in Young Animal, HAKUSENSHA, Inc., 2008

This is a work of fiction.

ISBN-13: 978-1-63442-975-7
Library of Congress Control Number: 2022952307
Printed in China

First Edition

Denpa, LLC.
625 NW 17th Ave
Portland, OR 97209
www.denpa.pub

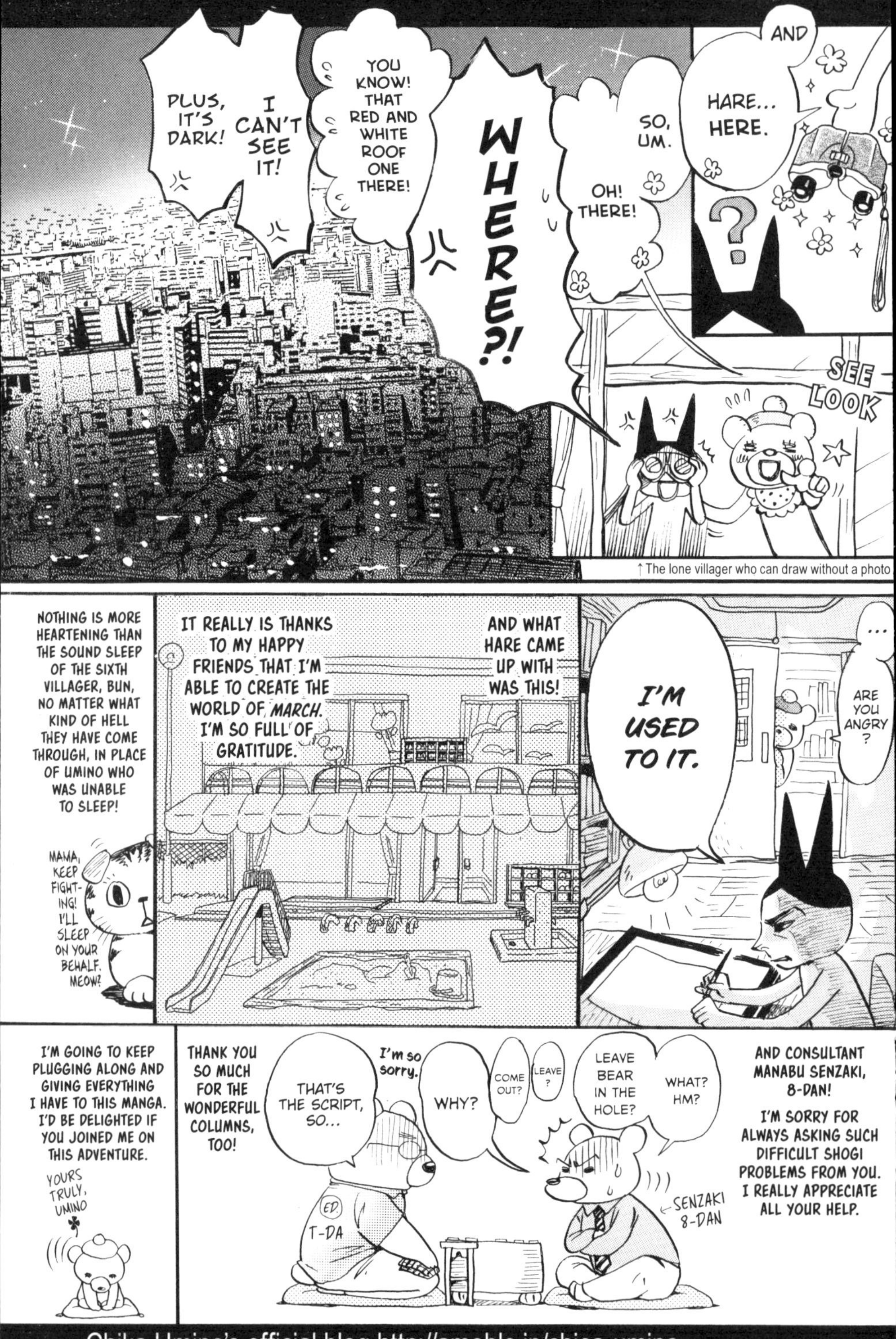
AND
HARE... HERE.
SO, UM.
OH! THERE!
SEE LOOK
WHERE?!
YOU KNOW! THAT RED AND WHITE ROOF ONE THERE!
I CAN'T SEE IT!
PLUS, IT'S DARK!
↑The lone villager who can draw without a photo
...
ARE YOU ANGRY?
I'M USED TO IT.
AND WHAT HARE CAME UP WITH WAS THIS!
IT REALLY IS THANKS TO MY HAPPY FRIENDS THAT I'M ABLE TO CREATE THE WORLD OF *MARCH*. I'M SO FULL OF GRATITUDE.
NOTHING IS MORE HEARTENING THAN THE SOUND SLEEP OF THE SIXTH VILLAGER, BUN, NO MATTER WHAT KIND OF HELL THEY HAVE COME THROUGH, IN PLACE OF UMINO WHO WAS UNABLE TO SLEEP!
MAMA, KEEP FIGHTING! I'LL SLEEP ON YOUR BEHALF. MEOW?
AND CONSULTANT MANABU SENZAKI, 8-DAN!
I'M SORRY FOR ALWAYS ASKING SUCH DIFFICULT SHOGI PROBLEMS FROM YOU. I REALLY APPRECIATE ALL YOUR HELP.
WHAT? HM?
LEAVE BEAR IN THE HOLE?
LEAVE?
COME OUT?
WHY?
I'm so sorry.
THAT'S THE SCRIPT, SO...
← SENZAKI 8-DAN
ED.
T-DA
THANK YOU SO MUCH FOR THE WONDERFUL COLUMNS, TOO!
I'M GOING TO KEEP PLUGGING ALONG AND GIVING EVERYTHING I HAVE TO THIS MANGA. I'D BE DELIGHTED IF YOU JOINED ME ON THIS ADVENTURE.
YOURS TRULY, UMINO

Chika Umino's official blog http://ameblo.jp/chica-umino

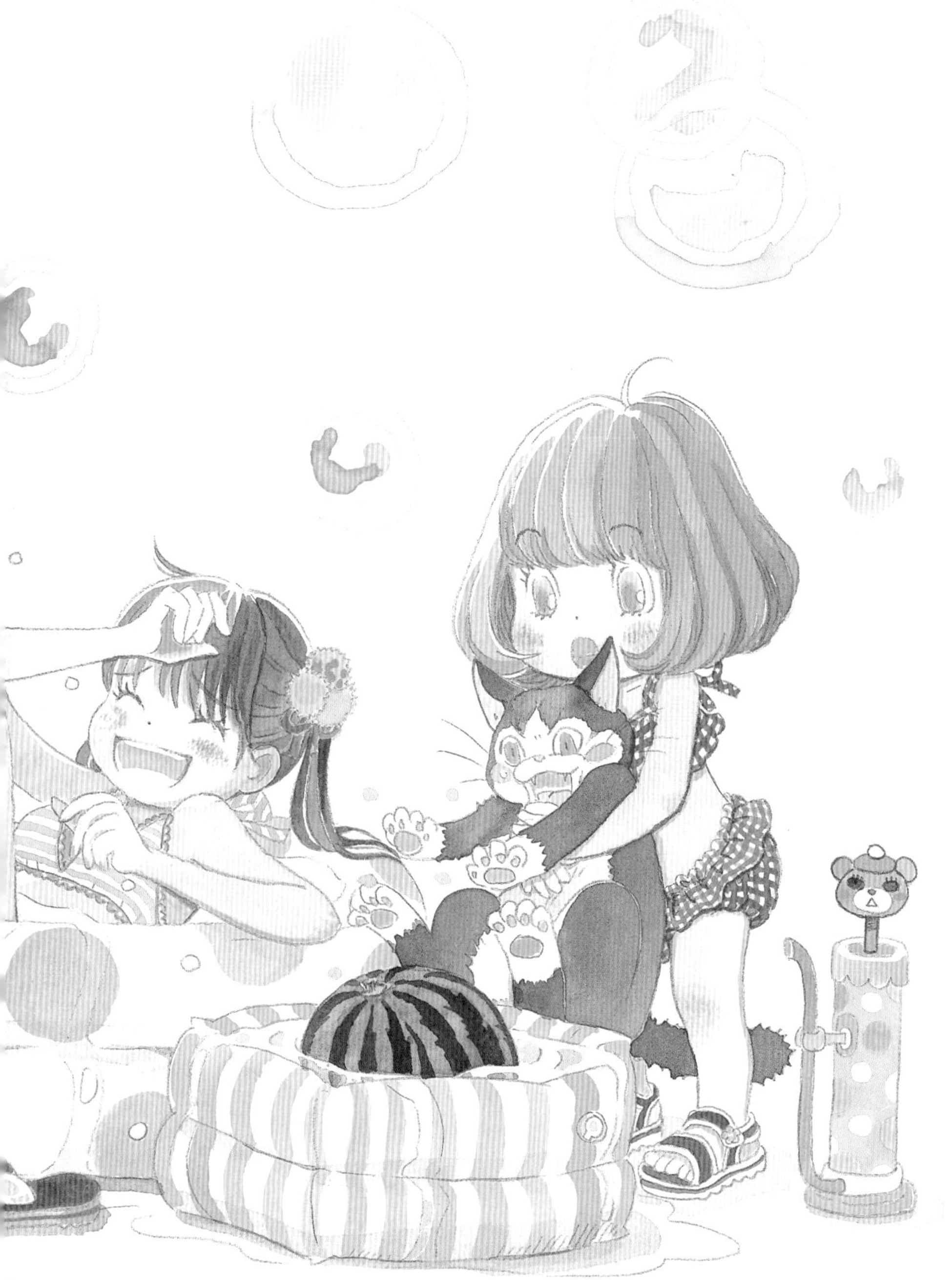

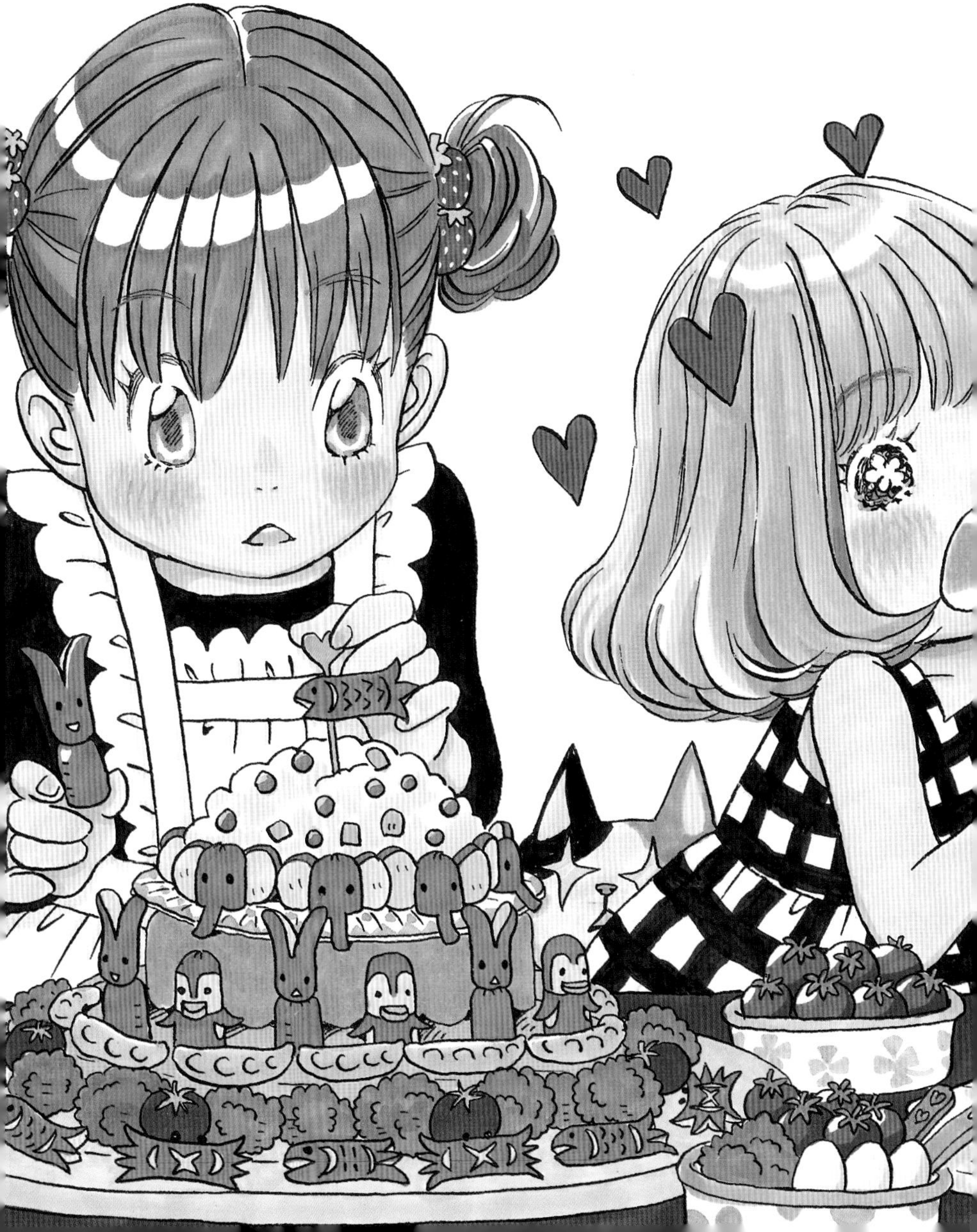

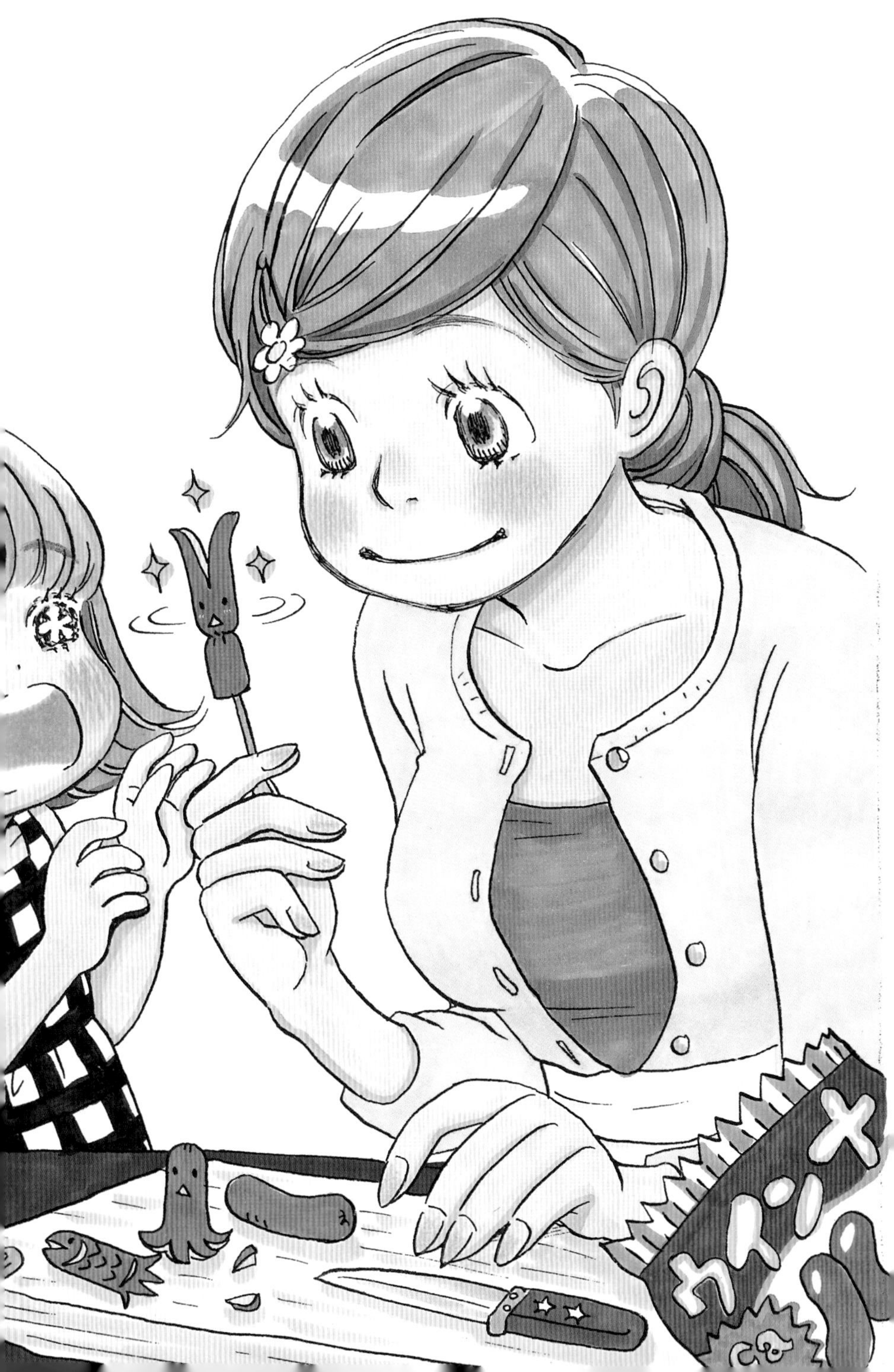

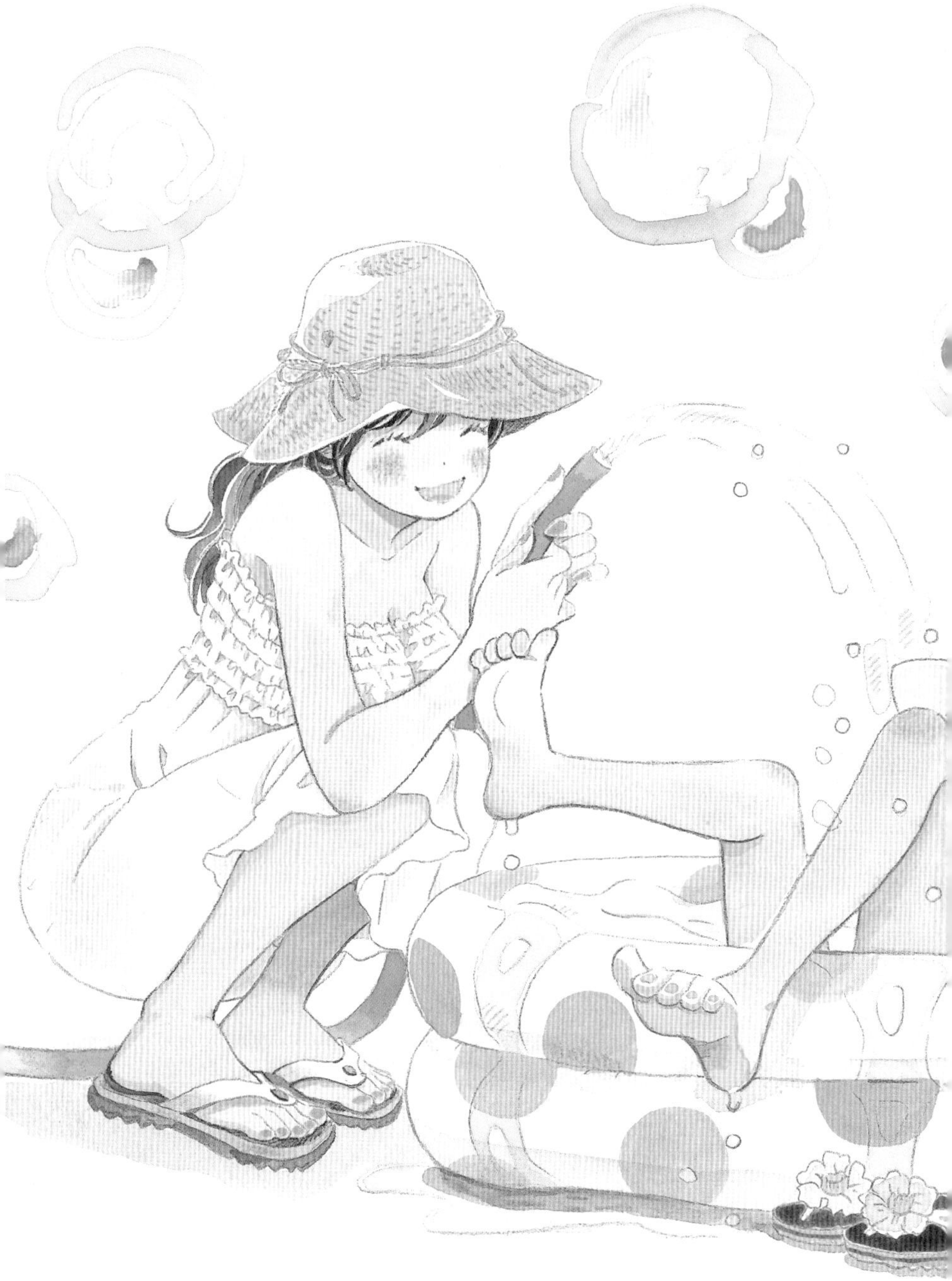

March Comes In Like a Lion

CHICA UMINO

Shogi Consultant: Manabu Senzaki

2

March Comes In Like a Lion ❷ contents

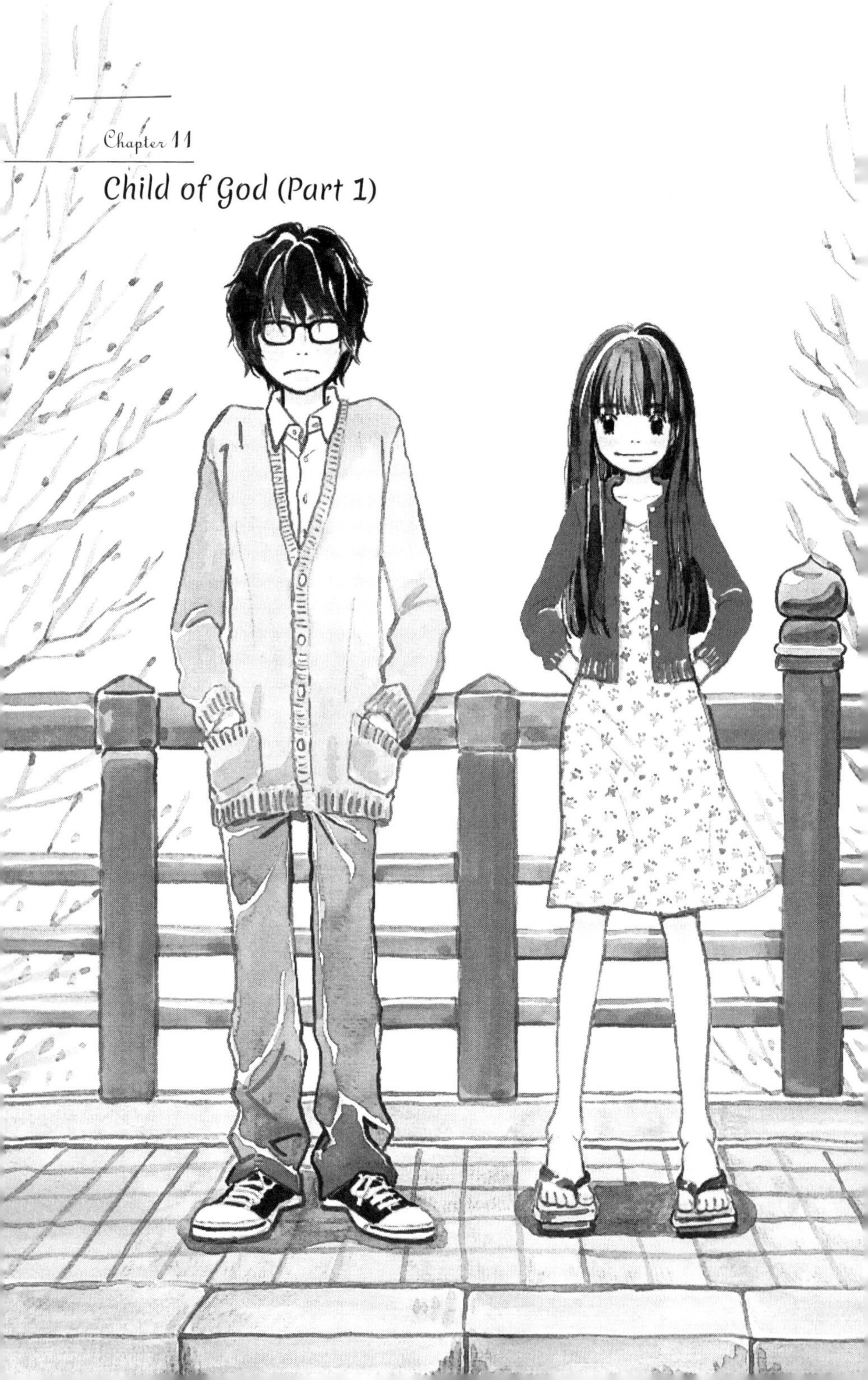
Chapter 11
Child of God (Part 1)

March Comes In Like a Lion

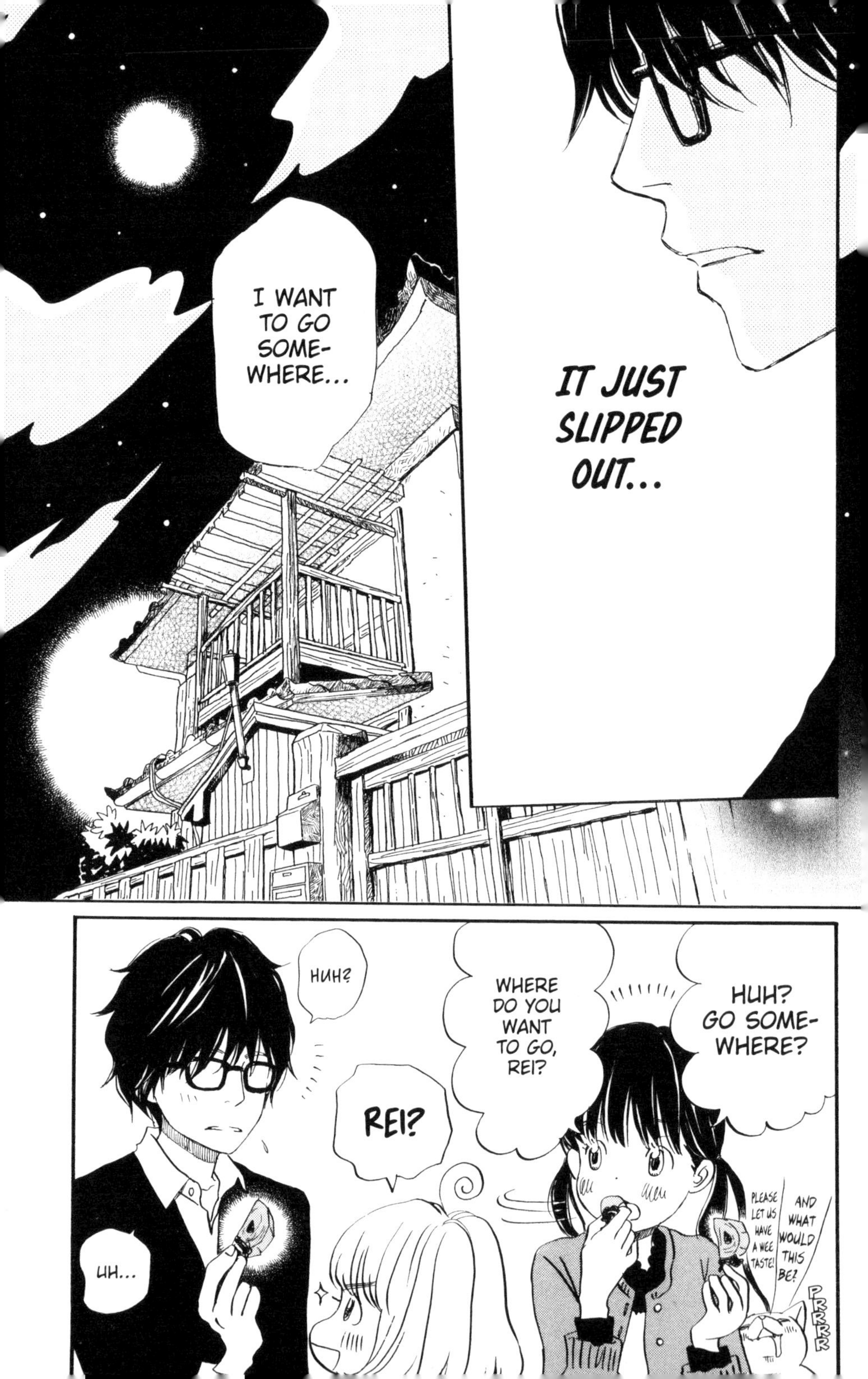
IT JUST SLIPPED OUT...
I WANT TO GO SOME-WHERE...
HUH? GO SOME-WHERE?
WHERE DO YOU WANT TO GO, REI?
HUH?
REI?
AND WHAT WOULD THIS BE?
PLEASE LET US HAVE A WEE TASTE!
PRRRR
UH...

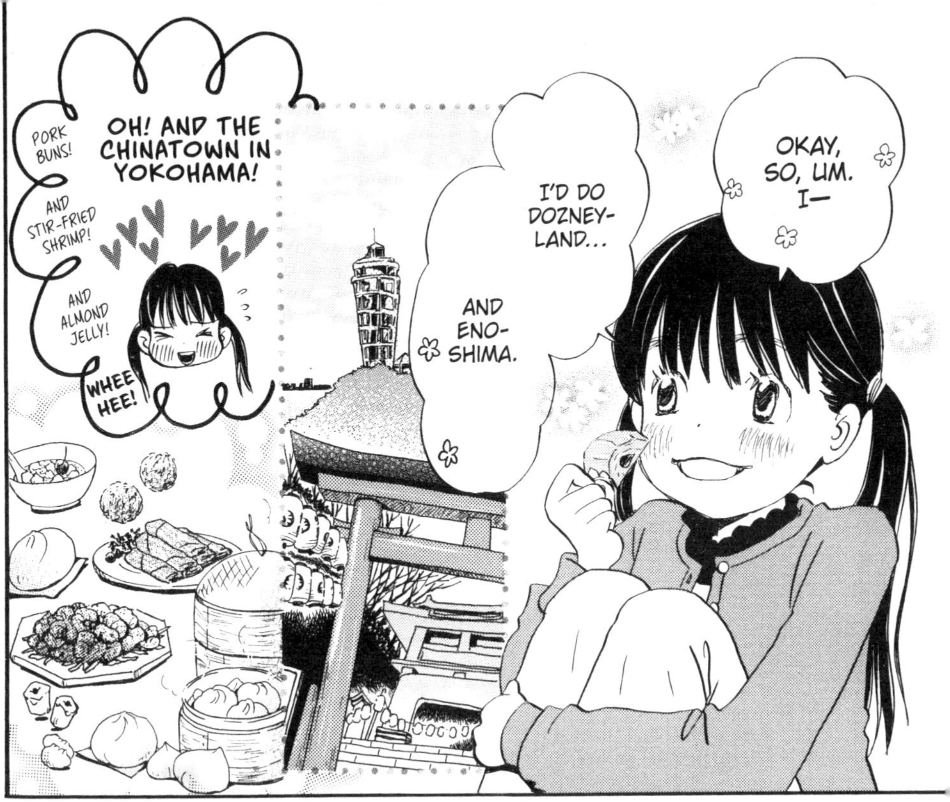
OKAY, SO, UM. I—
I'D DO DOZNEY-LAND...
AND ENO-SHIMA.
OH! AND THE CHINATOWN IN YOKOHAMA!
PORK BUNS!
AND STIR-FRIED SHRIMP!
AND ALMOND JELLY!
WHEE HEE!
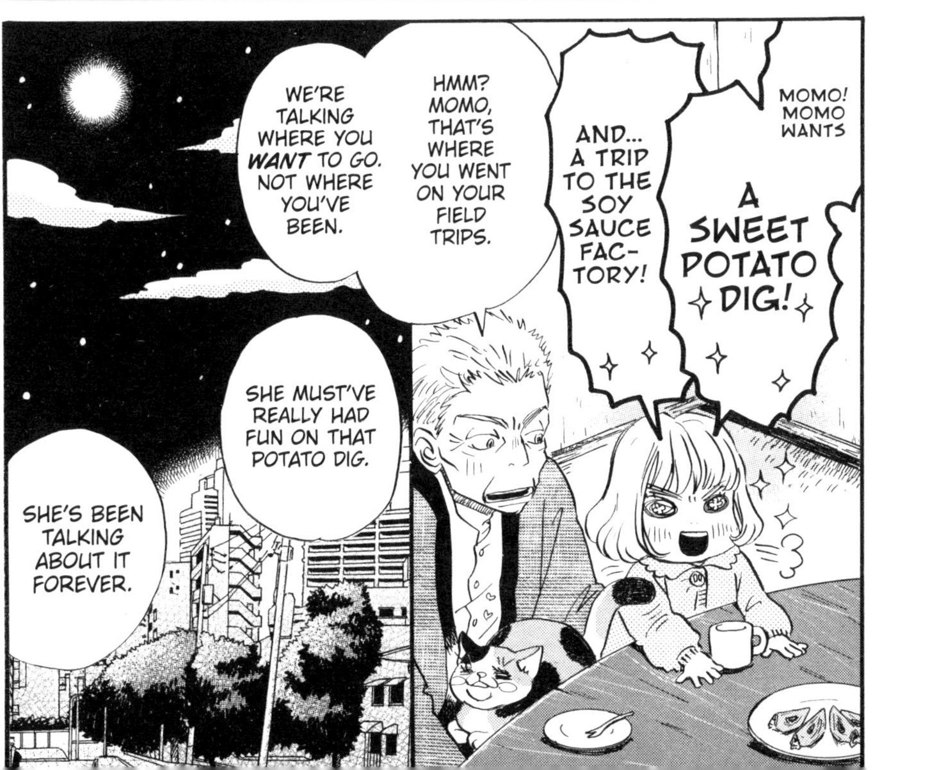
MOMO! MOMO WANTS
A SWEET POTATO DIG!
AND... A TRIP TO THE SOY SAUCE FAC-TORY!
HMM? MOMO, THAT'S WHERE YOU WENT ON YOUR FIELD TRIPS.
WE'RE TALKING WHERE YOU *WANT* TO GO. NOT WHERE YOU'VE BEEN.
SHE MUST'VE REALLY HAD FUN ON THAT POTATO DIG.
SHE'S BEEN TALKING ABOUT IT FOREVER.

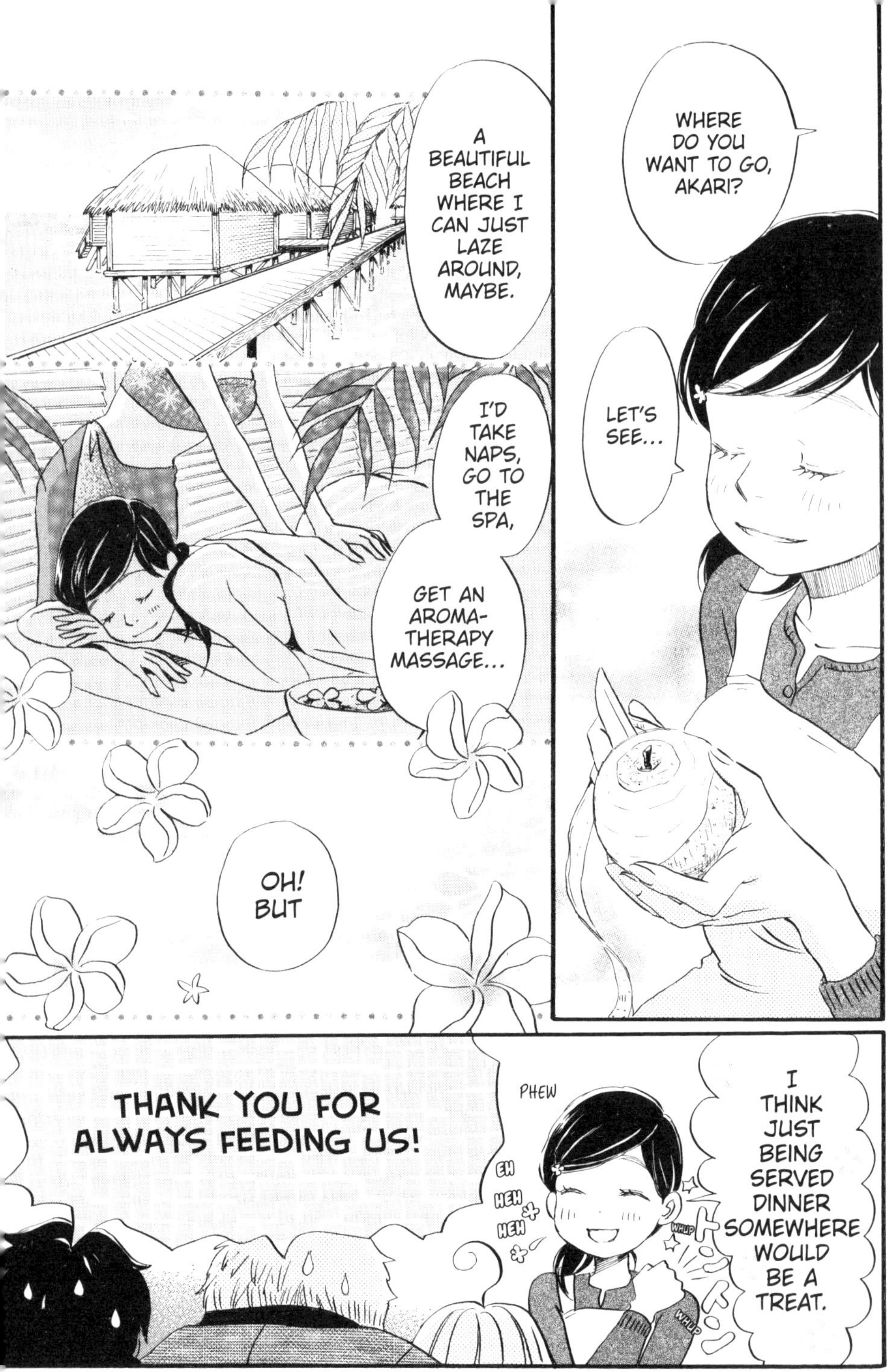
WHERE DO YOU WANT TO GO, AKARI?
LET'S SEE...
A BEAUTIFUL BEACH WHERE I CAN JUST LAZE AROUND, MAYBE.
I'D TAKE NAPS, GO TO THE SPA,
GET AN AROMA-THERAPY MASSAGE...
OH! BUT
I THINK JUST BEING SERVED DINNER SOMEWHERE WOULD BE A TREAT.
WHUP
WHUP
EH HEH HEH
PHEW
THANK YOU FOR ALWAYS FEEDING US!

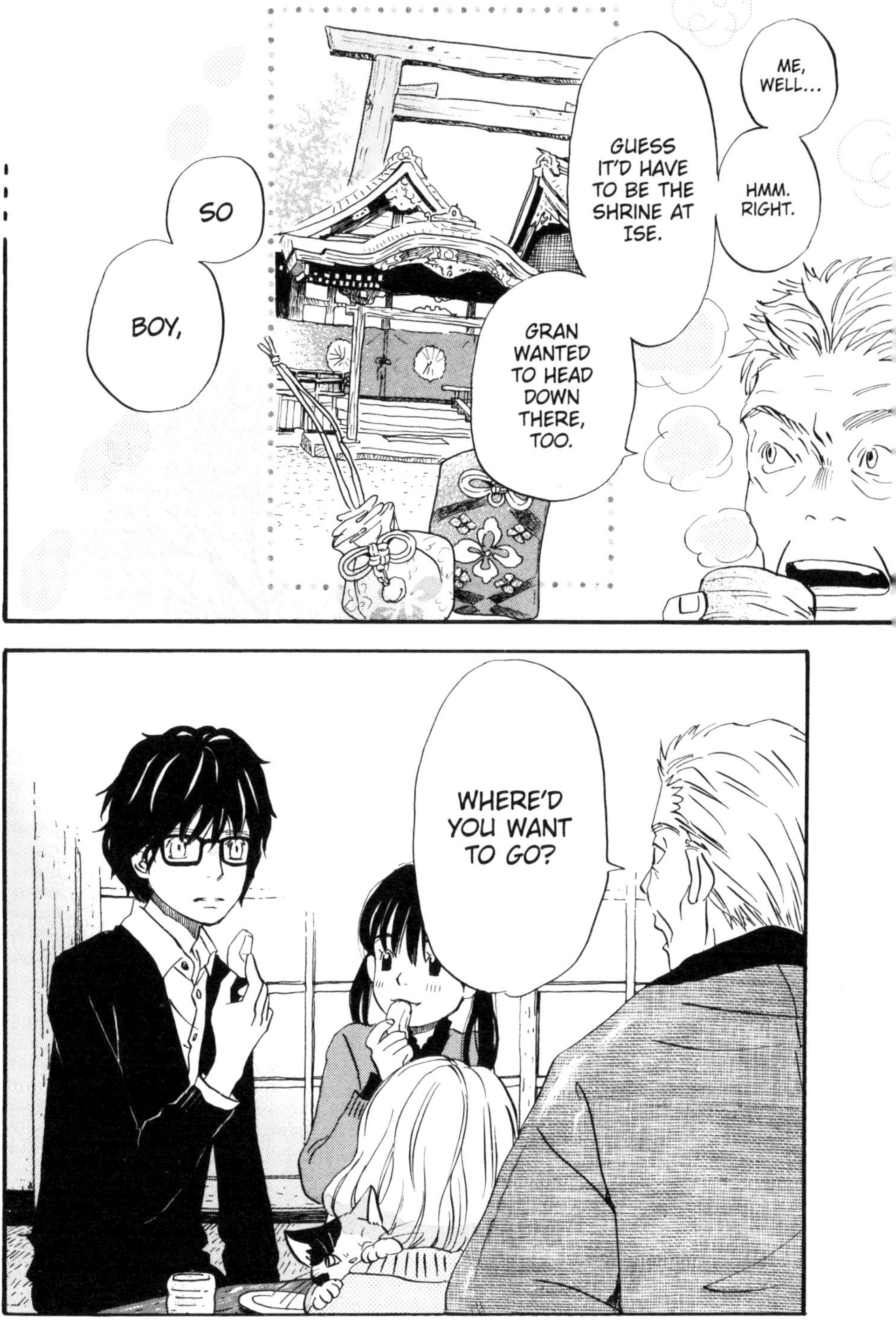
ME, WELL...
HMM. RIGHT.
GUESS IT'D HAVE TO BE THE SHRINE AT ISE.
GRAN WANTED TO HEAD DOWN THERE, TOO.
SO
BOY,
WHERE'D YOU WANT TO GO?

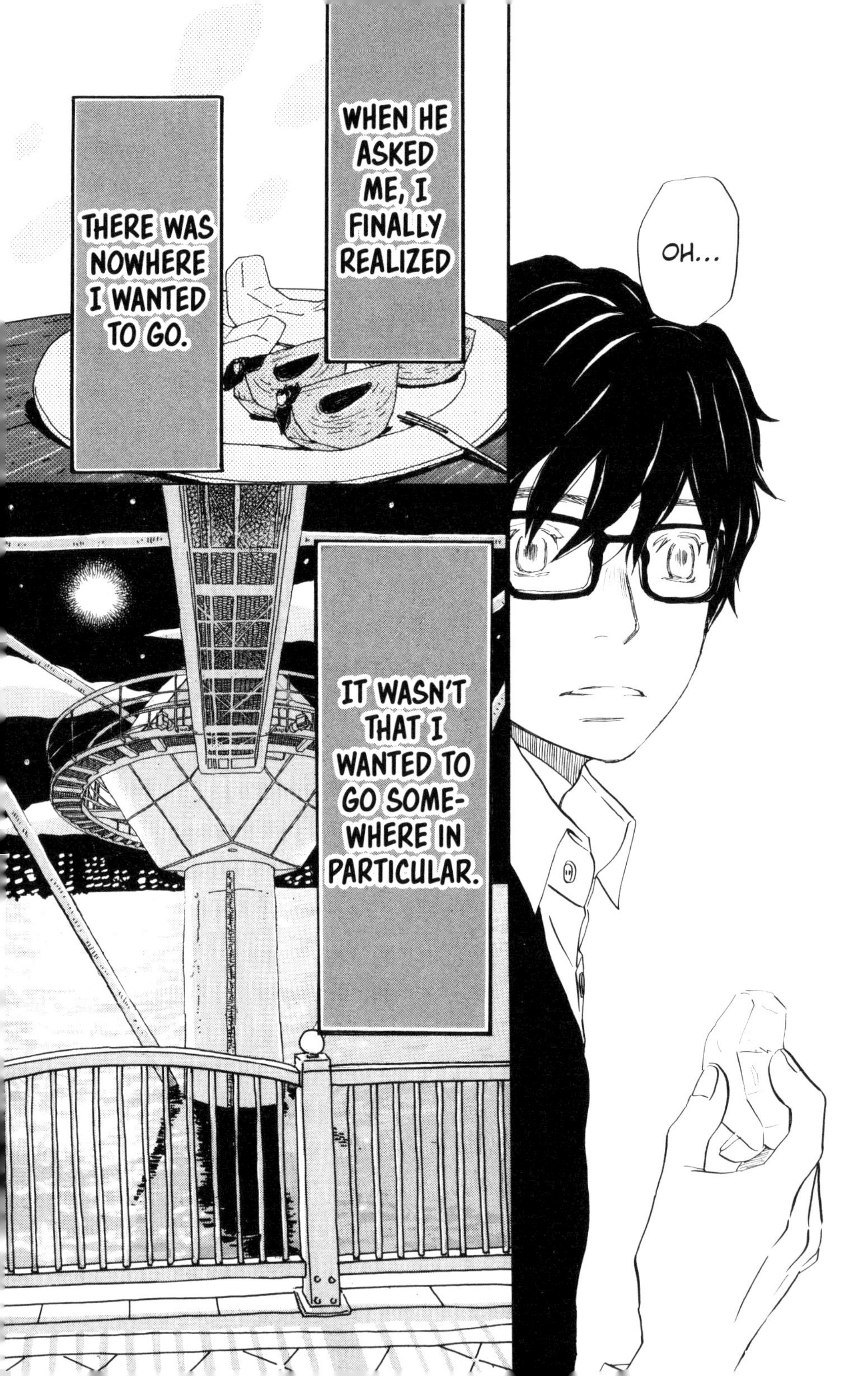
OH...
WHEN HE ASKED ME, I FINALLY REALIZED
THERE WAS NOWHERE I WANTED TO GO.
IT WASN'T THAT I WANTED TO GO SOME-WHERE IN PARTICULAR.

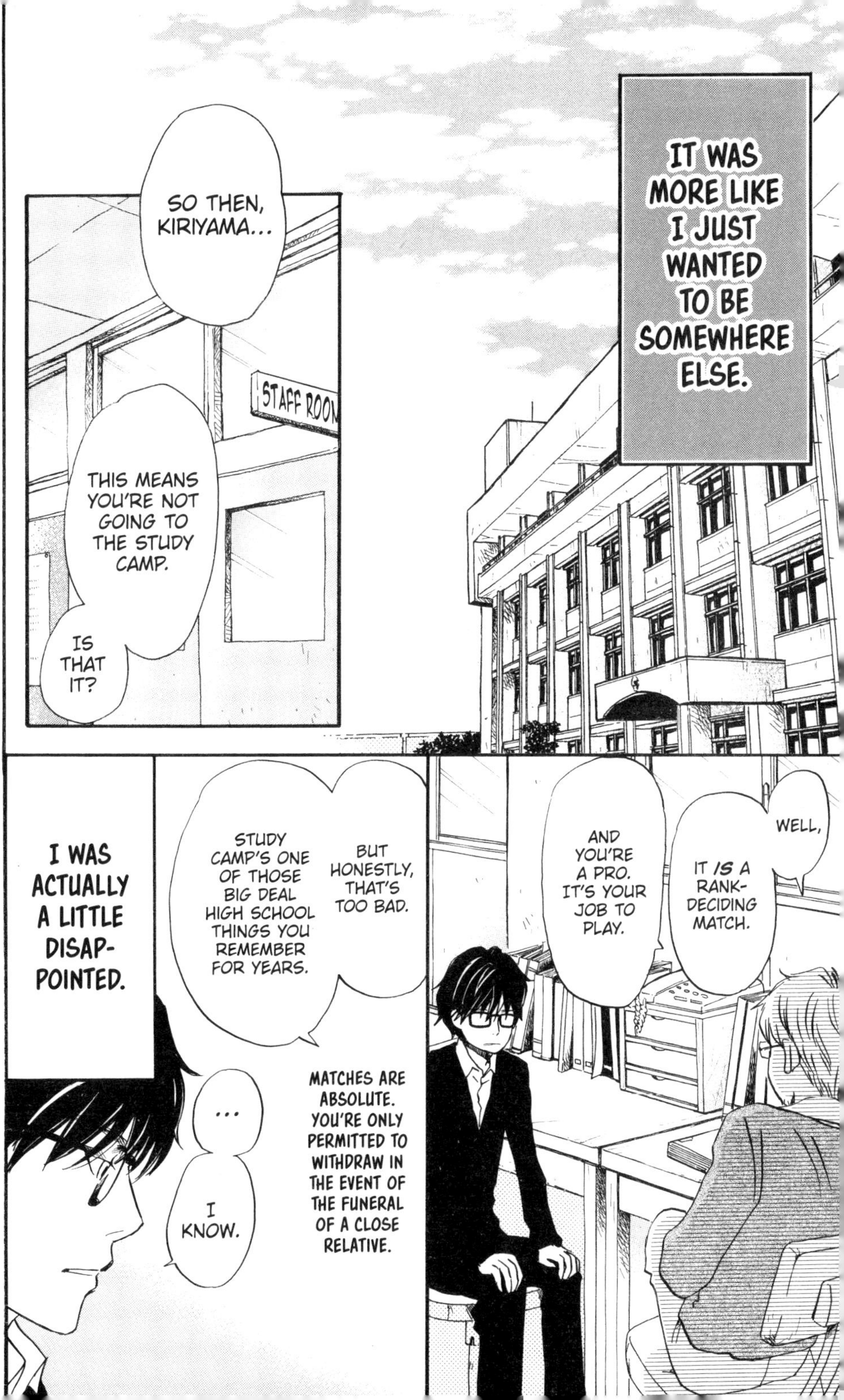
IT WAS MORE LIKE I JUST WANTED TO BE SOMEWHERE ELSE.
STAFF ROOM
SO THEN, KIRIYAMA...
THIS MEANS YOU'RE NOT GOING TO THE STUDY CAMP.
IS THAT IT?
WELL,
IT *IS* A RANK-DECIDING MATCH.
AND YOU'RE A PRO. IT'S YOUR JOB TO PLAY.
BUT HONESTLY, THAT'S TOO BAD.
STUDY CAMP'S ONE OF THOSE BIG DEAL HIGH SCHOOL THINGS YOU REMEMBER FOR YEARS.
MATCHES ARE ABSOLUTE. YOU'RE ONLY PERMITTED TO WITHDRAW IN THE EVENT OF THE FUNERAL OF A CLOSE RELATIVE.
...
I KNOW.
I WAS ACTUALLY A LITTLE DISAPPOINTED.

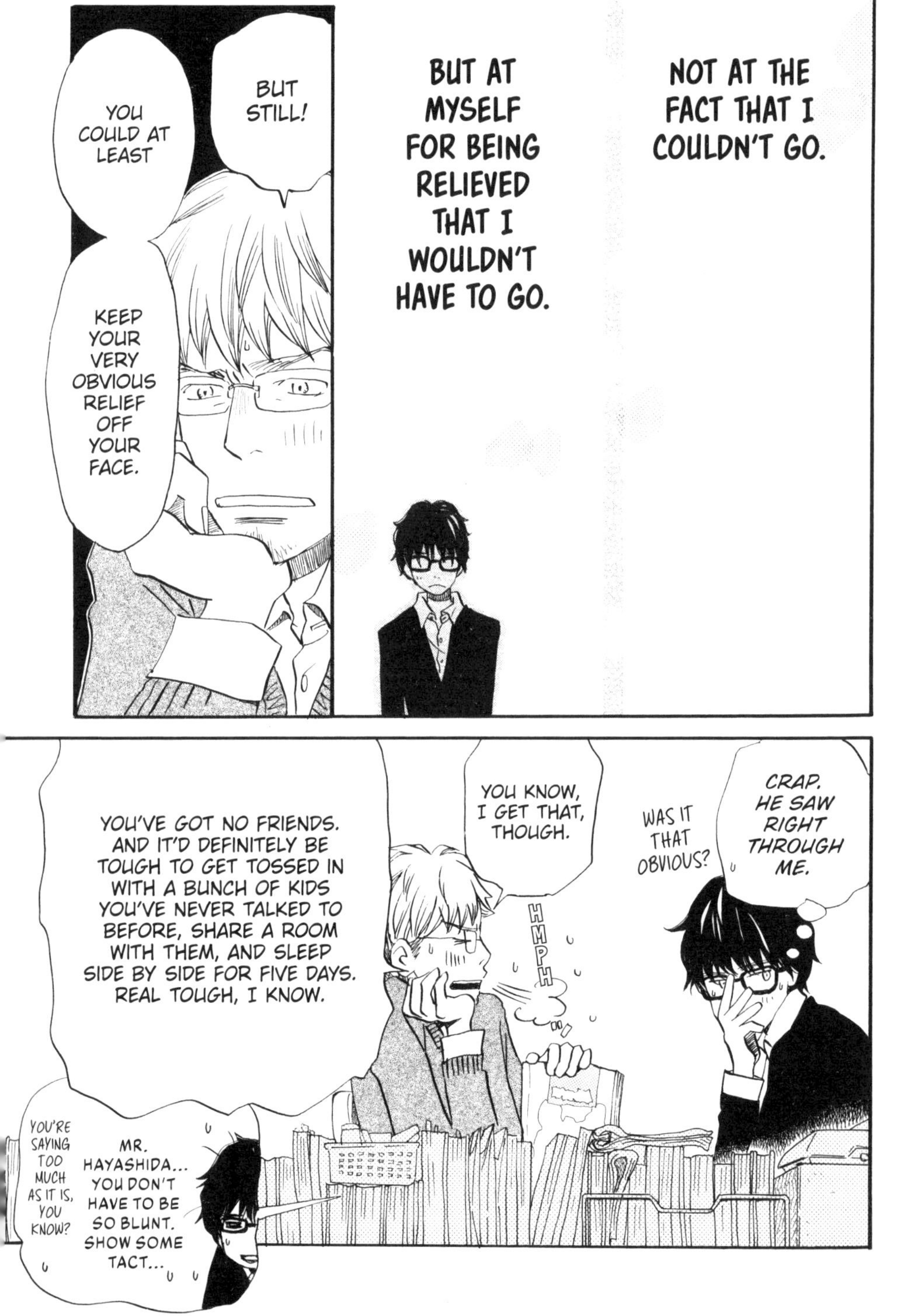
NOT AT THE FACT THAT I COULDN'T GO.
BUT AT MYSELF FOR BEING RELIEVED THAT I WOULDN'T HAVE TO GO.
BUT STILL!
YOU COULD AT LEAST
KEEP YOUR VERY OBVIOUS RELIEF OFF YOUR FACE.
CRAP. HE SAW RIGHT THROUGH ME.
WAS IT THAT OBVIOUS?
YOU KNOW, I GET THAT, THOUGH.
HMPH
YOU'VE GOT NO FRIENDS. AND IT'D DEFINITELY BE TOUGH TO GET TOSSED IN WITH A BUNCH OF KIDS YOU'VE NEVER TALKED TO BEFORE, SHARE A ROOM WITH THEM, AND SLEEP SIDE BY SIDE FOR FIVE DAYS. REAL TOUGH, I KNOW.
MR. HAYASHIDA... YOU DON'T HAVE TO BE SO BLUNT. SHOW SOME TACT...
YOU'RE SAYING TOO MUCH AS IT IS, YOU KNOW?

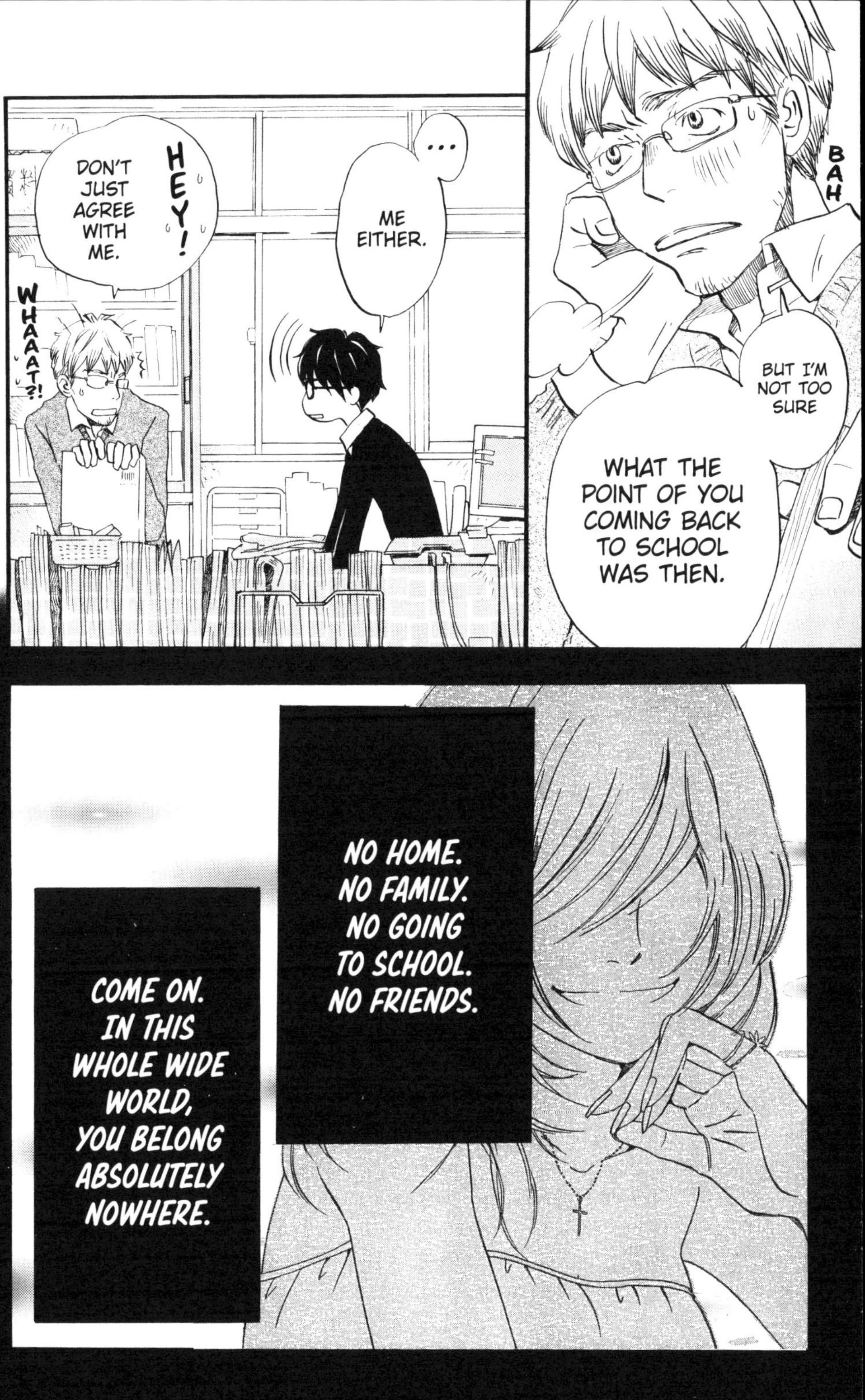
BAH
BUT I'M NOT TOO SURE
WHAT THE POINT OF YOU COMING BACK TO SCHOOL WAS THEN.
...
ME EITHER.
HEY!
DON'T JUST AGREE WITH ME.
WHAAAAT?!
NO HOME. NO FAMILY. NO GOING TO SCHOOL. NO FRIENDS.
COME ON. IN THIS WHOLE WIDE WORLD, YOU BELONG ABSOLUTELY NOWHERE.

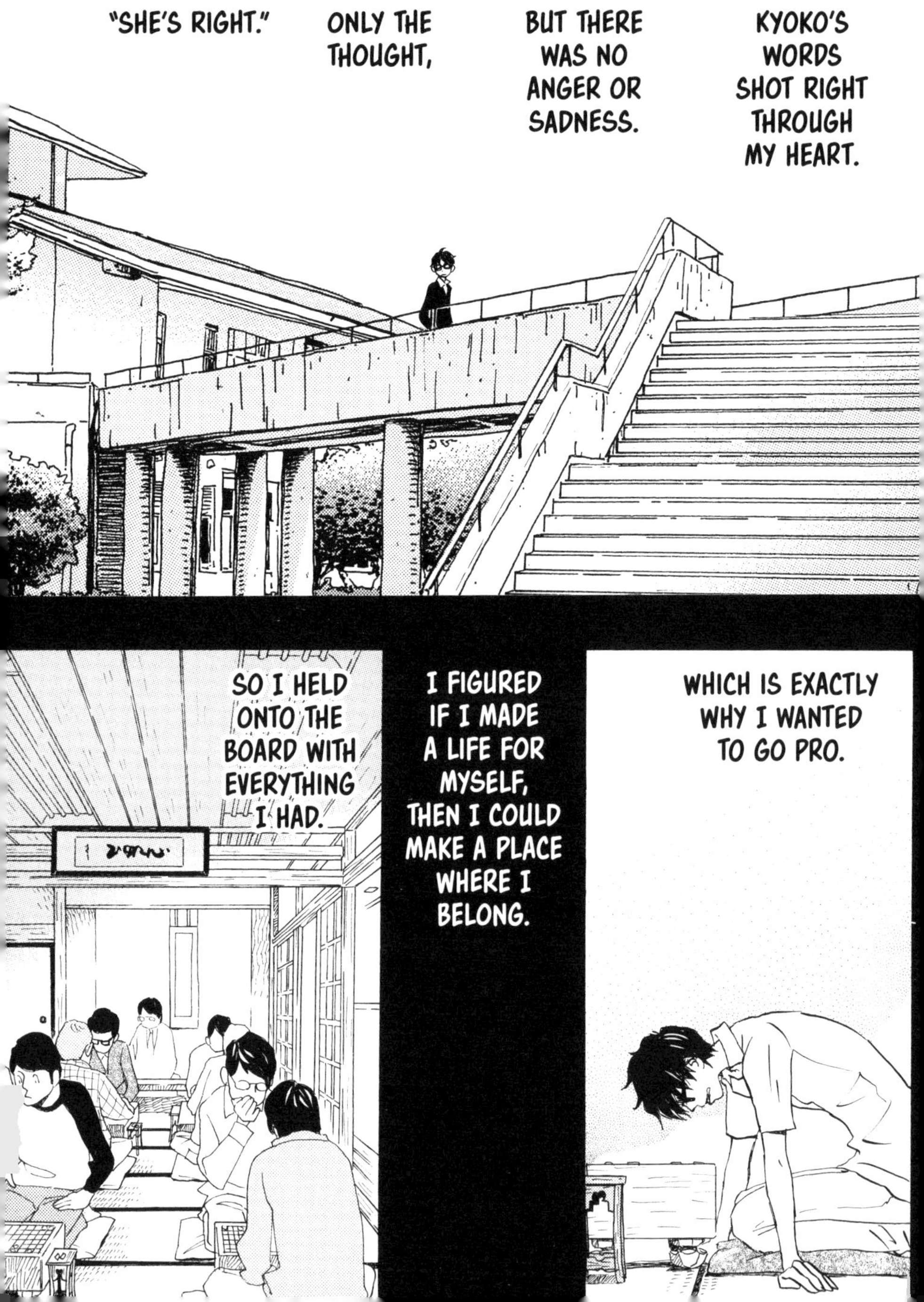
KYOKO'S WORDS SHOT RIGHT THROUGH MY HEART.
BUT THERE WAS NO ANGER OR SADNESS.
ONLY THE THOUGHT,
"SHE'S RIGHT."
WHICH IS EXACTLY WHY I WANTED TO GO PRO.
I FIGURED IF I MADE A LIFE FOR MYSELF, THEN I COULD MAKE A PLACE WHERE I BELONG.
SO I HELD ONTO THE BOARD WITH EVERYTHING I HAD.

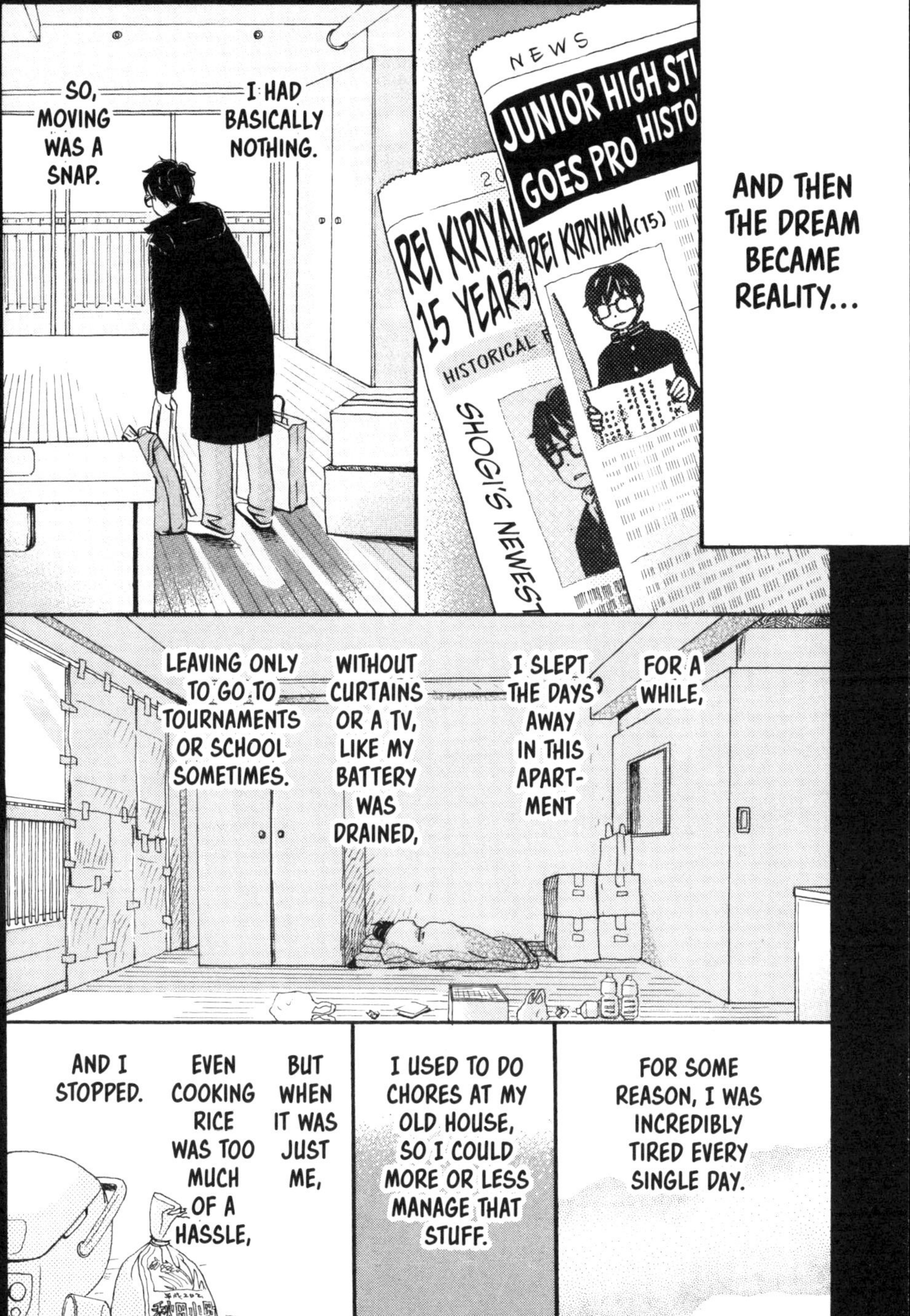
AND THEN THE DREAM BECAME REALITY...
NEWS
JUNIOR HIGH ST
GOES PRO HISTO
REI KIRIYAMA (15)
REI KIRIYA
15 YEARS
HISTORICAL
SHOGI'S NEWEST
I HAD BASICALLY NOTHING.
SO, MOVING WAS A SNAP.
FOR A WHILE,
I SLEPT THE DAYS AWAY IN THIS APARTMENT
WITHOUT CURTAINS OR A TV, LIKE MY BATTERY WAS DRAINED,
LEAVING ONLY TO GO TO TOURNAMENTS OR SCHOOL SOMETIMES.
FOR SOME REASON, I WAS INCREDIBLY TIRED EVERY SINGLE DAY.
I USED TO DO CHORES AT MY OLD HOUSE, SO I COULD MORE OR LESS MANAGE THAT STUFF.
BUT WHEN IT WAS JUST ME,
EVEN COOKING RICE WAS TOO MUCH OF A HASSLE,
AND I STOPPED.

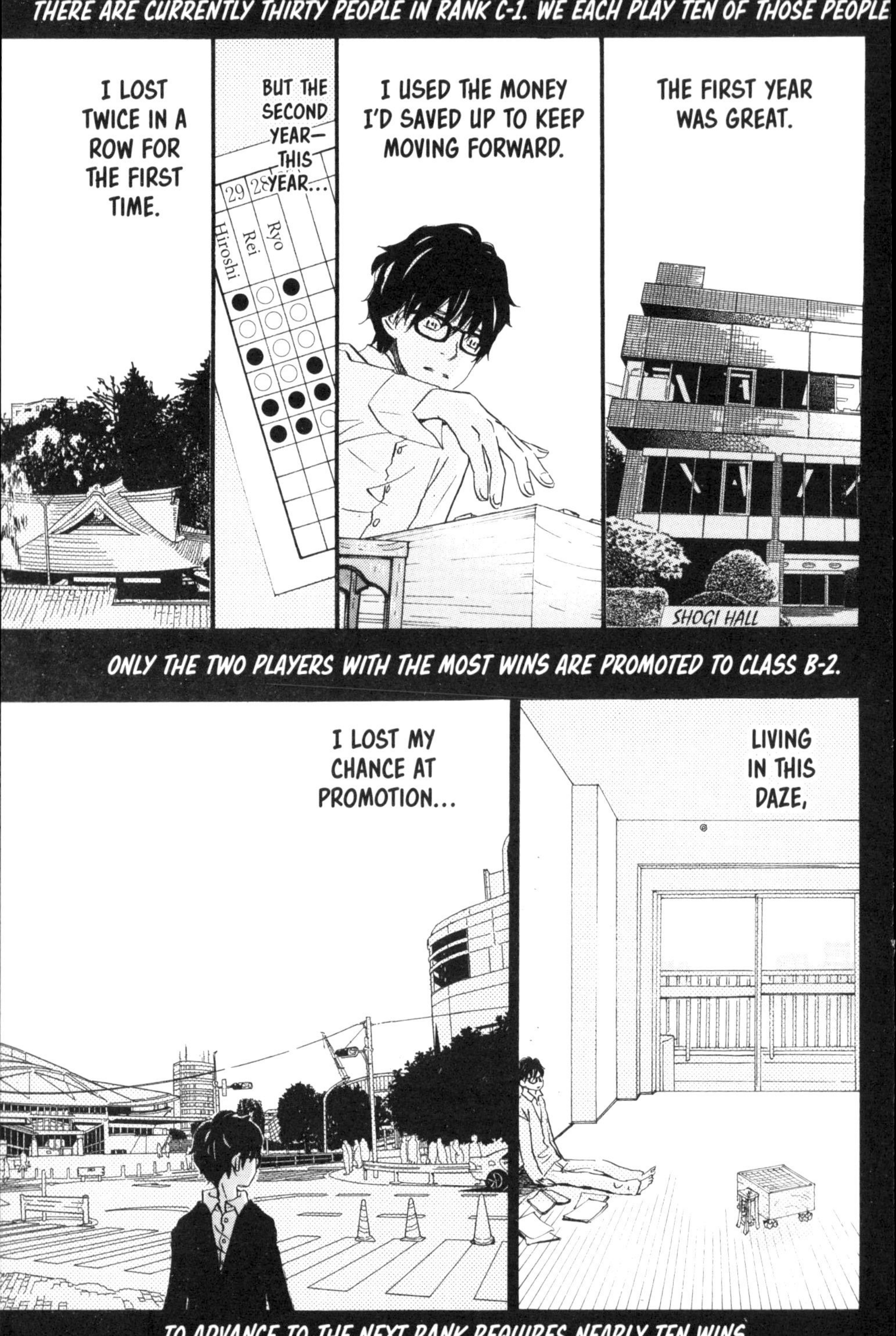
THERE ARE CURRENTLY THIRTY PEOPLE IN RANK C-1. WE EACH PLAY TEN OF THOSE PEOPLE
THE FIRST YEAR WAS GREAT.
SHOGI HALL
I USED THE MONEY I'D SAVED UP TO KEEP MOVING FORWARD.
BUT THE SECOND YEAR—THIS YEAR...
29 28
Ryo
Rei
Hiroshi
I LOST TWICE IN A ROW FOR THE FIRST TIME.
ONLY THE TWO PLAYERS WITH THE MOST WINS ARE PROMOTED TO CLASS B-2.
LIVING IN THIS DAZE,
I LOST MY CHANCE AT PROMOTION...
TO ADVANCE TO THE NEXT RANK REQUIRES NEARLY TEN WINS.

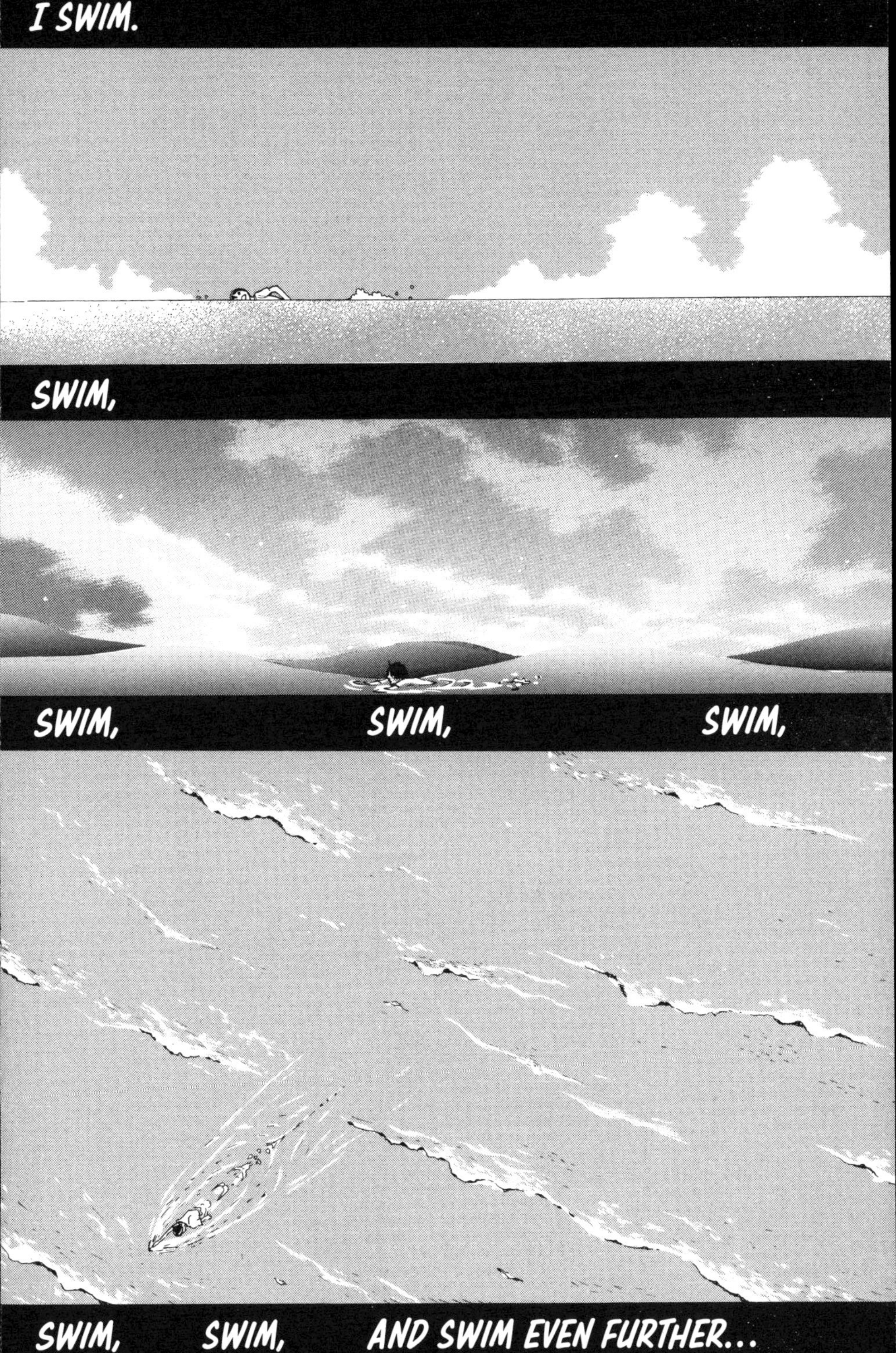
I SWIM.
SWIM,
SWIM, SWIM, SWIM,
SWIM, SWIM, AND SWIM EVEN FURTHER...

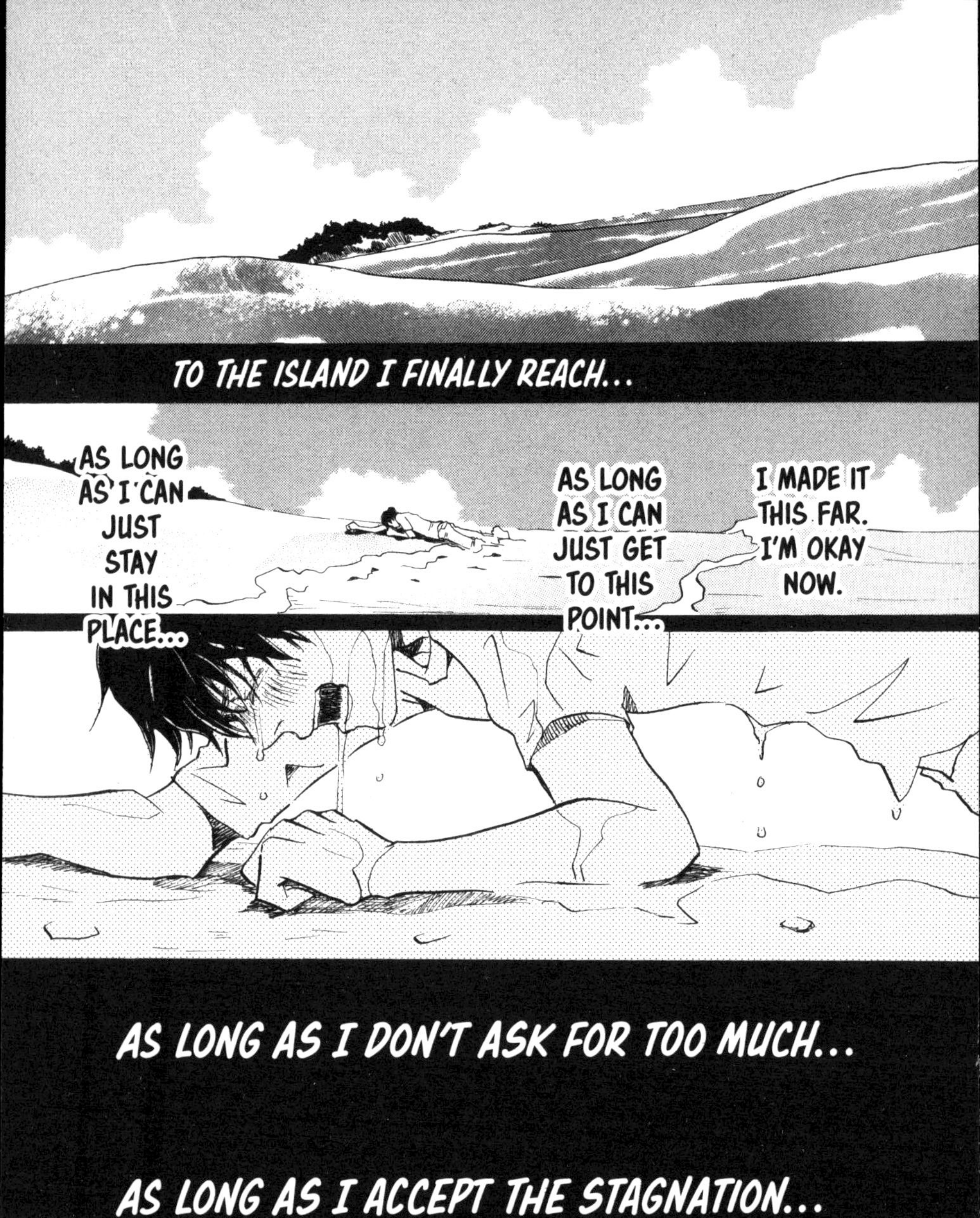
TO THE ISLAND I FINALLY REACH...
I MADE IT THIS FAR. I'M OKAY NOW.
AS LONG AS I CAN JUST GET TO THIS POINT...
AS LONG AS I CAN JUST STAY IN THIS PLACE...
AS LONG AS I DON'T ASK FOR TOO MUCH...
AS LONG AS I ACCEPT THE STAGNATION...

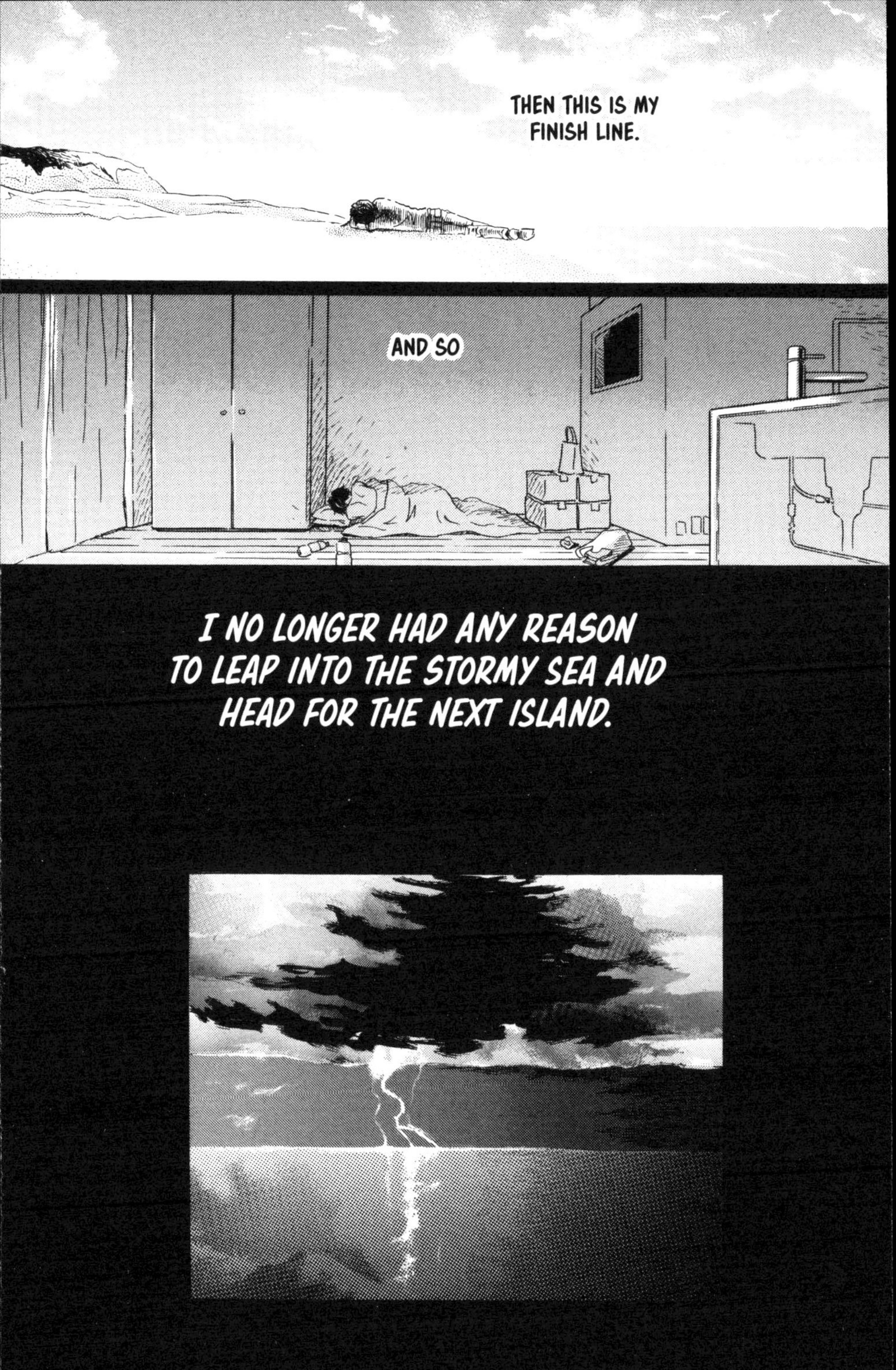
THEN THIS IS MY FINISH LINE.
AND SO
I NO LONGER HAD ANY REASON TO LEAP INTO THE STORMY SEA AND HEAD FOR THE NEXT ISLAND.

Chapter 12

Child of God (Part 2)

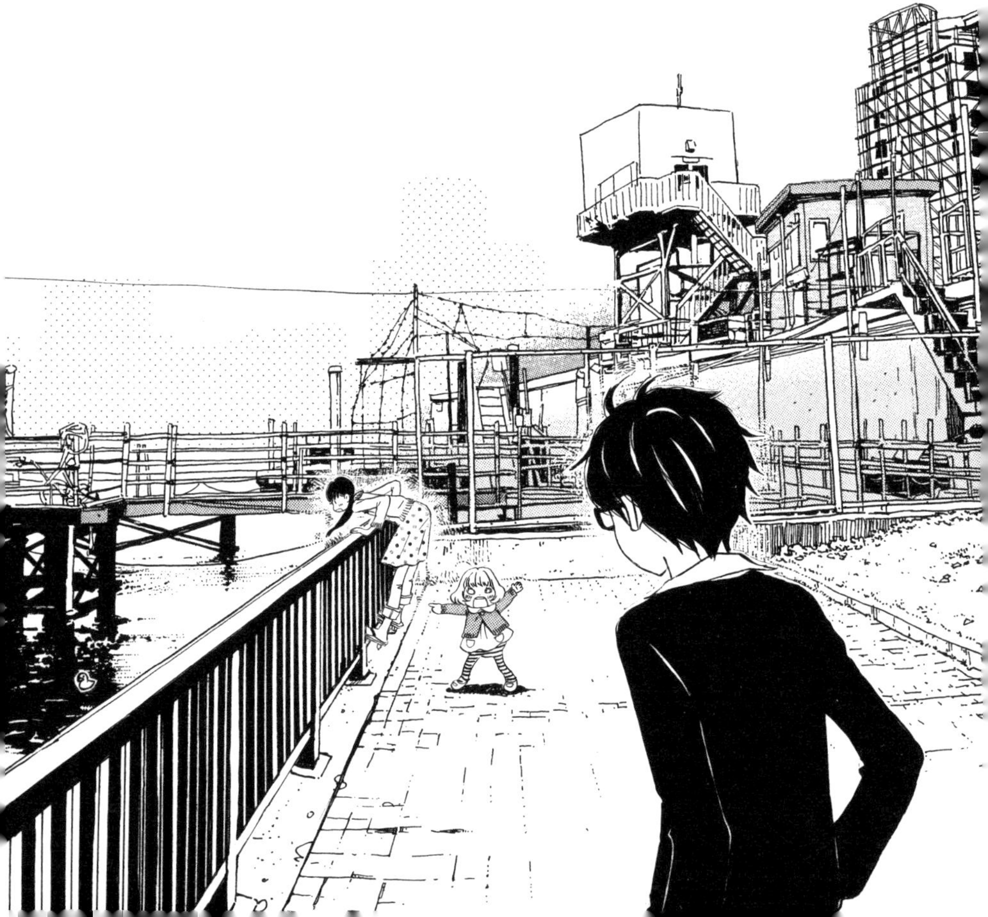

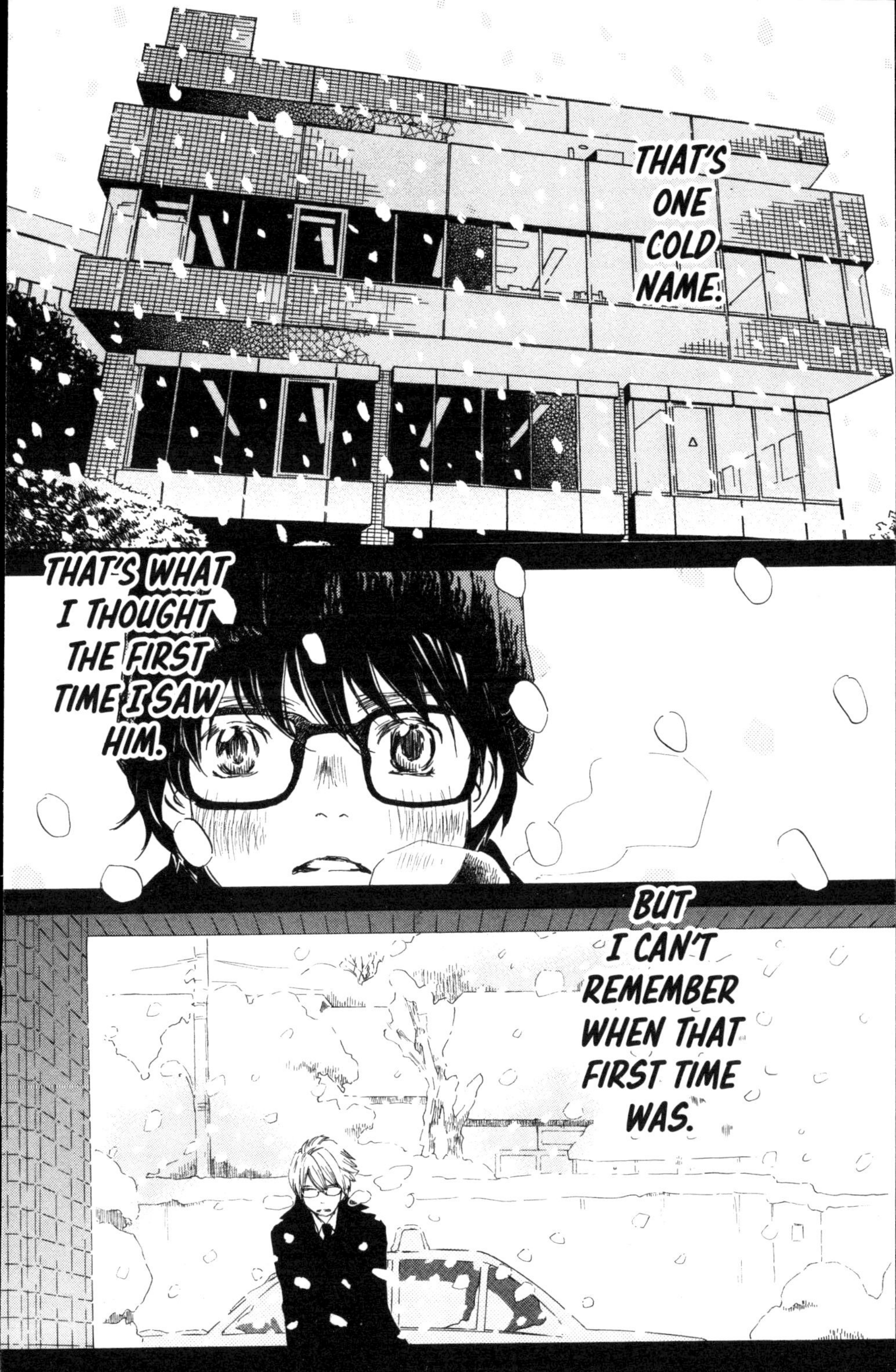
THAT'S ONE COLD NAME.
THAT'S WHAT I THOUGHT THE FIRST TIME I SAW HIM.
BUT I CAN'T REMEMBER WHEN THAT FIRST TIME WAS.

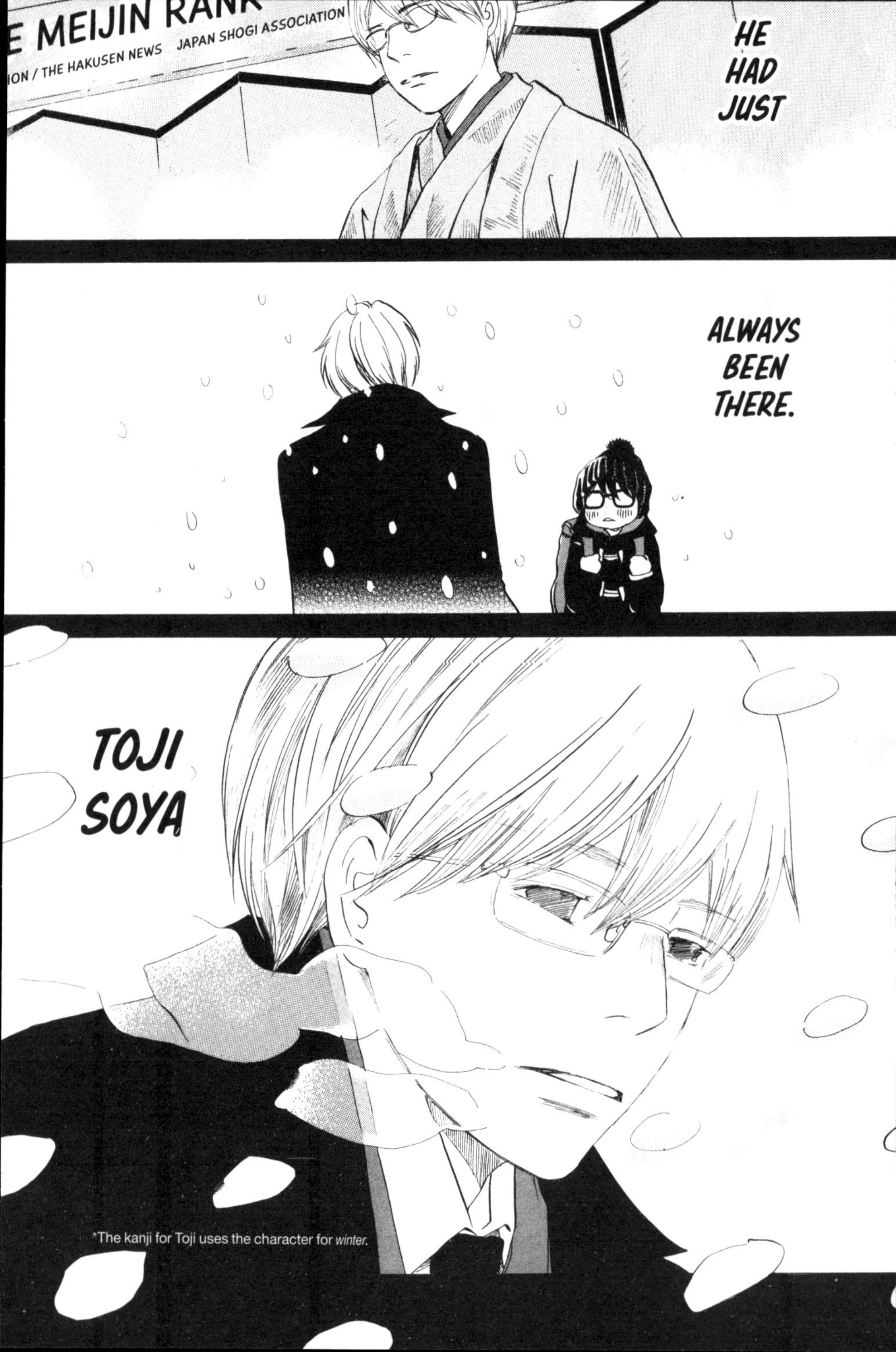
E MEIJIN RANK
ION / THE HAKUSEN NEWS JAPAN SHOGI ASSOCIATION
HE HAD JUST
ALWAYS BEEN THERE.
TOJI SOYA
*The kanji for Toji uses the character for *winter*.

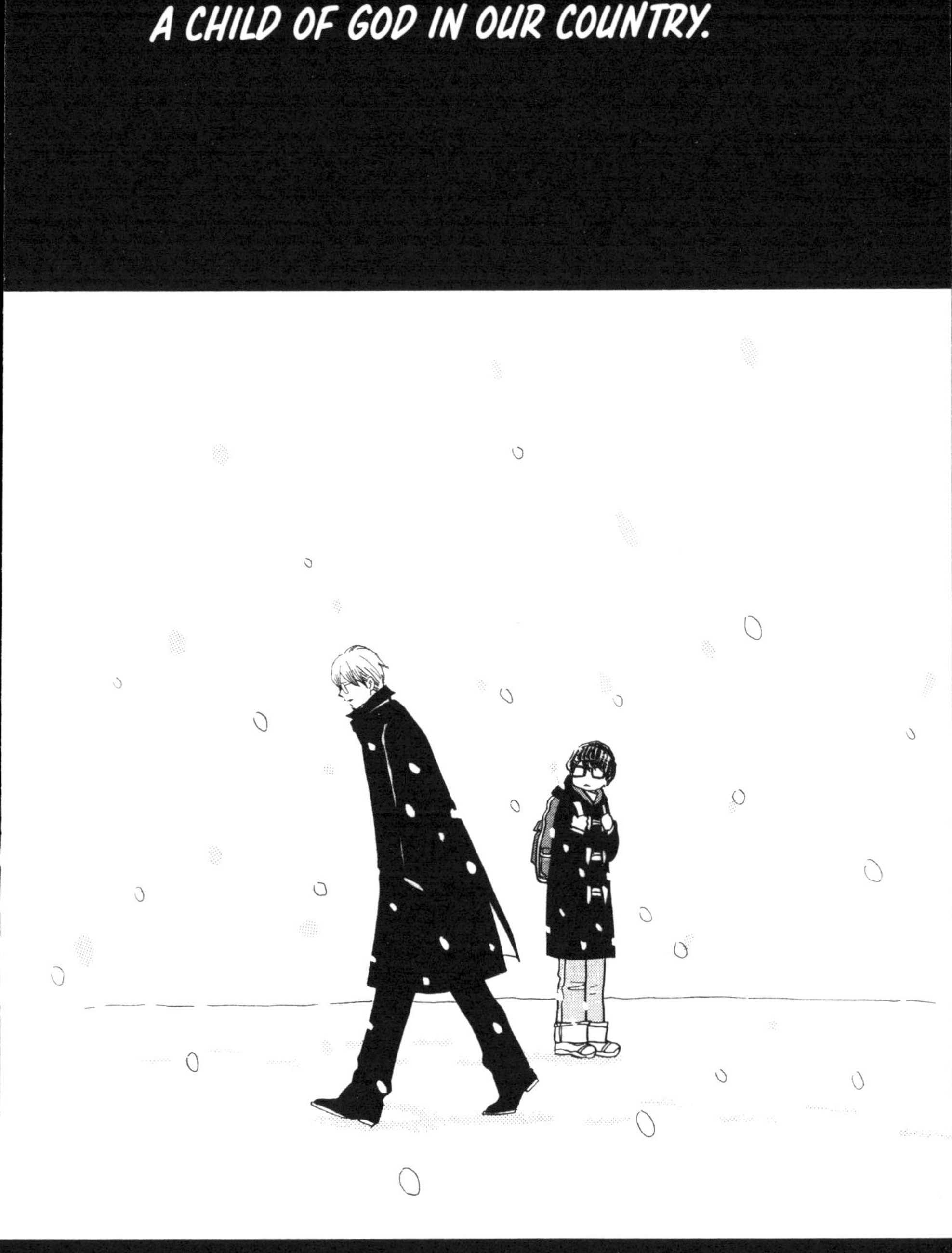
A CHILD OF GOD IN OUR COUNTRY.

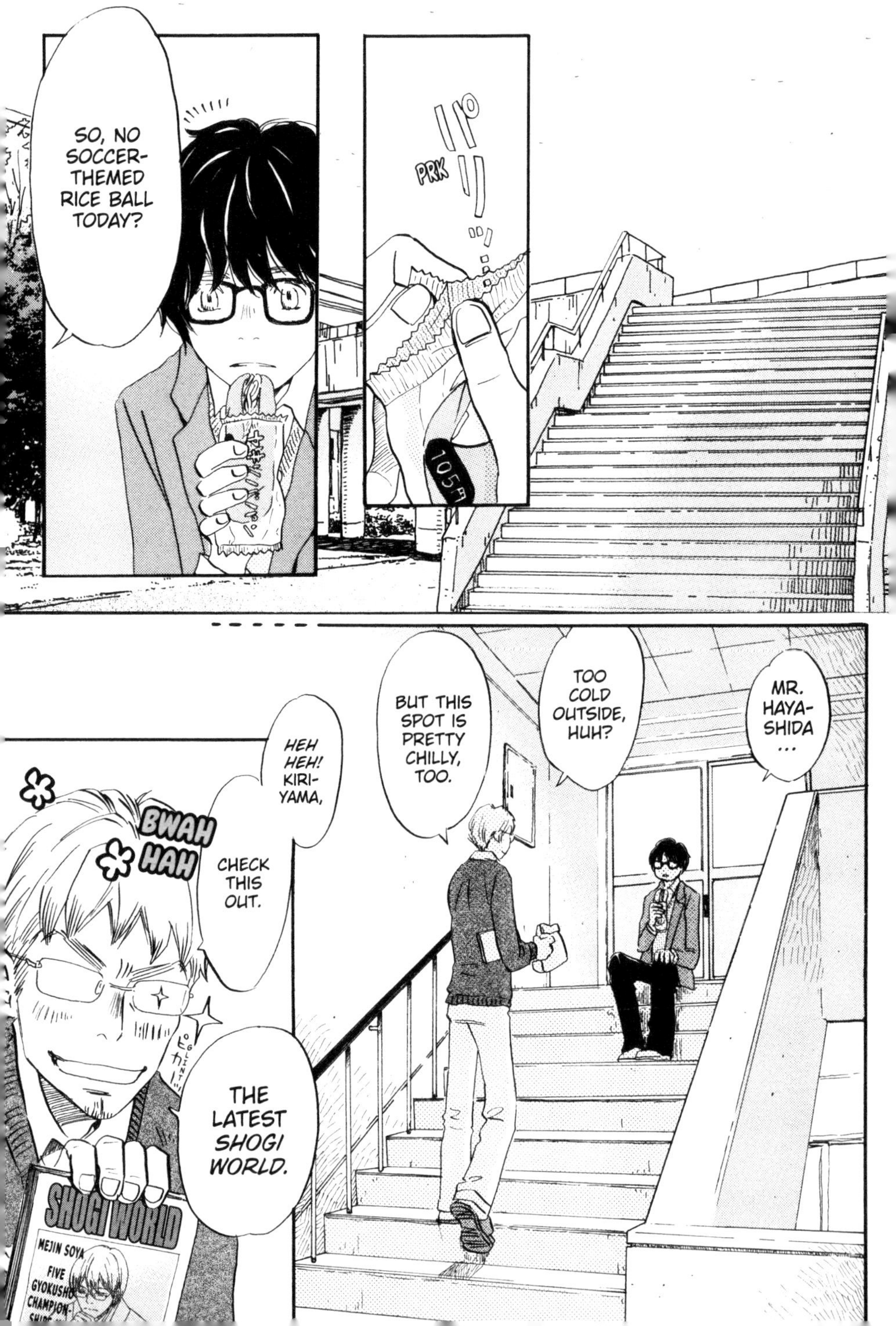

PRK
105円
SO, NO SOCCER-THEMED RICE BALL TODAY?
MR. HAYA-SHIDA...
TOO COLD OUTSIDE, HUH?
BUT THIS SPOT IS PRETTY CHILLY, TOO.
HEH HEH! KIRI-YAMA,
BWAH HAH
CHECK THIS OUT.
GLINT
THE LATEST SHOGI WORLD.
SHOGI WORLD
MEJIN SOYA
FIVE GYOKUSHO CHAMPION-

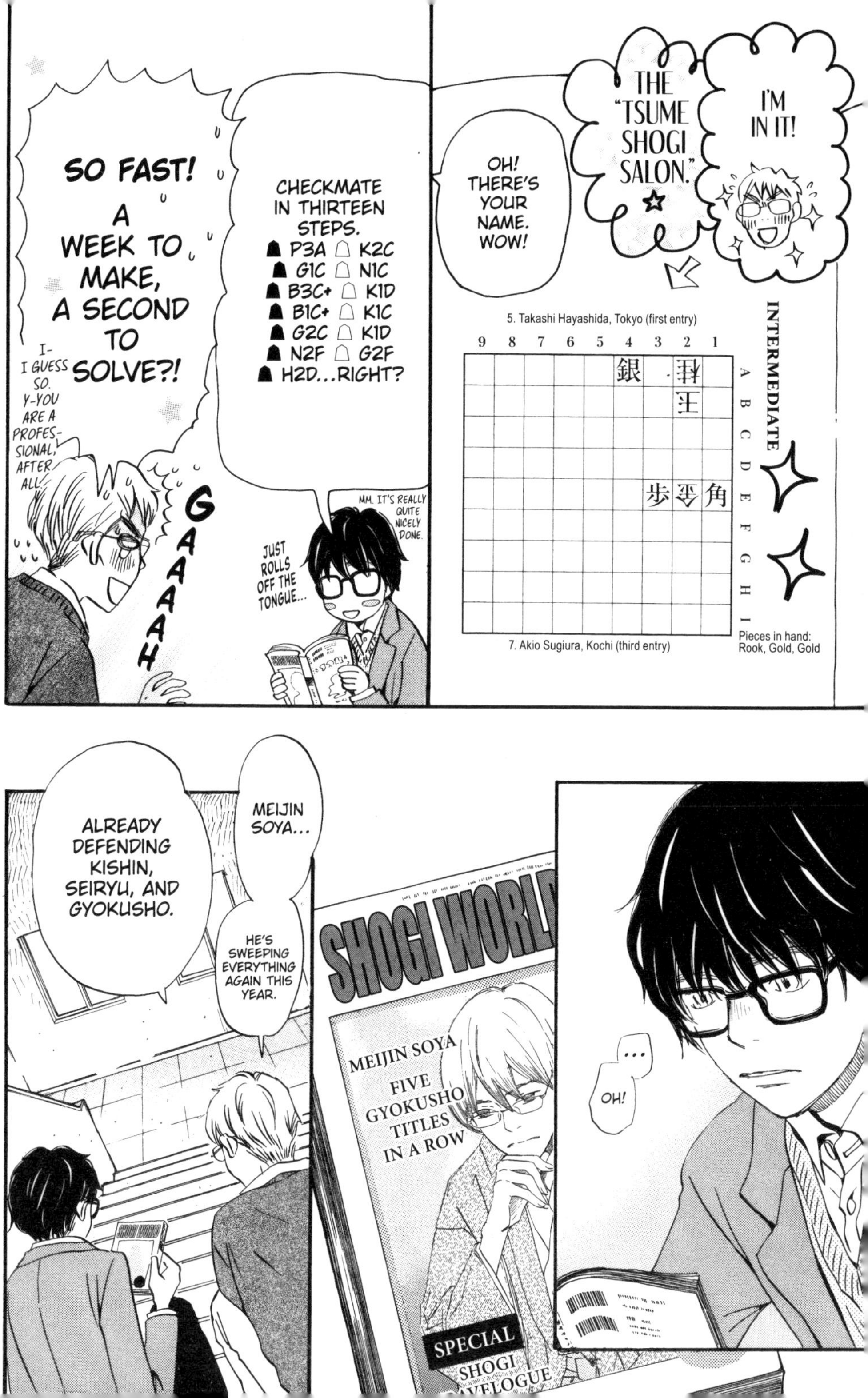
I'M IN IT!
THE "TSUME SHOGI SALON." ☆
OH! THERE'S YOUR NAME. WOW!
INTERMEDIATE
5. Takashi Hayashida, Tokyo (first entry)
9 8 7 6 5 4 3 2 1
A B C D E F G H I
銀 王 歩 角
7. Akio Sugiura, Kochi (third entry)
Pieces in hand: Rook, Gold, Gold
CHECKMATE IN THIRTEEN STEPS. ☗P3A ☖K2C ☗G1C ☖N1C ☗B3C+ ☖K1D ☗B1C+ ☖K1C ☗G2C ☖K1D ☗N2F ☖G2F ☗H2D...RIGHT?
SO FAST! A WEEK TO MAKE, A SECOND TO SOLVE?!
MM. IT'S REALLY QUITE NICELY DONE.
JUST ROLLS OFF THE TONGUE...
I- I GUESS SO. Y-YOU ARE A PROFESSIONAL, AFTER ALL.
GAAAAAH
...
OH!
SHOGI WORLD
MEIJIN SOYA
FIVE GYOKUSHO TITLES IN A ROW
SPECIAL
SHOGI
MEIJIN SOYA...
ALREADY DEFENDING KISHIN, SEIRYU, AND GYOKUSHO.
HE'S SWEEPING EVERYTHING AGAIN THIS YEAR.

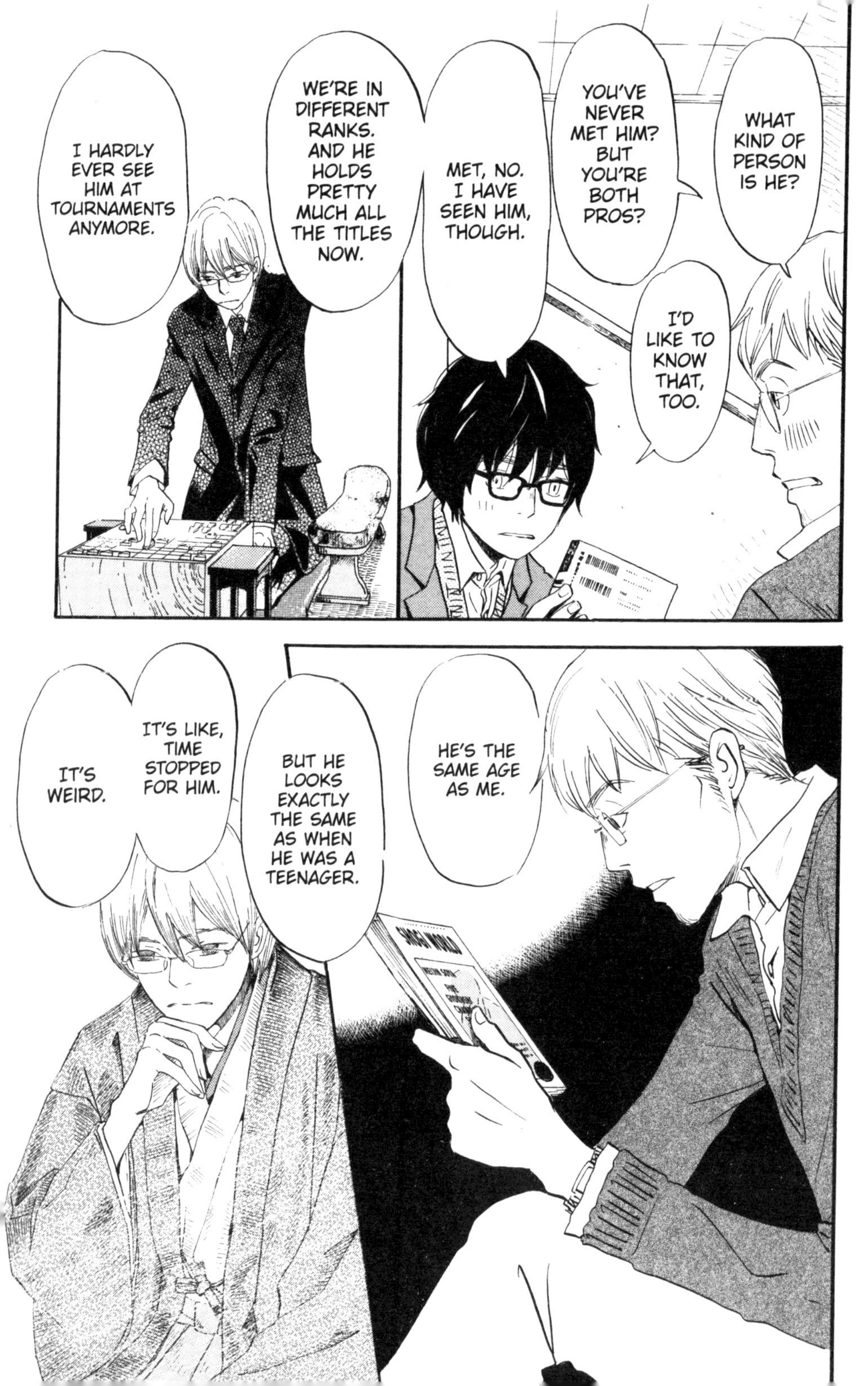
WHAT KIND OF PERSON IS HE?
I'D LIKE TO KNOW THAT, TOO.
YOU'VE NEVER MET HIM? BUT YOU'RE BOTH PROS?
MET, NO. I HAVE SEEN HIM, THOUGH.
WE'RE IN DIFFERENT RANKS. AND HE HOLDS PRETTY MUCH ALL THE TITLES NOW.
I HARDLY EVER SEE HIM AT TOURNAMENTS ANYMORE.
HE'S THE SAME AGE AS ME.
BUT HE LOOKS EXACTLY THE SAME AS WHEN HE WAS A TEENAGER.
IT'S LIKE, TIME STOPPED FOR HIM.
IT'S WEIRD.

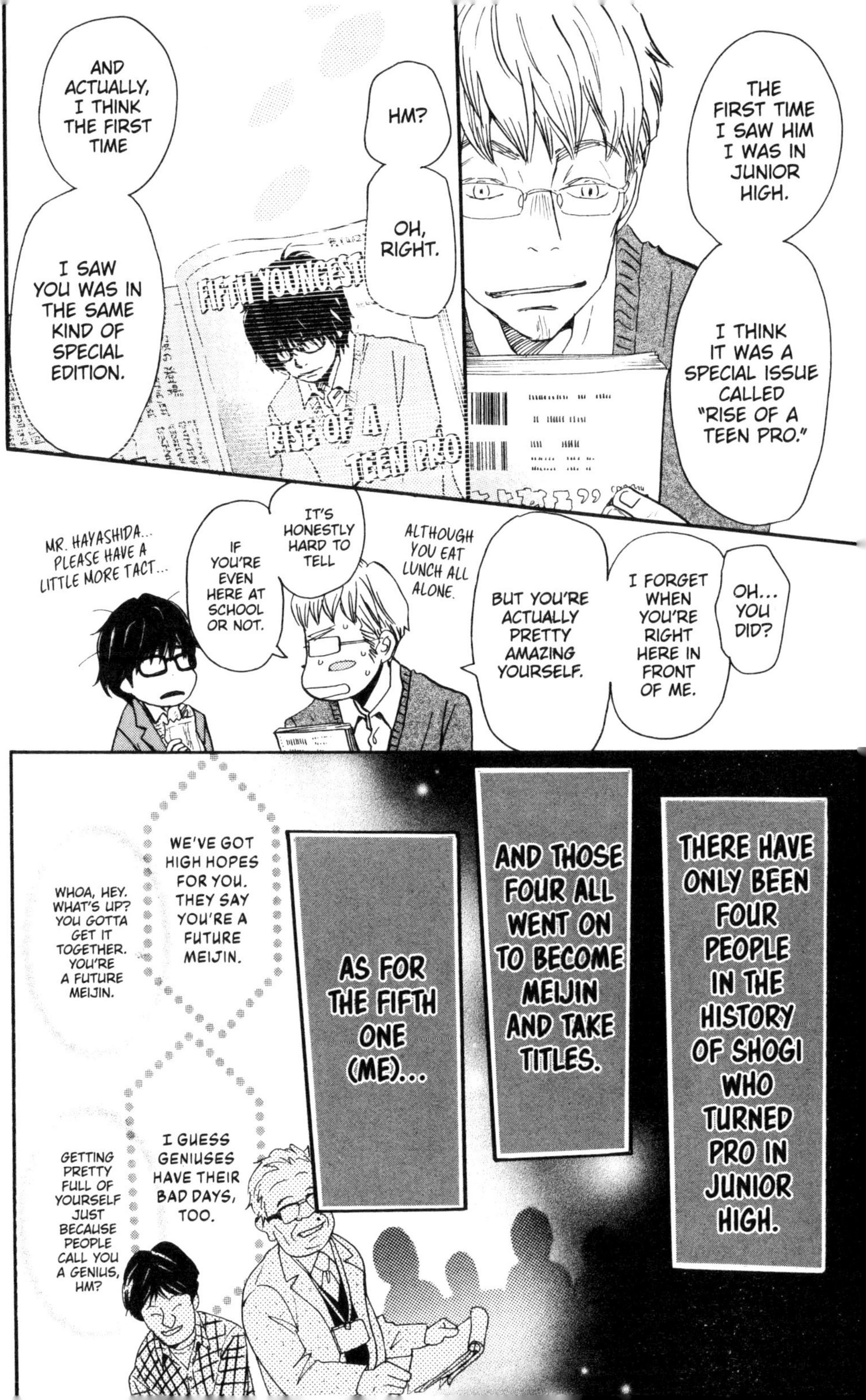
THE FIRST TIME I SAW HIM I WAS IN JUNIOR HIGH.
I THINK IT WAS A SPECIAL ISSUE CALLED "RISE OF A TEEN PRO."
HM?
OH, RIGHT.
FIFTH YOUNGEST
RISE OF A TEEN PRO
AND ACTUALLY, I THINK THE FIRST TIME
I SAW YOU WAS IN THE SAME KIND OF SPECIAL EDITION.
OH... YOU DID?
I FORGET WHEN YOU'RE RIGHT HERE IN FRONT OF ME.
BUT YOU'RE ACTUALLY PRETTY AMAZING YOURSELF.
ALTHOUGH YOU EAT LUNCH ALL ALONE.
IT'S HONESTLY HARD TO TELL
IF YOU'RE EVEN HERE AT SCHOOL OR NOT.
MR. HAYASHIDA... PLEASE HAVE A LITTLE MORE TACT...
THERE HAVE ONLY BEEN FOUR PEOPLE IN THE HISTORY OF SHOGI WHO TURNED PRO IN JUNIOR HIGH.
AND THOSE FOUR ALL WENT ON TO BECOME MEIJIN AND TAKE TITLES.
AS FOR THE FIFTH ONE (ME)...
WE'VE GOT HIGH HOPES FOR YOU. THEY SAY YOU'RE A FUTURE MEIJIN.
WHOA, HEY. WHAT'S UP? YOU GOTTA GET IT TOGETHER. YOU'RE A FUTURE MEIJIN.
I GUESS GENIUSES HAVE THEIR BAD DAYS, TOO.
GETTING PRETTY FULL OF YOURSELF JUST BECAUSE PEOPLE CALL YOU A GENIUS, HM?

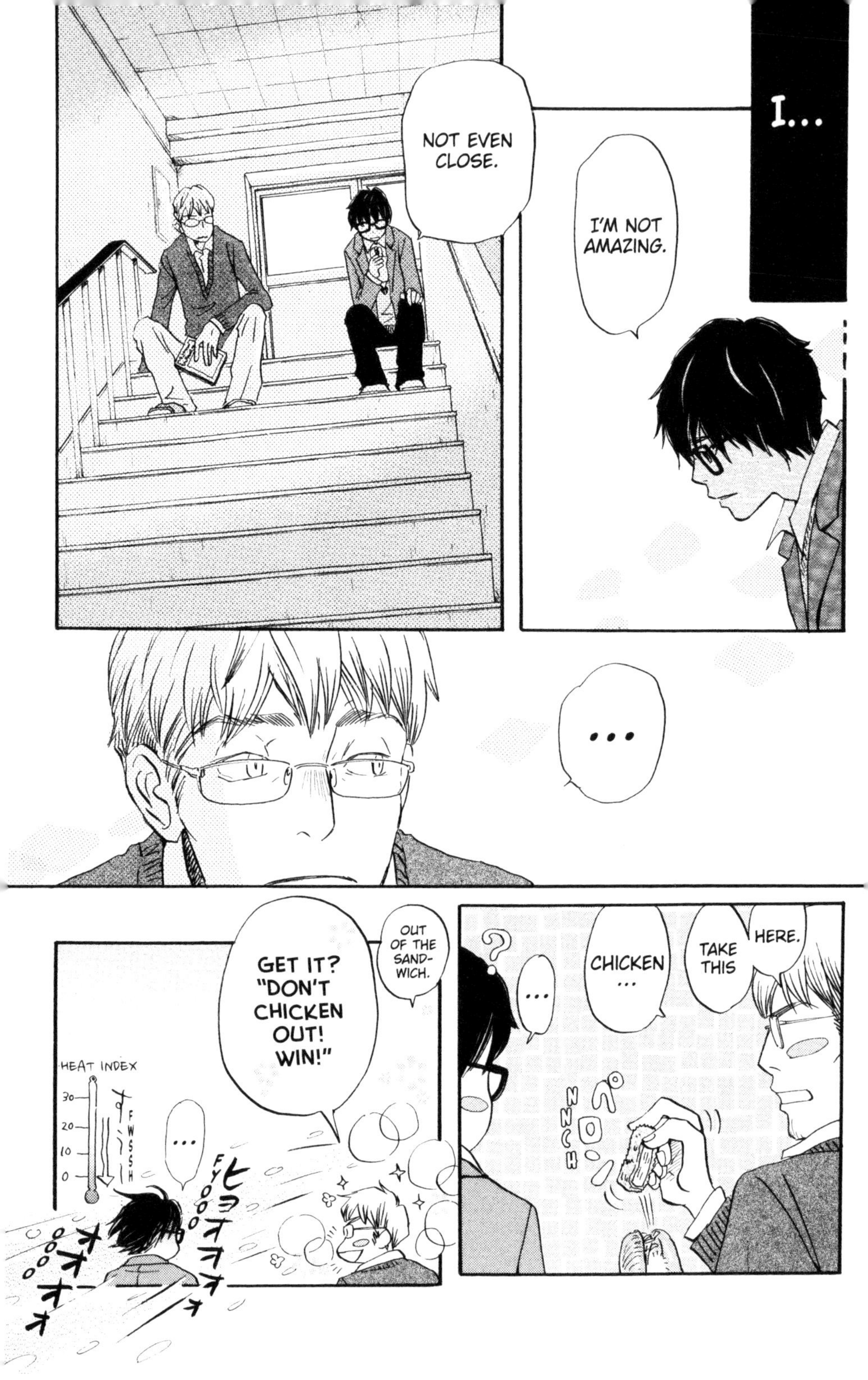

I...
I'M NOT AMAZING.
NOT EVEN CLOSE.
...
HERE.
TAKE THIS
CHICKEN ...
...
ぺ
NNCH
OUT OF THE SANDWICH.
GET IT? "DON'T CHICKEN OUT! WIN!"
...
HEAT INDEX
30
20
10
0
FWSSH
FYOOOO

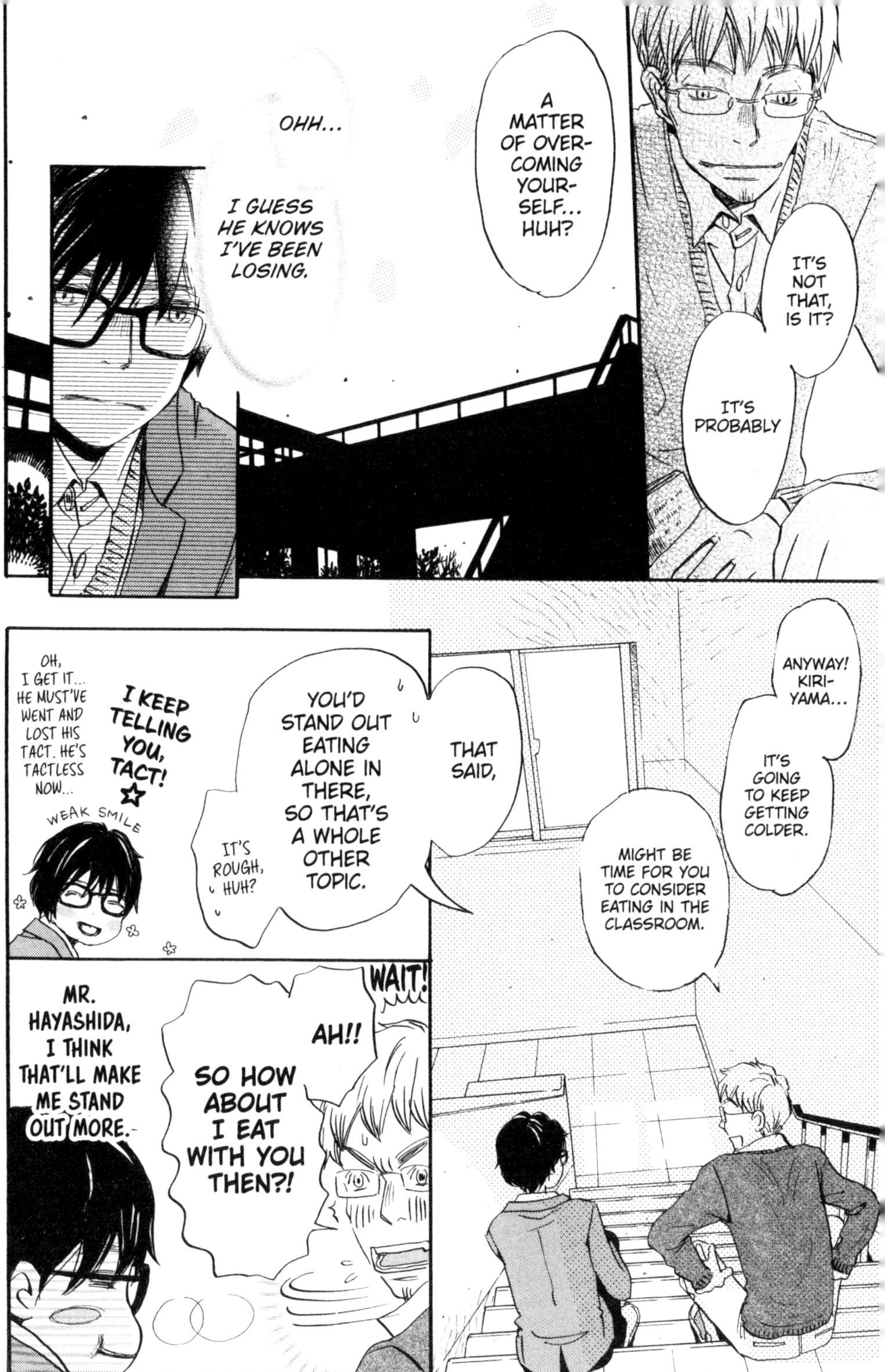
IT'S NOT THAT, IS IT?
IT'S PROBABLY
A MATTER OF OVER-COMING YOUR-SELF... HUH?
OHH...
I GUESS HE KNOWS I'VE BEEN LOSING.
ANYWAY! KIRI-YAMA...
IT'S GOING TO KEEP GETTING COLDER.
MIGHT BE TIME FOR YOU TO CONSIDER EATING IN THE CLASSROOM.
THAT SAID,
YOU'D STAND OUT EATING ALONE IN THERE, SO THAT'S A WHOLE OTHER TOPIC.
IT'S ROUGH, HUH?
I KEEP TELLING YOU, TACT! ☆
OH, I GET IT... HE MUST'VE WENT AND LOST HIS TACT. HE'S TACTLESS NOW...
WEAK SMILE
SO HOW ABOUT I EAT WITH YOU THEN?!
MR. HAYASHIDA, I THINK THAT'LL MAKE ME STAND OUT MORE.
AH!!
WAIT!

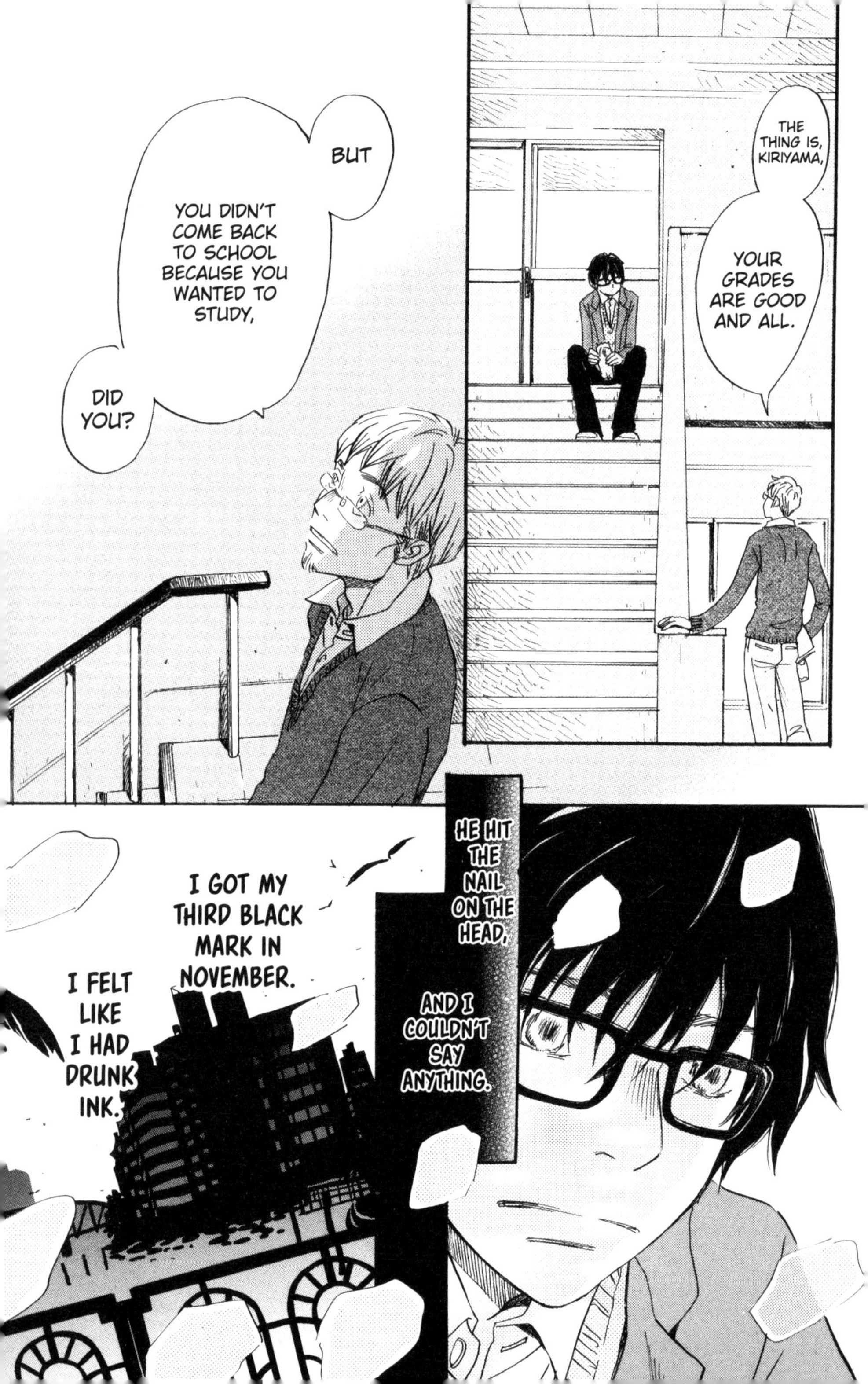
THE THING IS, KIRIYAMA,
YOUR GRADES ARE GOOD AND ALL.
BUT
YOU DIDN'T COME BACK TO SCHOOL BECAUSE YOU WANTED TO STUDY,
DID YOU?
HE HIT THE NAIL ON THE HEAD,
AND I COULDN'T SAY ANYTHING.
I GOT MY THIRD BLACK MARK IN NOVEMBER.
I FELT LIKE I HAD DRUNK INK.

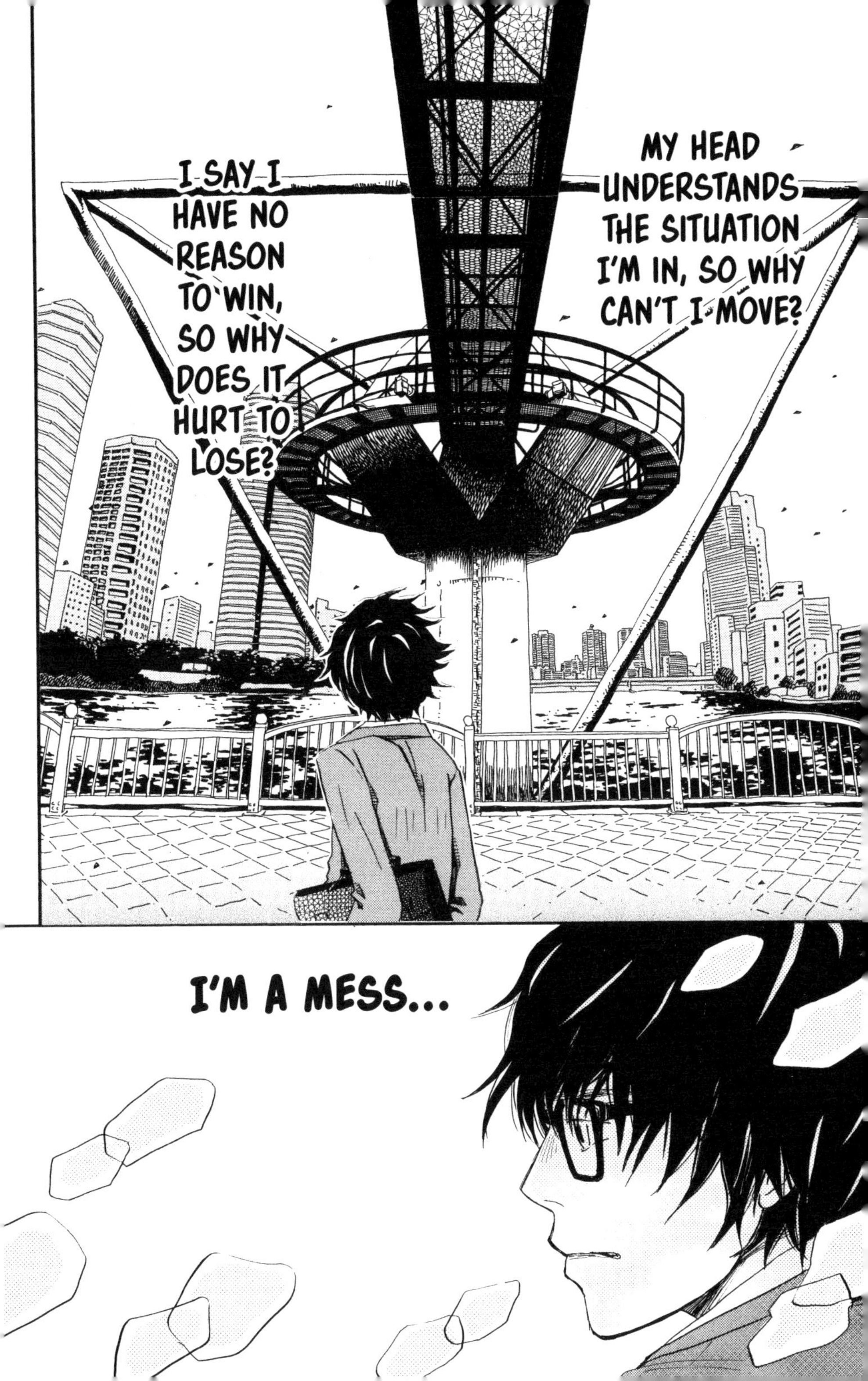
MY HEAD UNDERSTANDS THE SITUATION I'M IN, SO WHY CAN'T I MOVE?
I SAY I HAVE NO REASON TO WIN, SO WHY DOES IT HURT TO LOSE?
I'M A MESS...

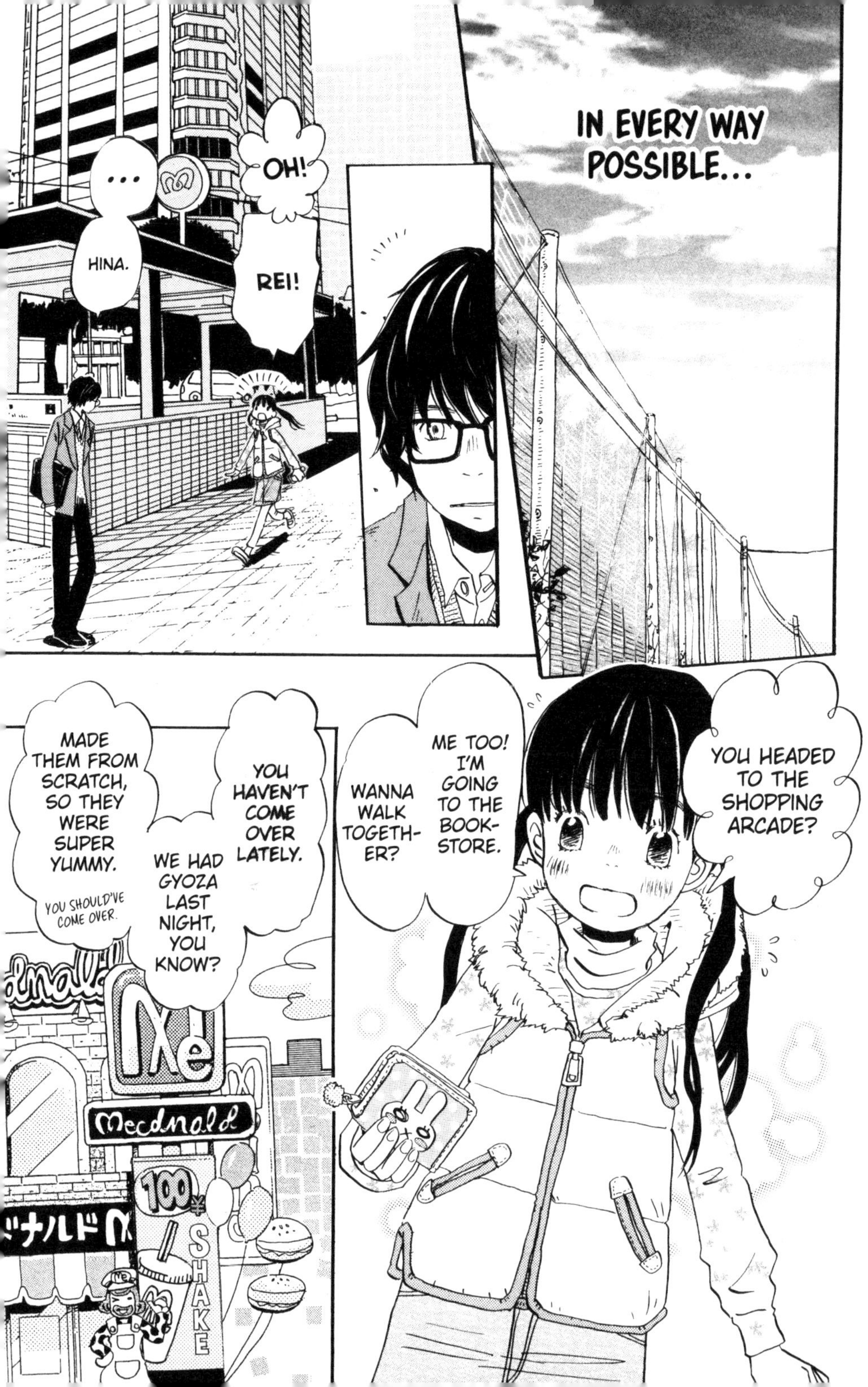
IN EVERY WAY POSSIBLE...
OH!
REI!
...
HINA.
YOU HEADED TO THE SHOPPING ARCADE?
ME TOO! I'M GOING TO THE BOOK-STORE.
WANNA WALK TOGETH-ER?
YOU HAVEN'T COME OVER LATELY.
WE HAD GYOZA LAST NIGHT, YOU KNOW?
MADE THEM FROM SCRATCH, SO THEY WERE SUPER YUMMY.
YOU SHOULD'VE COME OVER.
Mecdnald
100¥
SHAKE

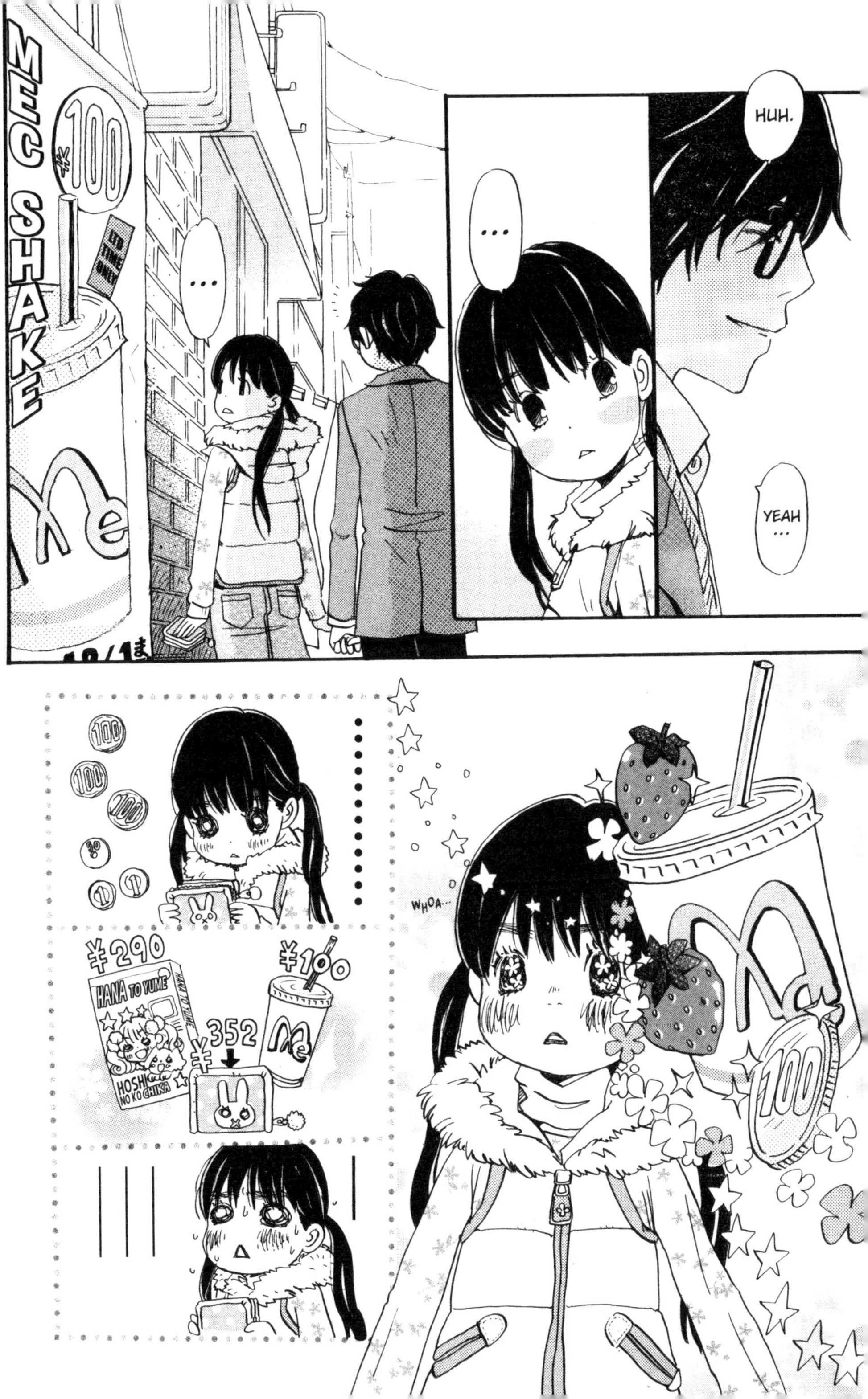
HUH.
...
YEAH ...
...
MEC SHAKE
¥100
LTD TIME ONLY!
WHOA...
100
¥290
HANA TO YUME
HOSHI NO KO CHIKA
¥100
¥352

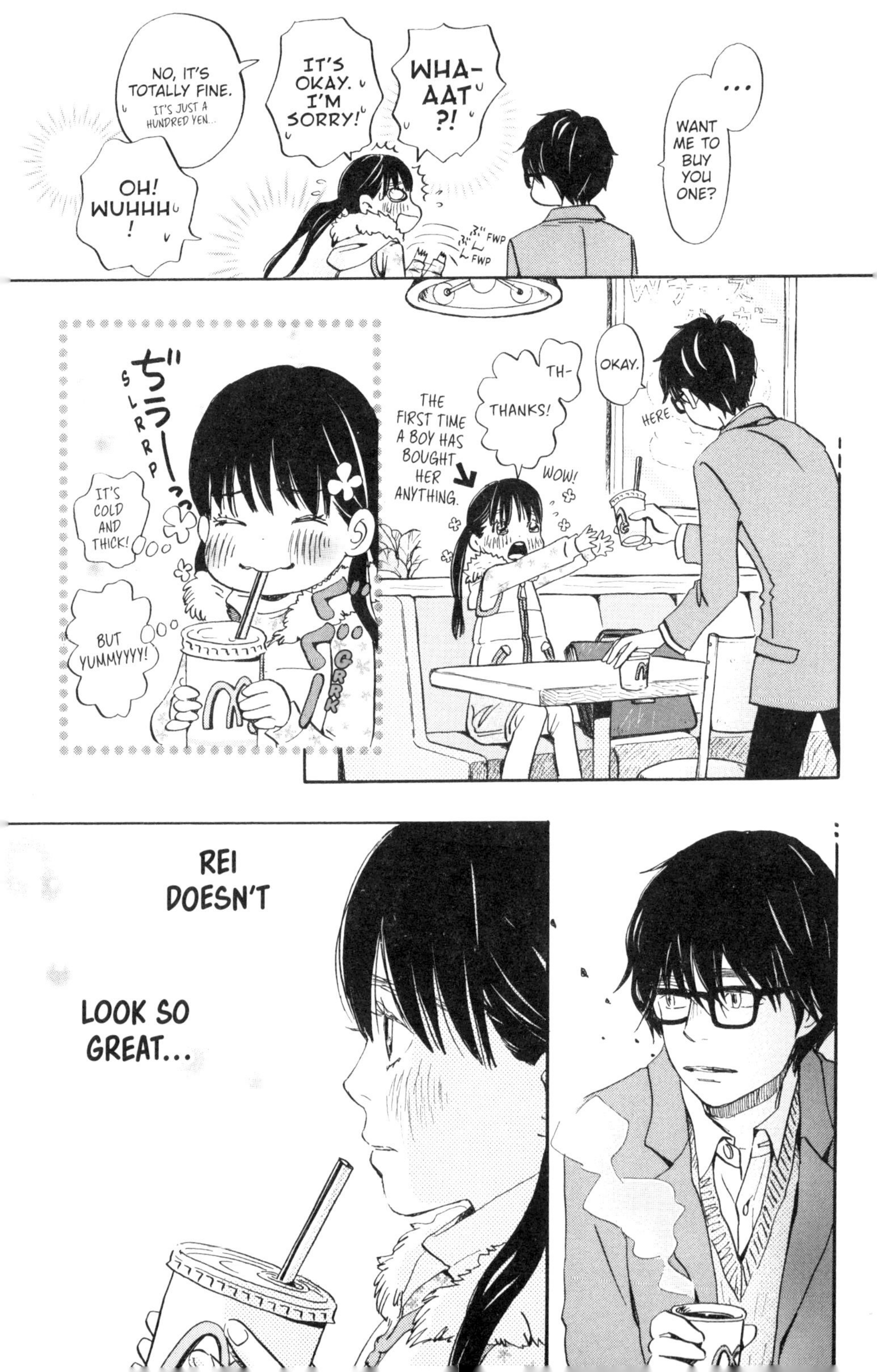
...
WANT ME TO BUY YOU ONE?
WHA-AAT?!
IT'S OKAY. I'M SORRY!
NO, IT'S TOTALLY FINE. IT'S JUST A HUNDRED YEN...
OH! WUHHH!
ぶぶ FWP FWP
OKAY.
HERE.
TH- THANKS!
WOW!
THE FIRST TIME A BOY HAS BOUGHT HER ANYTHING.
ぢラーっ SLRRP
IT'S COLD AND THICK!
BUT YUMMYYYY!
GRRK
REI DOESN'T
LOOK SO GREAT...

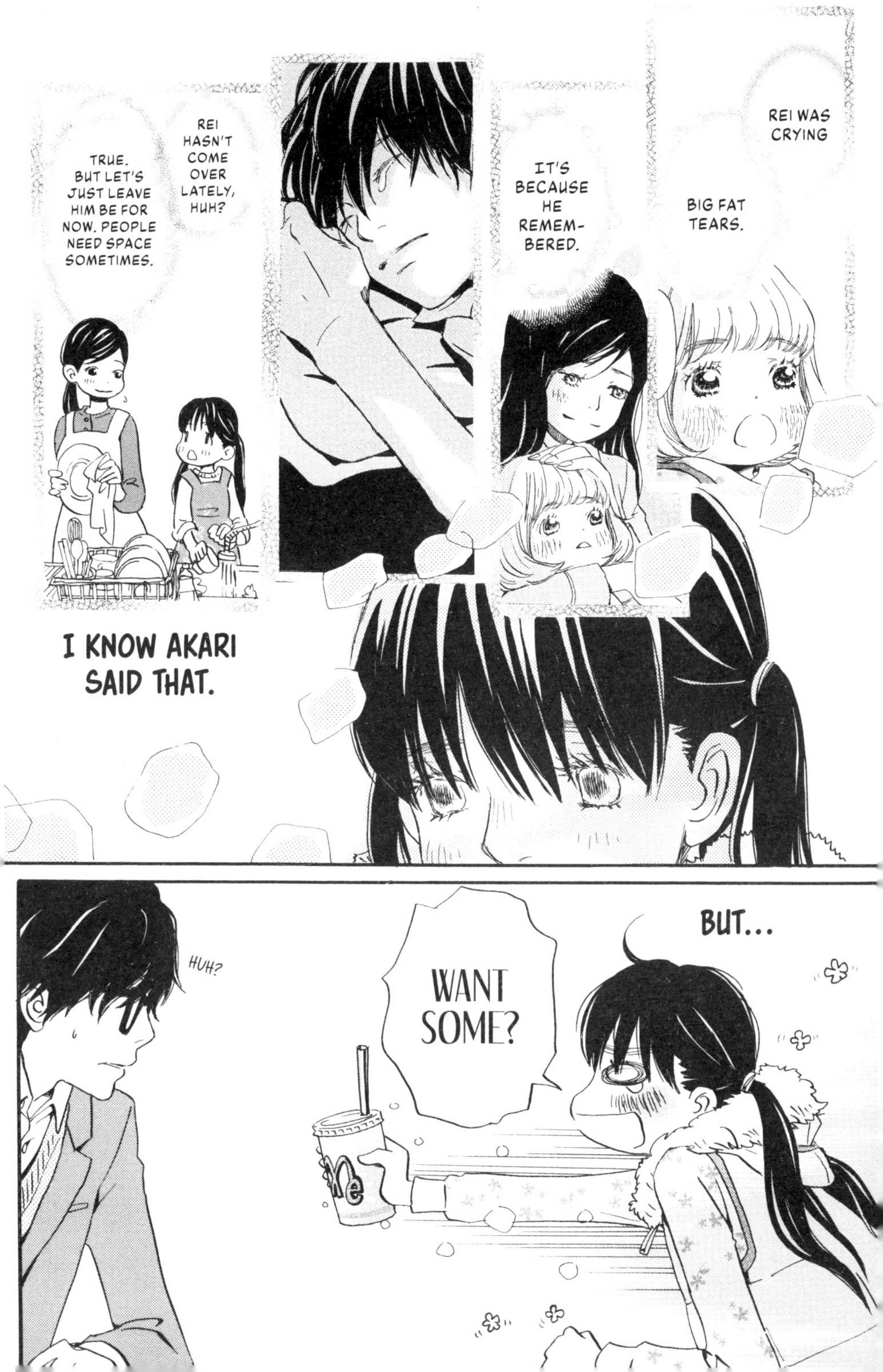
REI WAS CRYING
BIG FAT TEARS.
IT'S BECAUSE HE REMEMBERED.
REI HASN'T COME OVER LATELY, HUH?
TRUE. BUT LET'S JUST LEAVE HIM BE FOR NOW. PEOPLE NEED SPACE SOMETIMES.
I KNOW AKARI SAID THAT.
BUT...
WANT SOME?
HUH?

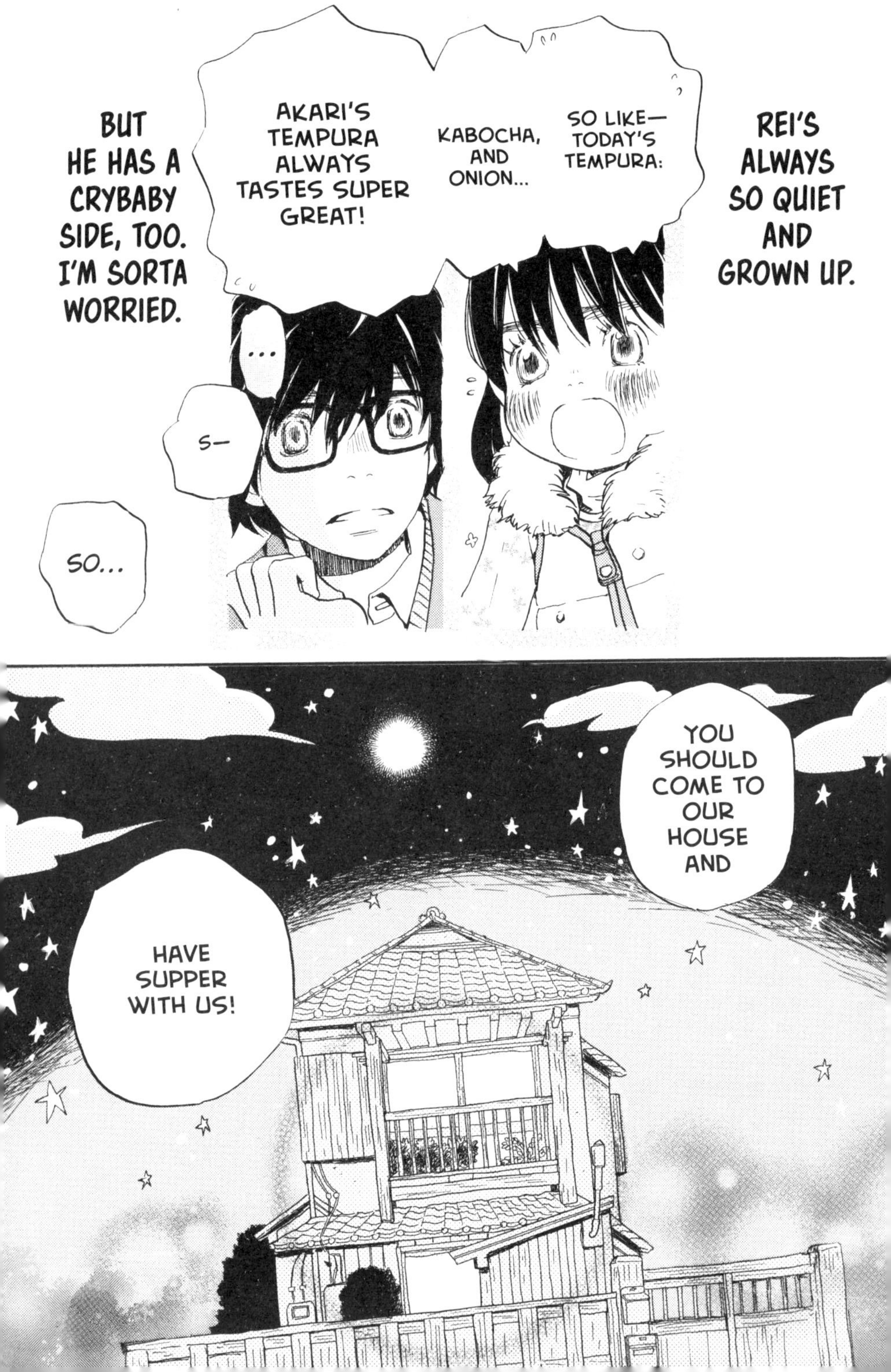
REI'S ALWAYS SO QUIET AND GROWN UP.
SO LIKE— TODAY'S TEMPURA:
KABOCHA, AND ONION...
AKARI'S TEMPURA ALWAYS TASTES SUPER GREAT!
BUT HE HAS A CRYBABY SIDE, TOO. I'M SORTA WORRIED.
...
S—
SO...
YOU SHOULD COME TO OUR HOUSE AND
HAVE SUPPER WITH US!

An Art Form in Itself! Creating Tsume Shogi is Hard.

Tsume shogi shows up quite a bit in *March Comes in Like a Lion*. In the game of shogi, the ultimate objective is to checkmate your opponent's king, and tsume shogi are puzzles to hone your technique. You checkmate the king with a series of checks, but there is boundless depth within this simple rule. Tsume shogi also made an appearance in this column in volume one.

The tsume shogi scene in volume two is on page 28 (Chapter 12). We see "Tsume Shogi Salon" and a diagram below it. This is in fact patterned after the tsume shogi reader submission column in *Shogi World*. This industry magazine is put out by the Japan Shogi Association and is a must-have for hardcore shogi fans.

In the manga, Kiriyama solves the 13-step tsume shogi problem created by Mr. Hayashida with a quick glance. And the truth is, a professional really could find checkmate this fast in this level of problem *(small self-satisfied chuckle)*.

So then, who created this problem? Naturally, me... or so you'd think. But I actually didn't. I'm quite good at solving these problems, but I'm terrible at coming up with them *(deep, depressed sigh)*. Well, the two *are* different beasts, and plenty of other professional players can't create tsume shogi, either.

So what did I do? I asked the famed Osakan player, Masahiko Urano, 7-*dan*. I explained the situation to him over the phone and waited a minute or two—well, I wasn't waiting, we were chatting the whole time, and then *bam!* He just came up with this tsume shogi. Quite impressive.

For another project, I had previously asked him for twelve problems. He was quite magnificent then, too. He said, "I'm just going to the barber," and an hour later, the twelve problems were ready. He was apparently imagining them while he was getting his hair cut. You do have to wonder how his brain works exactly.

An art that Urano is particularly good at is "nigiri-zume." You grab a handful of the forty pieces in the game and then use all of them to create a tsume shogi. He often shows off this talent at events, as the sort of thing you can do if you have a minute to spare. Urano has also been selected for the Kanjusho Prize, awarded annually to the most highly rated tsume shogi.

That creation is below. If you can get to checkmate, you too are on the professional level. ☗

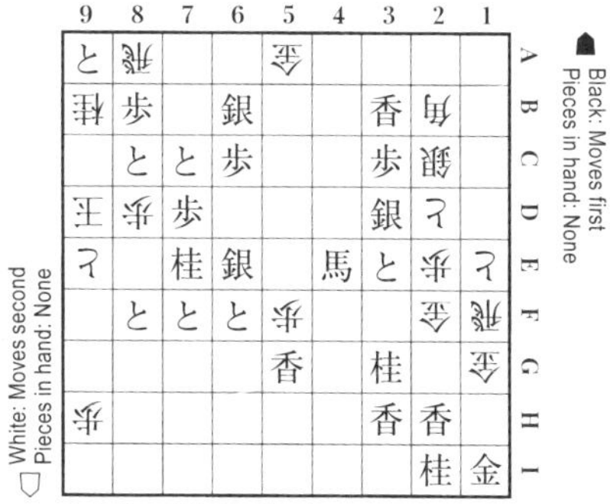
9 8 7 6 5 4 3 2 1
A B C D E F G H I
☗ Black: Moves first
Pieces in hand: None
☖ White: Moves second
Pieces in hand: None
Kanju Award Winning Board

Chapter 13

Child of God (Part 3)

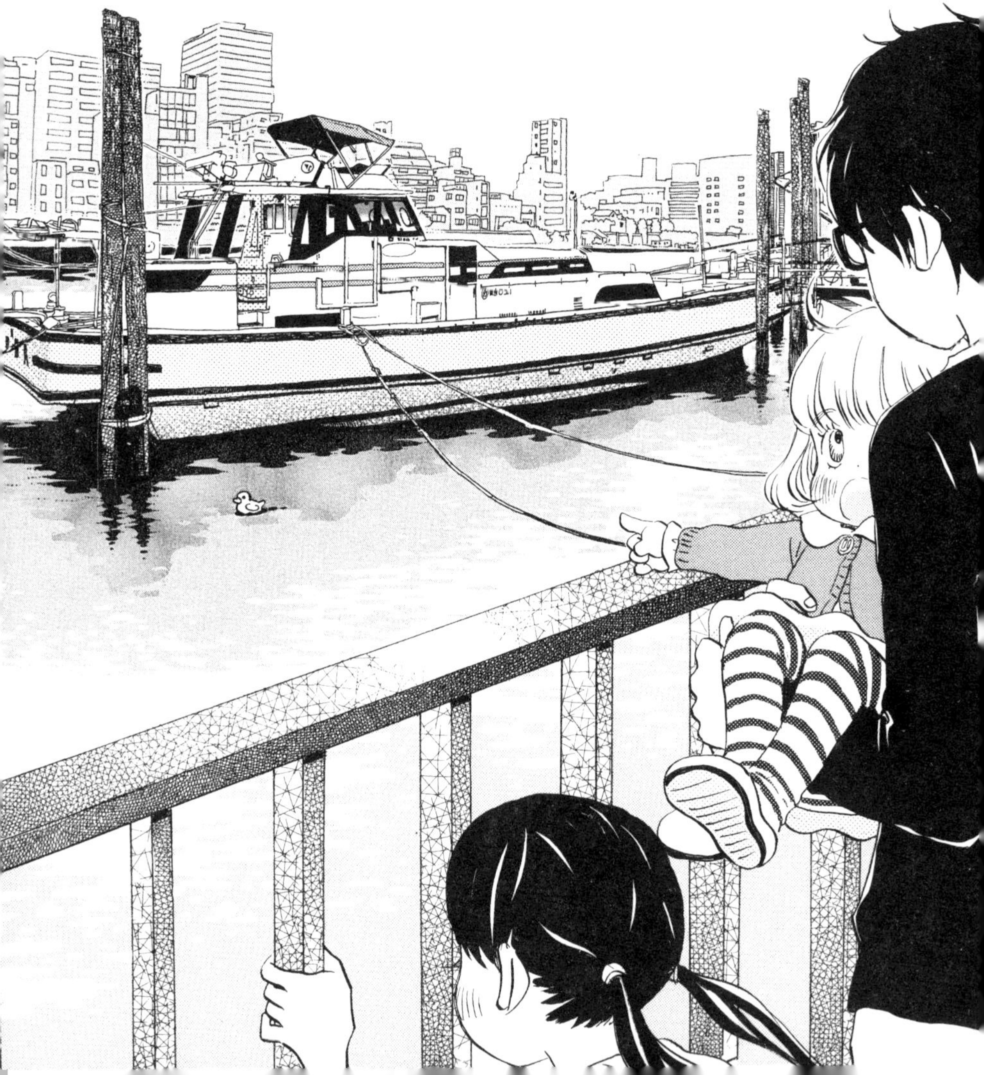

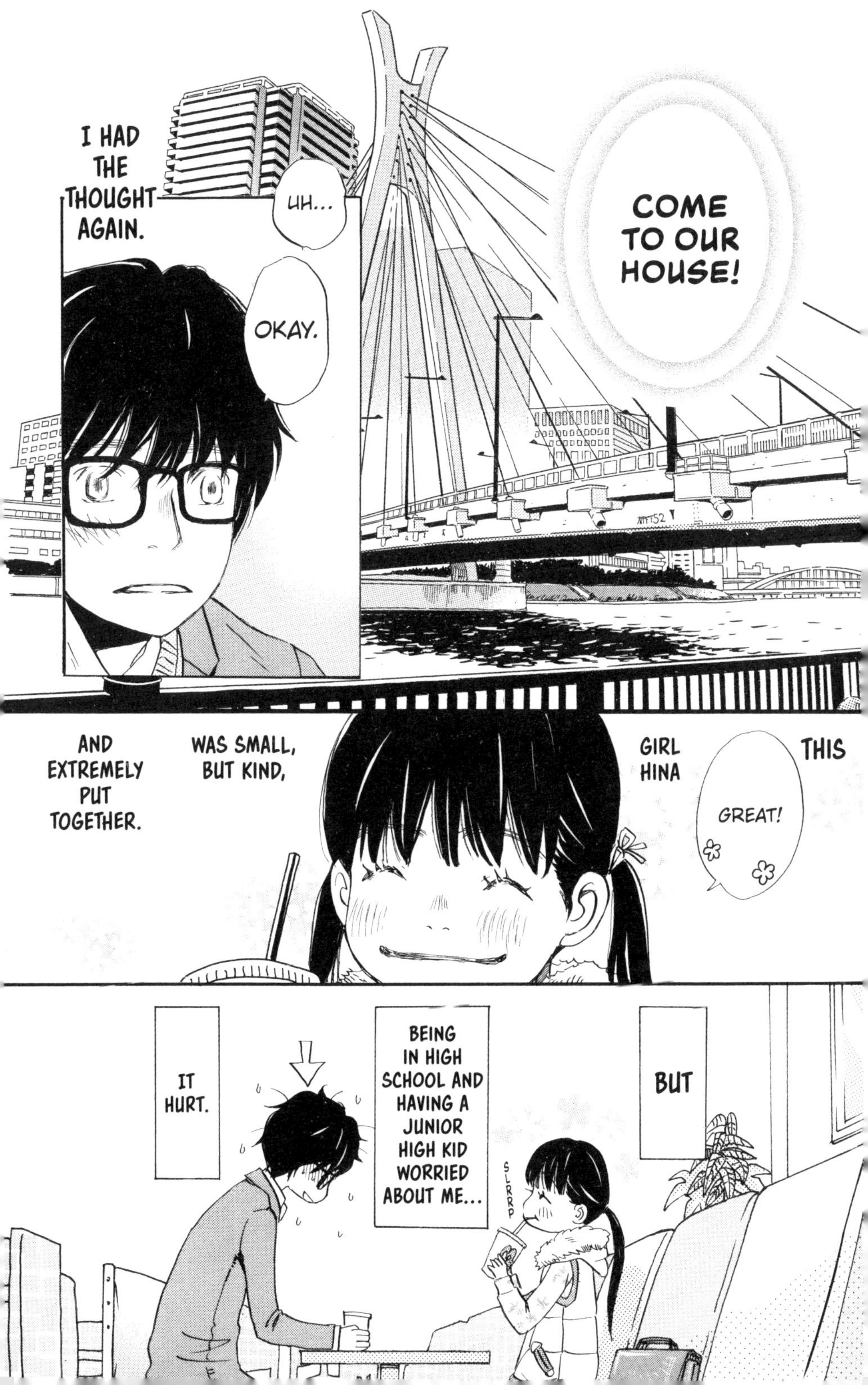
COME TO OUR HOUSE!
UH...
OKAY.
I HAD THE THOUGHT AGAIN.
THIS
GREAT!
GIRL HINA
WAS SMALL, BUT KIND,
AND EXTREMELY PUT TOGETHER.
BUT
BEING IN HIGH SCHOOL AND HAVING A JUNIOR HIGH KID WORRIED ABOUT ME...
SLRRP
IT HURT.

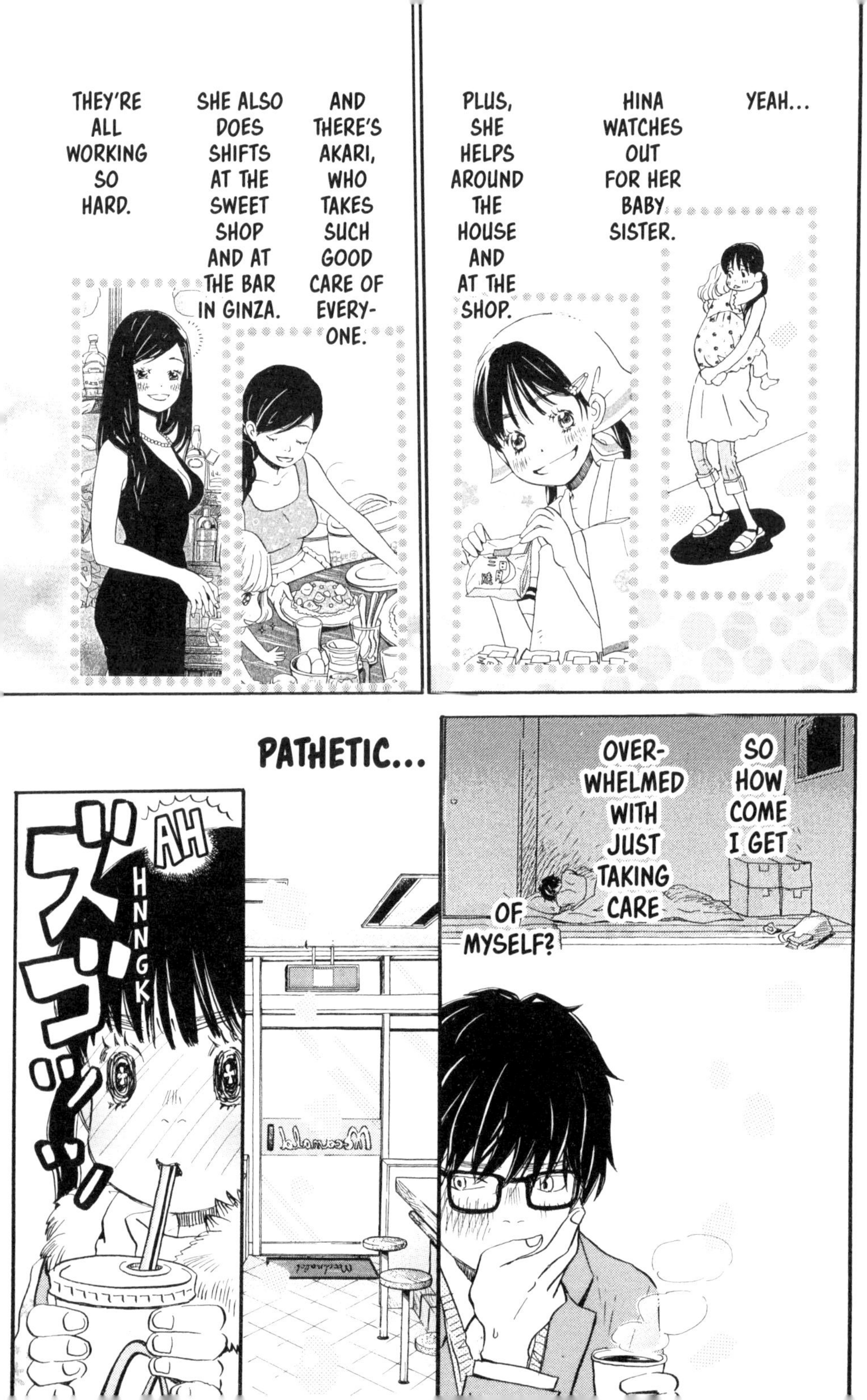
YEAH...
HINA WATCHES OUT FOR HER BABY SISTER.
PLUS, SHE HELPS AROUND THE HOUSE AND AT THE SHOP.
AND THERE'S AKARI, WHO TAKES SUCH GOOD CARE OF EVERYONE.
SHE ALSO DOES SHIFTS AT THE SWEET SHOP AND AT THE BAR IN GINZA.
THEY'RE ALL WORKING SO HARD.
SO HOW COME I GET
OVERWHELMED WITH JUST TAKING CARE OF MYSELF?
PATHETIC...
AH
HNNGK
ズゴ

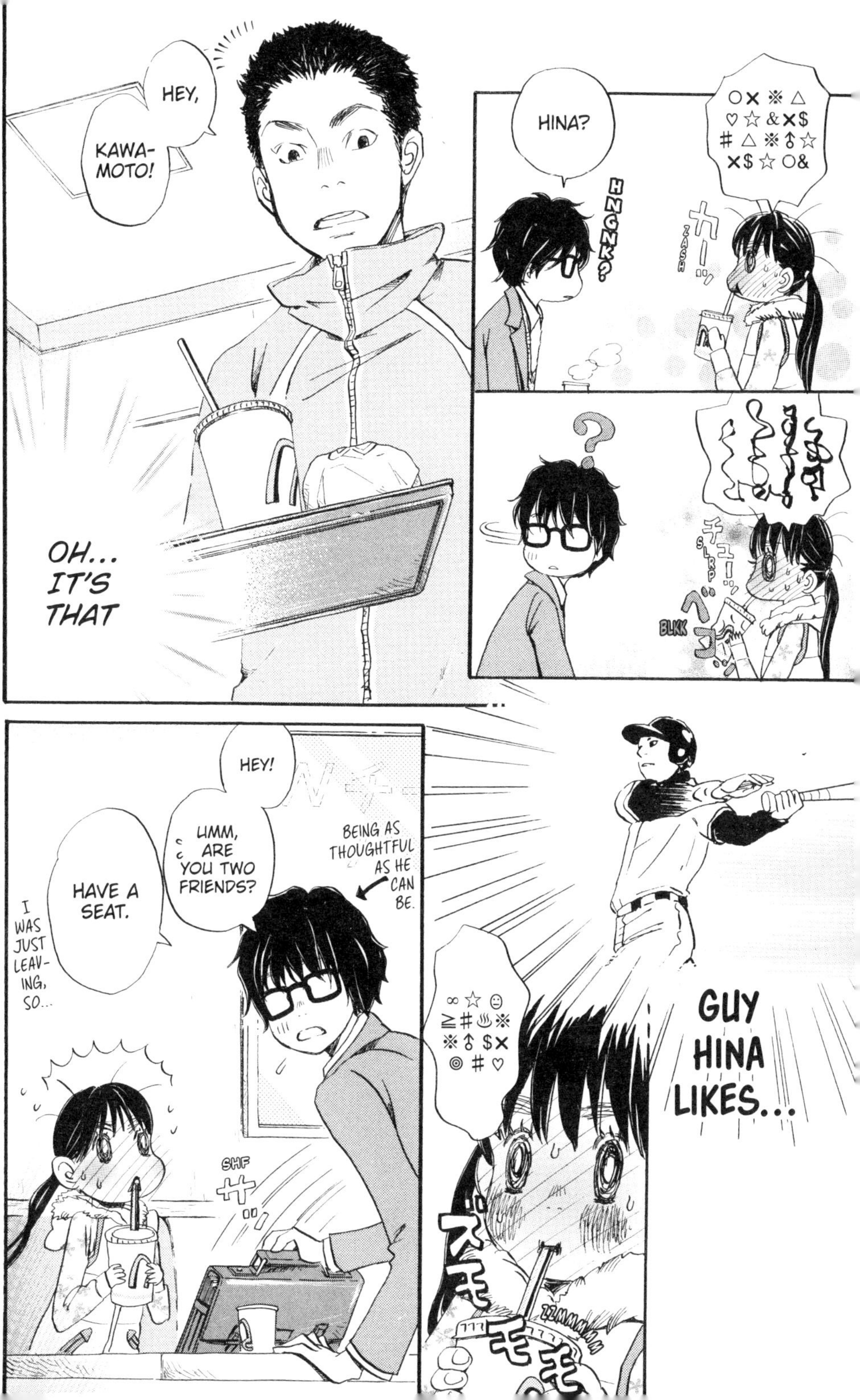
○×※△
♡☆&×$
#△※♂☆
×$☆○&
HINA?
カーッ
ZAASH
HNGNK?
チューッ
SLRP
ベコ
BLKK
HEY,
KAWA-MOTO!
OH... IT'S THAT
GUY HINA LIKES...
∞☆☺
≧#♨※
※♂$×
◎#♡
ズモモモ
ZZMMMMM
HEY!
BEING AS THOUGHTFUL AS HE CAN BE.
UMM, ARE YOU TWO FRIENDS?
HAVE A SEAT.
I WAS JUST LEAV-ING, SO...
サッ
SHF

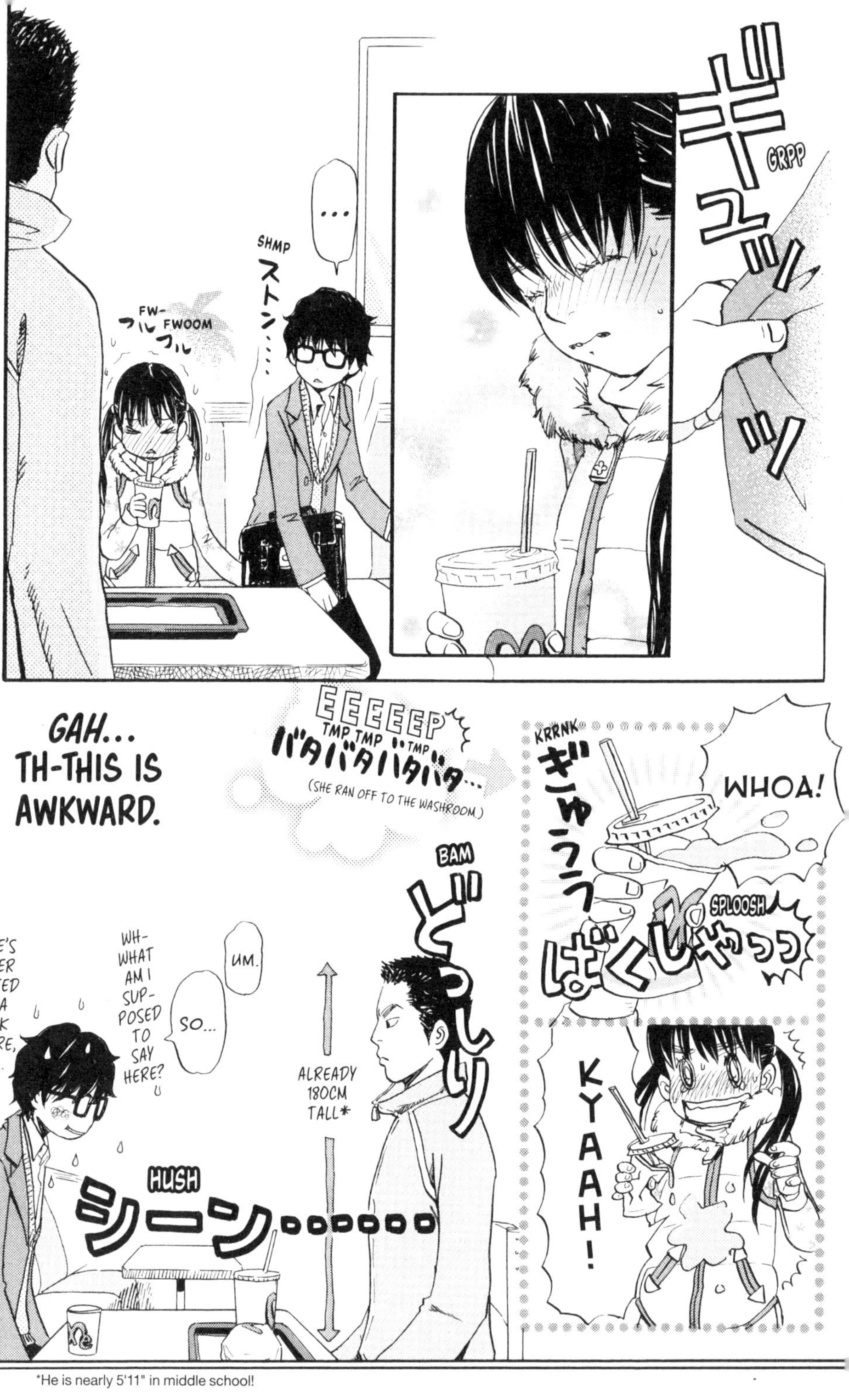
ギュッ
GRPP
...
SHMP
ストン…
FW-
フル
FWOOM
フル
KRRNK
ぎゅううう
WHOA!
SPLOOSH
ばくしゃっっっ
KYAAH!
EEEEEP
TMP TMP TMP
バタバタバタバタ…
(SHE RAN OFF TO THE WASHROOM.)
GAH... TH-THIS IS AWKWARD.
BAM
どっしり
ALREADY 180CM TALL*
UM.
SO...
WH-WHAT AM I SUPPOSED TO SAY HERE?
*HE'S NEVER TALKED TO A JOCK BEFORE, SO...
HUSH
シーン…….

*He is nearly 5'11" in middle school!

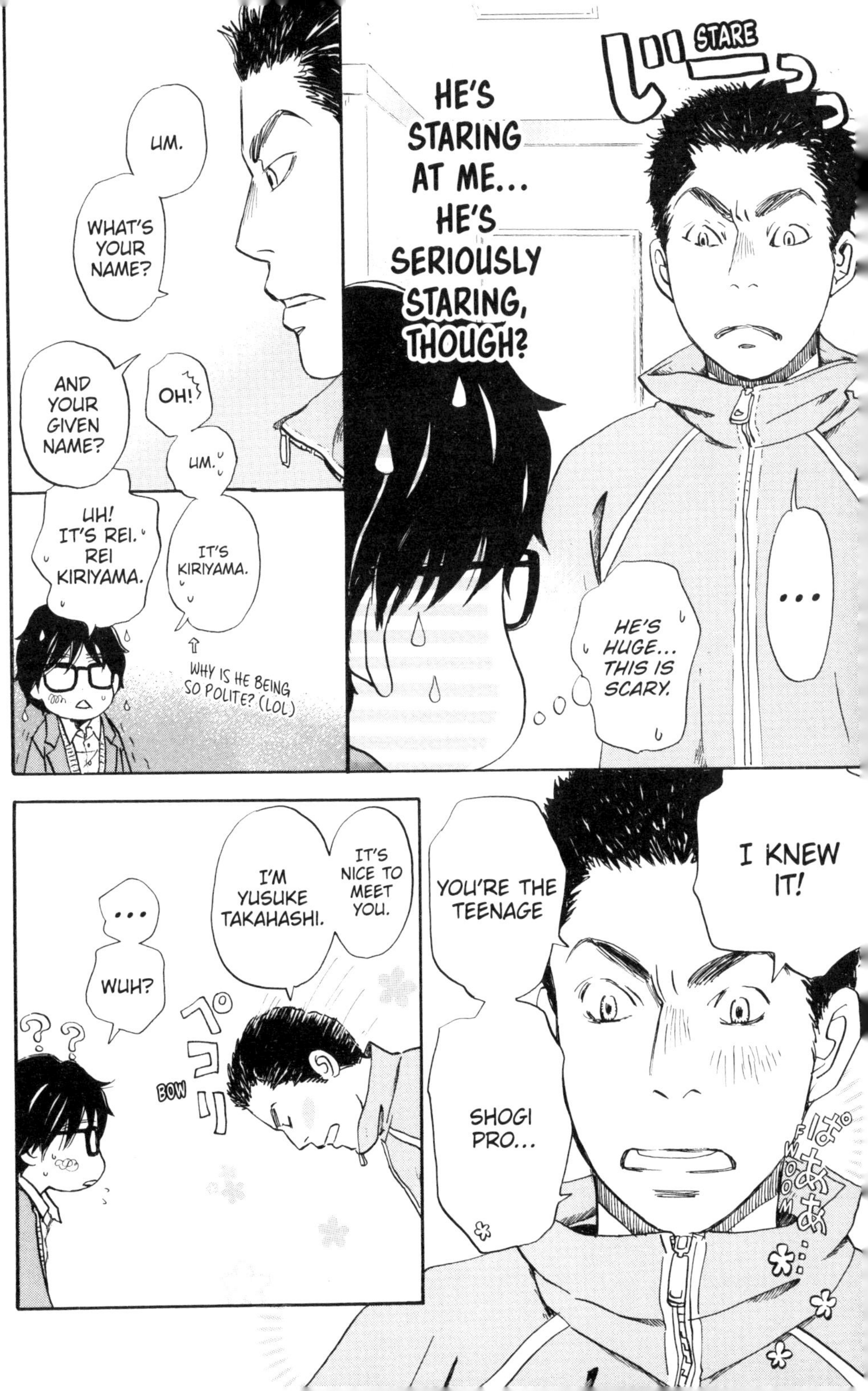
STARE
HE'S STARING AT ME... HE'S SERIOUSLY STARING, THOUGH?
...
HE'S HUGE... THIS IS SCARY.
UM.
WHAT'S YOUR NAME?
OH!
UM.
AND YOUR GIVEN NAME?
IT'S KIRIYAMA.
UH! IT'S REI. REI KIRIYAMA.
WHY IS HE BEING SO POLITE? (LOL)
I KNEW IT!
YOU'RE THE TEENAGE
SHOGI PRO...
FWOOM
IT'S NICE TO MEET YOU.
I'M YUSUKE TAKAHASHI.
BOW
...
WUH?

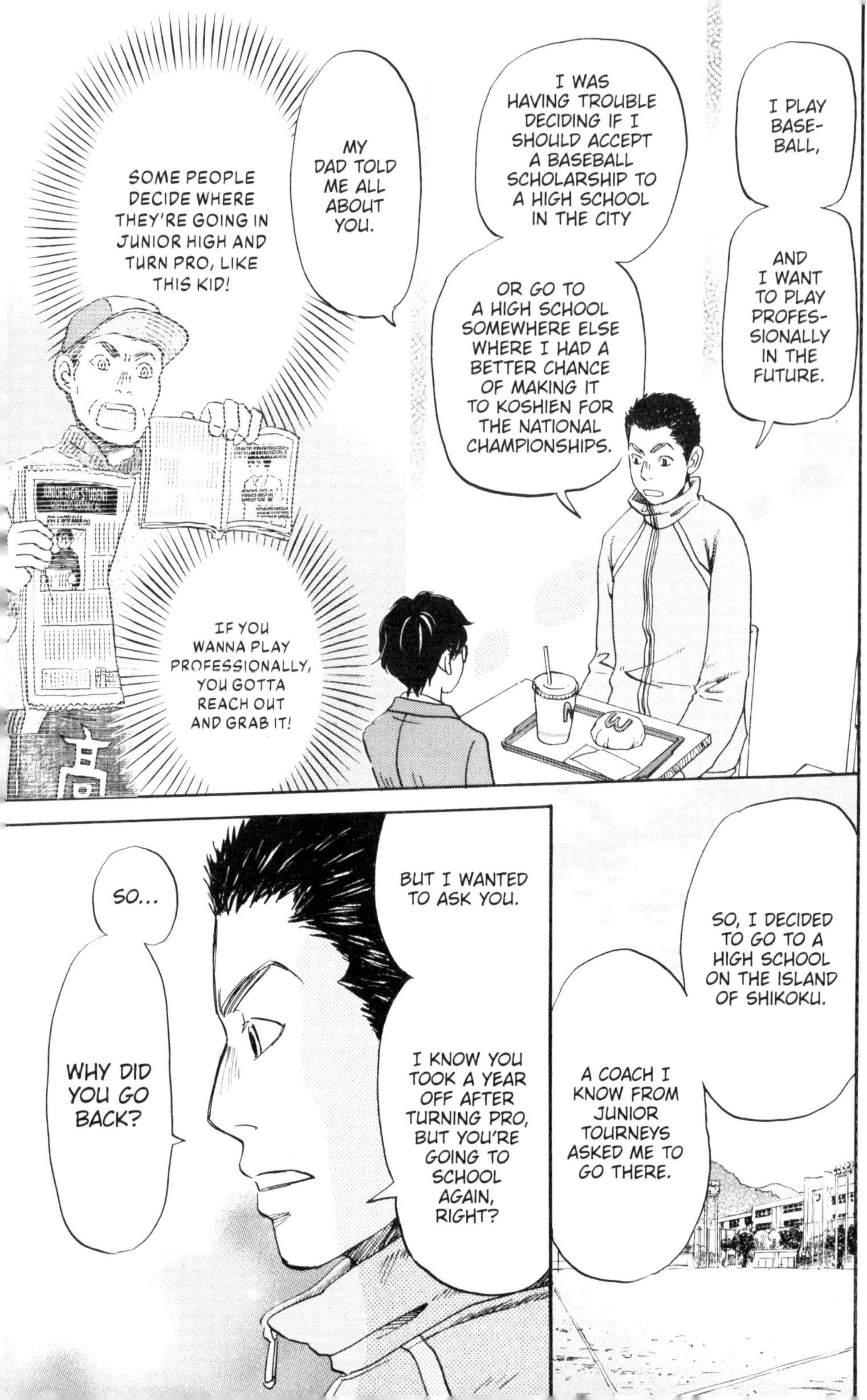
I PLAY BASE-BALL,
AND I WANT TO PLAY PROFES-SIONALLY IN THE FUTURE.
I WAS HAVING TROUBLE DECIDING IF I SHOULD ACCEPT A BASEBALL SCHOLARSHIP TO A HIGH SCHOOL IN THE CITY
OR GO TO A HIGH SCHOOL SOMEWHERE ELSE WHERE I HAD A BETTER CHANCE OF MAKING IT TO KOSHIEN FOR THE NATIONAL CHAMPIONSHIPS.
MY DAD TOLD ME ALL ABOUT YOU.
SOME PEOPLE DECIDE WHERE THEY'RE GOING IN JUNIOR HIGH AND TURN PRO, LIKE THIS KID!
IF YOU WANNA PLAY PROFESSIONALLY, YOU GOTTA REACH OUT AND GRAB IT!
SO, I DECIDED TO GO TO A HIGH SCHOOL ON THE ISLAND OF SHIKOKU.
A COACH I KNOW FROM JUNIOR TOURNEYS ASKED ME TO GO THERE.
BUT I WANTED TO ASK YOU.
I KNOW YOU TOOK A YEAR OFF AFTER TURNING PRO, BUT YOU'RE GOING TO SCHOOL AGAIN, RIGHT?
SO...
WHY DID YOU GO BACK?

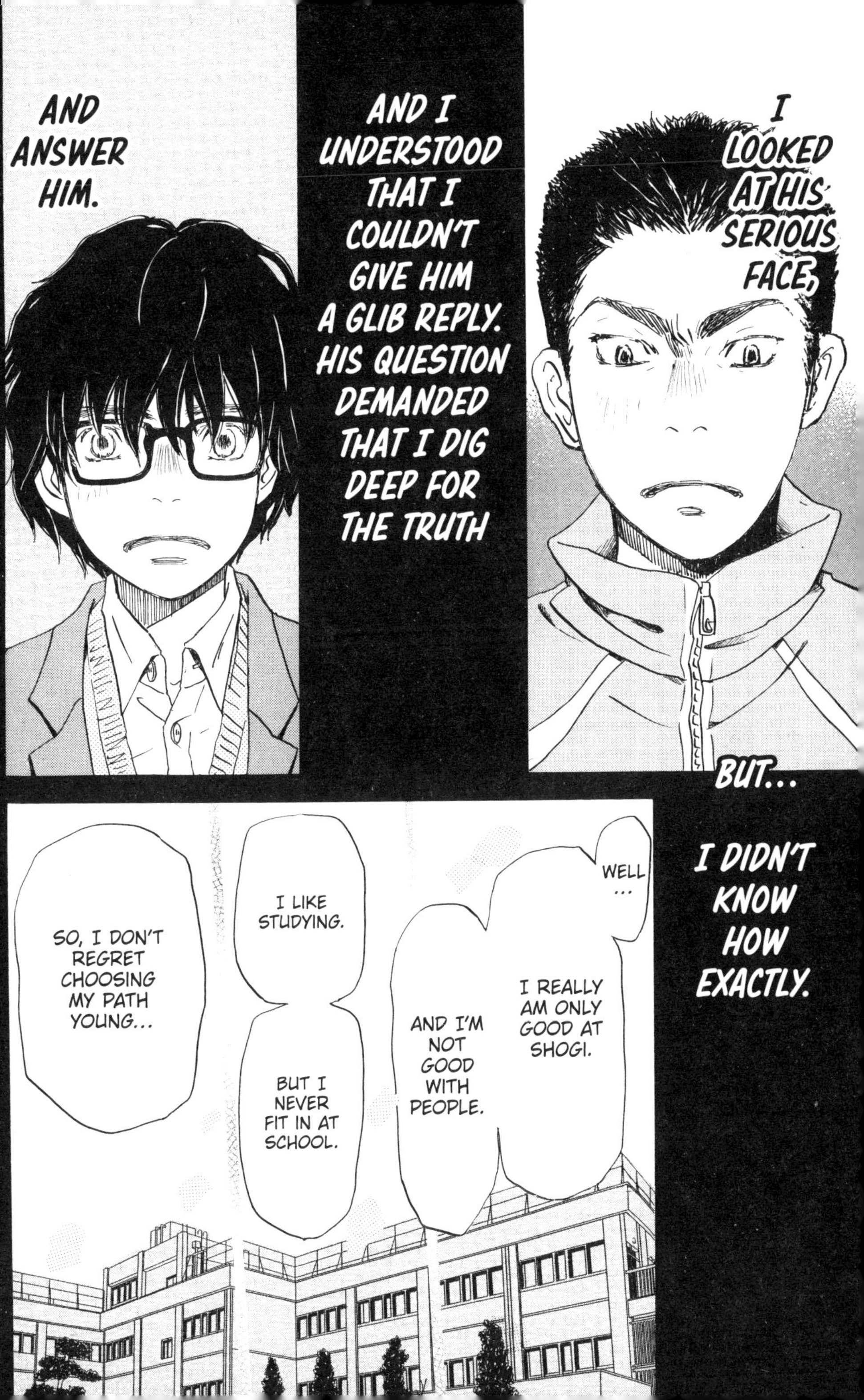
I LOOKED AT HIS SERIOUS FACE,
AND I UNDERSTOOD THAT I COULDN'T GIVE HIM A GLIB REPLY. HIS QUESTION DEMANDED THAT I DIG DEEP FOR THE TRUTH
AND ANSWER HIM.
BUT...
I DIDN'T KNOW HOW EXACTLY.
WELL ...
I REALLY AM ONLY GOOD AT SHOGI.
AND I'M NOT GOOD WITH PEOPLE.
I LIKE STUDYING.
BUT I NEVER FIT IN AT SCHOOL.
SO, I DON'T REGRET CHOOSING MY PATH YOUNG...

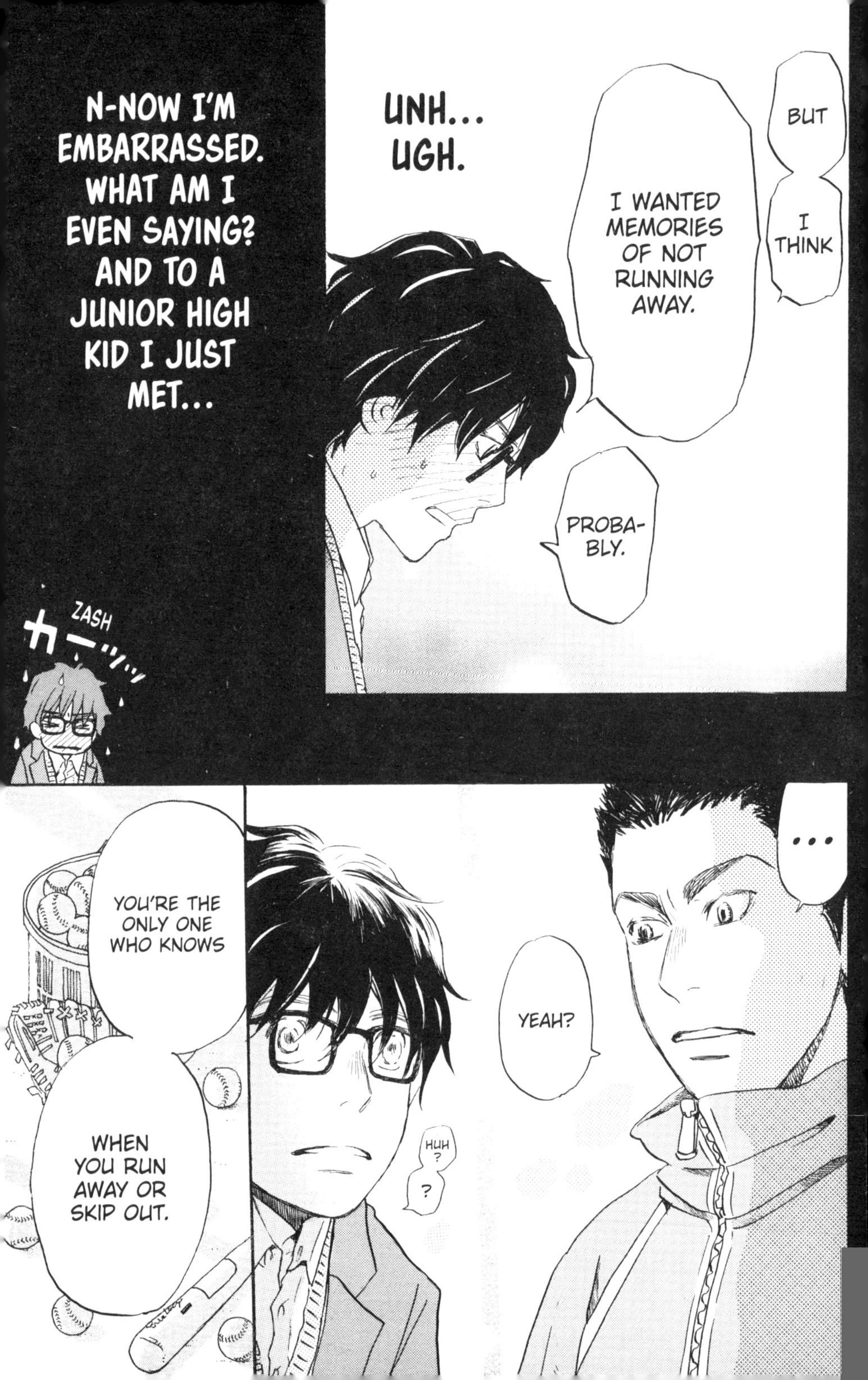
BUT
I THINK
I WANTED MEMORIES OF NOT RUNNING AWAY.
PROBABLY.
UNH... UGH.
N-NOW I'M EMBARRASSED. WHAT AM I EVEN SAYING? AND TO A JUNIOR HIGH KID I JUST MET...
ZASH
...
YEAH?
YOU'RE THE ONLY ONE WHO KNOWS
WHEN YOU RUN AWAY OR SKIP OUT.
HUH? ?

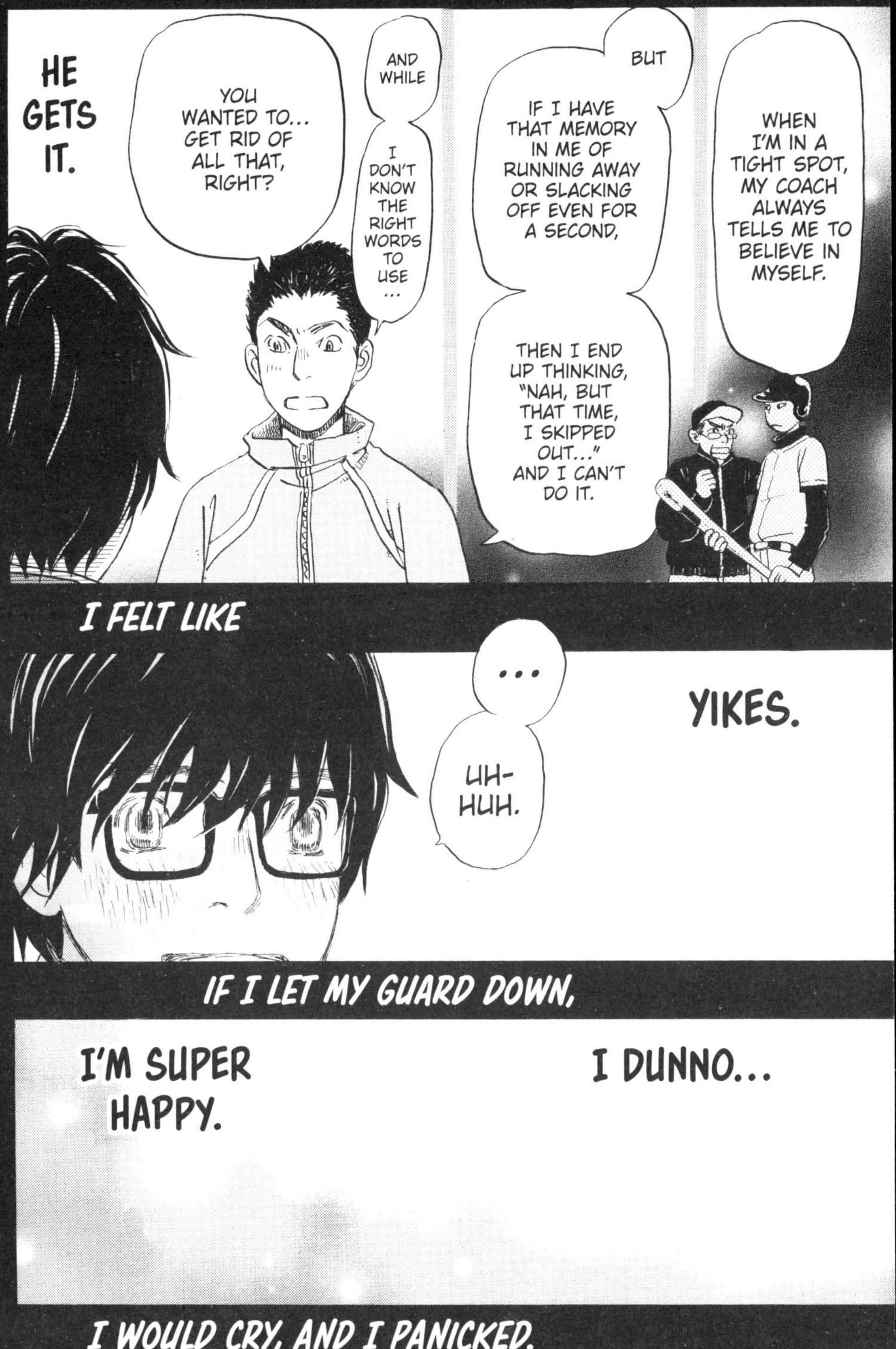
WHEN I'M IN A TIGHT SPOT, MY COACH ALWAYS TELLS ME TO BELIEVE IN MYSELF.
BUT
IF I HAVE THAT MEMORY IN ME OF RUNNING AWAY OR SLACKING OFF EVEN FOR A SECOND,
THEN I END UP THINKING, "NAH, BUT THAT TIME, I SKIPPED OUT..." AND I CAN'T DO IT.
AND WHILE
I DON'T KNOW THE RIGHT WORDS TO USE...
YOU WANTED TO... GET RID OF ALL THAT, RIGHT?
HE GETS IT.
I FELT LIKE
YIKES.
...
UH-HUH.
IF I LET MY GUARD DOWN,
I DUNNO...
I'M SUPER HAPPY.
I WOULD CRY, AND I PANICKED.

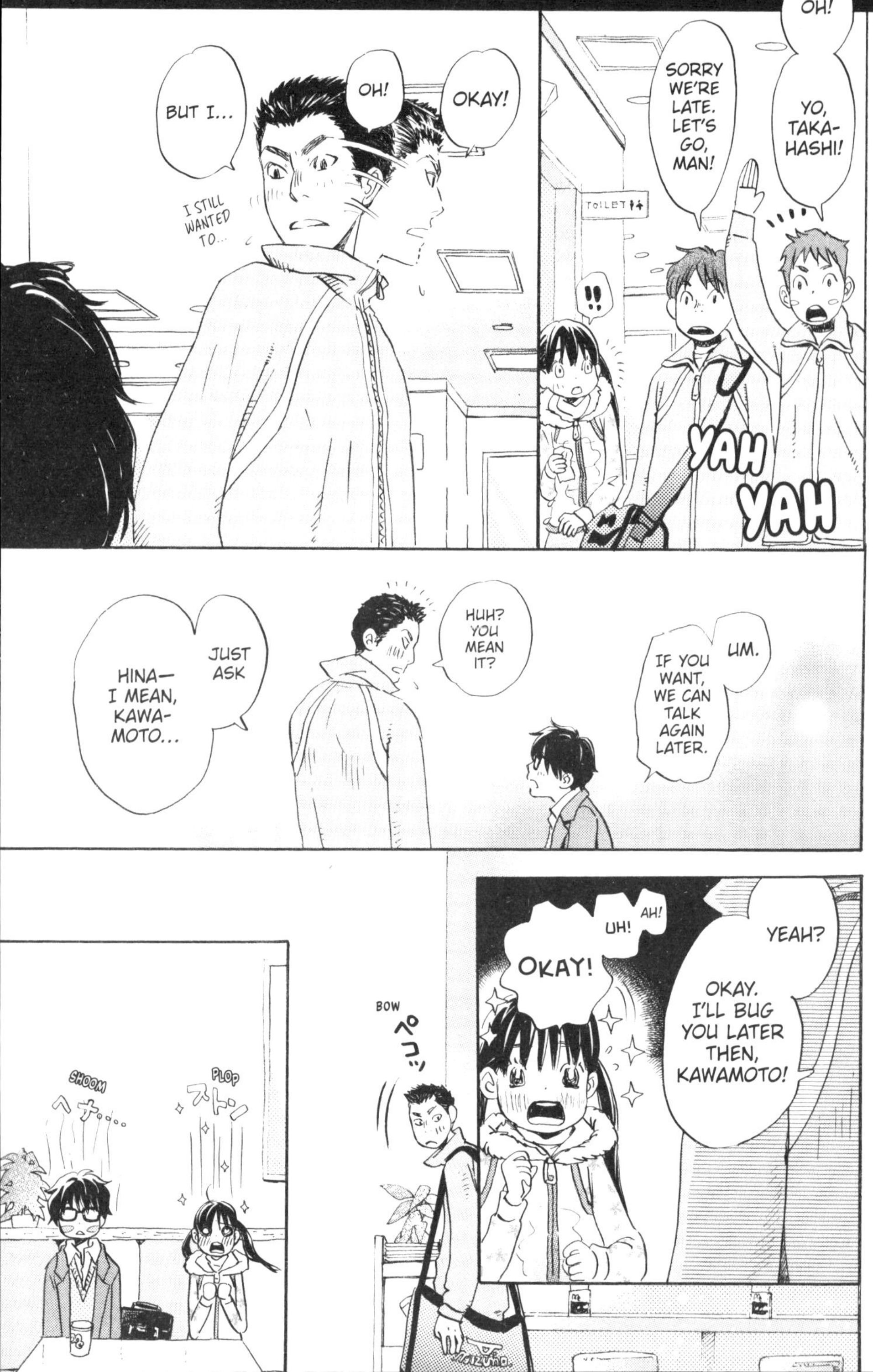
OH!
YO, TAKA-HASHI!
SORRY WE'RE LATE. LET'S GO, MAN!
!!
TOILET
YAH YAH
OKAY!
OH!
BUT I...
I STILL WANTED TO...
UM.
IF YOU WANT, WE CAN TALK AGAIN LATER.
HUH? YOU MEAN IT?
JUST ASK
HINA— I MEAN, KAWAMOTO...
YEAH?
OKAY. I'LL BUG YOU LATER THEN, KAWAMOTO!
AH!
UH!
OKAY!
BOW
ペコッ
PLOP
ストン
SHOOM
ヘナ....

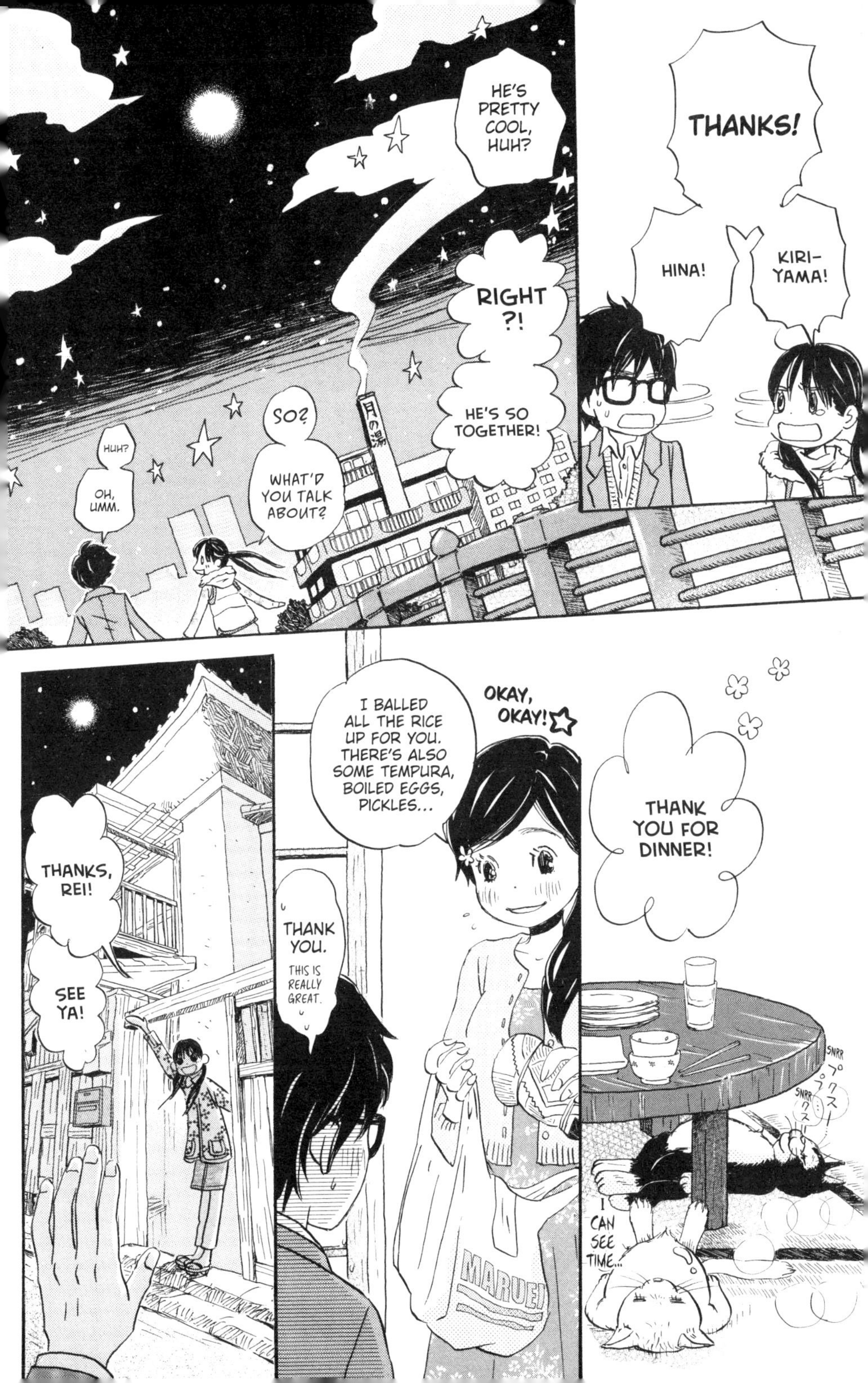
THANKS!
KIRI-YAMA!
HINA!
HE'S PRETTY COOL, HUH?
RIGHT?!
HE'S SO TOGETHER!
月の湯
SO?
WHAT'D YOU TALK ABOUT?
HUH?
OH, UMM.
THANK YOU FOR DINNER!
SNRR
プクスー
SNRR
クスー
I CAN SEE TIME...
OKAY, OKAY!
I BALLED ALL THE RICE UP FOR YOU. THERE'S ALSO SOME TEMPURA, BOILED EGGS, PICKLES...
THANK YOU.
THIS IS REALLY GREAT.
MARUEI
THANKS, REI!
SEE YA!

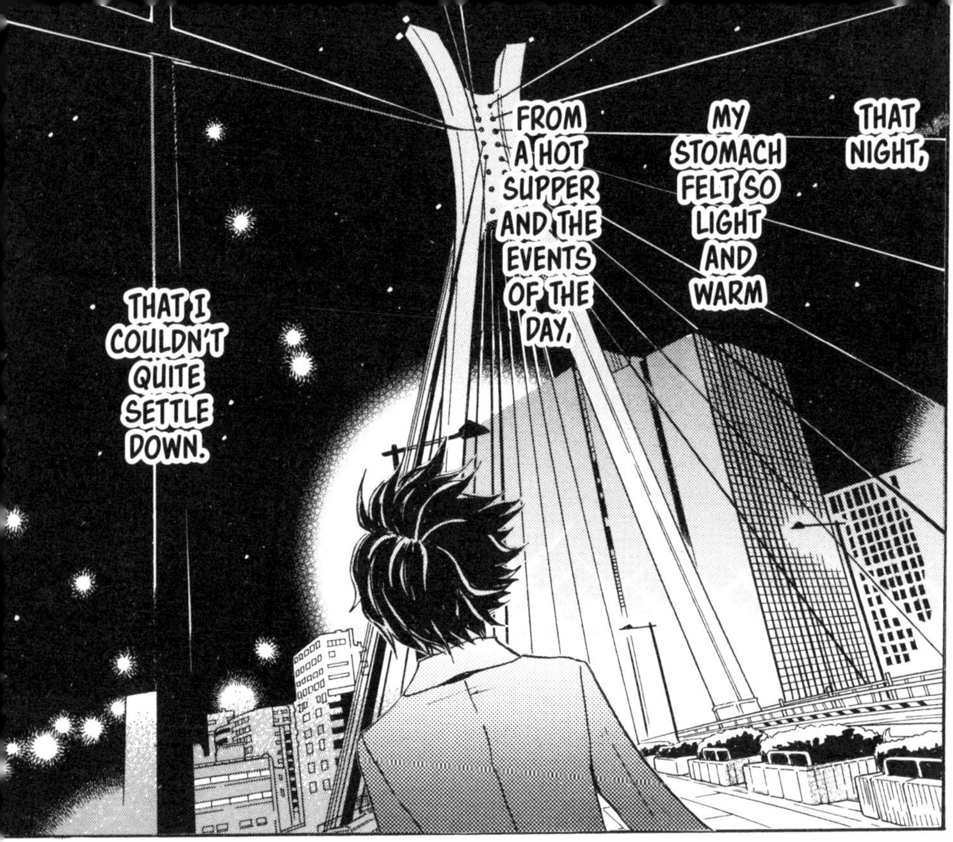
THAT NIGHT,
MY STOMACH FELT SO LIGHT AND WARM
FROM A HOT SUPPER AND THE EVENTS OF THE DAY,
THAT I COULDN'T QUITE SETTLE DOWN.
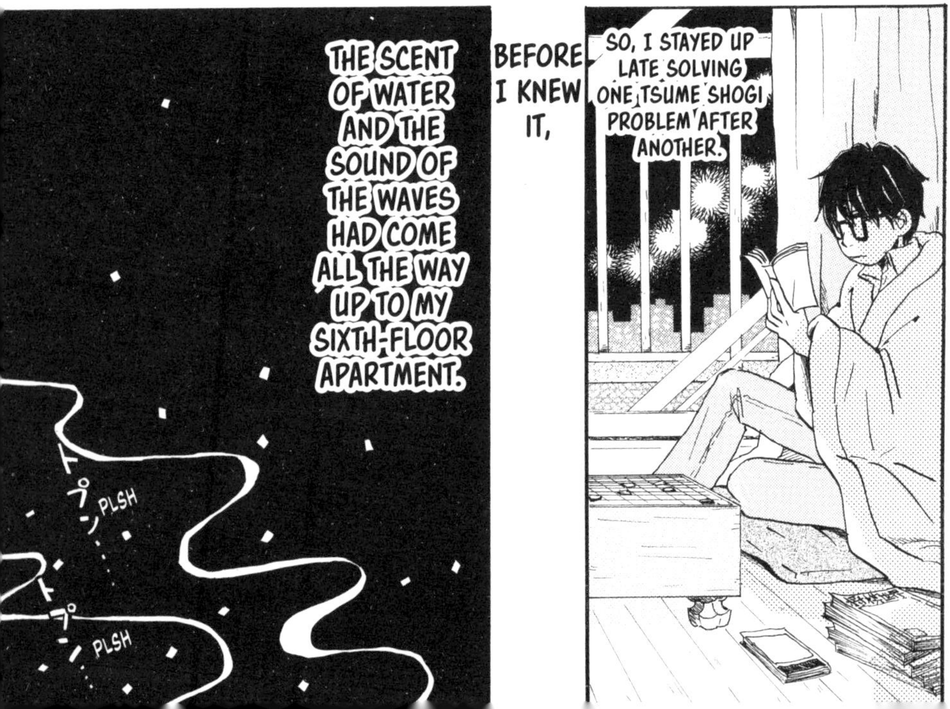
SO, I STAYED UP LATE SOLVING ONE TSUME SHOGI PROBLEM AFTER ANOTHER.
BEFORE I KNEW IT,
THE SCENT OF WATER AND THE SOUND OF THE WAVES HAD COME ALL THE WAY UP TO MY SIXTH-FLOOR APARTMENT.
トプン… PLSH
トプン… PLSH

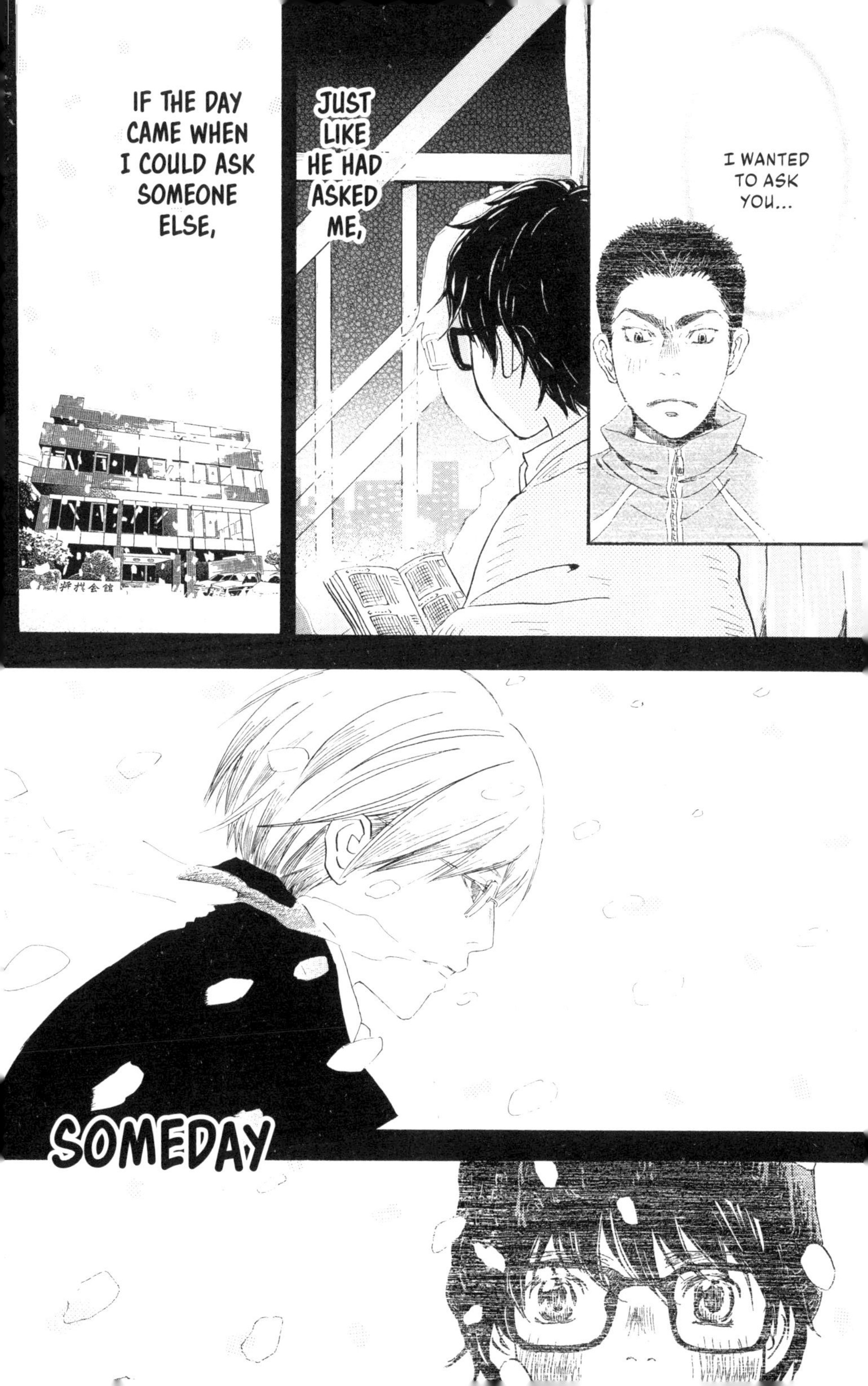
I WANTED TO ASK YOU...
JUST LIKE HE HAD ASKED ME,
IF THE DAY CAME WHEN I COULD ASK SOMEONE ELSE,
SOMEDAY

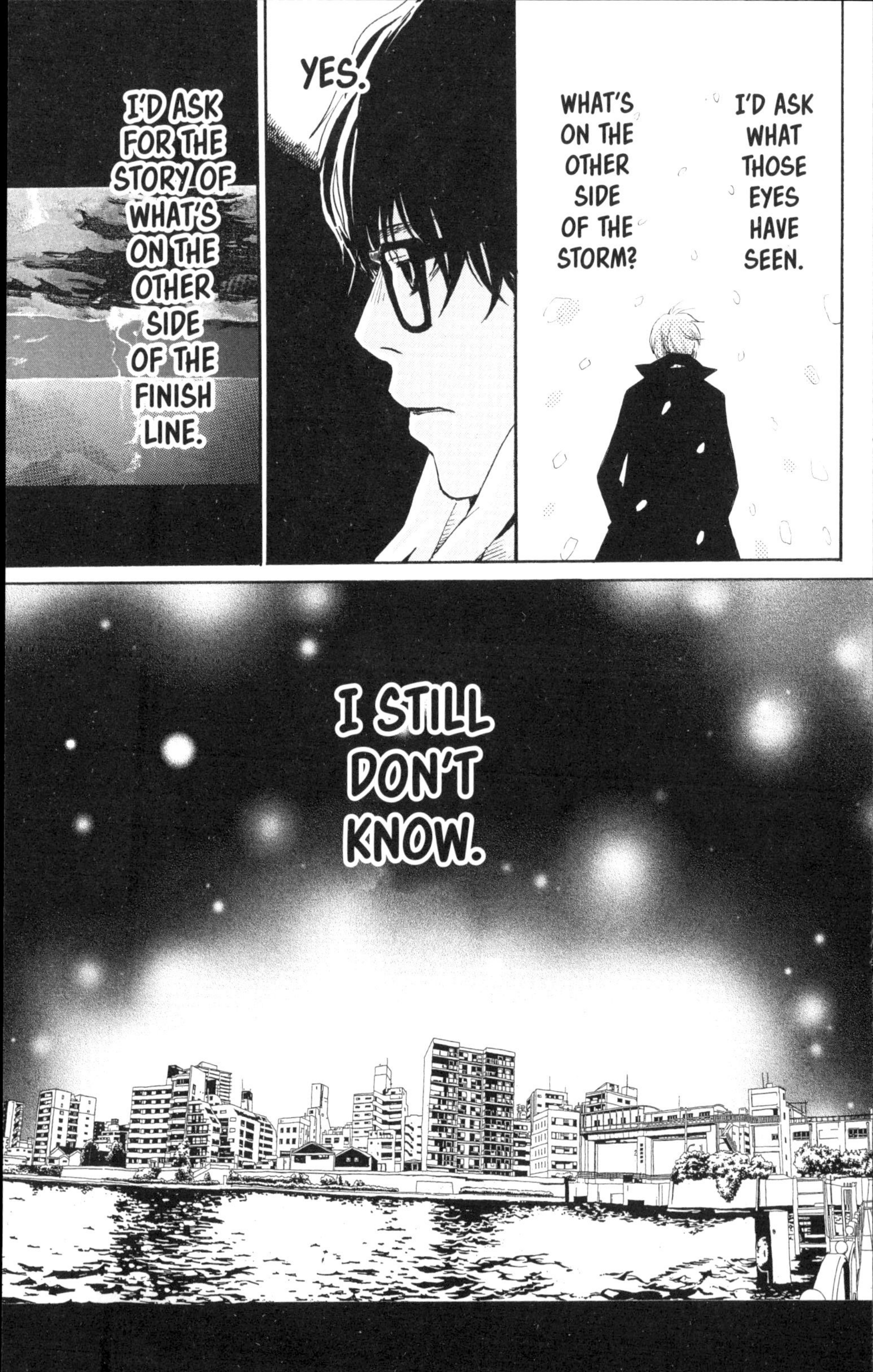
I'D ASK WHAT THOSE EYES HAVE SEEN.
WHAT'S ON THE OTHER SIDE OF THE STORM?
YES.
I'D ASK FOR THE STORY OF WHAT'S ON THE OTHER SIDE OF THE FINISH LINE.
I STILL DON'T KNOW.

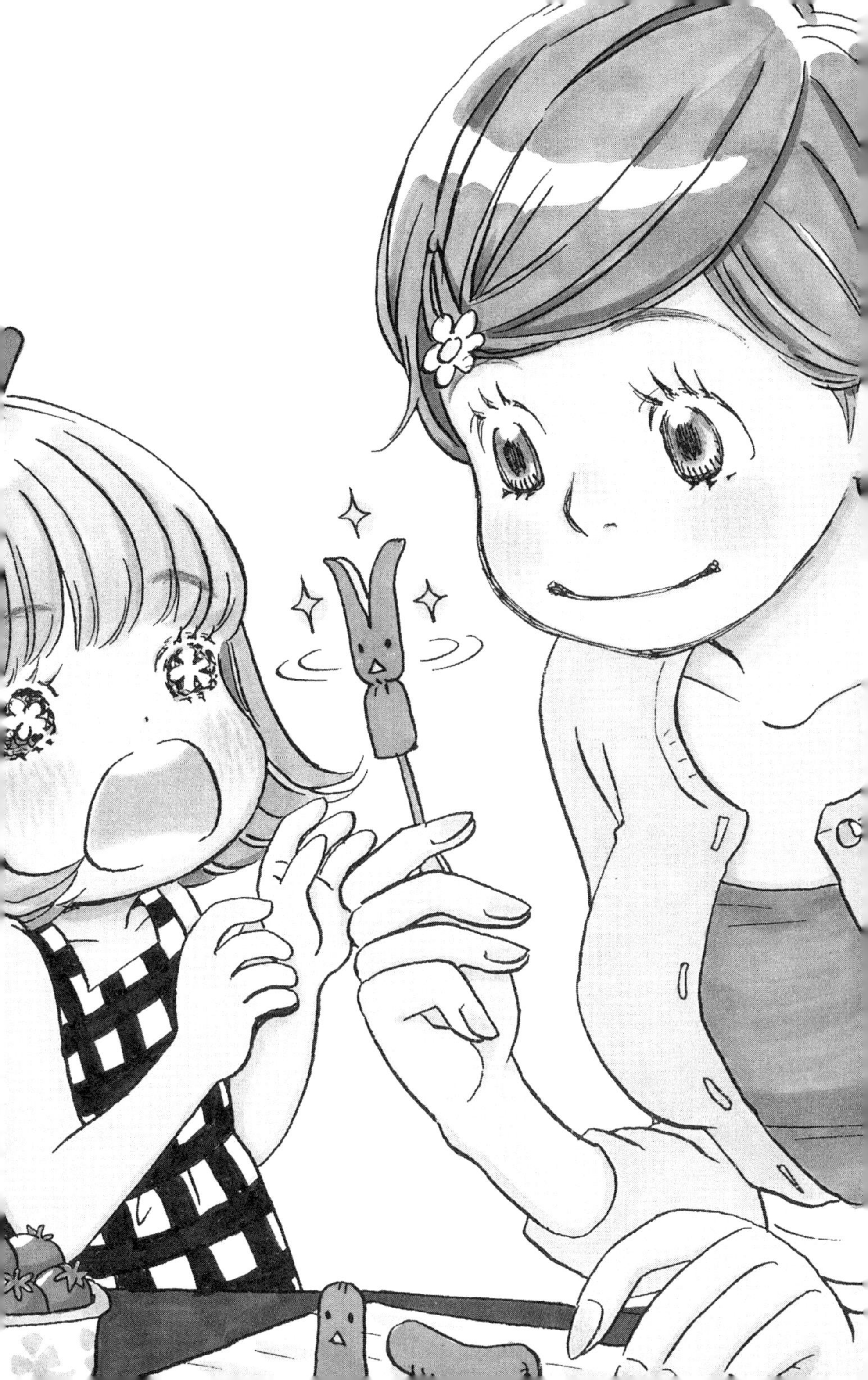

Chapter 14

Important Things, Important Matters

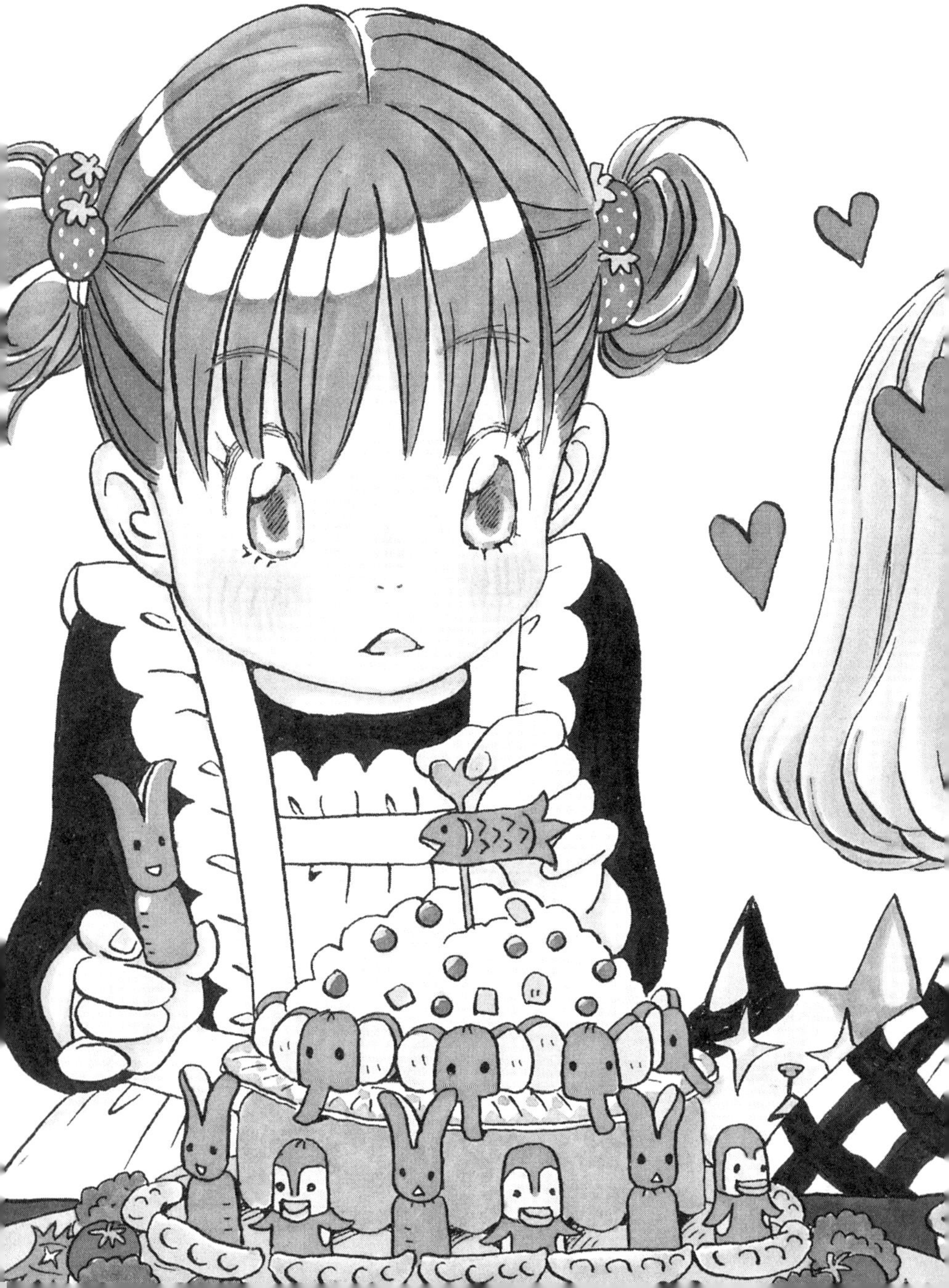

March Comes In Like a Lion

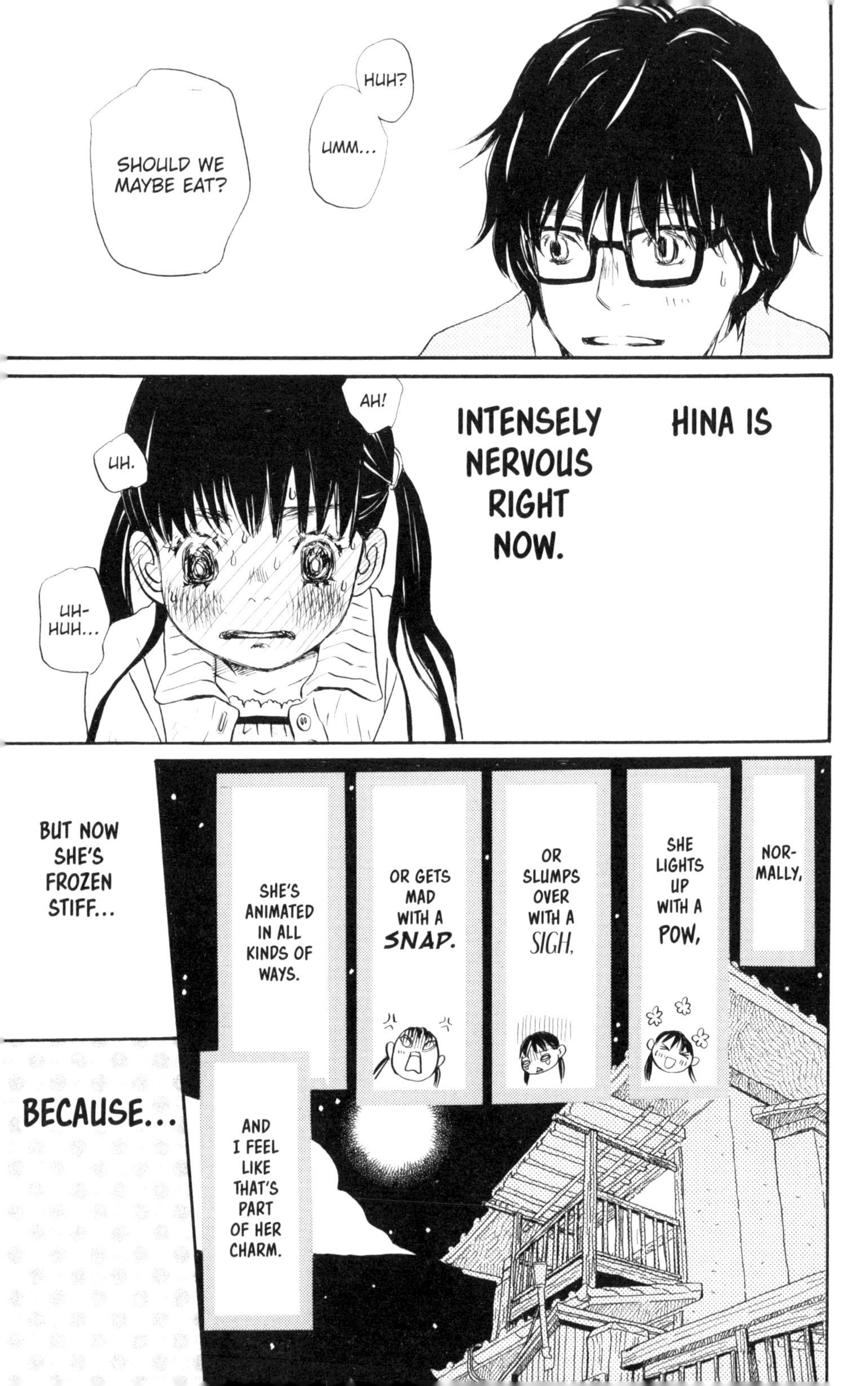
HUH?
UMM...
SHOULD WE MAYBE EAT?
HINA IS
INTENSELY NERVOUS RIGHT NOW.
AH!
UH.
UH-HUH...
NOR-MALLY,
SHE LIGHTS UP WITH A POW,
OR SLUMPS OVER WITH A SIGH,
OR GETS MAD WITH A SNAP.
SHE'S ANIMATED IN ALL KINDS OF WAYS.
BUT NOW SHE'S FROZEN STIFF...
AND I FEEL LIKE THAT'S PART OF HER CHARM.
BECAUSE...

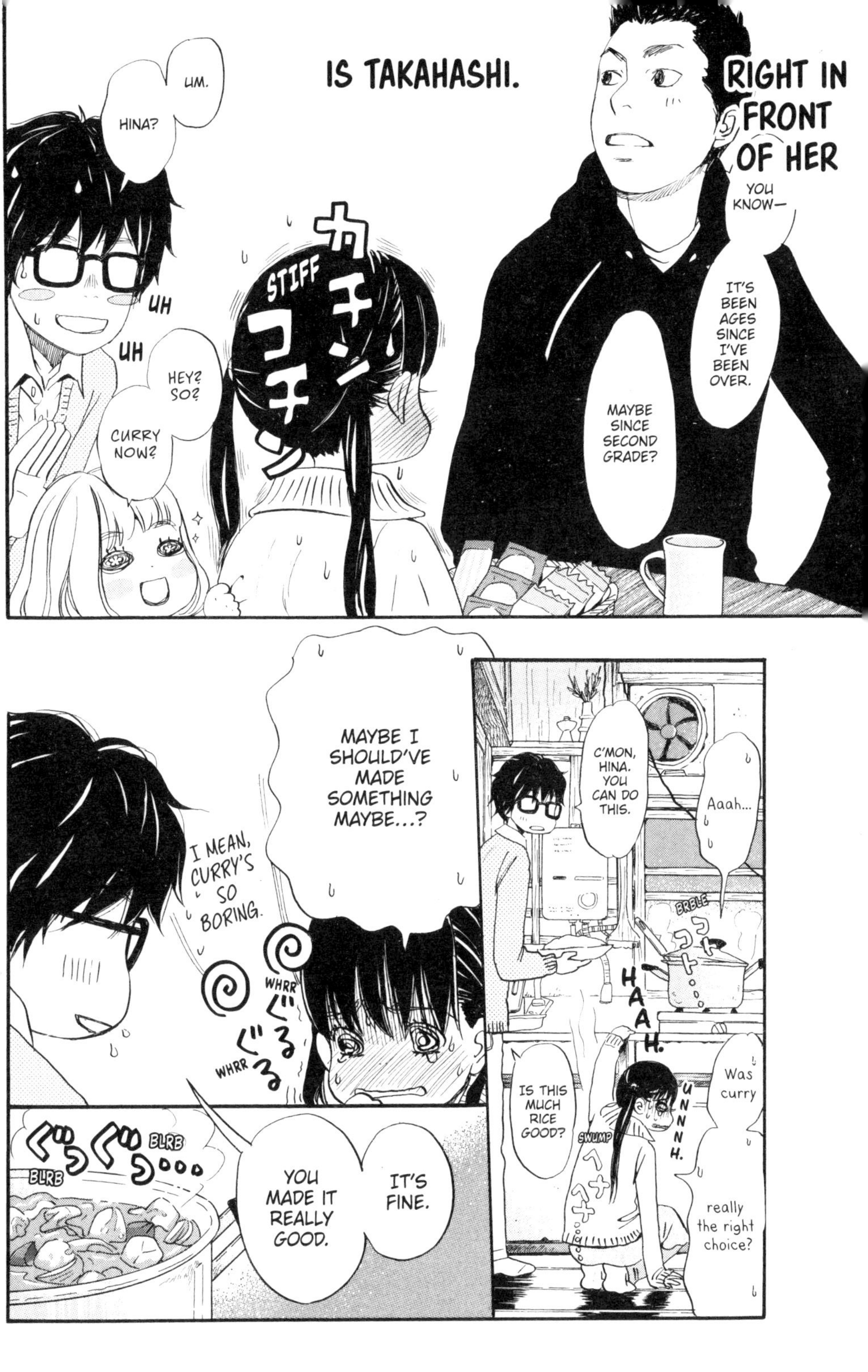
RIGHT IN FRONT OF HER
IS TAKAHASHI.
YOU KNOW—
IT'S BEEN AGES SINCE I'VE BEEN OVER.
MAYBE SINCE SECOND GRADE?
STIFF
カチンコチン
UM.
HINA?
UH
UH
HEY? SO?
CURRY NOW?
Aaah...
C'MON, HINA. YOU CAN DO THIS.
BRBLE
コトコト
HAAAH.
Was curry
really the right choice?
UNNNH.
IS THIS MUCH RICE GOOD?
SWUMP
ヘナヘナ
MAYBE I SHOULD'VE MADE SOMETHING MAYBE...?
I MEAN, CURRY'S SO BORING.
WHRR
ぐるぐる
WHRR
IT'S FINE.
YOU MADE IT REALLY GOOD.
BLRB
ぐつぐつ
BLRB

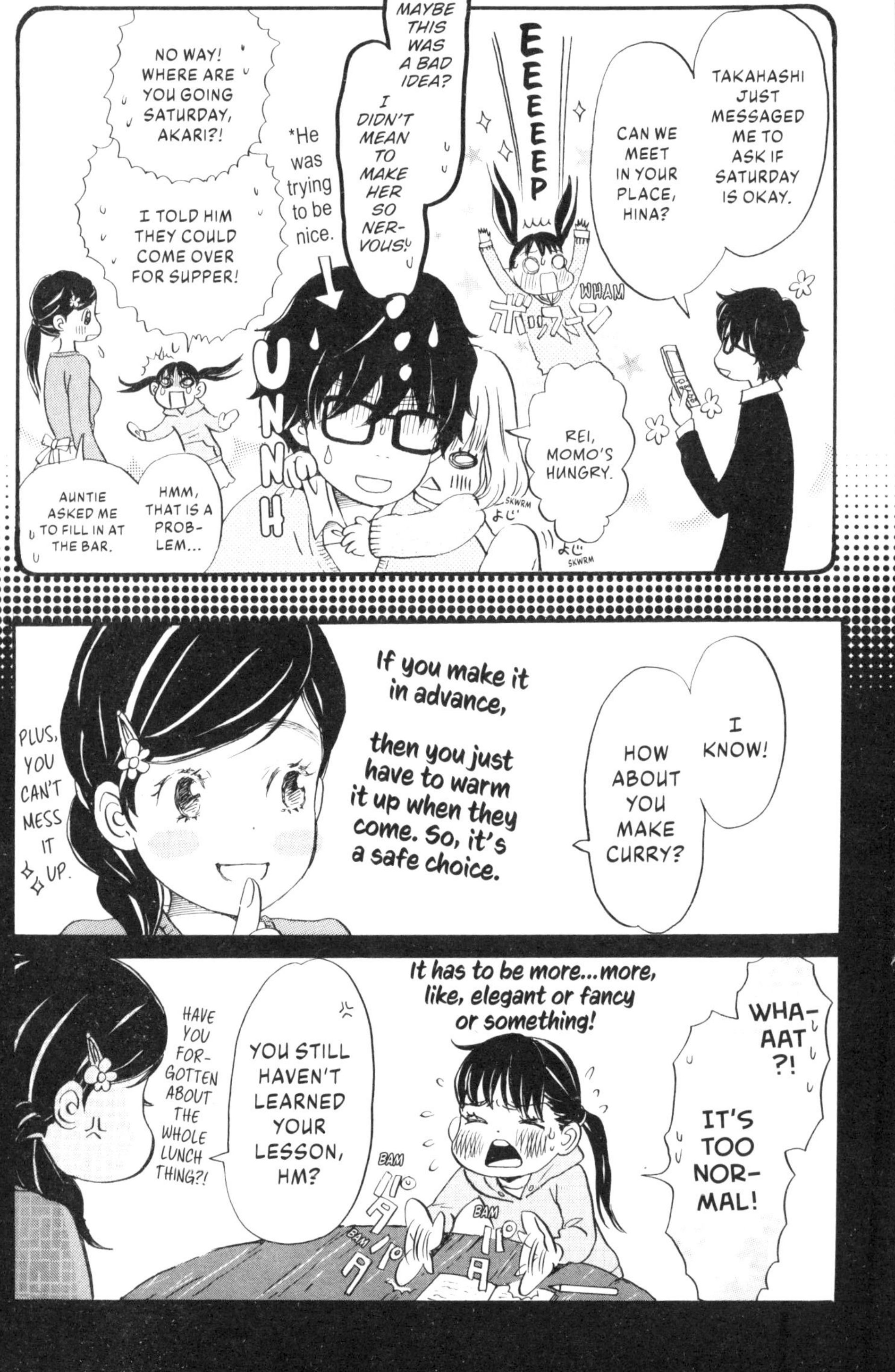
TAKAHASHI JUST MESSAGED ME TO ASK IF SATURDAY IS OKAY.
CAN WE MEET IN YOUR PLACE, HINA?
EEEEEEEP
WHAM
MAYBE THIS WAS A BAD IDEA?
I DIDN'T MEAN TO MAKE HER SO NERVOUS!
*He was trying to be nice.
UNNNH
REI, MOMO'S HUNGRY.
SKWRM
SKWRM
NO WAY! WHERE ARE YOU GOING SATURDAY, AKARI?!
I TOLD HIM THEY COULD COME OVER FOR SUPPER!
HMM, THAT IS A PROBLEM...
AUNTIE ASKED ME TO FILL IN AT THE BAR.
I KNOW!
HOW ABOUT YOU MAKE CURRY?
If you make it in advance,
then you just have to warm it up when they come. So, it's a safe choice.
PLUS, YOU CAN'T MESS IT UP.
WHA-AAT?!
IT'S TOO NOR-MAL!
It has to be more...more, like, elegant or fancy or something!
BAM
BAM
BAM
YOU STILL HAVEN'T LEARNED YOUR LESSON, HM?
HAVE YOU FORGOTTEN ABOUT THE WHOLE LUNCH THING?!

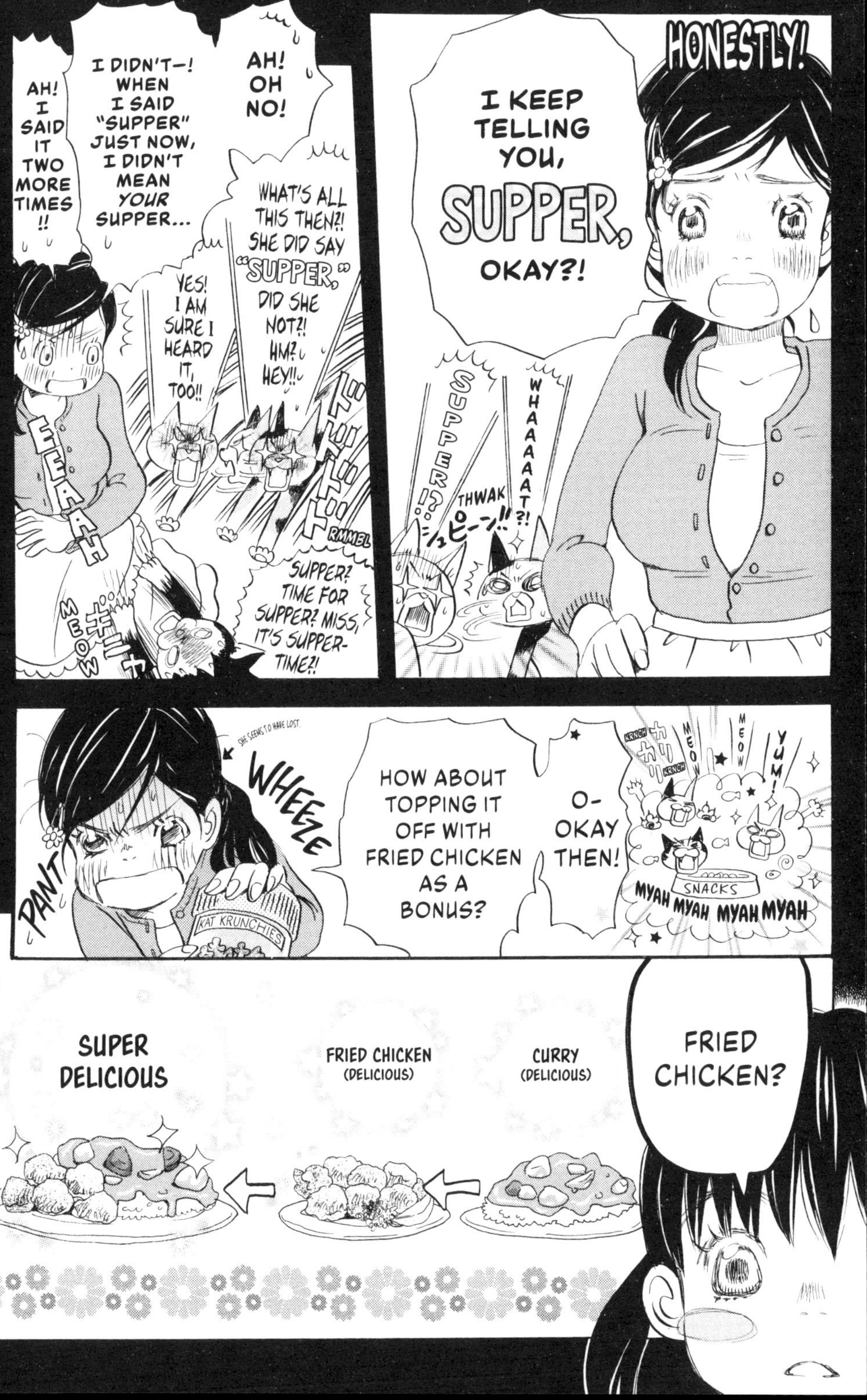
HONESTLY!
I KEEP TELLING YOU, SUPPER, OKAY?!
WHAAAAAAAT?!
SUPPER!?
THWAK
AH! OH NO!
I DIDN'T—! WHEN I SAID "SUPPER" JUST NOW, I DIDN'T MEAN YOUR SUPPER...
AH! I SAID IT TWO MORE TIMES!!
WHAT'S ALL THIS THEN?! SHE DID SAY "SUPPER," DID SHE NOT?! HM? HEY!!
YES! I AM SURE I HEARD IT, TOO!!
RMMBL
SUPPER? TIME FOR SUPPER? MISS, IT'S SUPPER-TIME?!
EEEAAAH
MEOW
KRNCH
KRNCH
MEOW
MEOW
YUM!
SNACKS
MYAH MYAH MYAH MYAH
O-OKAY THEN!
HOW ABOUT TOPPING IT OFF WITH FRIED CHICKEN AS A BONUS?
SHE SEEMS TO HAVE LOST.
WHEEZE
PANT
KAT KRUNCHIES
FRIED CHICKEN?
CURRY (DELICIOUS)
FRIED CHICKEN (DELICIOUS)
SUPER DELICIOUS

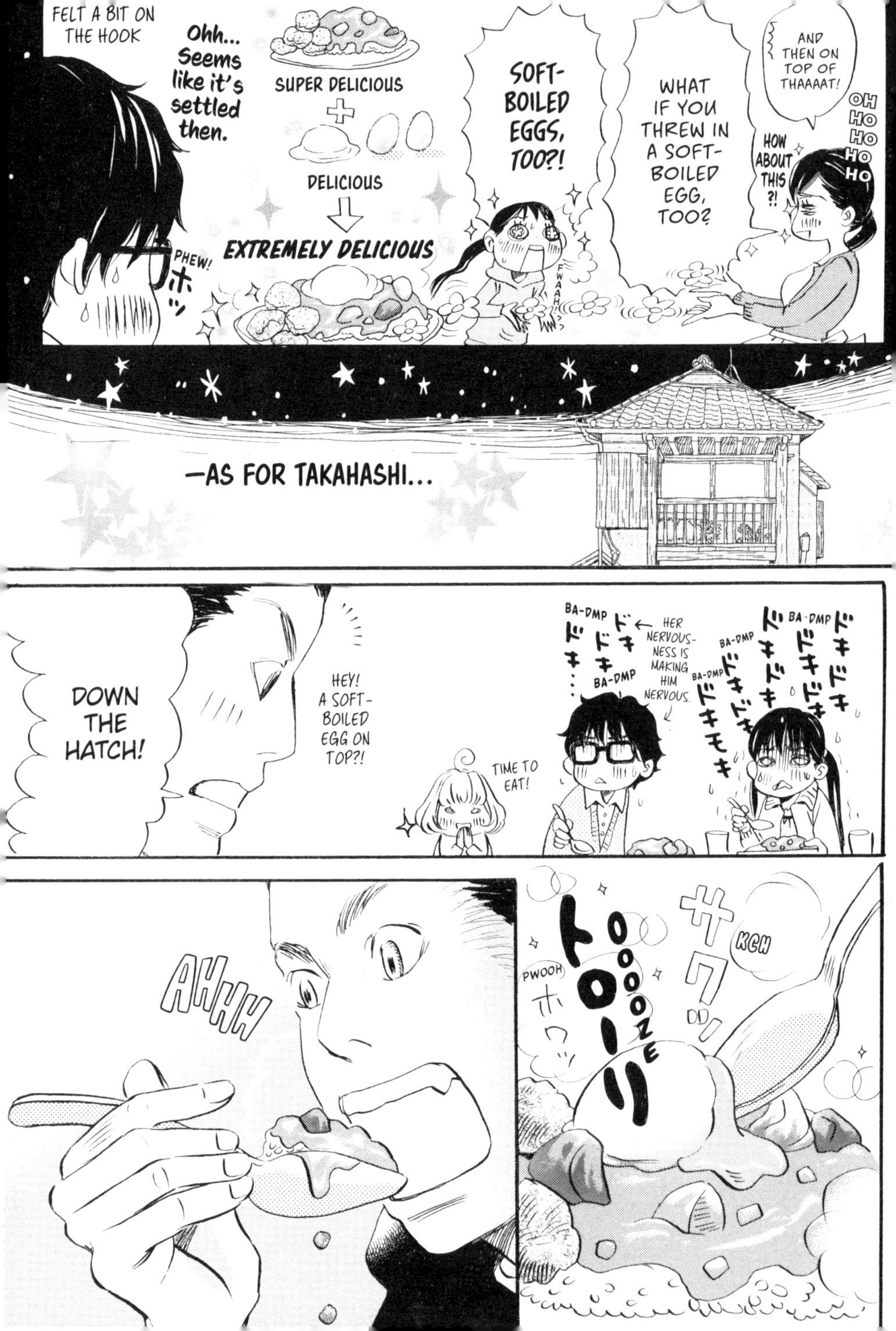
AND THEN ON TOP OF THAAAAT!
OH HO HO HO HO
HOW ABOUT THIS?!
WHAT IF YOU THREW IN A SOFT-BOILED EGG, TOO?
SOFT-BOILED EGGS, TOO?!
FWAAH!!
SUPER DELICIOUS
+
DELICIOUS
⇩
EXTREMELY DELICIOUS
Ohh... Seems like it's settled then.
FELT A BIT ON THE HOOK
PHEW!
ホッ
—AS FOR TAKAHASHI...
ドキドキドキ BA-DMP
ドキドキドキ BA-DMP
ドキドキドキ BA-DMP
ドキモキ BA-DMP
HER NERVOUSNESS IS MAKING HIM NERVOUS.
ドキドキ BA-DMP
ドキ... BA-DMP
TIME TO EAT!
HEY! A SOFT-BOILED EGG ON TOP?!
DOWN THE HATCH!
サク KCH
トローリ OOOOOZE
ホワッ PWOOH
AHHHH

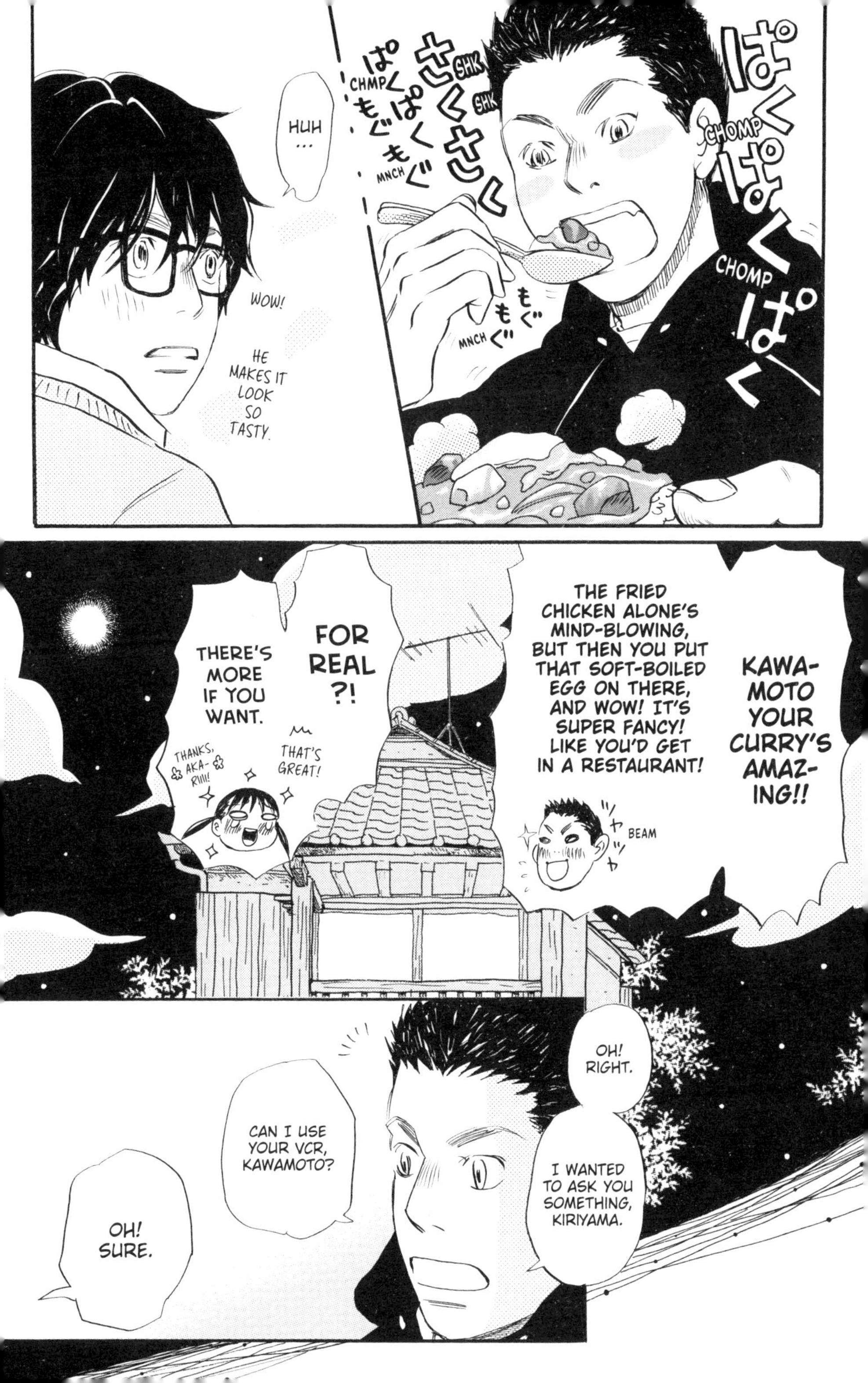

ぱくぱくぱく
CHOMP
CHOMP
さくさく
SHK
SHK
ぱくぱく
CHMP
もぐもぐ
MNCH
もぐもぐ
MNCH
HUH ...
WOW!
HE MAKES IT LOOK SO TASTY.
KAWA-MOTO YOUR CURRY'S AMAZ-ING!!
THE FRIED CHICKEN ALONE'S MIND-BLOWING, BUT THEN YOU PUT THAT SOFT-BOILED EGG ON THERE, AND WOW! IT'S SUPER FANCY! LIKE YOU'D GET IN A RESTAURANT!
BEAM
FOR REAL?!
THERE'S MORE IF YOU WANT.
THAT'S GREAT!
THANKS, AKA-RIIII!
OH! RIGHT.
I WANTED TO ASK YOU SOMETHING, KIRIYAMA.
CAN I USE YOUR VCR, KAWAMOTO?
OH! SURE.

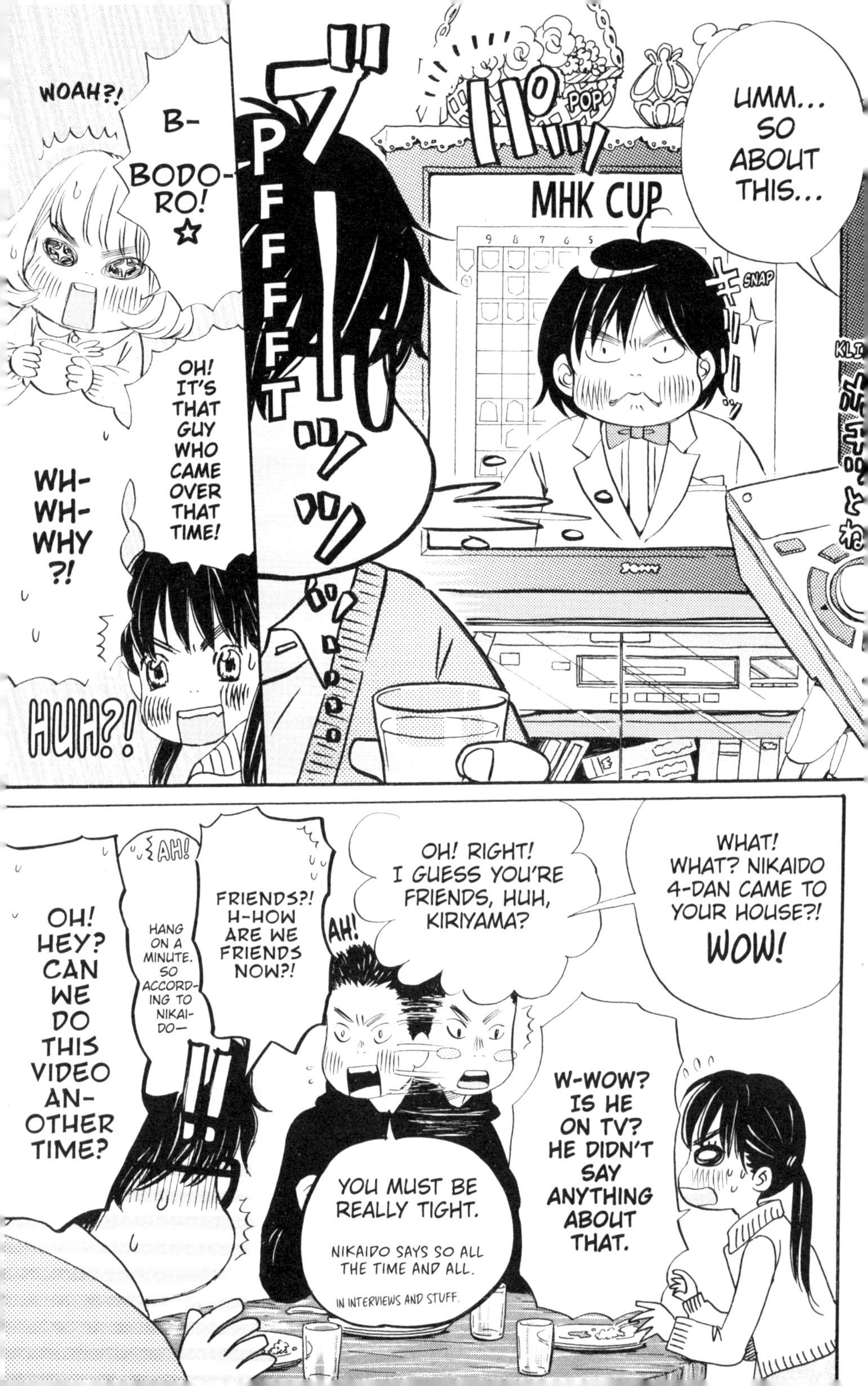
UMM... SO ABOUT THIS...
MHK CUP
SNAP
KLI
POP
PFFFFT
B-BODO-RO! ☆
WOAH?!
OH! IT'S THAT GUY WHO CAME OVER THAT TIME!
WH-WH-WHY?!
HUH?!
WHAT! WHAT? NIKAIDO 4-DAN CAME TO YOUR HOUSE?! WOW!
OH! RIGHT! I GUESS YOU'RE FRIENDS, HUH, KIRIYAMA?
W-WOW? IS HE ON TV? HE DIDN'T SAY ANYTHING ABOUT THAT.
YOU MUST BE REALLY TIGHT.
NIKAIDO SAYS SO ALL THE TIME AND ALL.
IN INTERVIEWS AND STUFF.
AH!
FRIENDS?! H-HOW ARE WE FRIENDS NOW?!
AH!
HANG ON A MINUTE. SO ACCORDING TO NIKAIDO—
OH! HEY? CAN WE DO THIS VIDEO AN-OTHER TIME?

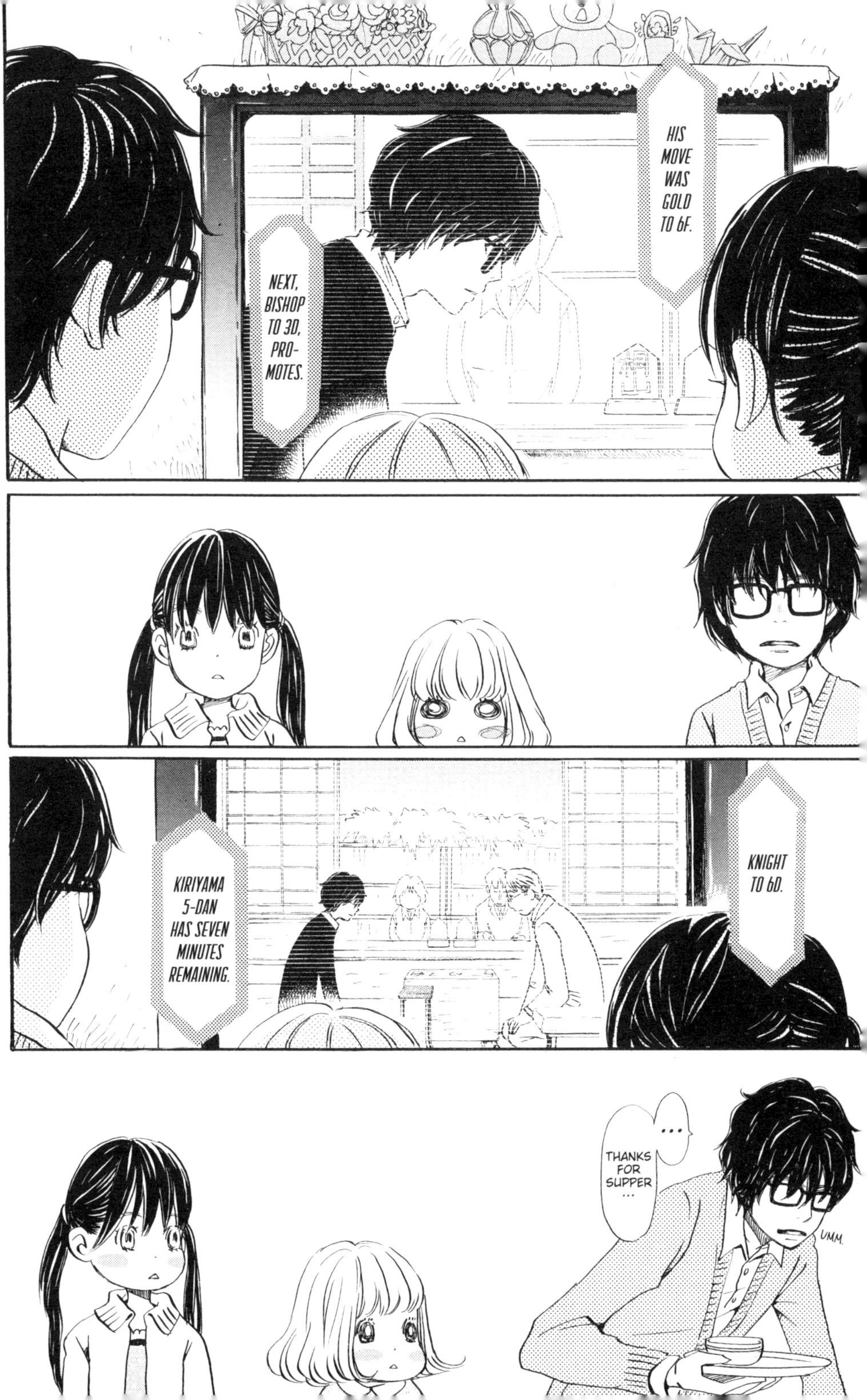
HIS MOVE WAS GOLD TO 6F.
NEXT, BISHOP TO 3D, PRO-MOTES.
KNIGHT TO 6D.
KIRIYAMA 5-DAN HAS SEVEN MINUTES REMAINING.
...
THANKS FOR SUPPER ...
UMM.

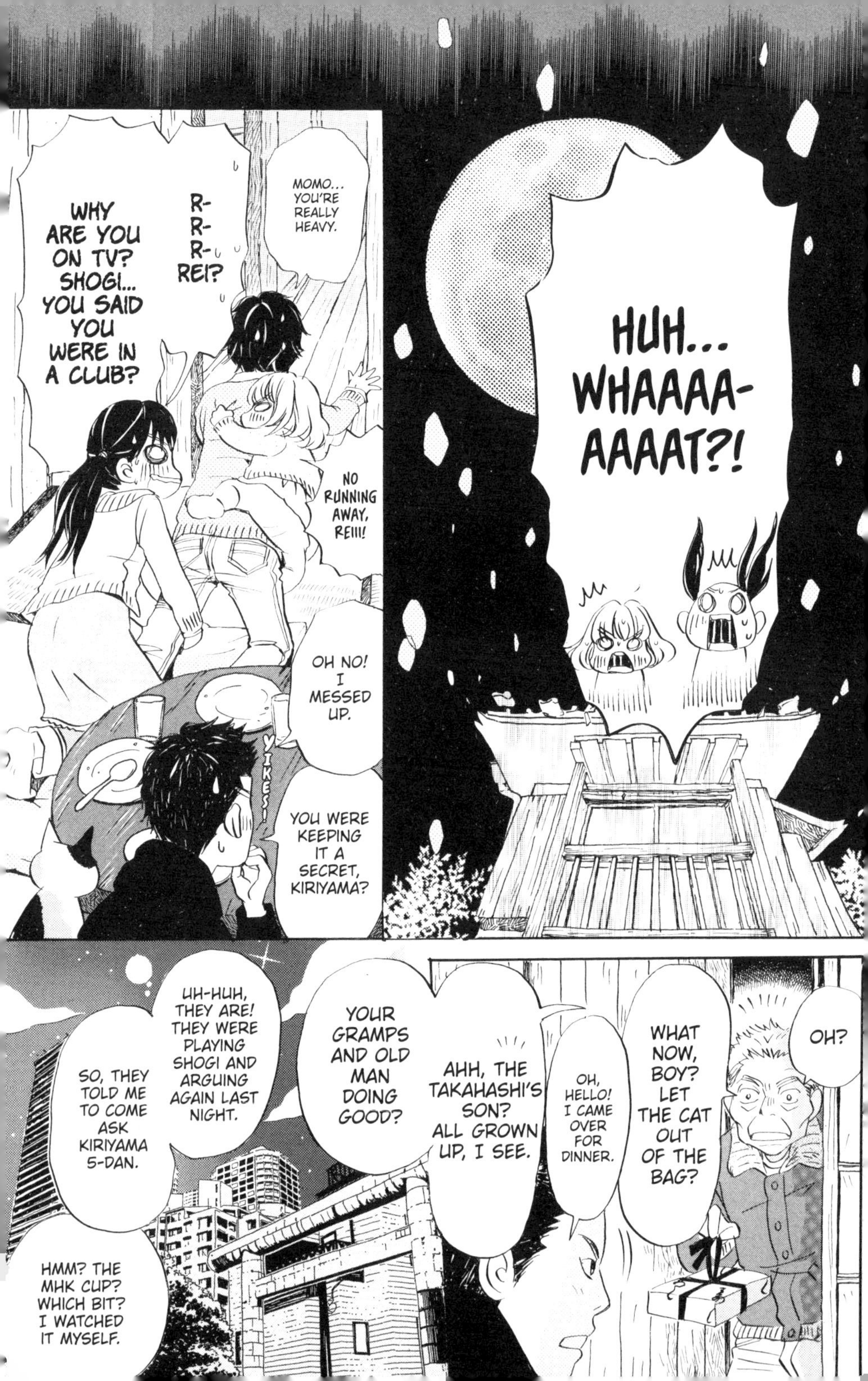
HUH... WHAAAA-AAAAT?!
MOMO... YOU'RE REALLY HEAVY.
R-R-R-REI?
WHY ARE YOU ON TV? SHOGI... YOU SAID YOU WERE IN A CLUB?
NO RUNNING AWAY, REIII!
OH NO! I MESSED UP.
YIKES!
YOU WERE KEEPING IT A SECRET, KIRIYAMA?
OH?
WHAT NOW, BOY? LET THE CAT OUT OF THE BAG?
OH, HELLO! I CAME OVER FOR DINNER.
AHH, THE TAKAHASHI'S SON? ALL GROWN UP, I SEE.
YOUR GRAMPS AND OLD MAN DOING GOOD?
UH-HUH, THEY ARE! THEY WERE PLAYING SHOGI AND ARGUING AGAIN LAST NIGHT.
SO, THEY TOLD ME TO COME ASK KIRIYAMA 5-DAN.
HMM? THE MHK CUP? WHICH BIT? I WATCHED IT MYSELF.

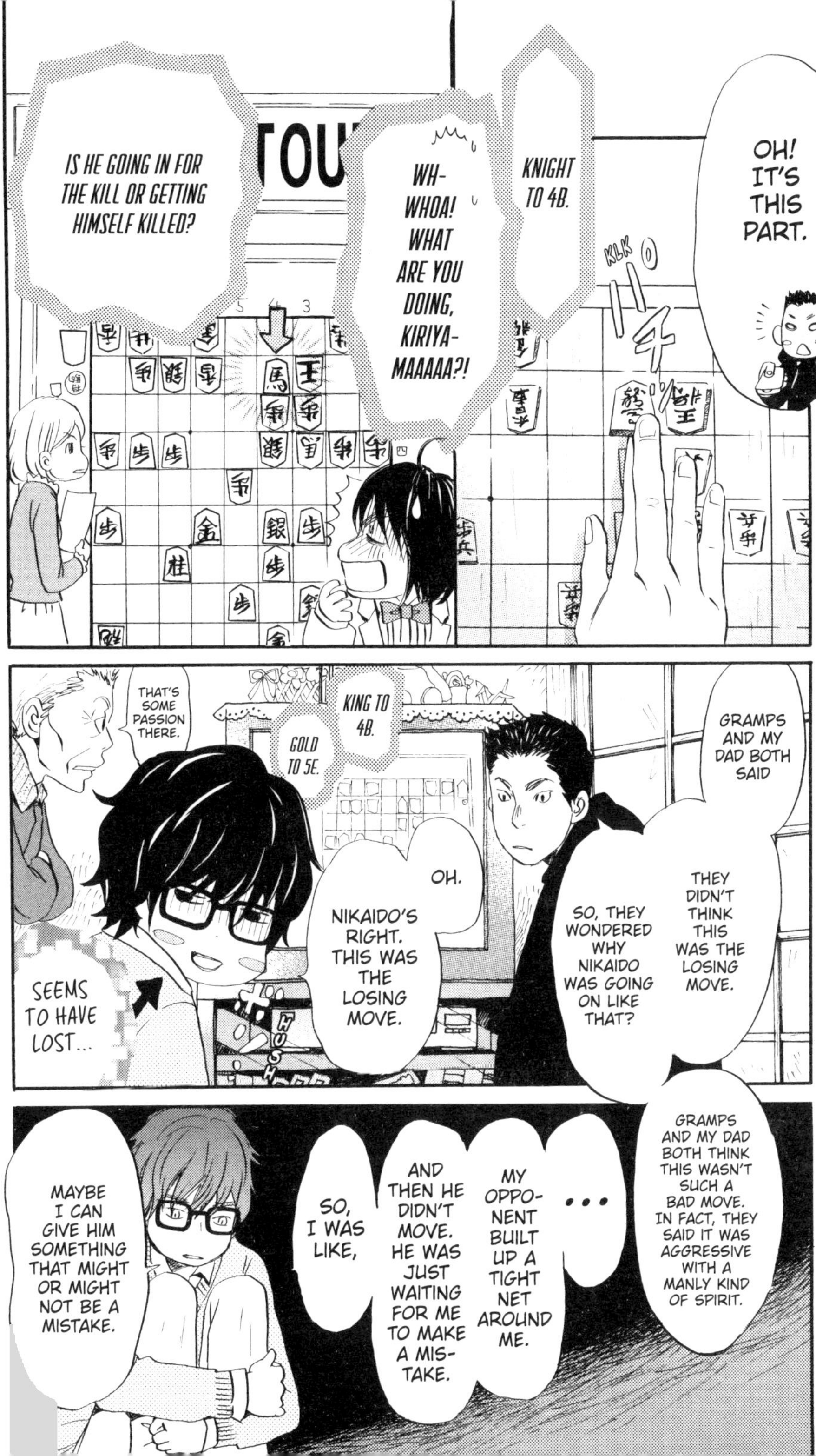
OH! IT'S THIS PART.
KLK
KNIGHT TO 4B.
WH-WHOA! WHAT ARE YOU DOING, KIRIYA-MAAAAA?!
TOU
IS HE GOING IN FOR THE KILL OR GETTING HIMSELF KILLED?
GRAMPS AND MY DAD BOTH SAID
THEY DIDN'T THINK THIS WAS THE LOSING MOVE.
SO, THEY WONDERED WHY NIKAIDO WAS GOING ON LIKE THAT?
KING TO 4B.
GOLD TO 5E.
THAT'S SOME PASSION THERE.
OH.
NIKAIDO'S RIGHT. THIS WAS THE LOSING MOVE.
HUSH
SEEMS TO HAVE LOST...
GRAMPS AND MY DAD BOTH THINK THIS WASN'T SUCH A BAD MOVE. IN FACT, THEY SAID IT WAS AGGRESSIVE WITH A MANLY KIND OF SPIRIT.
...
MY OPPONENT BUILT UP A TIGHT NET AROUND ME.
AND THEN HE DIDN'T MOVE. HE WAS JUST WAITING FOR ME TO MAKE A MISTAKE.
SO, I WAS LIKE,
MAYBE I CAN GIVE HIM SOMETHING THAT MIGHT OR MIGHT NOT BE A MISTAKE.

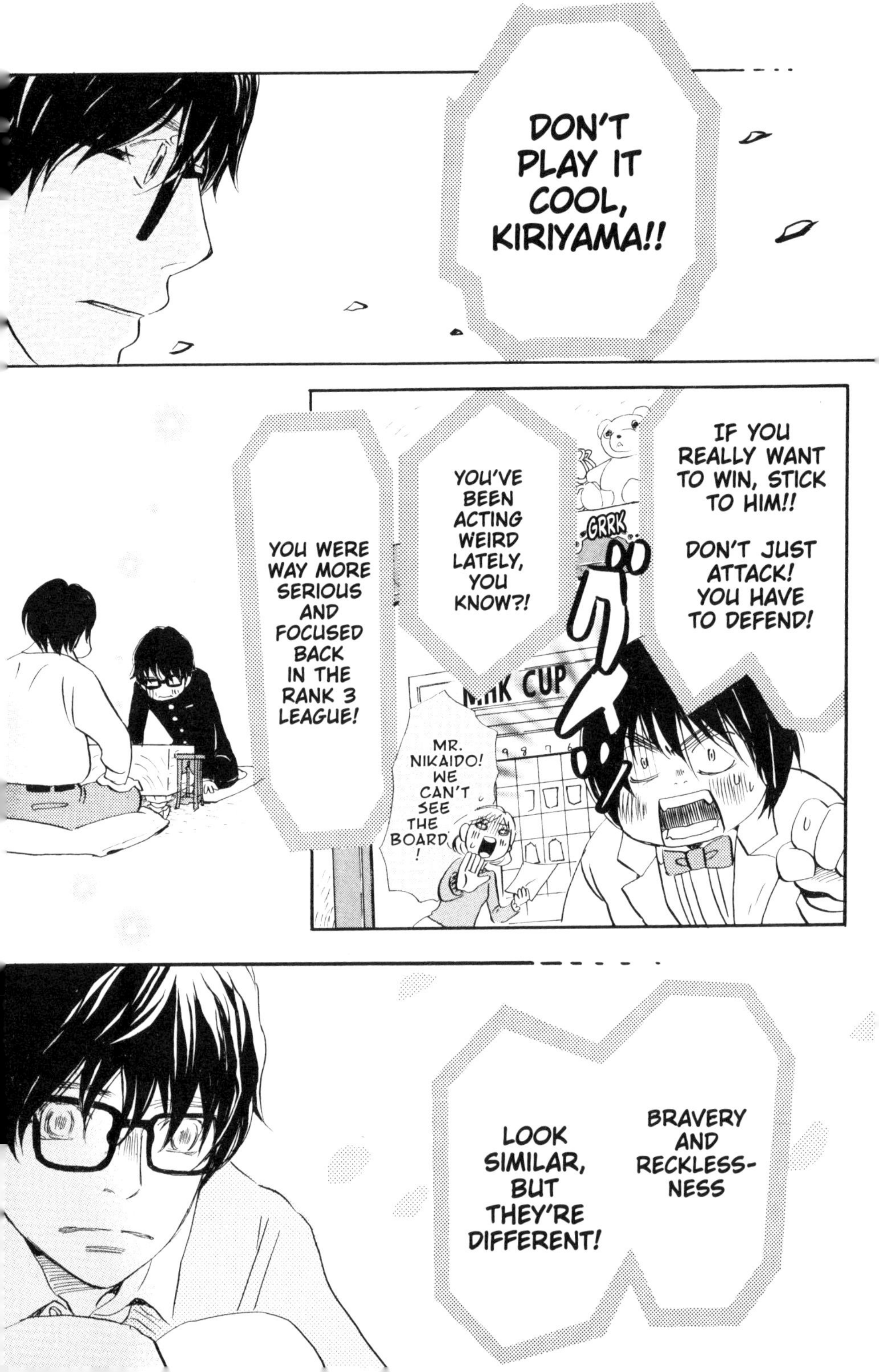
DON'T PLAY IT COOL, KIRIYAMA!!
IF YOU REALLY WANT TO WIN, STICK TO HIM!!
DON'T JUST ATTACK! YOU HAVE TO DEFEND!
GRRK
YOU'VE BEEN ACTING WEIRD LATELY, YOU KNOW?!
MR. NIKAIDO! WE CAN'T SEE THE BOARD!
YOU WERE WAY MORE SERIOUS AND FOCUSED BACK IN THE RANK 3 LEAGUE!
BRAVERY AND RECKLESS-NESS
LOOK SIMILAR, BUT THEY'RE DIFFERENT!

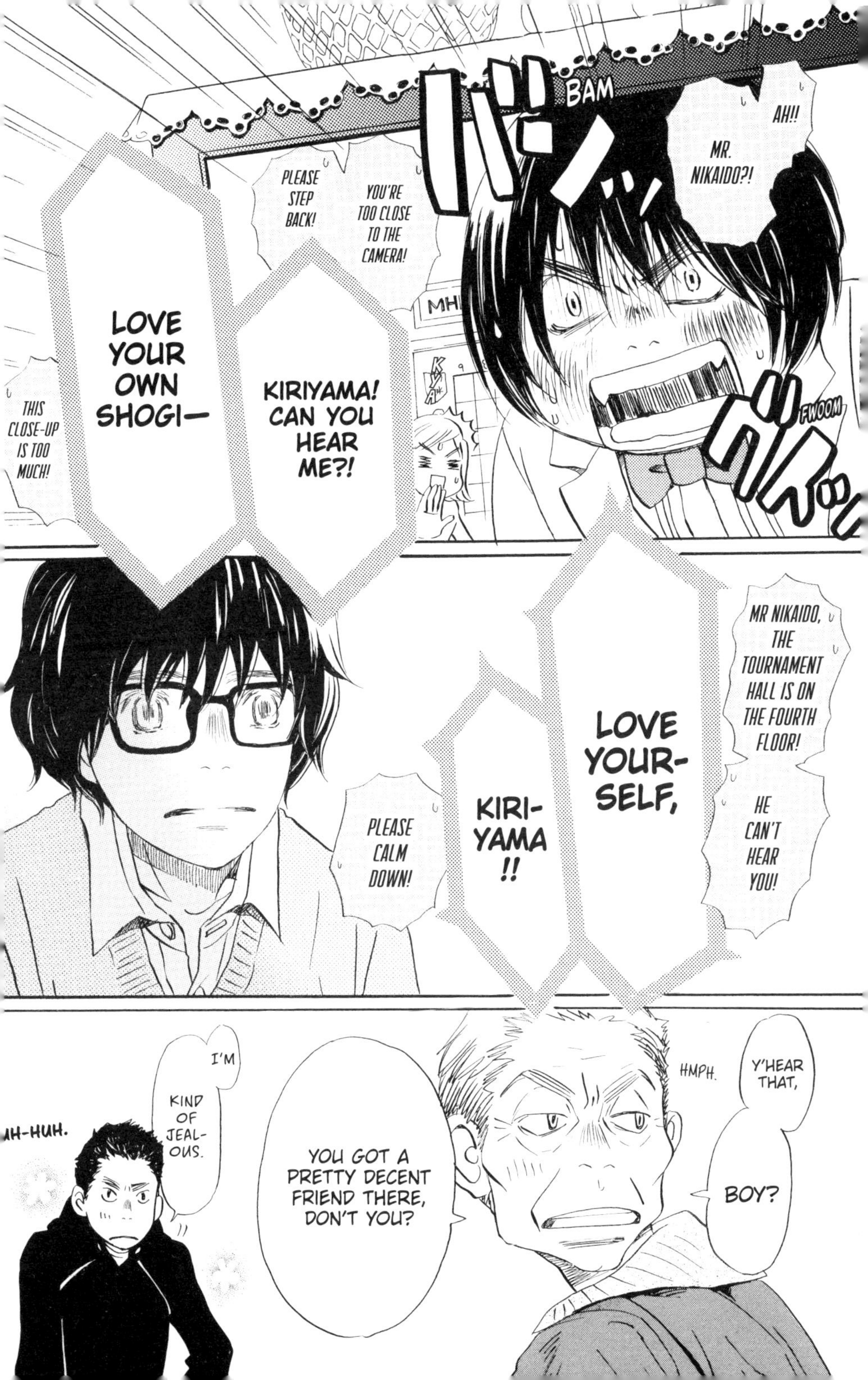
BAM
AH!!
MR. NIKAIDO?!
FWOOM
YOU'RE TOO CLOSE TO THE CAMERA!
PLEASE STEP BACK!
KIRIYAMA! CAN YOU HEAR ME?!
LOVE YOUR OWN SHOGI—
THIS CLOSE-UP IS TOO MUCH!
MR NIKAIDO, THE TOURNAMENT HALL IS ON THE FOURTH FLOOR!
HE CAN'T HEAR YOU!
LOVE YOUR-SELF,
KIRI-YAMA!!
PLEASE CALM DOWN!
Y'HEAR THAT,
BOY?
HMPH.
YOU GOT A PRETTY DECENT FRIEND THERE, DON'T YOU?
I'M KIND OF JEAL-OUS.

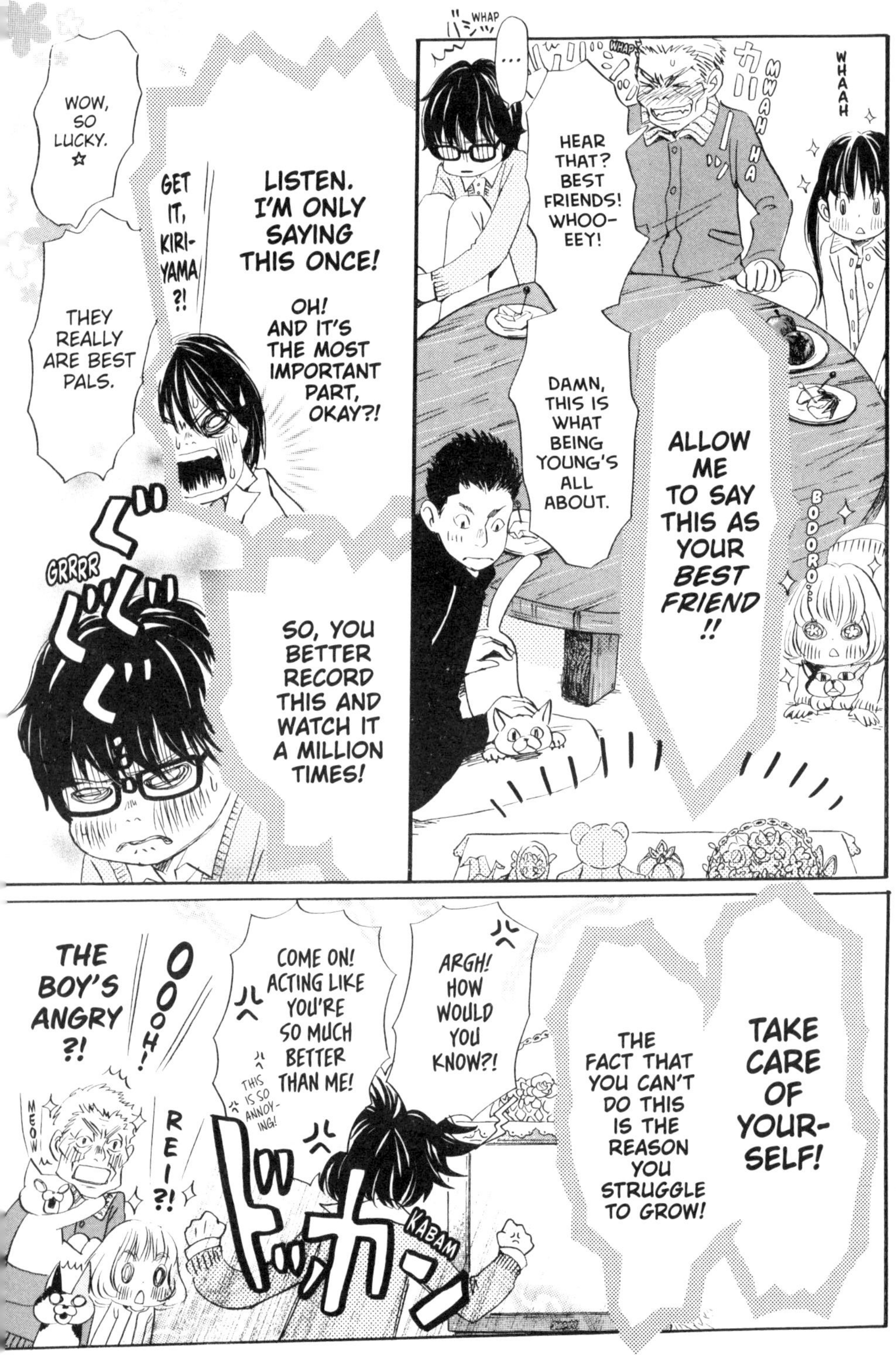

WHAAAH
MWAAH HA
WHAP
WHAP
...
HEAR THAT? BEST FRIENDS! WHOOO-EEY!
ALLOW ME TO SAY THIS AS YOUR BEST FRIEND!!
DAMN, THIS IS WHAT BEING YOUNG'S ALL ABOUT.
BODORO...
LISTEN. I'M ONLY SAYING THIS ONCE!
GET IT, KIRI-YAMA?!
WOW, SO LUCKY. ☆
OH! AND IT'S THE MOST IMPORTANT PART, OKAY?!
THEY REALLY ARE BEST PALS.
SO, YOU BETTER RECORD THIS AND WATCH IT A MILLION TIMES!
GRRRR
TAKE CARE OF YOUR-SELF!
THE FACT THAT YOU CAN'T DO THIS IS THE REASON YOU STRUGGLE TO GROW!
ARGH! HOW WOULD YOU KNOW?!
COME ON! ACTING LIKE YOU'RE SO MUCH BETTER THAN ME!
OOOOH!
THE BOY'S ANGRY?!
THIS IS SO ANNOY-ING!
KABAM
REI?!
MEOW

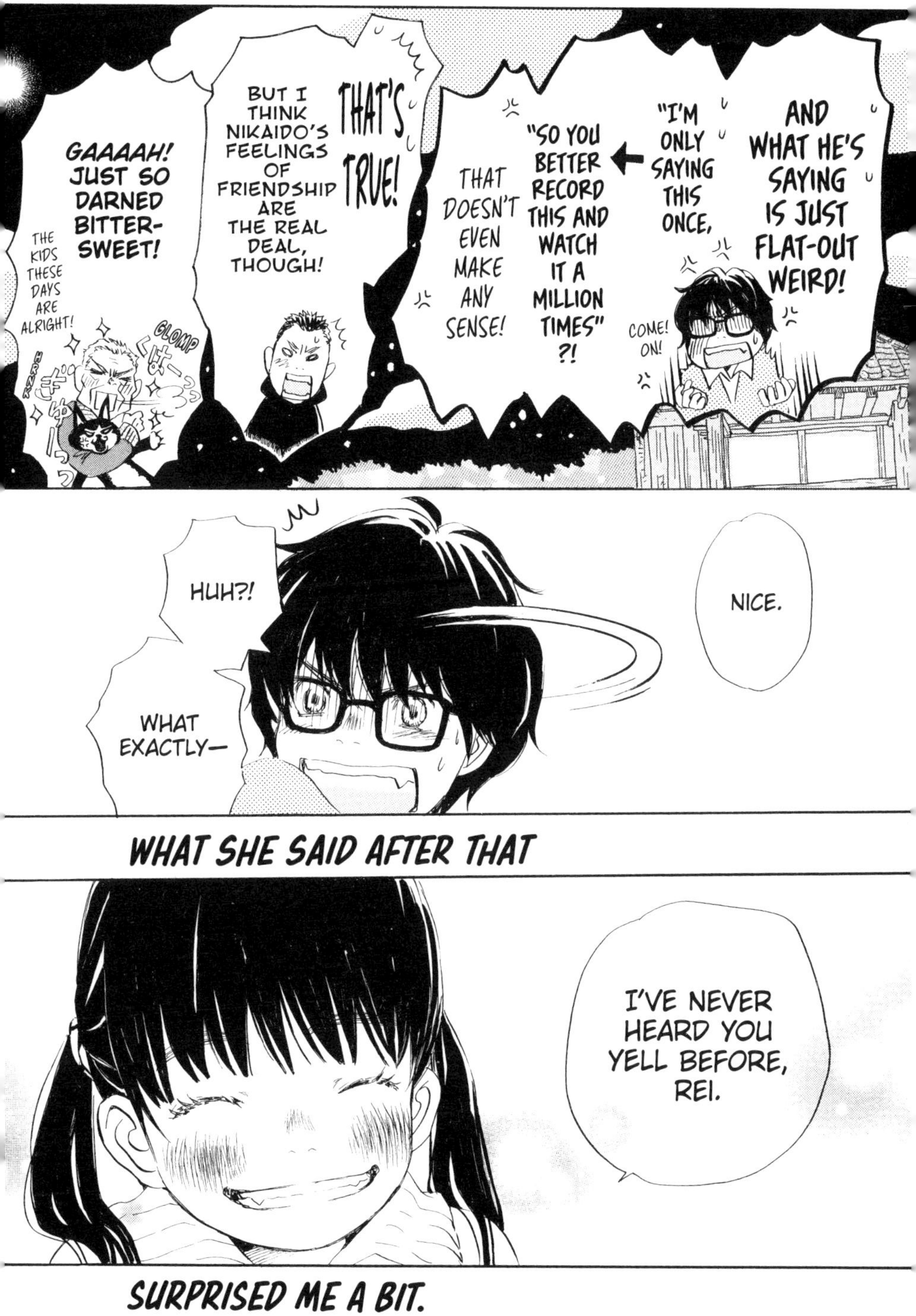
AND WHAT HE'S SAYING IS JUST FLAT-OUT WEIRD!
"I'M ONLY SAYING THIS ONCE,
COME! ON!
"SO YOU BETTER RECORD THIS AND WATCH IT A MILLION TIMES"?!
THAT DOESN'T EVEN MAKE ANY SENSE!
THAT'S TRUE!
BUT I THINK NIKAIDO'S FEELINGS OF FRIENDSHIP ARE THE REAL DEAL, THOUGH!
GAAAAH! JUST SO DARNED BITTER-SWEET!
GLOMP
THE KIDS THESE DAYS ARE ALRIGHT!
NICE.
HUH?!
WHAT EXACTLY—
WHAT SHE SAID AFTER THAT
I'VE NEVER HEARD YOU YELL BEFORE, REI.
SURPRISED ME A BIT.

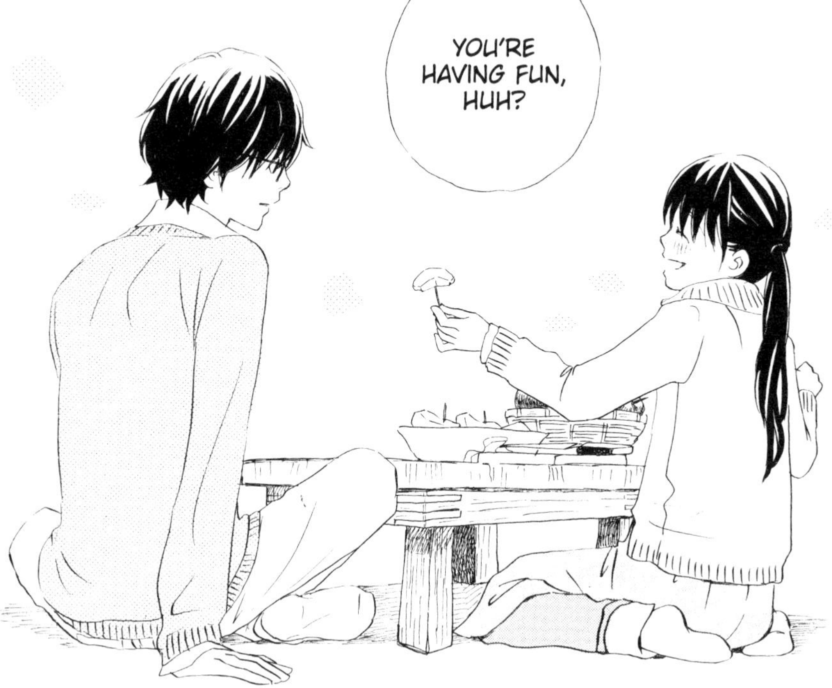
YOU'RE HAVING FUN, HUH?

AFTER ALL, IT WAS THE FIRST TIME

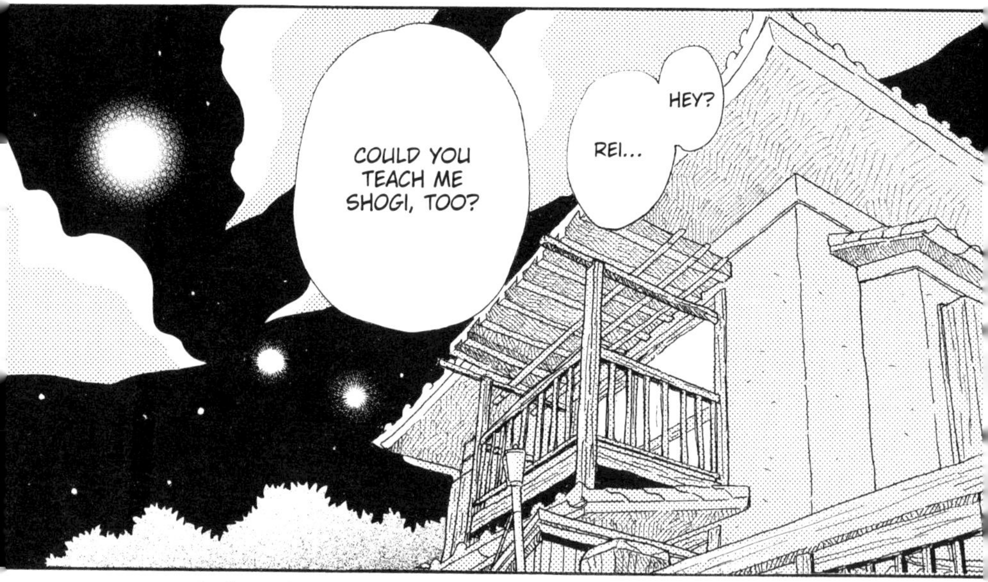
HEY?
REI...
COULD YOU TEACH ME SHOGI, TOO?

ANYONE HAD EVER SAID THAT TO ME.

Manabu Senzaki's *by Manabu Senzaki*
Lion Shogi

② 2

It's Hard Playing Shogi on TV!

A formal professional match basically takes a whole day. It starts at ten in the morning, and sometimes goes well into the night, with even the earliest matches lasting until early evening. But there are exceptions: TV tournaments are one of these, with each match set up to end in around two hours so that it can fit into the TV broadcast framework. This means that the time control (the limited time you're allowed to think) is very short, and in the industry, this is called "hayasashi," or quick play. There are two major televised tournaments: the NHK Tournament, and the Ginga Tournament aired on cable TV's Go/Shogi channel.

On page 65 of this manga (Chapter 14) is... the MHK Cup for some reason, but well, I suppose this is meant to be the NHK Cup. (Nikaido is also shown in extreme close-up in this panel, too. In reality, there would never be this kind of close-up.)

Now then, in the manga, because Takahashi puts on this video, Hina finds out the truth about Kiriyama and there is a big commotion, and in fact, this sort of scene does occasionally actually happen.

Shogi players don't particularly stand out in everyday life. In fact, they're usually quite unassuming. However, the moment they appear on TV, their visibility goes up quite a bit.

The impact of TV really is impressive. When I meet children, the first thing out of their mouths is, "You're a professional player? Are you on TV?"

If you lose on TV, you will be told, "You're not doing so well, hm?" even by your fans, no matter how many tournaments you win after that. There are actually qualifiers for the NHK Cup, but if you lose there, you can't appear on NHK for a year, so in years like that, I've been asked by people I know, completely seriously,

"You haven't retired, have you?"

Shogi players are not entertainers, so it's not the case that our incomes increase because our name sells, but as long as you're a player, it's only natural to want to win and have your name be bankable. We are all fighting as hard as we can.

The chart below is a list of NHK Cup winners. I actually won it myself back in 1990. But that was ages and ages ago, and I've forgotten all about it now. ▲

PAST WINNERS

1990	Manabu Senzaki, 5-*dan*	1999	Daisuke Suzuki, 6-*dan*
1991	Yoshiharu Habu, *Kioh*	2000	Yoshiharu Habu, five crowns
1992	Makoto Nakahara, *Meijin*	2001	Toshiyuki Moriuchi, 8-*dan*
1993	Hifumi Kato, 9-*dan*	2002	Hiroyuki Miura, 8-*dan*
1994	Makoto Nakahara, lifetime 10-*dan*	2003	Toshiaki Kubo, 8-*dan*
1995	Yoshiharu Habu, *Ryuoh/Meijin*	2004	Takayuki Yamazaki, 6-*dan*
1996	Toshiyuki Moriuchi, 8-*dan*	2005	Tadahisa Maruyama, 9-*dan*
1997	Yoshiharu Habu, four crowns	2006	Yasumitsu Sato, *Kisei*
1998	Yoshiharu Habu, four crowns	2007	Yasumitsu Sato, two crowns

(Rankings and titles are at the time of winning.)

Chapter 15

Teach Me Shogi

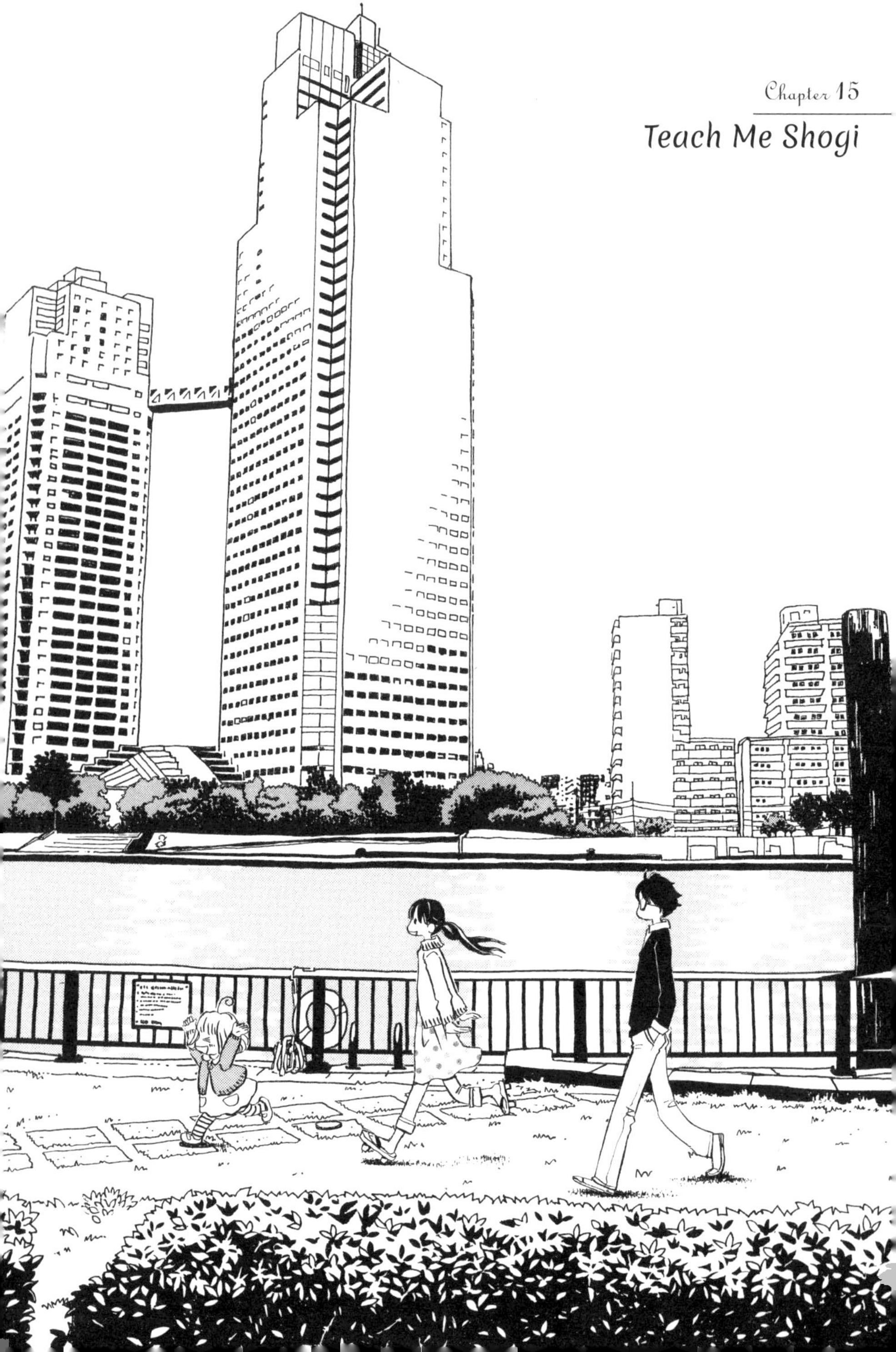

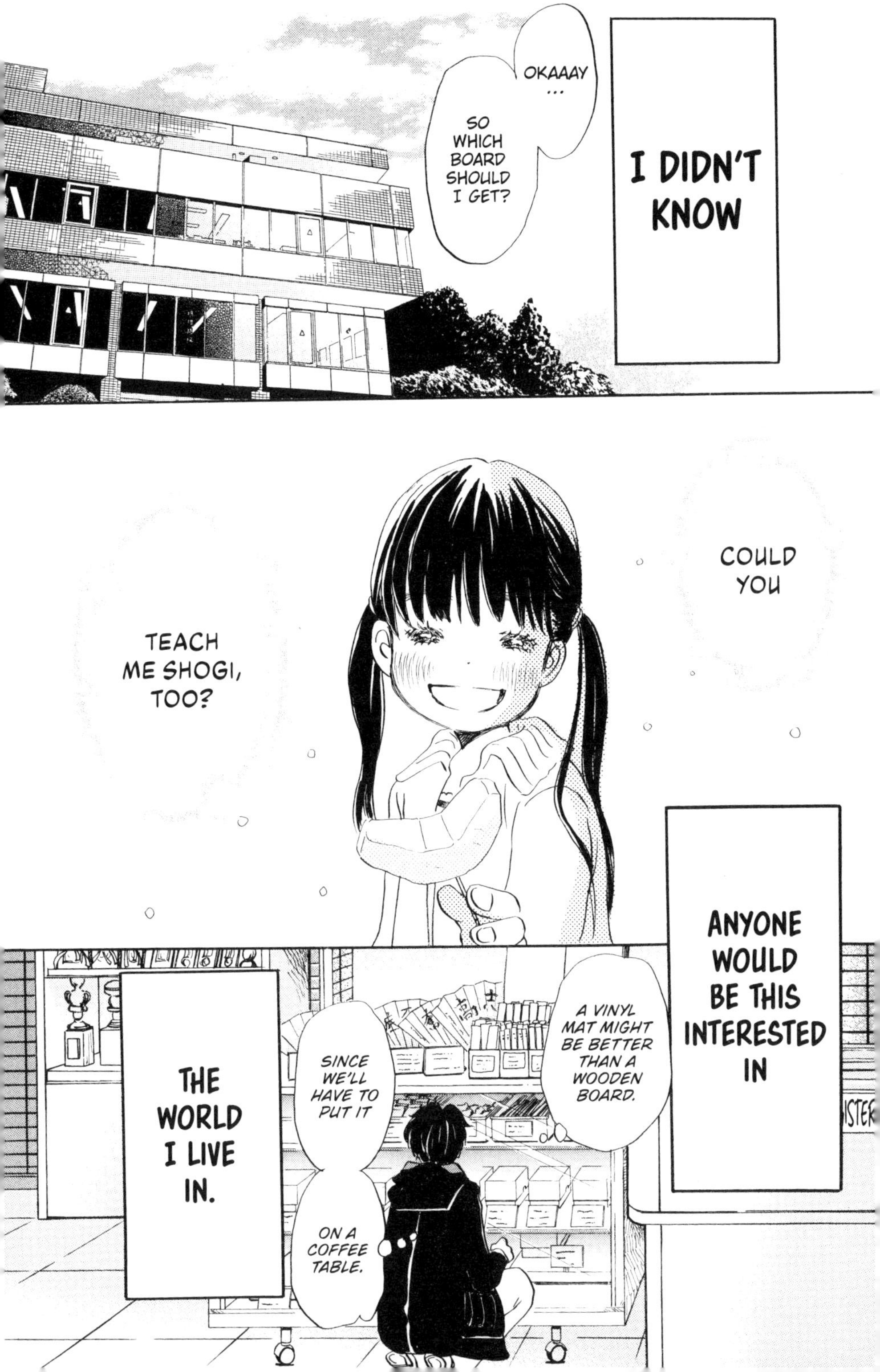
I DIDN'T KNOW
OKAAAY...
SO WHICH BOARD SHOULD I GET?
COULD YOU
TEACH ME SHOGI, TOO?
ANYONE WOULD BE THIS INTERESTED IN
A VINYL MAT MIGHT BE BETTER THAN A WOODEN BOARD.
SINCE WE'LL HAVE TO PUT IT
ON A COFFEE TABLE.
THE WORLD I LIVE IN.

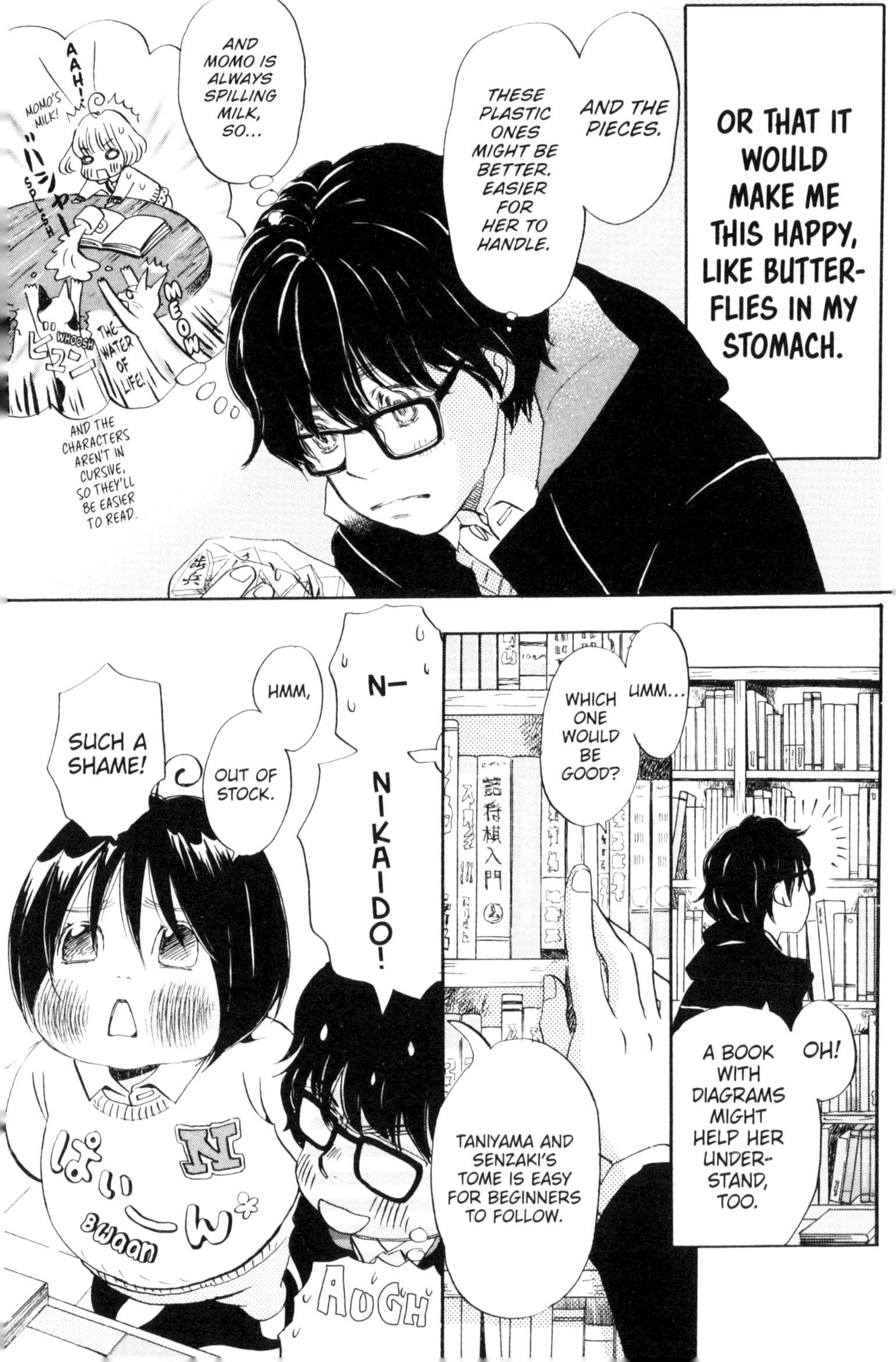
OR THAT IT WOULD MAKE ME THIS HAPPY, LIKE BUTTERFLIES IN MY STOMACH.
AND THE PIECES.
THESE PLASTIC ONES MIGHT BE BETTER. EASIER FOR HER TO HANDLE.
AND MOMO IS ALWAYS SPILLING MILK, SO...
AAH!
MOMO'S MILK!
SPLISH
MEOW
WHOOSH
THE WATER OF LIFE!
AND THE CHARACTERS AREN'T IN CURSIVE, SO THEY'LL BE EASIER TO READ.
UMM...
WHICH ONE WOULD BE GOOD?
OH!
A BOOK WITH DIAGRAMS MIGHT HELP HER UNDER-STAND, TOO.
TANIYAMA AND SENZAKI'S TOME IS EASY FOR BEGINNERS TO FOLLOW.
N—
N-NIKAIDO!
HMM,
OUT OF STOCK.
SUCH A SHAME!
Bwaan
AUGH

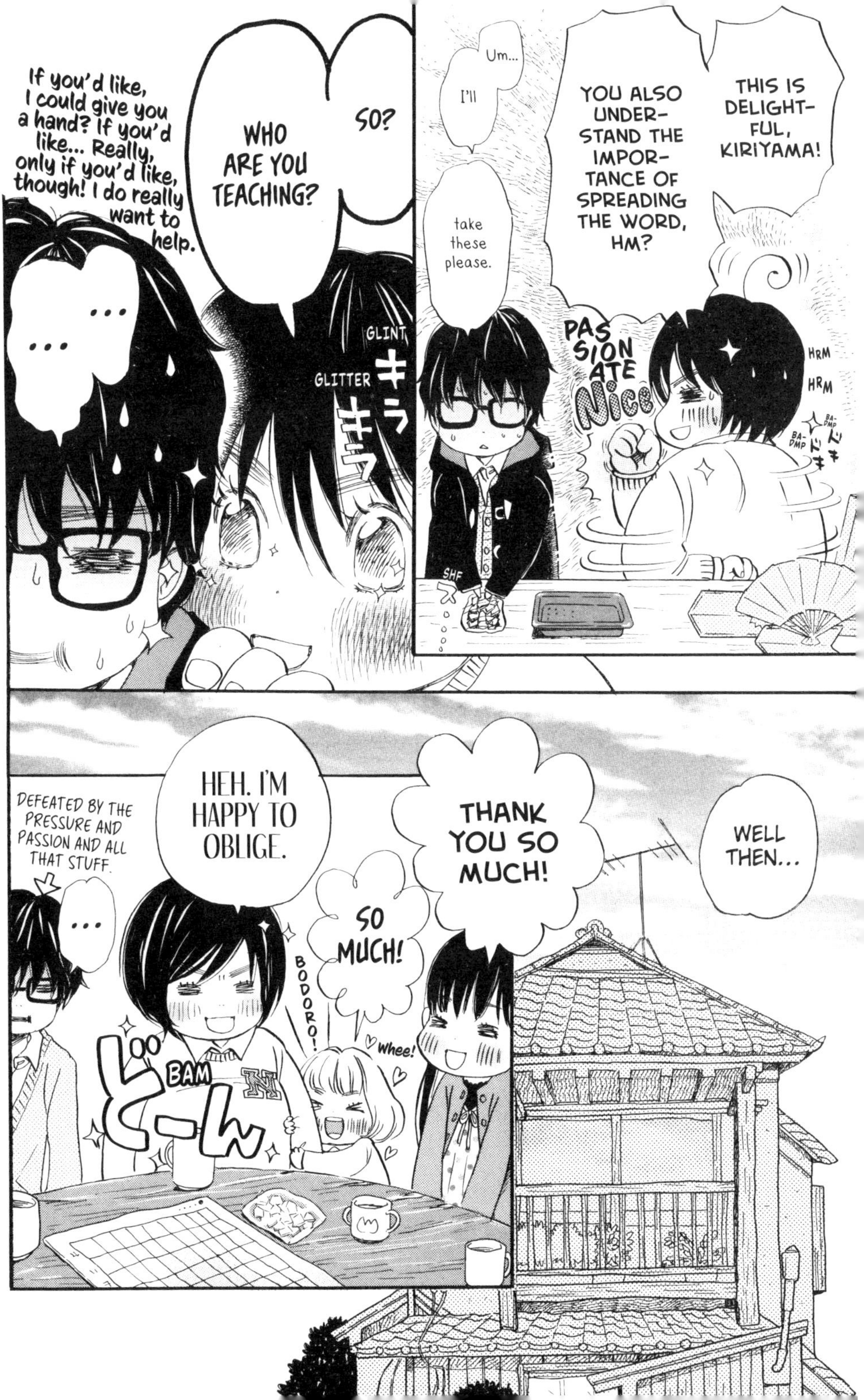
THIS IS DELIGHTFUL, KIRIYAMA!
YOU ALSO UNDERSTAND THE IMPORTANCE OF SPREADING THE WORD, HM?
Um...
I'll
take these please.
PASSIONATE Nice
HRM HRM
BA-DMP BA-DMP
ドキ ドキ
SHF
SO?
WHO ARE YOU TEACHING?
GLINT GLITTER
キラ キラ
If you'd like, I could give you a hand? If you'd like... Really, only if you'd like, though! I do really want to help.
...
...
WELL THEN...
THANK YOU SO MUCH!
SO MUCH!
Whee!
BODORO!
HEH. I'M HAPPY TO OBLIGE.
BAM
どーん
...
DEFEATED BY THE PRESSURE AND PASSION AND ALL THAT STUFF.

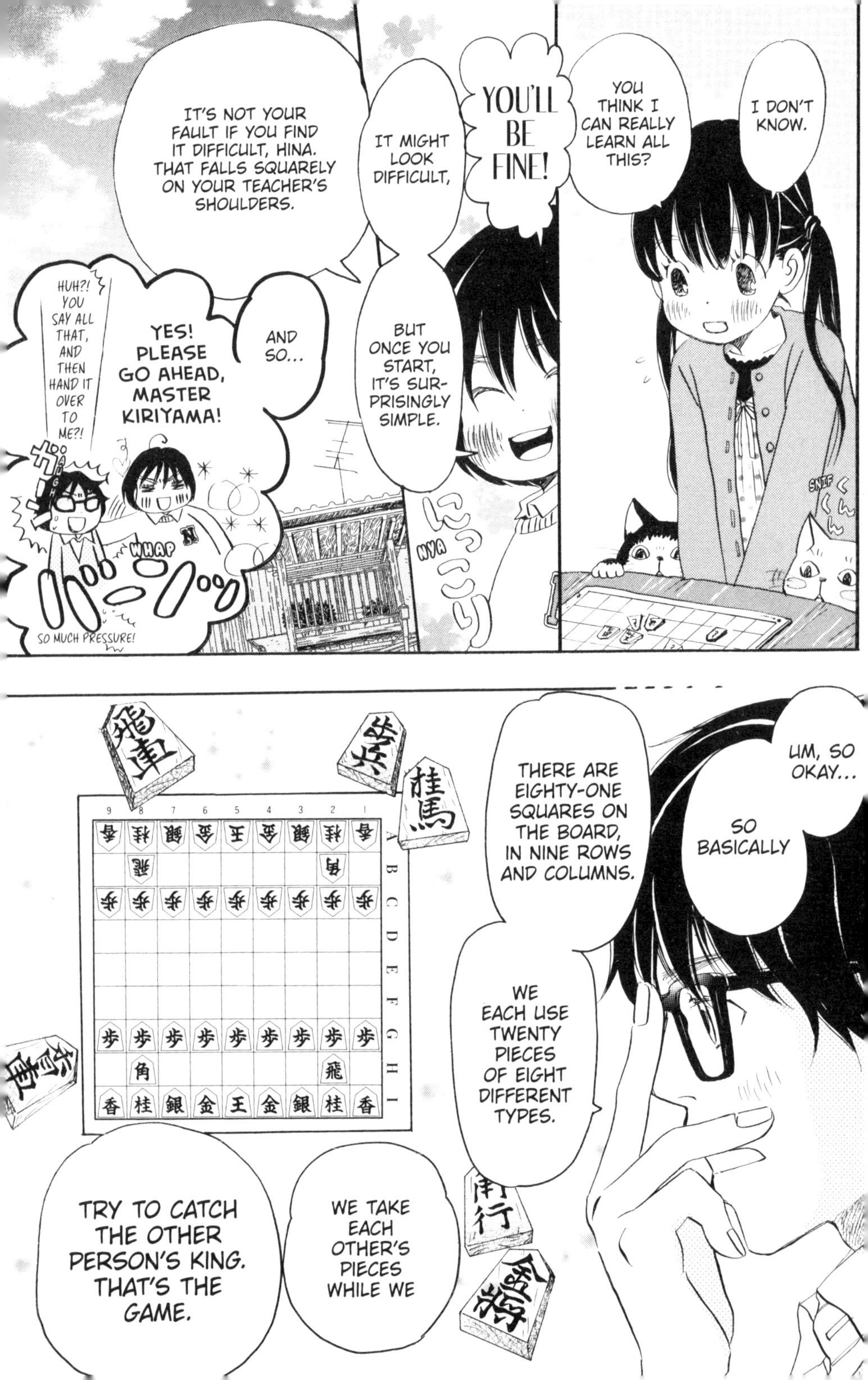
I DON'T KNOW.
YOU THINK I CAN REALLY LEARN ALL THIS?
SNIFF
くんくん
YOU'LL BE FINE!
IT MIGHT LOOK DIFFICULT,
BUT ONCE YOU START, IT'S SURPRISINGLY SIMPLE.
NYA
にっこり
IT'S NOT YOUR FAULT IF YOU FIND IT DIFFICULT, HINA. THAT FALLS SQUARELY ON YOUR TEACHER'S SHOULDERS.
AND SO...
YES! PLEASE GO AHEAD, MASTER KIRIYAMA!
HUH?! YOU SAY ALL THAT, AND THEN HAND IT OVER TO ME?!
WHAP
SO MUCH PRESSURE!
UM, SO OKAY...
SO BASICALLY
THERE ARE EIGHTY-ONE SQUARES ON THE BOARD, IN NINE ROWS AND COLUMNS.
WE EACH USE TWENTY PIECES OF EIGHT DIFFERENT TYPES.
WE TAKE EACH OTHER'S PIECES WHILE WE
TRY TO CATCH THE OTHER PERSON'S KING. THAT'S THE GAME.

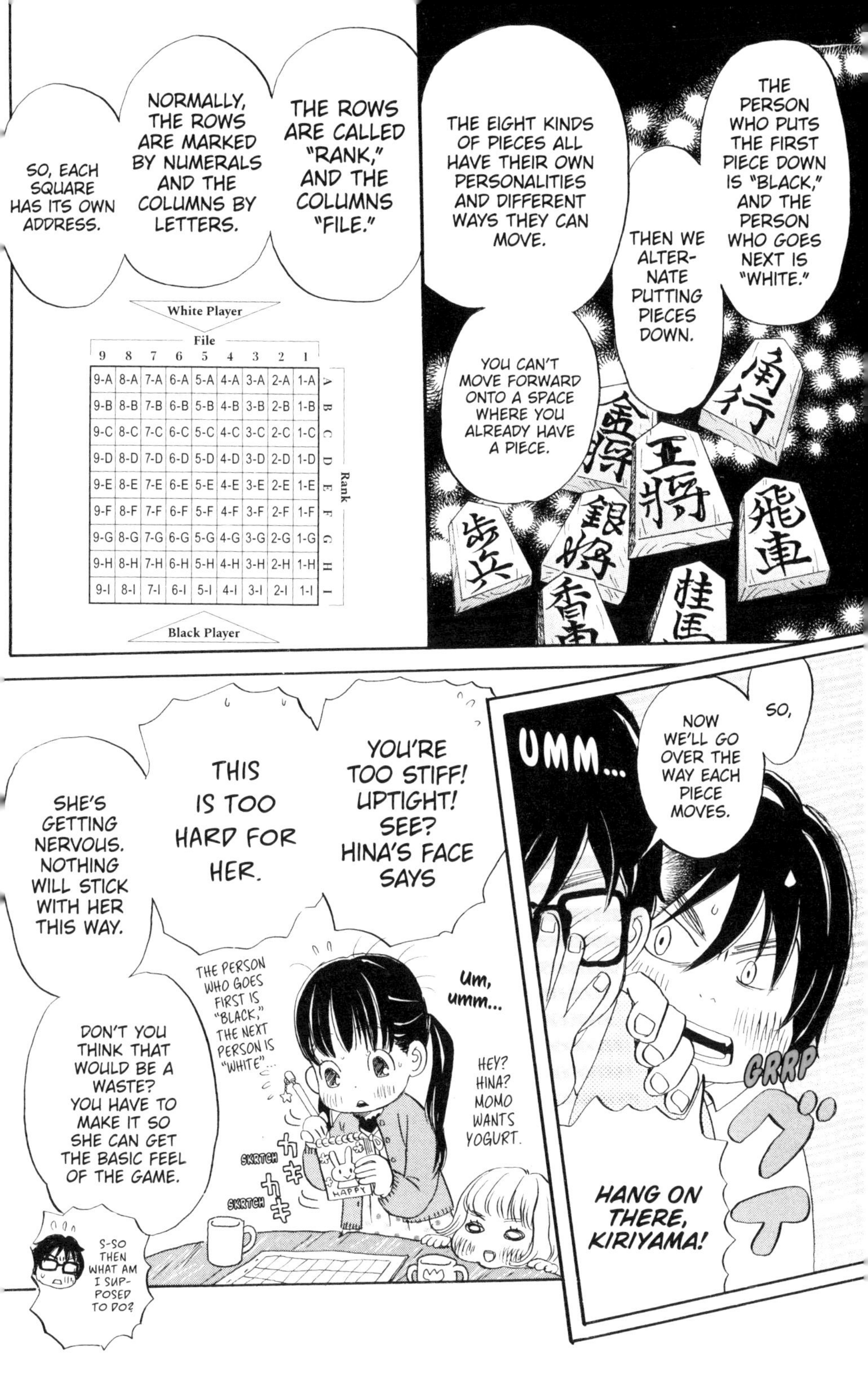
THE PERSON WHO PUTS THE FIRST PIECE DOWN IS "BLACK," AND THE PERSON WHO GOES NEXT IS "WHITE."
THEN WE ALTER-NATE PUTTING PIECES DOWN.
THE EIGHT KINDS OF PIECES ALL HAVE THEIR OWN PERSONALITIES AND DIFFERENT WAYS THEY CAN MOVE.
YOU CAN'T MOVE FORWARD ONTO A SPACE WHERE YOU ALREADY HAVE A PIECE.
角行
飛車
王将
金将
銀将
歩兵
THE ROWS ARE CALLED "RANK," AND THE COLUMNS "FILE."
NORMALLY, THE ROWS ARE MARKED BY NUMERALS AND THE COLUMNS BY LETTERS.
SO, EACH SQUARE HAS ITS OWN ADDRESS.
White Player
File
Rank
Black Player
SO,
NOW WE'LL GO OVER THE WAY EACH PIECE MOVES.
UMM...
GRRP
HANG ON THERE, KIRIYAMA!
YOU'RE TOO STIFF! UPTIGHT! SEE? HINA'S FACE SAYS
THIS IS TOO HARD FOR HER.
SHE'S GETTING NERVOUS. NOTHING WILL STICK WITH HER THIS WAY.
Um, umm...
THE PERSON WHO GOES FIRST IS "BLACK," THE NEXT PERSON IS "WHITE"...
HEY? HINA? MOMO WANTS YOGURT.
DON'T YOU THINK THAT WOULD BE A WASTE? YOU HAVE TO MAKE IT SO SHE CAN GET THE BASIC FEEL OF THE GAME.
SKRTCH カキ
SKRTCH カキ
HAPPY
S-SO THEN WHAT AM I SUP-POSED TO DO?

9	8	7	6	5	4	3	2	1	
9-A	8-A	7-A	6-A	5-A	4-A	3-A	2-A	1-A	A
9-B	8-B	7-B	6-B	5-B	4-B	3-B	2-B	1-B	B
9-C	8-C	7-C	6-C	5-C	4-C	3-C	2-C	1-C	C
9-D	8-D	7-D	6-D	5-D	4-D	3-D	2-D	1-D	D
9-E	8-E	7-E	6-E	5-E	4-E	3-E	2-E	1-E	E
9-F	8-F	7-F	6-F	5-F	4-F	3-F	2-F	1-F	F
9-G	8-G	7-G	6-G	5-G	4-G	3-G	2-G	1-G	G
9-H	8-H	7-H	6-H	5-H	4-H	3-H	2-H	1-H	H
9-I	8-I	7-I	6-I	5-I	4-I	3-I	2-I	1-I	I

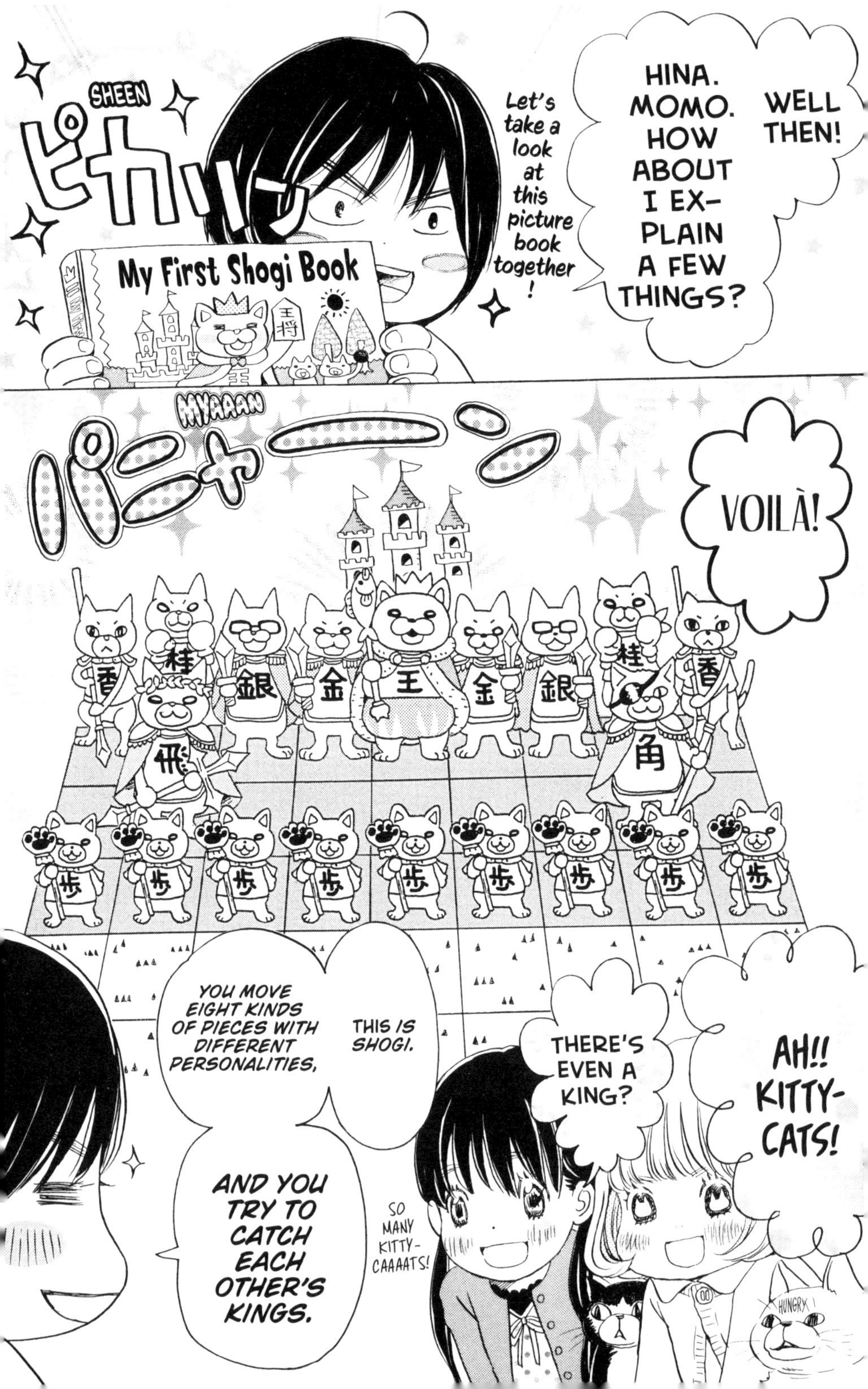
WELL THEN!
HINA. MOMO. HOW ABOUT I EX-PLAIN A FEW THINGS?
Let's take a look at this picture book together!
SHEEN
My First Shogi Book
VOILÀ!
MYAAAN
AH!! KITTY-CATS!
THERE'S EVEN A KING?
SO MANY KITTY-CAAAATS!
HUNGRY!
THIS IS SHOGI.
YOU MOVE EIGHT KINDS OF PIECES WITH DIFFERENT PERSONALITIES,
AND YOU TRY TO CATCH EACH OTHER'S KINGS.

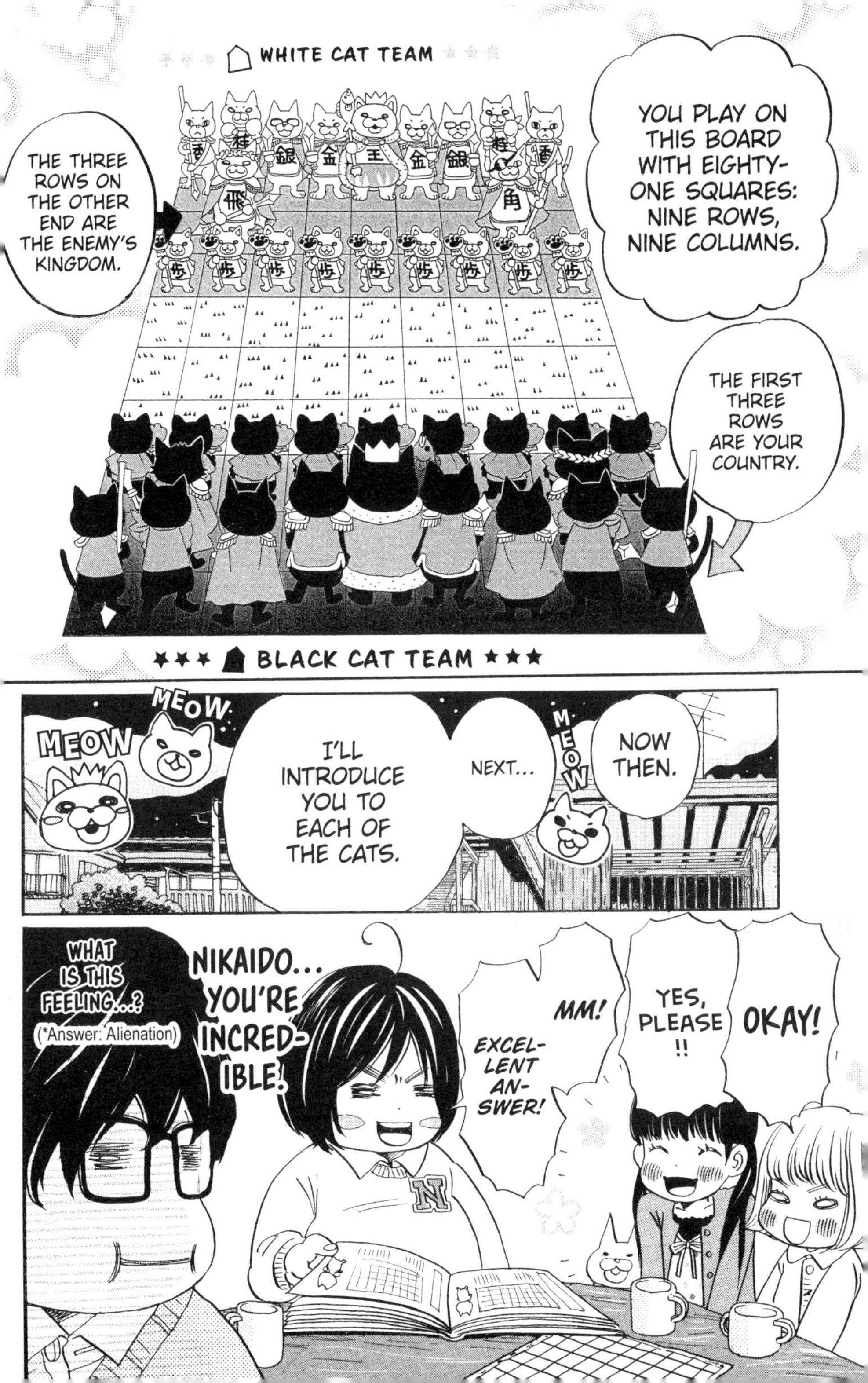
WHITE CAT TEAM
YOU PLAY ON THIS BOARD WITH EIGHTY-ONE SQUARES: NINE ROWS, NINE COLUMNS.
THE THREE ROWS ON THE OTHER END ARE THE ENEMY'S KINGDOM.
THE FIRST THREE ROWS ARE YOUR COUNTRY.
BLACK CAT TEAM
NOW THEN.
MEOW
NEXT...
I'LL INTRODUCE YOU TO EACH OF THE CATS.
MEOW
MEOW
OKAY!
YES, PLEASE!!
MM!
EXCELLENT ANSWER!
NIKAIDO... YOU'RE INCREDIBLE!
WHAT IS THIS FEELING...?
(*Answer: Alienation)

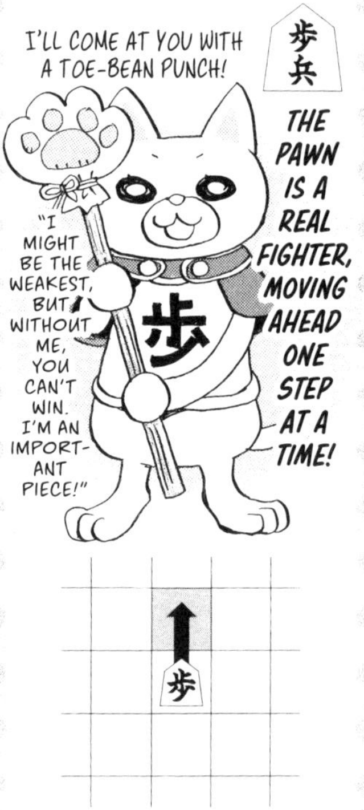
歩兵
I'LL COME AT YOU WITH A TOE-BEAN PUNCH!
THE PAWN IS A REAL FIGHTER, MOVING AHEAD ONE STEP AT A TIME!
"I MIGHT BE THE WEAKEST, BUT WITHOUT ME, YOU CAN'T WIN. I'M AN IMPORTANT PIECE!"
歩
歩

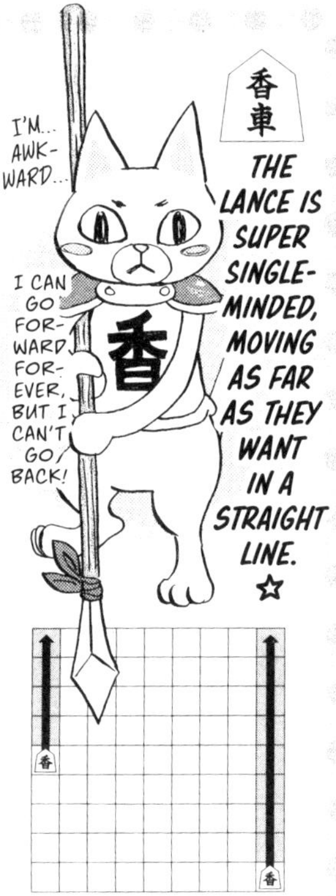
香車
I'M... AWKWARD...
THE LANCE IS SUPER SINGLE-MINDED, MOVING AS FAR AS THEY WANT IN A STRAIGHT LINE. ☆
I CAN GO FORWARD FOREVER, BUT I CAN'T GO BACK!
香
香
香

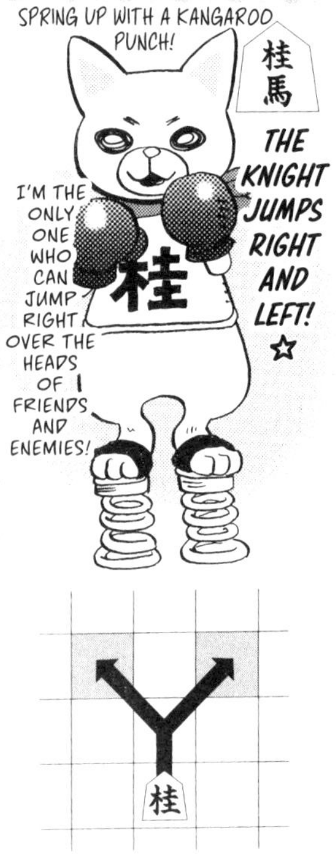
SPRING UP WITH A KANGAROO PUNCH!
桂馬
THE KNIGHT JUMPS RIGHT AND LEFT! ☆
I'M THE ONLY ONE WHO CAN JUMP RIGHT OVER THE HEADS OF FRIENDS AND ENEMIES!
桂
桂

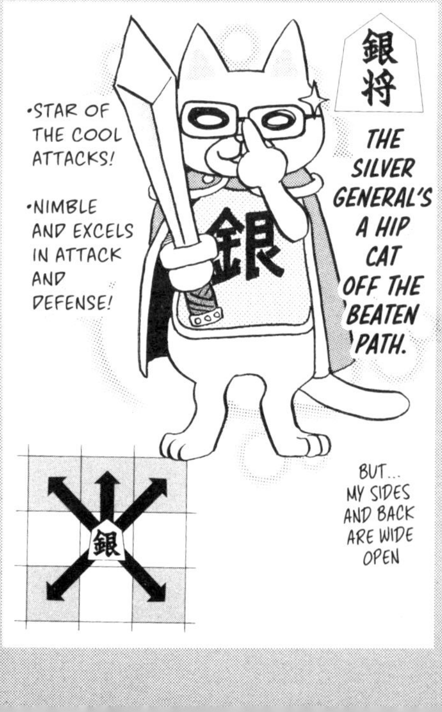
銀将
•STAR OF THE COOL ATTACKS!
•NIMBLE AND EXCELS IN ATTACK AND DEFENSE!
THE SILVER GENERAL'S A HIP CAT OFF THE BEATEN PATH.
銀
BUT... MY SIDES AND BACK ARE WIDE OPEN
銀

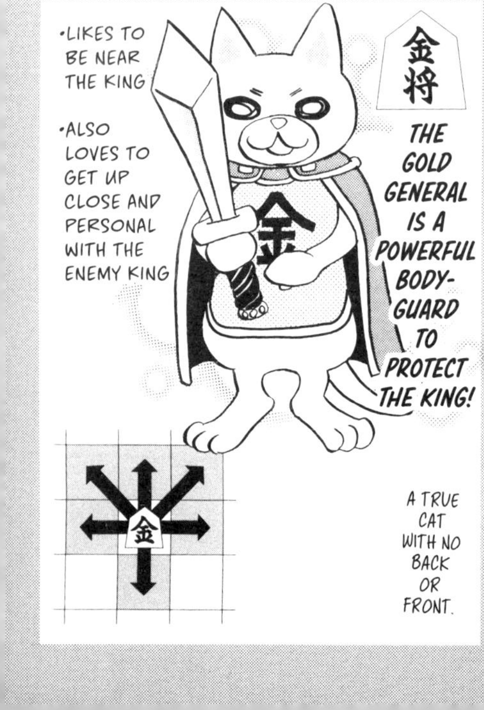
金将
•LIKES TO BE NEAR THE KING
•ALSO LOVES TO GET UP CLOSE AND PERSONAL WITH THE ENEMY KING
THE GOLD GENERAL IS A POWERFUL BODYGUARD TO PROTECT THE KING!
金
A TRUE CAT WITH NO BACK OR FRONT.
金

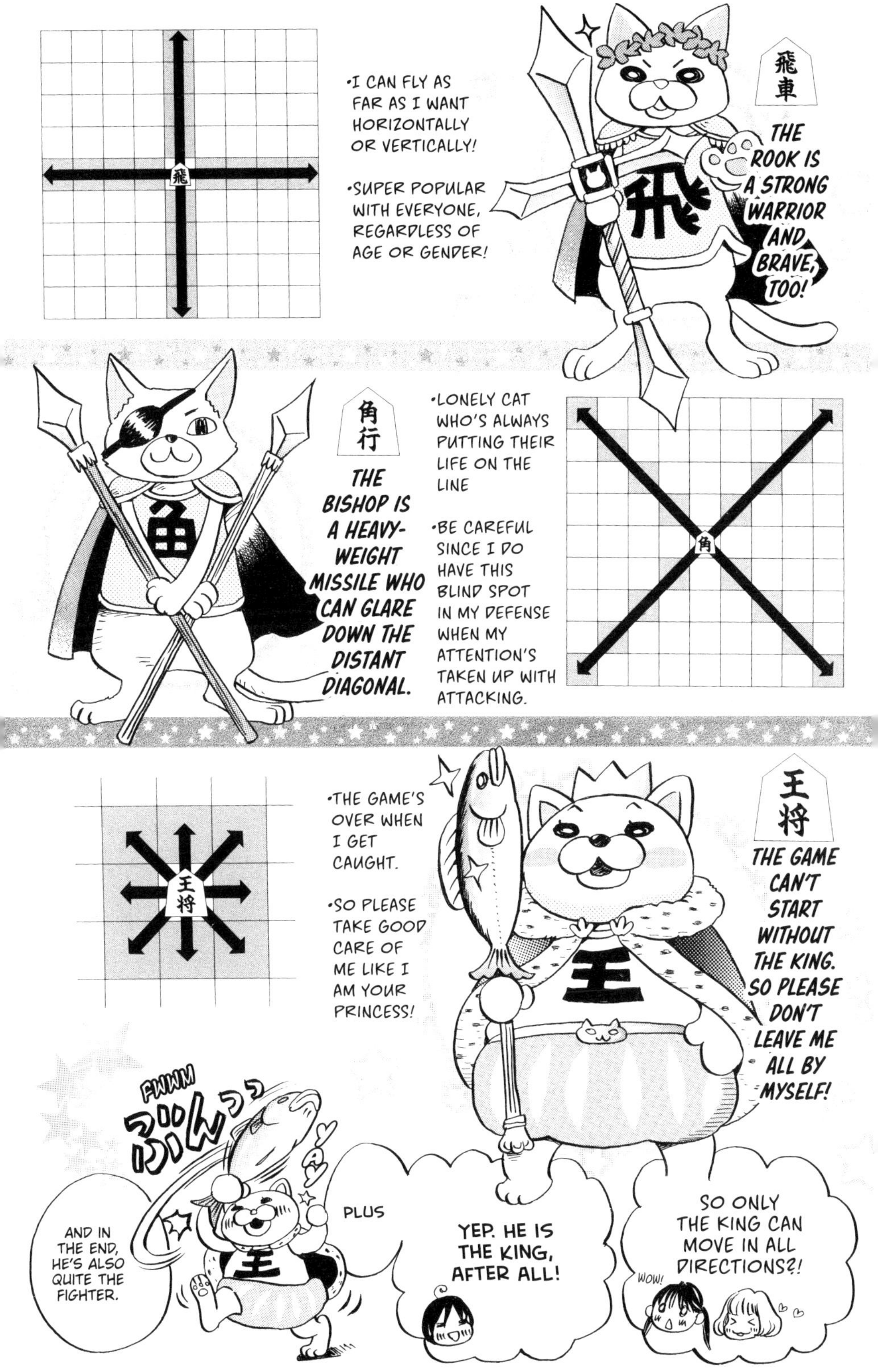

飛車
THE ROOK IS A STRONG WARRIOR AND BRAVE, TOO!
•I CAN FLY AS FAR AS I WANT HORIZONTALLY OR VERTICALLY!
•SUPER POPULAR WITH EVERYONE, REGARDLESS OF AGE OR GENDER!
飛
•LONELY CAT WHO'S ALWAYS PUTTING THEIR LIFE ON THE LINE
•BE CAREFUL SINCE I DO HAVE THIS BLIND SPOT IN MY DEFENSE WHEN MY ATTENTION'S TAKEN UP WITH ATTACKING.
角
角行
THE BISHOP IS A HEAVY-WEIGHT MISSILE WHO CAN GLARE DOWN THE DISTANT DIAGONAL.
角
王将
THE GAME CAN'T START WITHOUT THE KING. SO PLEASE DON'T LEAVE ME ALL BY MYSELF!
王
•THE GAME'S OVER WHEN I GET CAUGHT.
•SO PLEASE TAKE GOOD CARE OF ME LIKE I AM YOUR PRINCESS!
王将
SO ONLY THE KING CAN MOVE IN ALL DIRECTIONS?!
WOW!
YEP. HE IS THE KING, AFTER ALL!
PLUS
王
FWWM
ぶんっっ
AND IN THE END, HE'S ALSO QUITE THE FIGHTER.

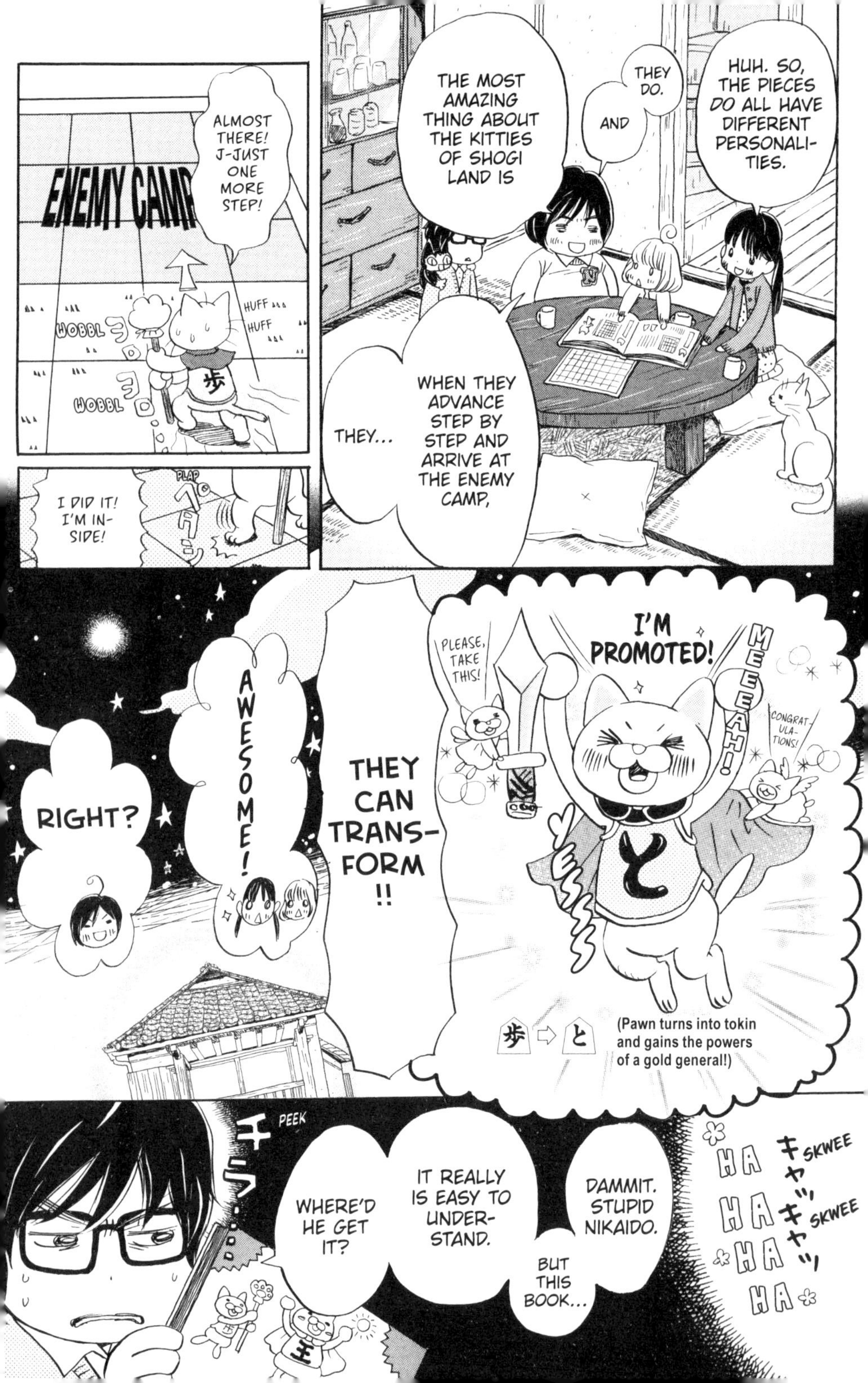
HUH. SO, THE PIECES DO ALL HAVE DIFFERENT PERSONALITIES.
THEY DO.
AND
THE MOST AMAZING THING ABOUT THE KITTIES OF SHOGI LAND IS
WHEN THEY ADVANCE STEP BY STEP AND ARRIVE AT THE ENEMY CAMP,
THEY...
ENEMY CAMP
ALMOST THERE! J-JUST ONE MORE STEP!
HUFF
HUFF
WOBBL
WOBBL
PLAP
I DID IT! I'M IN-SIDE!
I'M PROMOTED!
MEEEAH!
CONGRAT-ULATIONS!
PLEASE, TAKE THIS!
(Pawn turns into tokin and gains the powers of a gold general!)
THEY CAN TRANS-FORM !!
AWESOME!
RIGHT?
SKWEE
SKWEE
HA HA HA HA
DAMMIT. STUPID NIKAIDO.
BUT THIS BOOK...
IT REALLY IS EASY TO UNDER-STAND.
WHERE'D HE GET IT?
PEEK

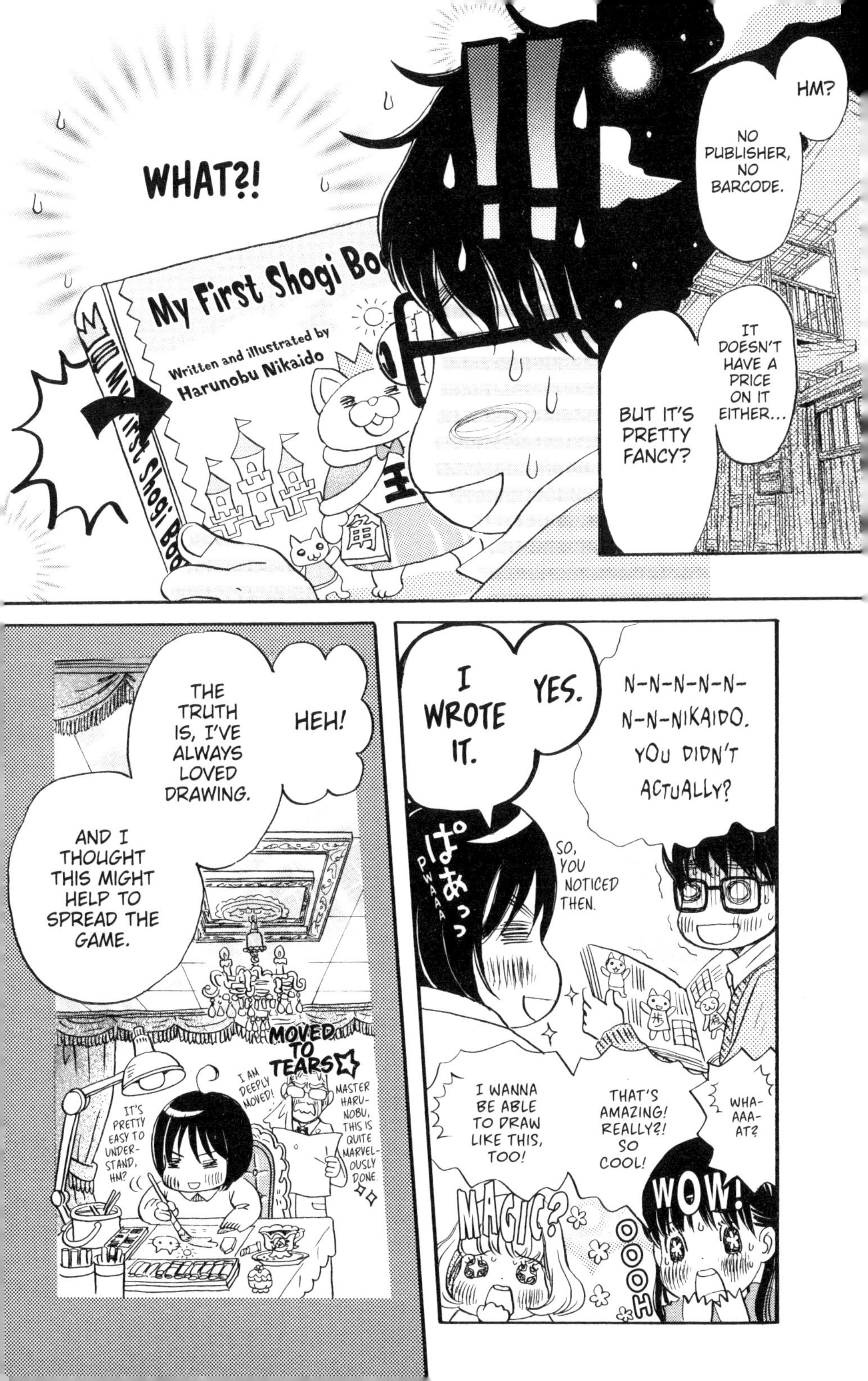

HM?
NO PUBLISHER, NO BARCODE.
IT DOESN'T HAVE A PRICE ON IT EITHER...
BUT IT'S PRETTY FANCY?
WHAT?!
My First Shogi Bo
Written and illustrated by
Harunobu Nikaido
N-N-N-N-N-N-N-NIKAIDO. YOU DIDN'T ACTUALLY?
YES.
I WROTE IT.
ぱあっ
PWAAA
SO, YOU NOTICED THEN.
WHA-AAA-AT?
THAT'S AMAZING! REALLY?! SO COOL!
I WANNA BE ABLE TO DRAW LIKE THIS, TOO!
WOW!
OOOOH
MAGIC?
HEH!
THE TRUTH IS, I'VE ALWAYS LOVED DRAWING.
AND I THOUGHT THIS MIGHT HELP TO SPREAD THE GAME.
MOVED TO TEARS
MASTER HARUNOBU, THIS IS QUITE MARVELOUSLY DONE.
I AM DEEPLY MOVED!
IT'S PRETTY EASY TO UNDERSTAND, HM?

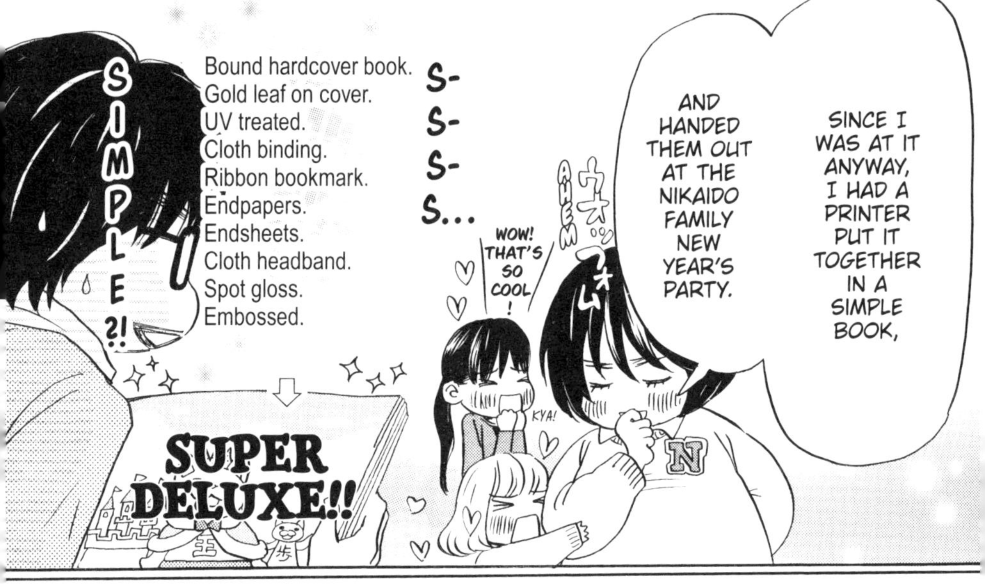
SINCE I WAS AT IT ANYWAY, I HAD A PRINTER PUT IT TOGETHER IN A SIMPLE BOOK,
AND HANDED THEM OUT AT THE NIKAIDO FAMILY NEW YEAR'S PARTY.
AHEM
WOW! THAT'S SO COOL!
KYA!
S- S- S- S...
Bound hardcover book.
Gold leaf on cover.
UV treated.
Cloth binding.
Ribbon bookmark.
Endpapers.
Endsheets.
Cloth headband.
Spot gloss.
Embossed.
SIMPLE?!
SUPER DELUXE!!
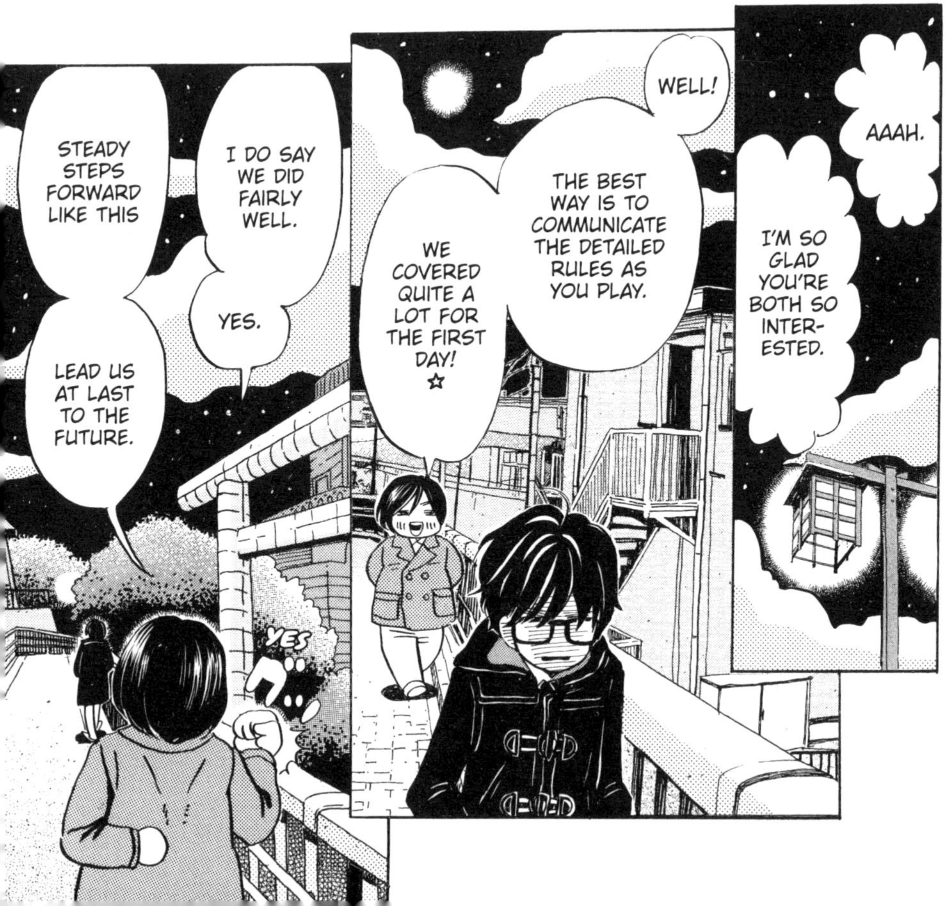
AAAH.
I'M SO GLAD YOU'RE BOTH SO INTER-ESTED.
WELL!
THE BEST WAY IS TO COMMUNICATE THE DETAILED RULES AS YOU PLAY.
WE COVERED QUITE A LOT FOR THE FIRST DAY! ☆
I DO SAY WE DID FAIRLY WELL.
YES.
STEADY STEPS FORWARD LIKE THIS
LEAD US AT LAST TO THE FUTURE.
YES

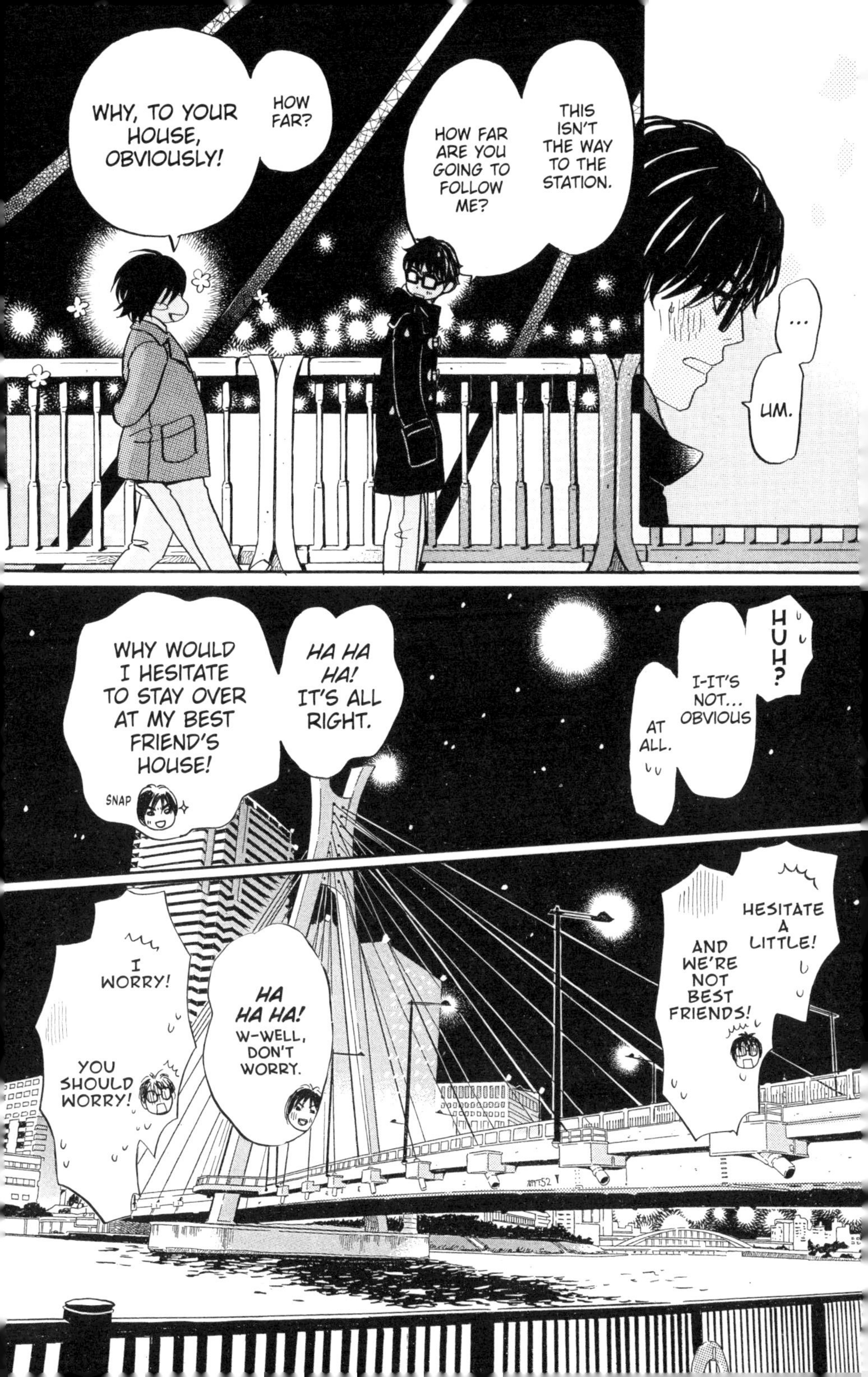
THIS ISN'T THE WAY TO THE STATION.
HOW FAR ARE YOU GOING TO FOLLOW ME?
HOW FAR?
WHY, TO YOUR HOUSE, OBVIOUSLY!
...
UM.
HUH?
I-IT'S NOT... OBVIOUS
AT ALL.
HA HA HA! IT'S ALL RIGHT.
WHY WOULD I HESITATE TO STAY OVER AT MY BEST FRIEND'S HOUSE!
SNAP
HESITATE A LITTLE!
AND WE'RE NOT BEST FRIENDS!
HA HA HA! W-WELL, DON'T WORRY.
I WORRY!
YOU SHOULD WORRY!

Chapter 16
Image

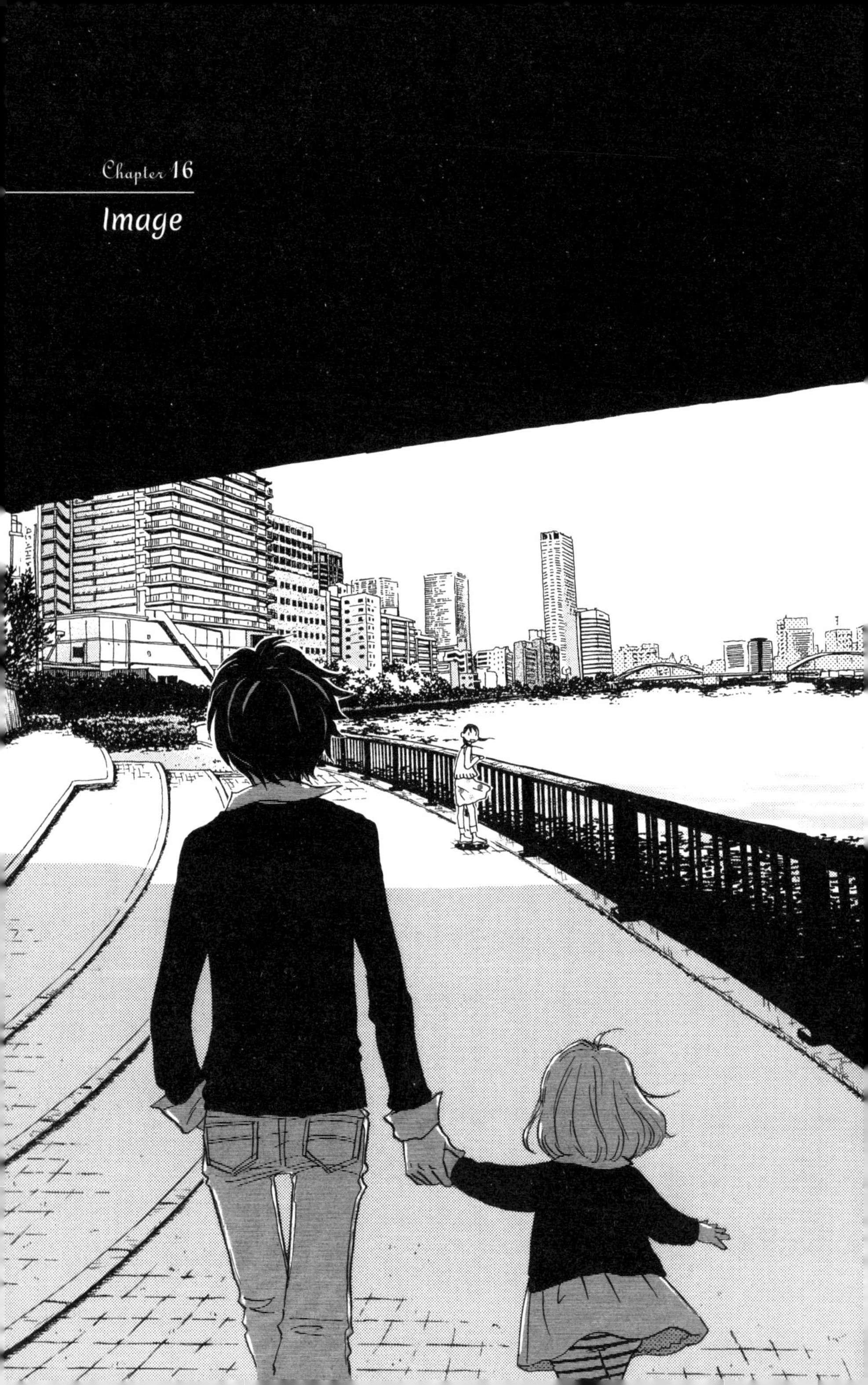

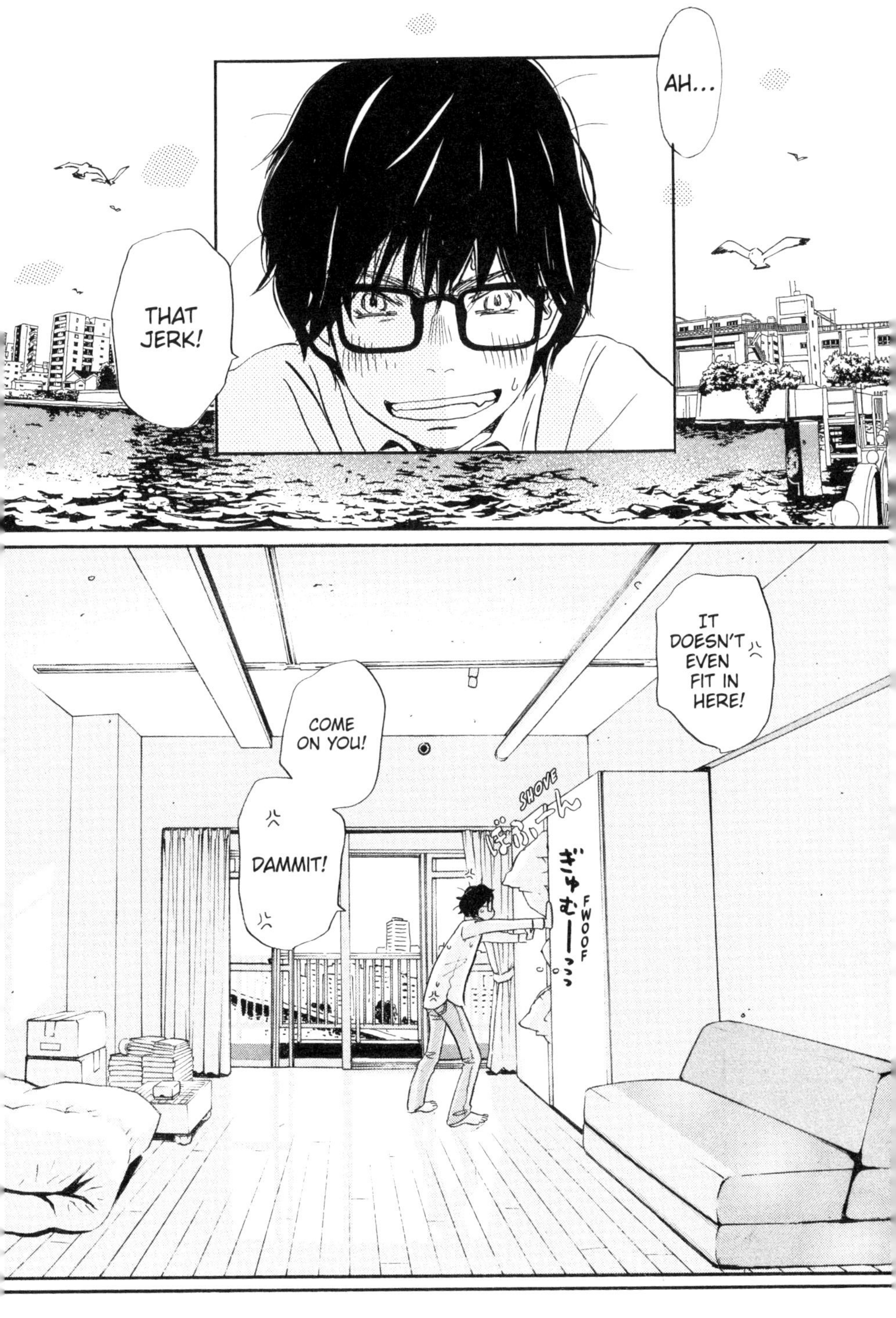
AH...
THAT JERK!
IT DOESN'T EVEN FIT IN HERE!
COME ON YOU!
DAMMIT!
SHOVE
ぎゅむーっっっ
FWOOF

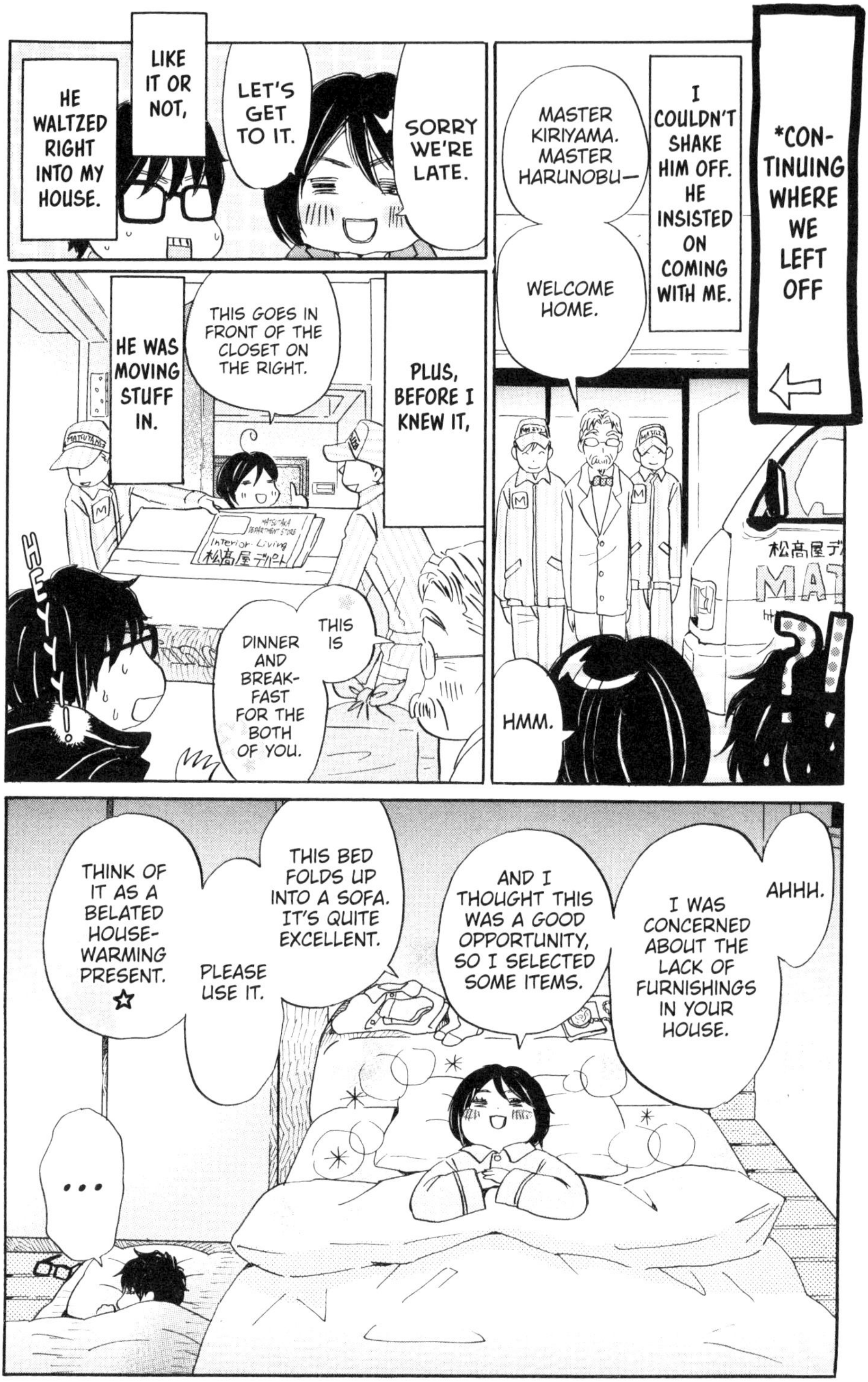
*CONTINUING WHERE WE LEFT OFF
I COULDN'T SHAKE HIM OFF. HE INSISTED ON COMING WITH ME.
MASTER KIRIYAMA. MASTER HARUNOBU—
WELCOME HOME.
HMM.
SORRY WE'RE LATE.
LET'S GET TO IT.
LIKE IT OR NOT,
HE WALTZED RIGHT INTO MY HOUSE.
PLUS, BEFORE I KNEW IT,
THIS GOES IN FRONT OF THE CLOSET ON THE RIGHT.
HE WAS MOVING STUFF IN.
MATSUTAKA DEPARTMENT STORE
Interior・Living
松高屋デパート
THIS IS DINNER AND BREAKFAST FOR THE BOTH OF YOU.
HEYYYY!
AHHH.
I WAS CONCERNED ABOUT THE LACK OF FURNISHINGS IN YOUR HOUSE.
AND I THOUGHT THIS WAS A GOOD OPPORTUNITY, SO I SELECTED SOME ITEMS.
THIS BED FOLDS UP INTO A SOFA. IT'S QUITE EXCELLENT.
PLEASE USE IT.
THINK OF IT AS A BELATED HOUSE-WARMING PRESENT. ☆
...

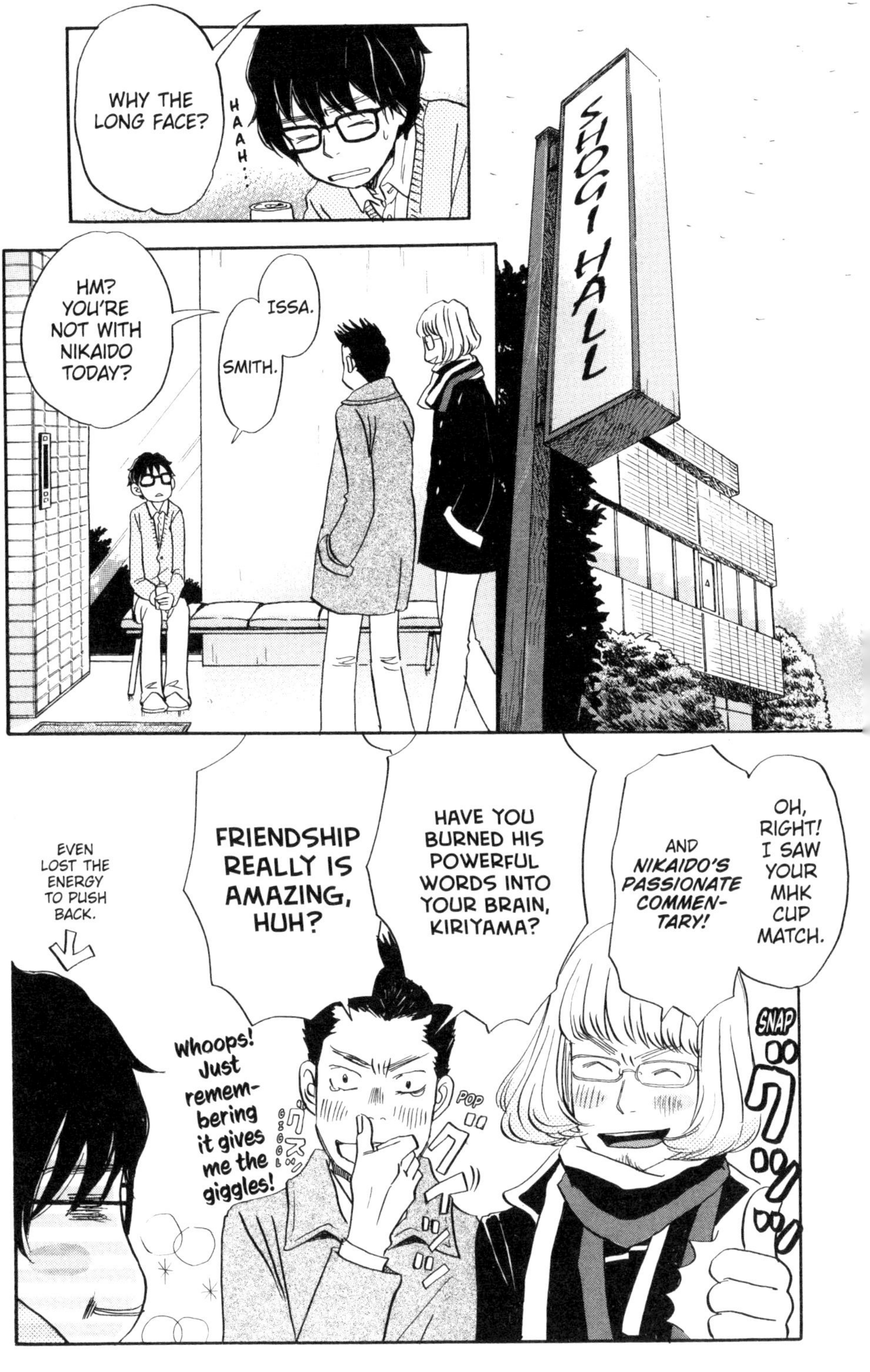
SHOGI HALL
WHY THE LONG FACE?
HAAH...
ISSA.
SMITH.
HM? YOU'RE NOT WITH NIKAIDO TODAY?
OH, RIGHT! I SAW YOUR MHK CUP MATCH.
AND NIKAIDO'S PASSIONATE COMMENTARY!
HAVE YOU BURNED HIS POWERFUL WORDS INTO YOUR BRAIN, KIRIYAMA?
FRIENDSHIP REALLY IS AMAZING, HUH?
SNAP
POP
GIGGLE
Whoops! Just remembering it gives me the giggles!
EVEN LOST THE ENERGY TO PUSH BACK.

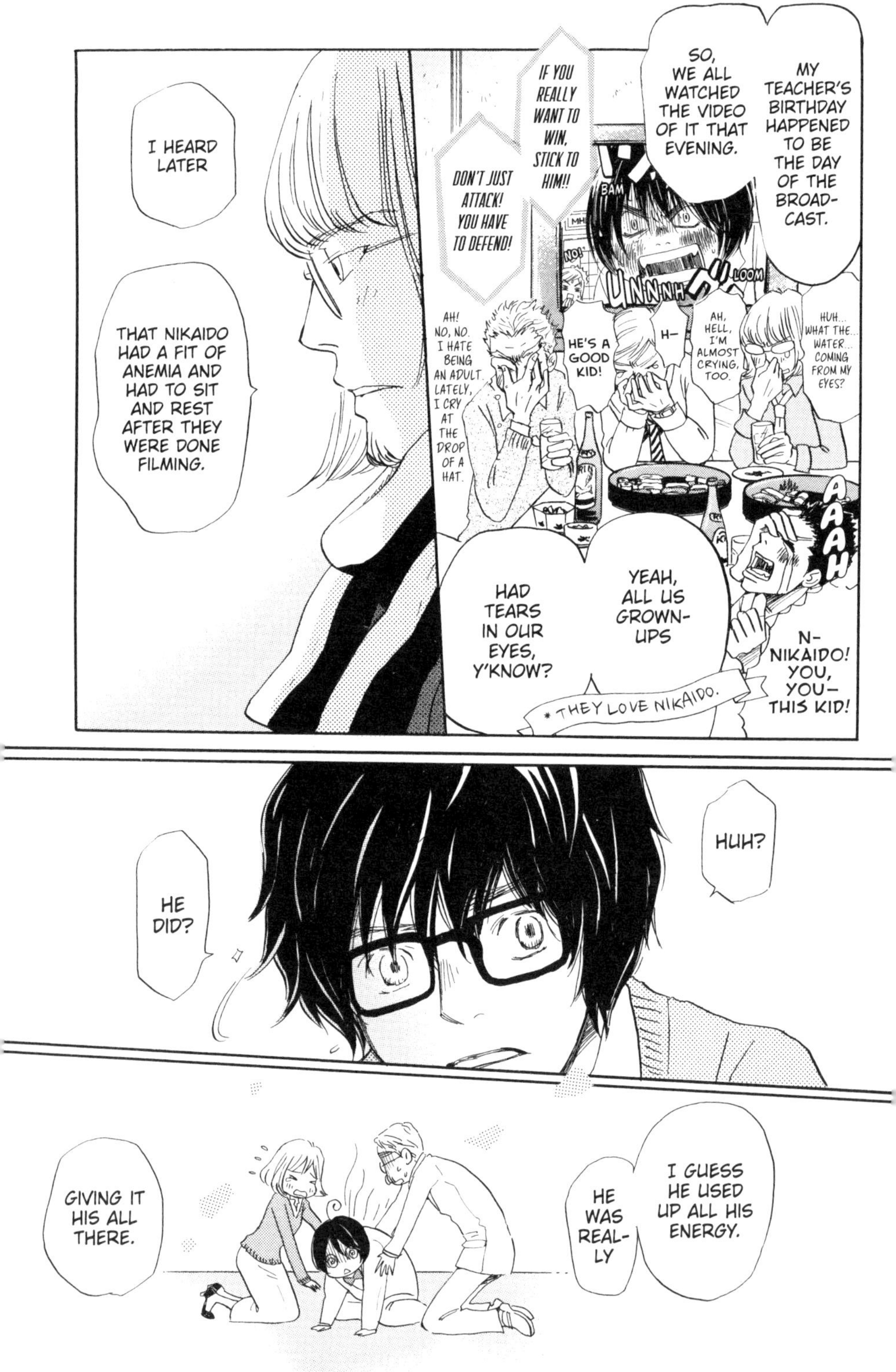
MY TEACHER'S BIRTHDAY HAPPENED TO BE THE DAY OF THE BROAD-CAST.
SO, WE ALL WATCHED THE VIDEO OF IT THAT EVENING.
IF YOU REALLY WANT TO WIN, STICK TO HIM!!
DON'T JUST ATTACK! YOU HAVE TO DEFEND!
BAM
NO!
UNNNH
LOOM
HUH... WHAT THE... WATER... COMING FROM MY EYES?
AH, HELL, I'M ALMOST CRYING, TOO.
H—
HE'S A GOOD KID!
AH! NO, NO. I HATE BEING AN ADULT. LATELY, I CRY AT THE DROP OF A HAT.
AAAAH
N-NIKAIDO! YOU, YOU— THIS KID!
YEAH, ALL US GROWN-UPS
HAD TEARS IN OUR EYES, Y'KNOW?
* THEY LOVE NIKAIDO.
I HEARD LATER
THAT NIKAIDO HAD A FIT OF ANEMIA AND HAD TO SIT AND REST AFTER THEY WERE DONE FILMING.
HUH?
HE DID?
I GUESS HE USED UP ALL HIS ENERGY.
HE WAS REAL-LY
GIVING IT HIS ALL THERE.

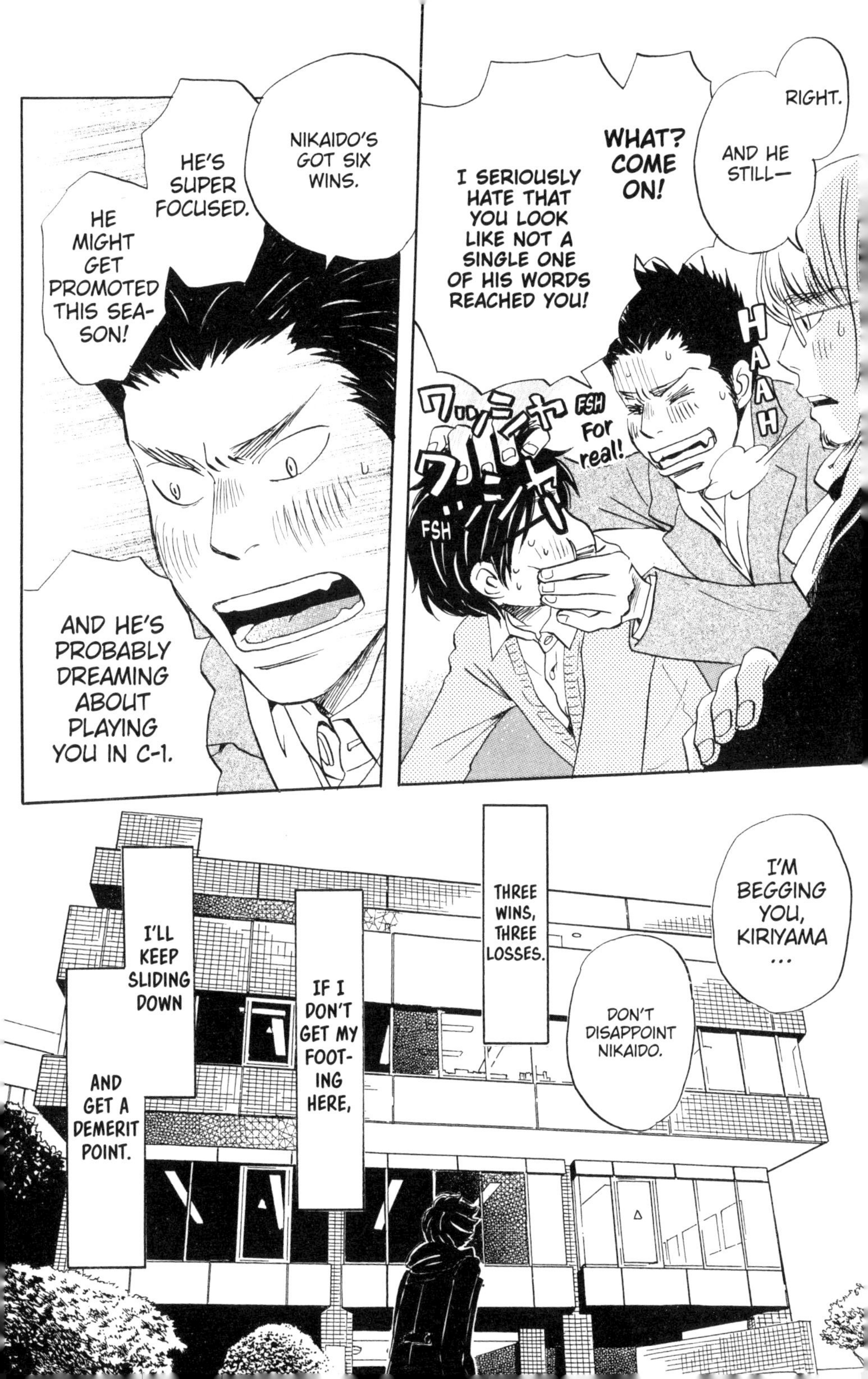
RIGHT.
AND HE STILL—
WHAT? COME ON!
I SERIOUSLY HATE THAT YOU LOOK LIKE NOT A SINGLE ONE OF HIS WORDS REACHED YOU!
HAAH
FSH
For real!
FSH
NIKAIDO'S GOT SIX WINS.
HE'S SUPER FOCUSED.
HE MIGHT GET PROMOTED THIS SEA-SON!
AND HE'S PROBABLY DREAMING ABOUT PLAYING YOU IN C-1.
I'M BEGGING YOU, KIRIYAMA ...
DON'T DISAPPOINT NIKAIDO.
THREE WINS, THREE LOSSES.
IF I DON'T GET MY FOOT-ING HERE,
I'LL KEEP SLIDING DOWN
AND GET A DEMERIT POINT.

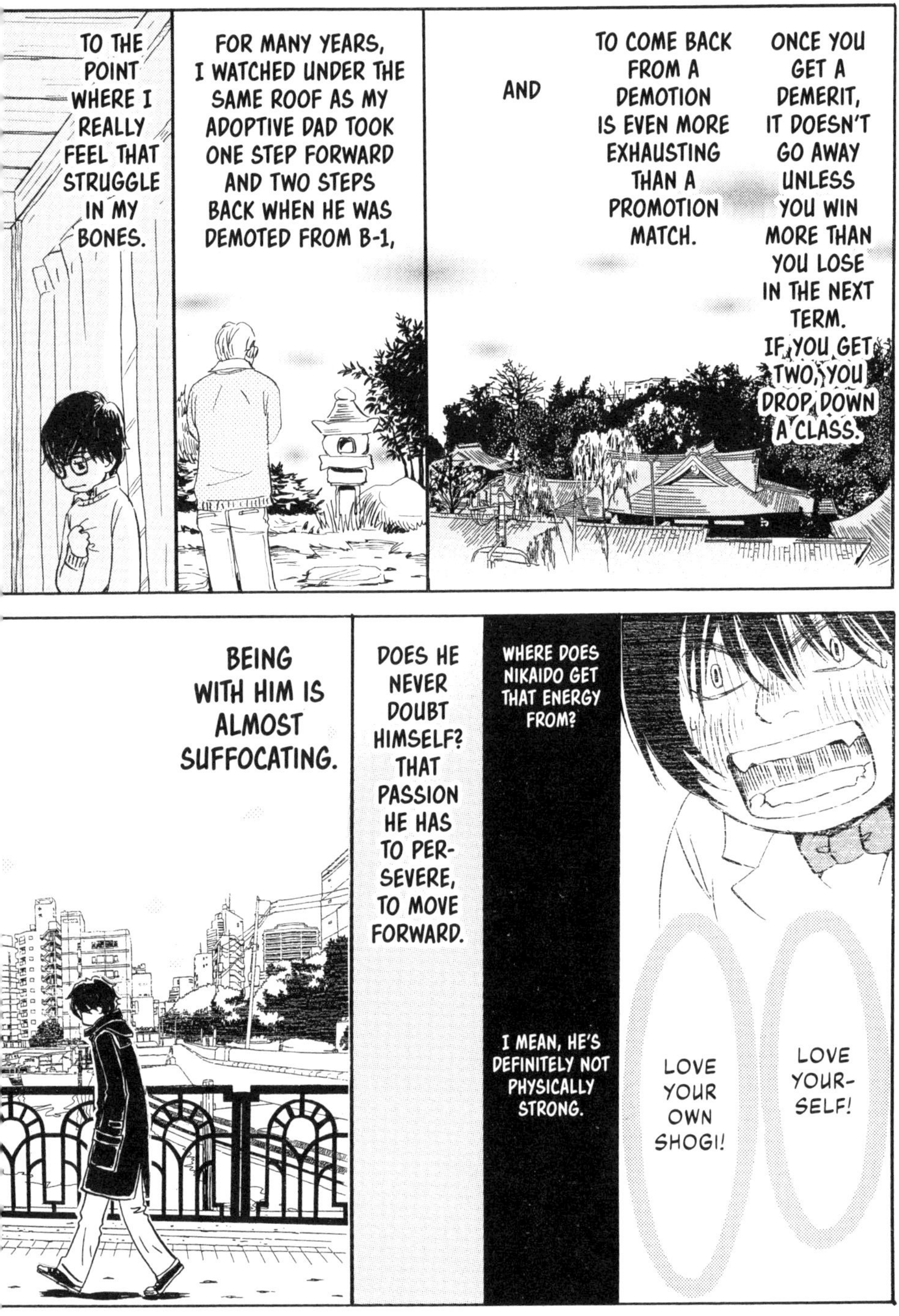
ONCE YOU GET A DEMERIT, IT DOESN'T GO AWAY UNLESS YOU WIN MORE THAN YOU LOSE IN THE NEXT TERM. IF YOU GET TWO, YOU DROP DOWN A CLASS.
TO COME BACK FROM A DEMOTION IS EVEN MORE EXHAUSTING THAN A PROMOTION MATCH.
AND
FOR MANY YEARS, I WATCHED UNDER THE SAME ROOF AS MY ADOPTIVE DAD TOOK ONE STEP FORWARD AND TWO STEPS BACK WHEN HE WAS DEMOTED FROM B-1,
TO THE POINT WHERE I REALLY FEEL THAT STRUGGLE IN MY BONES.
LOVE YOUR-SELF!
LOVE YOUR OWN SHOGI!
WHERE DOES NIKAIDO GET THAT ENERGY FROM?
I MEAN, HE'S DEFINITELY NOT PHYSICALLY STRONG.
DOES HE NEVER DOUBT HIMSELF? THAT PASSION HE HAS TO PER-SEVERE, TO MOVE FORWARD.
BEING WITH HIM IS ALMOST SUFFOCATING.

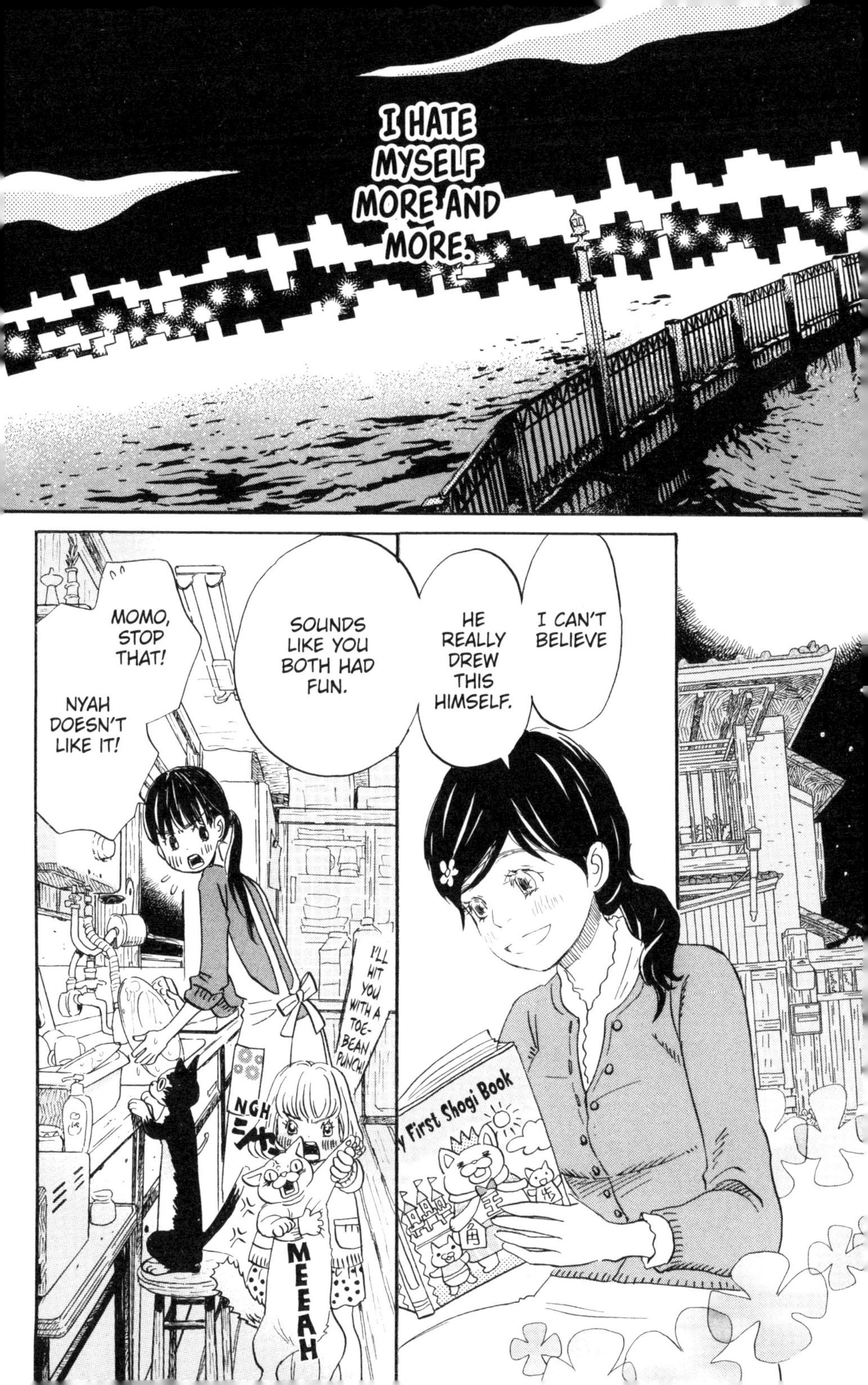
I HATE MYSELF MORE AND MORE.
I CAN'T BELIEVE
HE REALLY DREW THIS HIMSELF.
y First Shogi Book
SOUNDS LIKE YOU BOTH HAD FUN.
MOMO, STOP THAT!
NYAH DOESN'T LIKE IT!
I'LL HIT YOU WITH A TOE-BEAN PUNCH!
NGH
MEEEAH

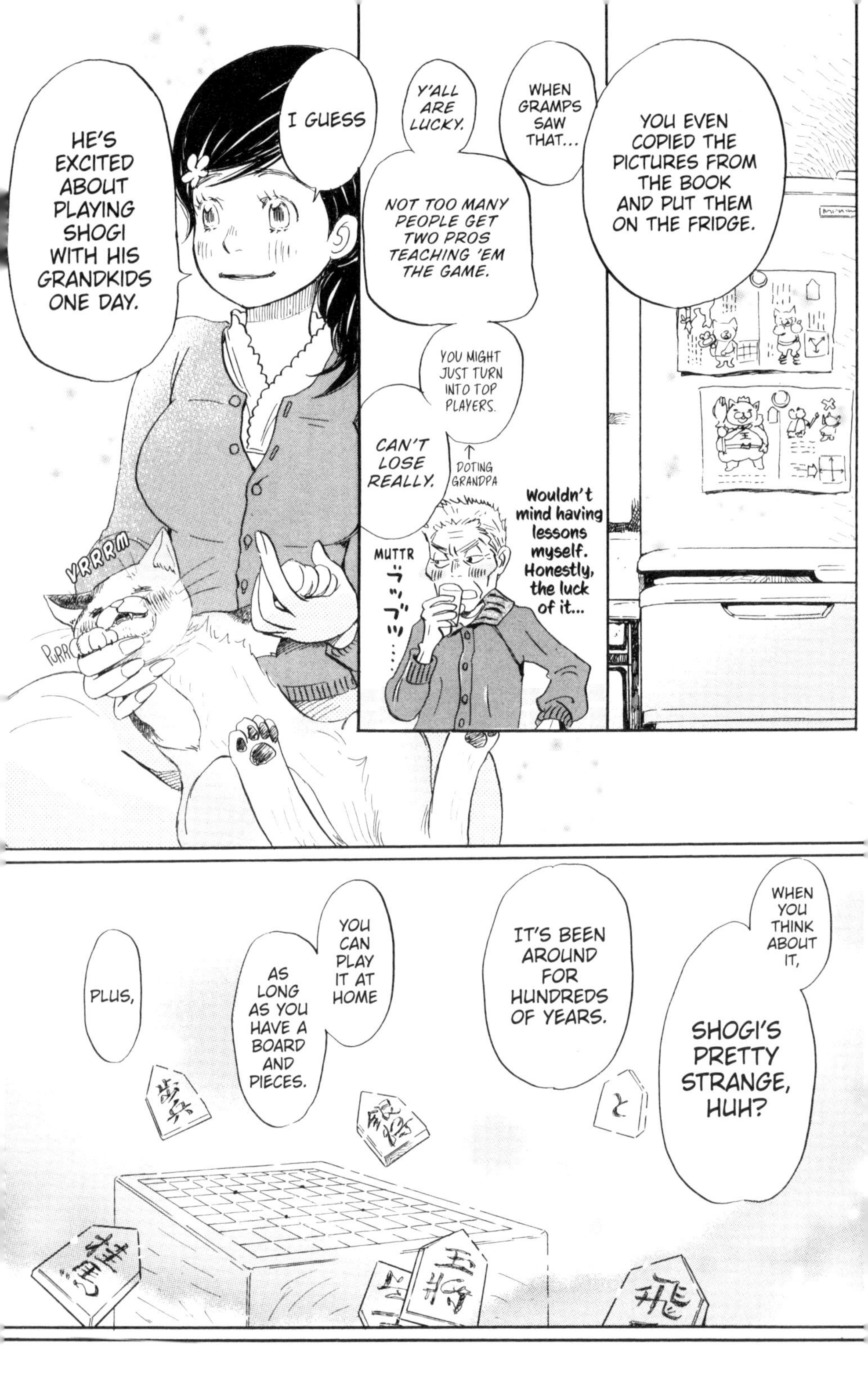
YOU EVEN COPIED THE PICTURES FROM THE BOOK AND PUT THEM ON THE FRIDGE.
WHEN GRAMPS SAW THAT...
Y'ALL ARE LUCKY.
NOT TOO MANY PEOPLE GET TWO PROS TEACHING 'EM THE GAME.
YOU MIGHT JUST TURN INTO TOP PLAYERS.
CAN'T LOSE REALLY.
↑ DOTING GRANDPA
Wouldn't mind having lessons myself. Honestly, the luck of it...
MUTTR
ブツブツ…
I GUESS
HE'S EXCITED ABOUT PLAYING SHOGI WITH HIS GRANDKIDS ONE DAY.
VRRRM
PURR
WHEN YOU THINK ABOUT IT,
SHOGI'S PRETTY STRANGE, HUH?
IT'S BEEN AROUND FOR HUNDREDS OF YEARS.
YOU CAN PLAY IT AT HOME
AS LONG AS YOU HAVE A BOARD AND PIECES.
PLUS,

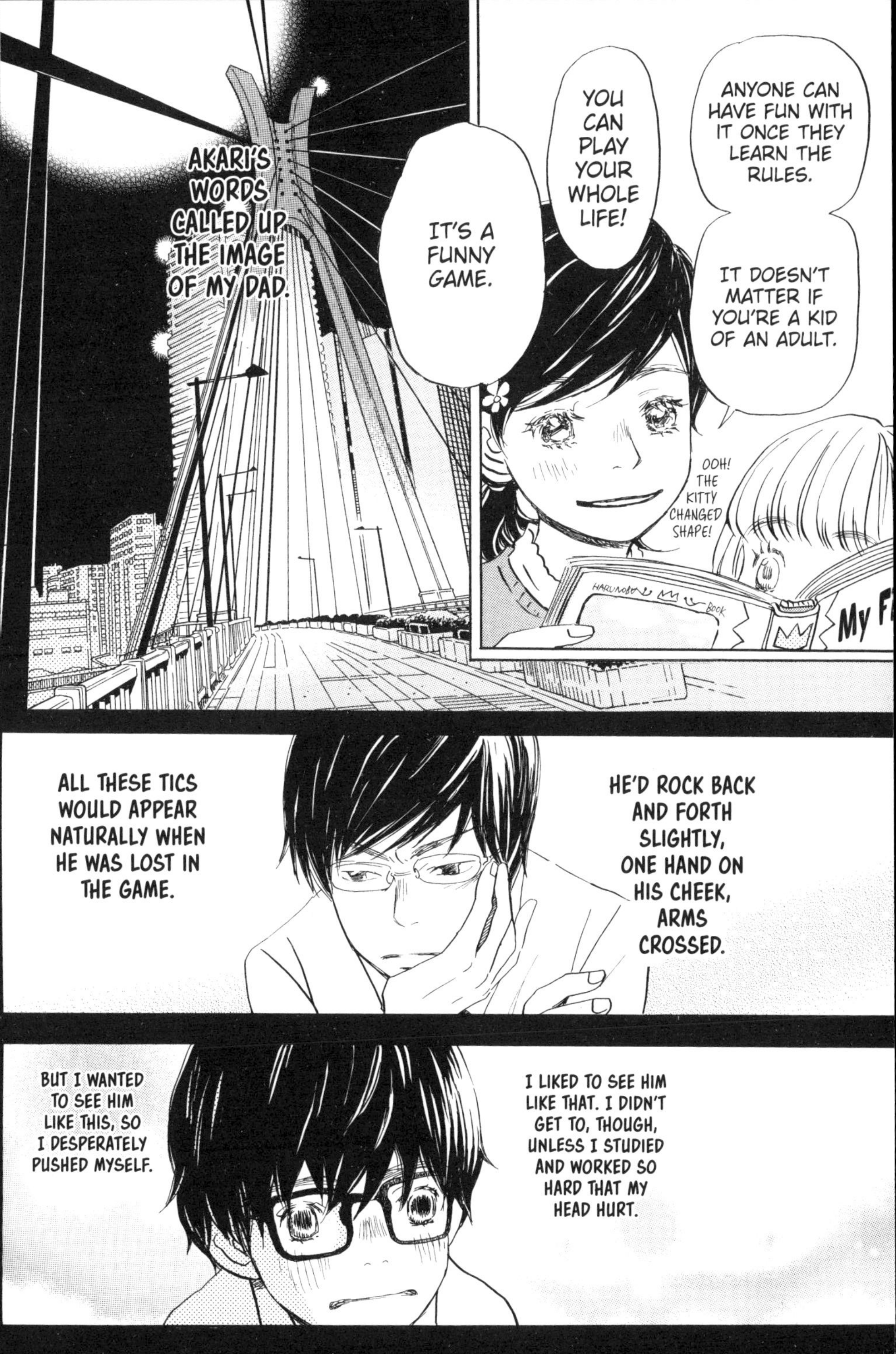
ANYONE CAN HAVE FUN WITH IT ONCE THEY LEARN THE RULES.
YOU CAN PLAY YOUR WHOLE LIFE!
IT DOESN'T MATTER IF YOU'RE A KID OF AN ADULT.
IT'S A FUNNY GAME.
OOH! THE KITTY CHANGED SHAPE!
AKARI'S WORDS CALLED UP THE IMAGE OF MY DAD.
HE'D ROCK BACK AND FORTH SLIGHTLY, ONE HAND ON HIS CHEEK, ARMS CROSSED.
ALL THESE TICS WOULD APPEAR NATURALLY WHEN HE WAS LOST IN THE GAME.
I LIKED TO SEE HIM LIKE THAT. I DIDN'T GET TO, THOUGH, UNLESS I STUDIED AND WORKED SO HARD THAT MY HEAD HURT.
BUT I WANTED TO SEE HIM LIKE THIS, SO I DESPERATELY PUSHED MYSELF.

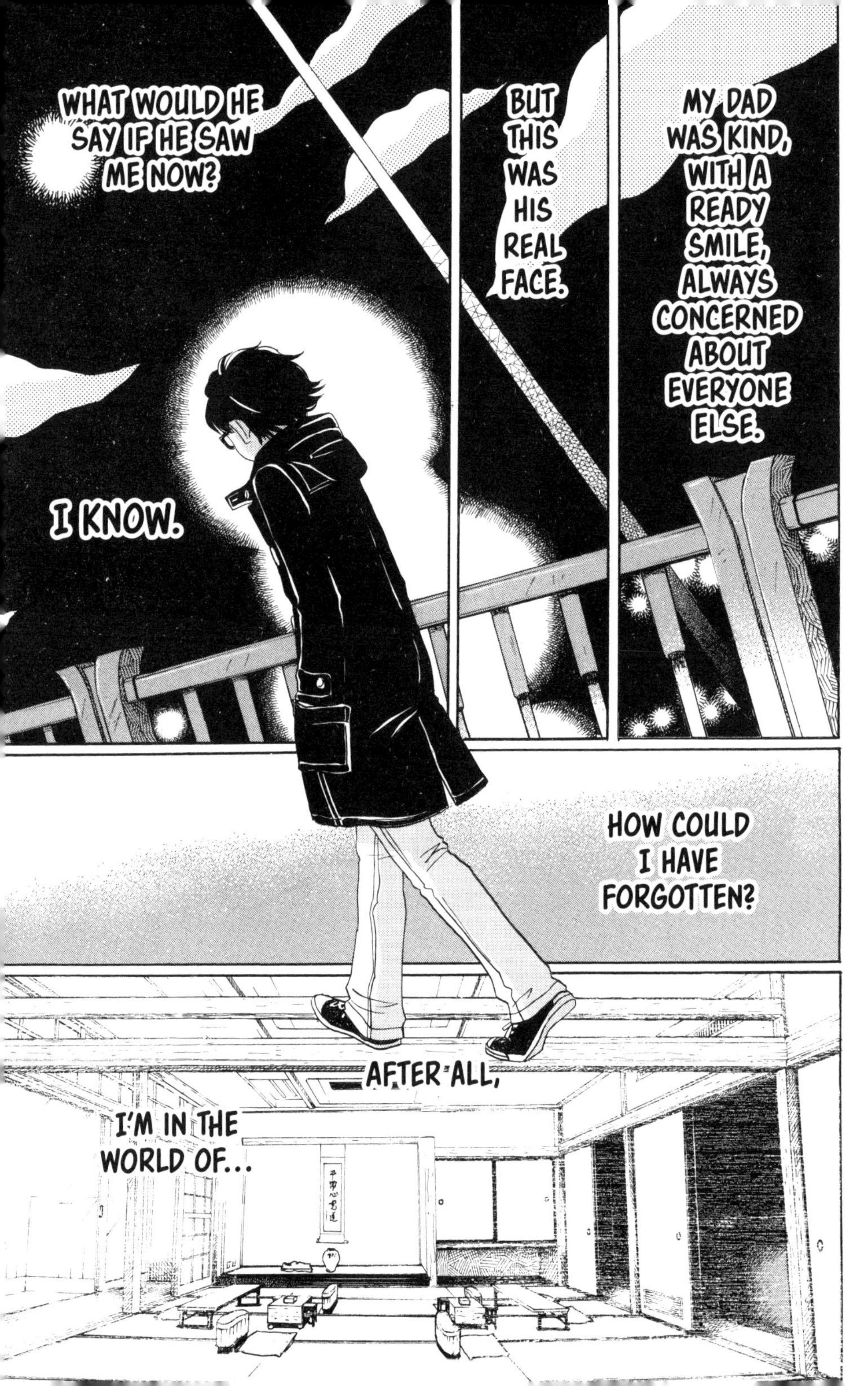
MY DAD WAS KIND, WITH A READY SMILE, ALWAYS CONCERNED ABOUT EVERYONE ELSE.
BUT THIS WAS HIS REAL FACE.
WHAT WOULD HE SAY IF HE SAW ME NOW?
I KNOW.
HOW COULD I HAVE FORGOTTEN?
AFTER ALL,
I'M IN THE WORLD OF...

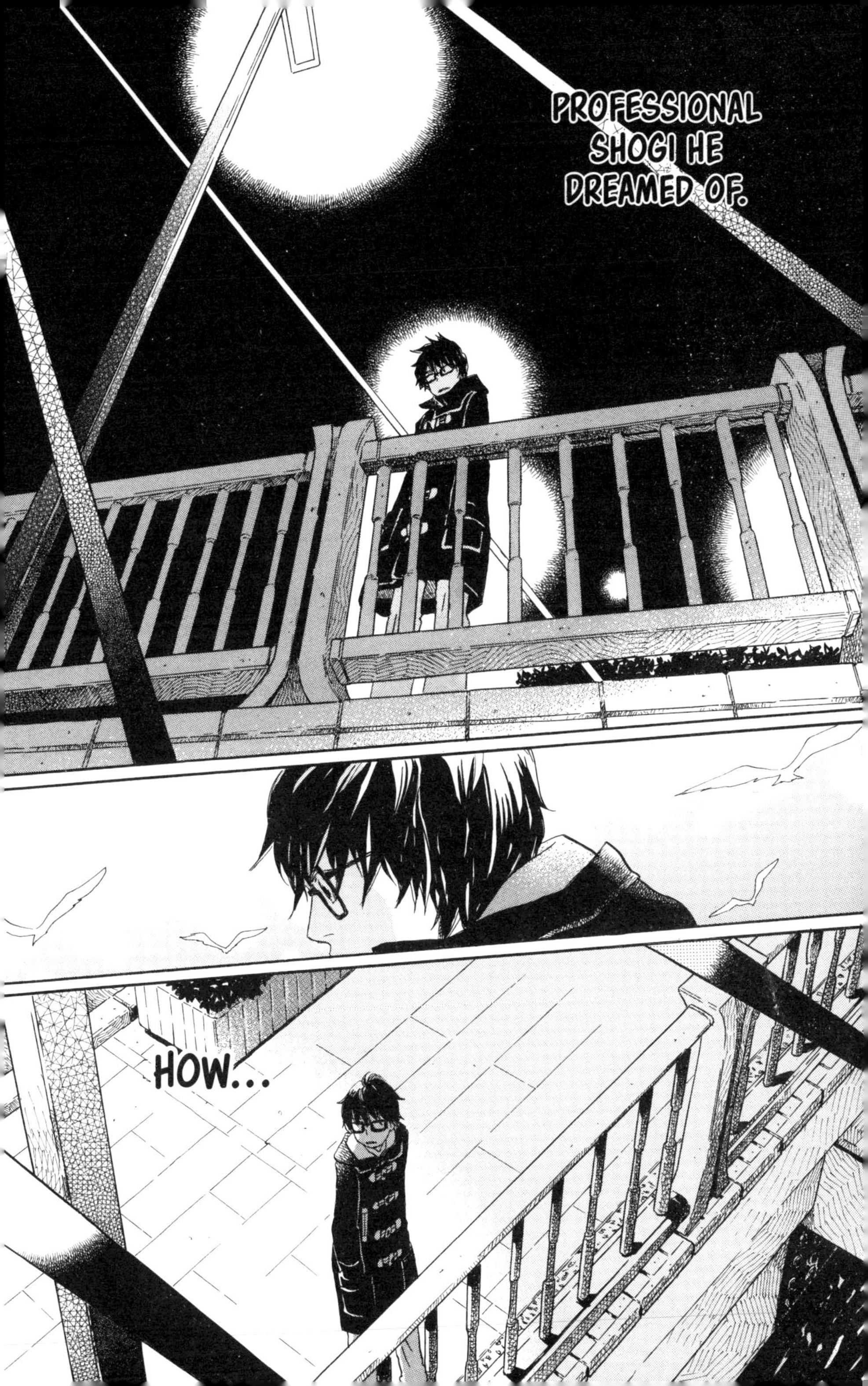
PROFESSIONAL SHOGI HE DREAMED OF.
HOW...

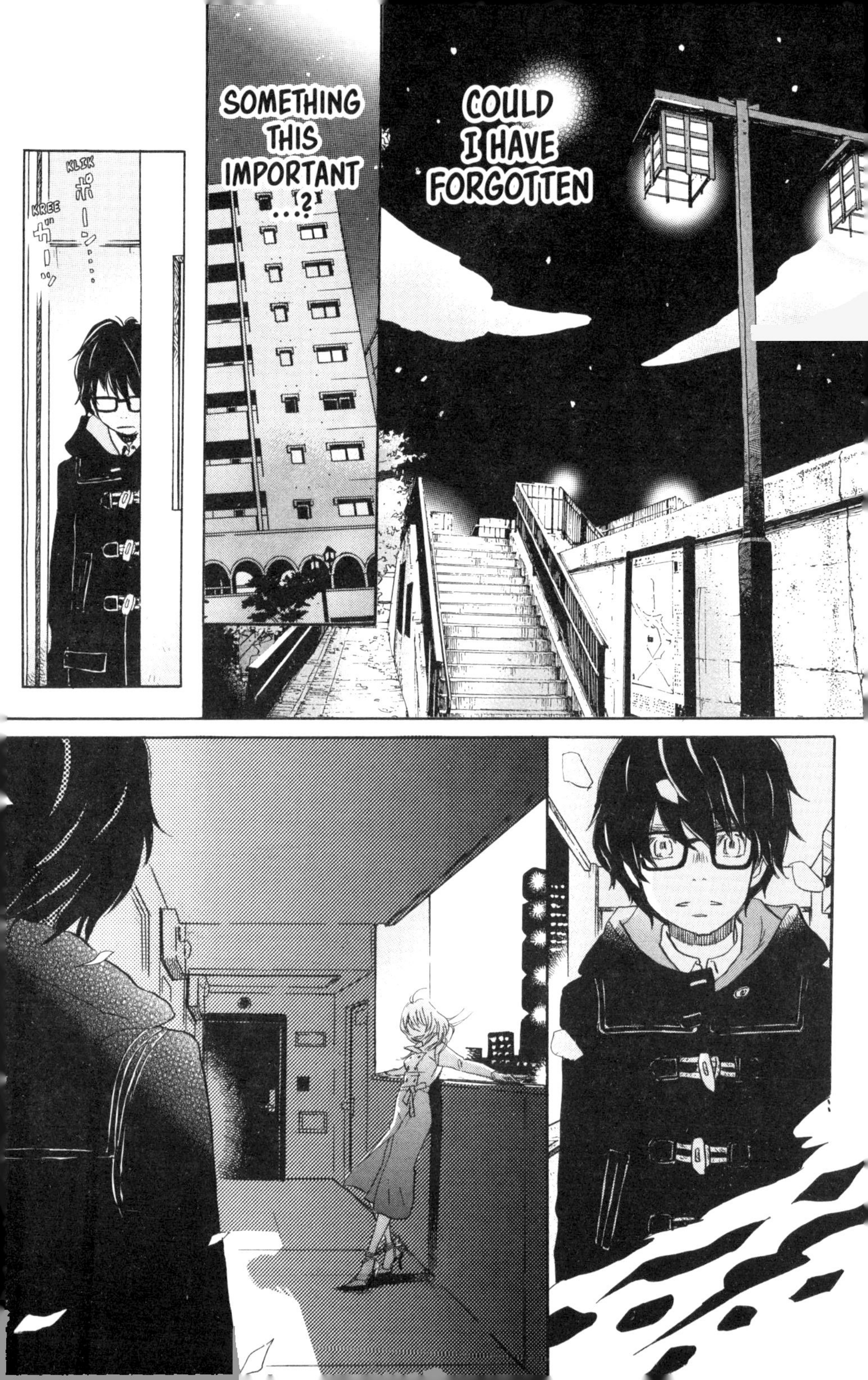
COULD I HAVE FORGOTTEN
SOMETHING THIS IMPORTANT ...?
KLIK
ポーン....
KREE
ガーッ

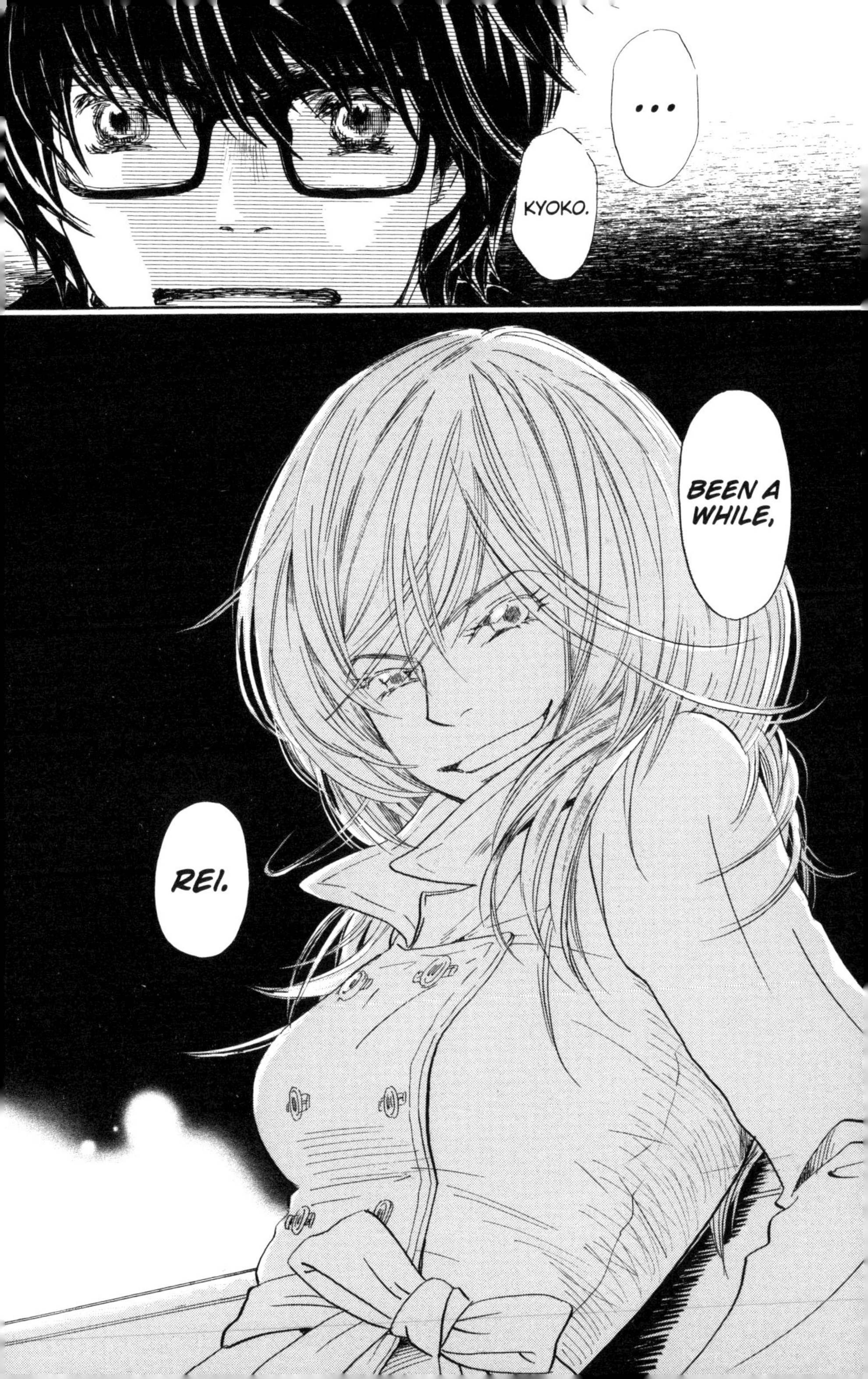
...
KYOKO.
BEEN A WHILE,
REI.

You Can Have Fun with Shogi No Matter How Old You Are When You Start!

Meow then!! (Ah! I slipped into cat talk there. Although I'm actually a dog person.) Some of you readers perhaps did not know the rules of shogi, but that situation has now been rectified. Chapter 15 is unique in *March*—a shogi beginners' class. Our intrepid artist Chica Umino really does love shogi, hm? Her desire to spread the shogi gospel practically leaps off of these pages. As a professional shogi player, it does bring tears to my eyes.

The pictures of shogi on page 81 and the following page, with the pieces as cats, are truly incredible. I suppose Umino never imagined that she would draw this many cats in one panel over the course of her manga career. When I picture all the cats each with their own distinctive face, my heart feels lighter.

Many shogi players learn the game as children, but of course, you can become quite the skilled player even if you start as an adult. Some people say it's best to start early, but that's really only if you're aiming to go pro or reach the highest ranks. Anyone can make it to shodan if they invest the time to work on their game. With just a bit of study, it's not too difficult to make it to 10-*kyu* or even 5-*kyu*, if you have a knack for the sport. Once you're at 5-*kyu* and up to the shodan level, you can more or less understand what the commentator is talking about during a televised shogi tournament. And shogi becomes a whole lot more fun after you've hit this level.

I myself have played countless people who had only just learned the game. Naturally, there is a difference in ability in such games, so I play with a handicap, such as the 2-piece handicap, in which my rook and bishop, two incredibly powerful pieces, are taken off the board right from the start. If you can win against me with this handicap, that would make you *shodan*. From there, I will drop even more pieces.

At first, I'll have only pawns and the king, and if you clear that, then I'll play with just the pawns, king, and gold general. The diagram below is of that. I'm black, with no rook, bishop, silver generals, or knights. If you can beat me from this starting point, then you're probably around 20-*kyu*. There are some little tricks you can play to win. I hope you all study hard and we get the chance to play somewhere. ☗

9 8 7 6 5 4 3 2 1
A B C D E F G H I
香 桂 銀 金 王 金 銀 桂 香
飛 角
歩 歩 歩 歩 歩 歩 歩 歩 歩
歩 歩 歩 歩 歩 歩 歩 歩 歩
金 王 金
☗ Black Pieces in hand: None
☖ White Pieces in hand: None

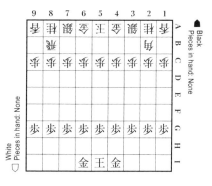

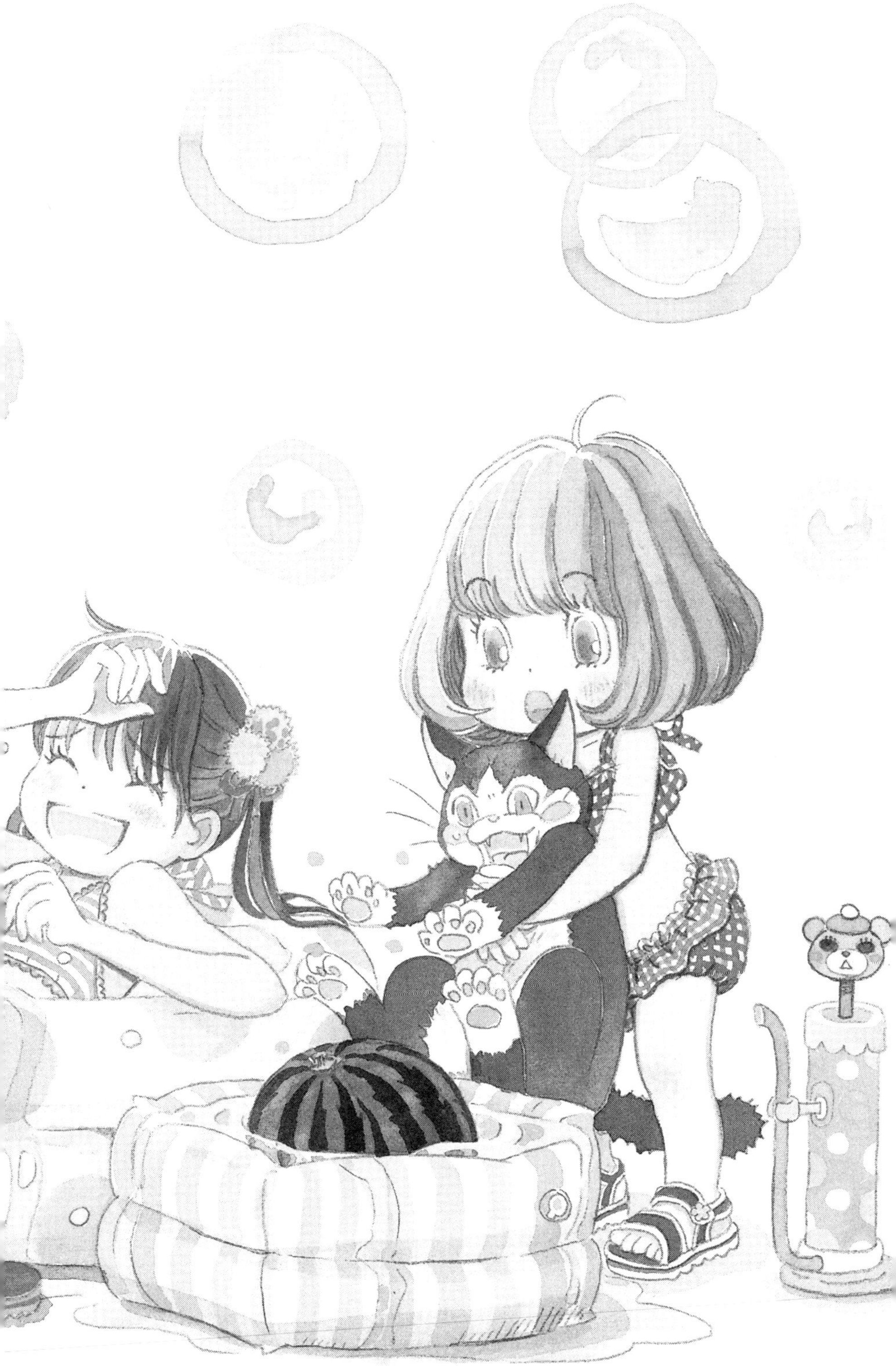

Chapter 17

Distant Thunder

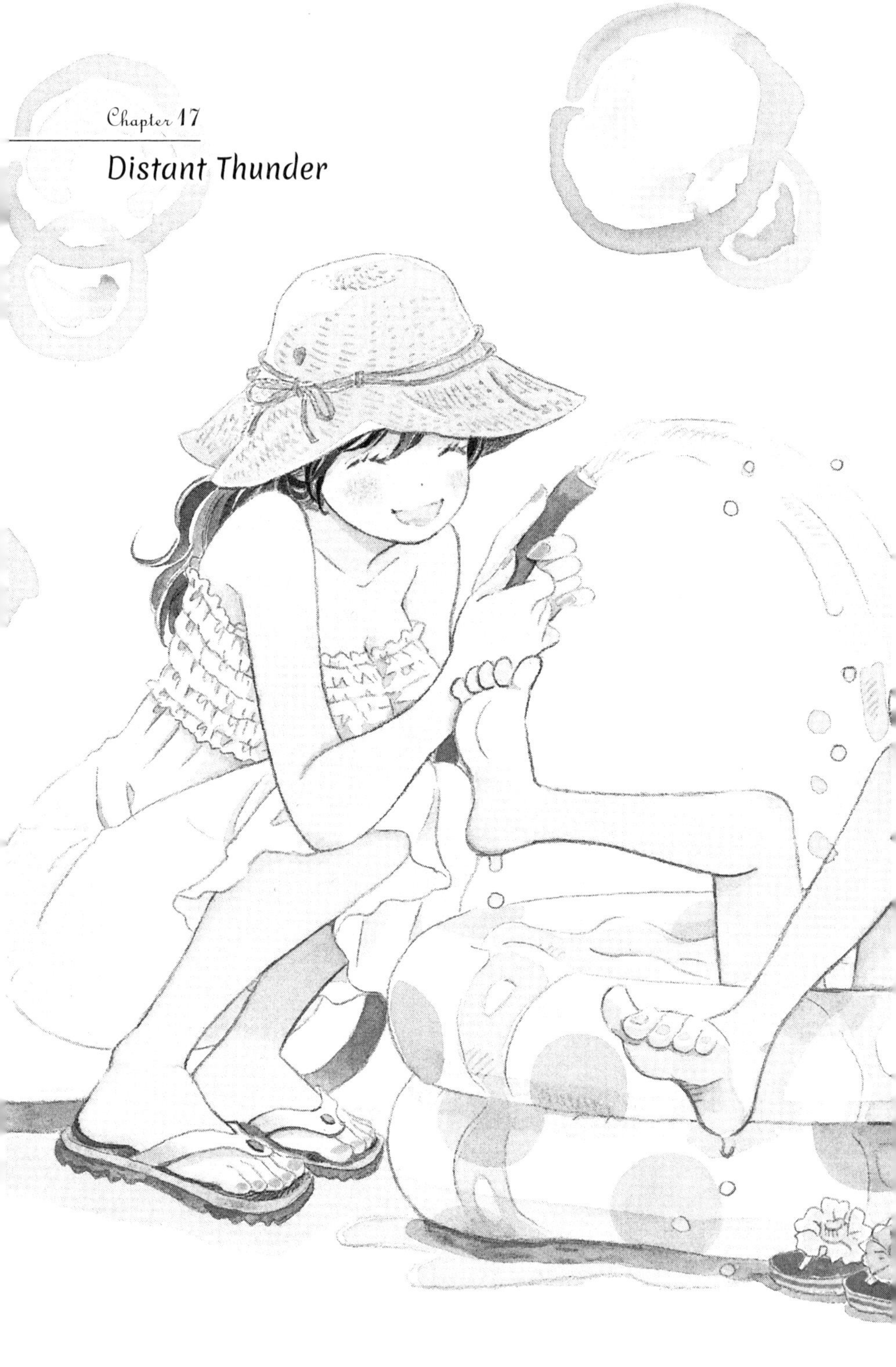

March Comes In
Like a Lion

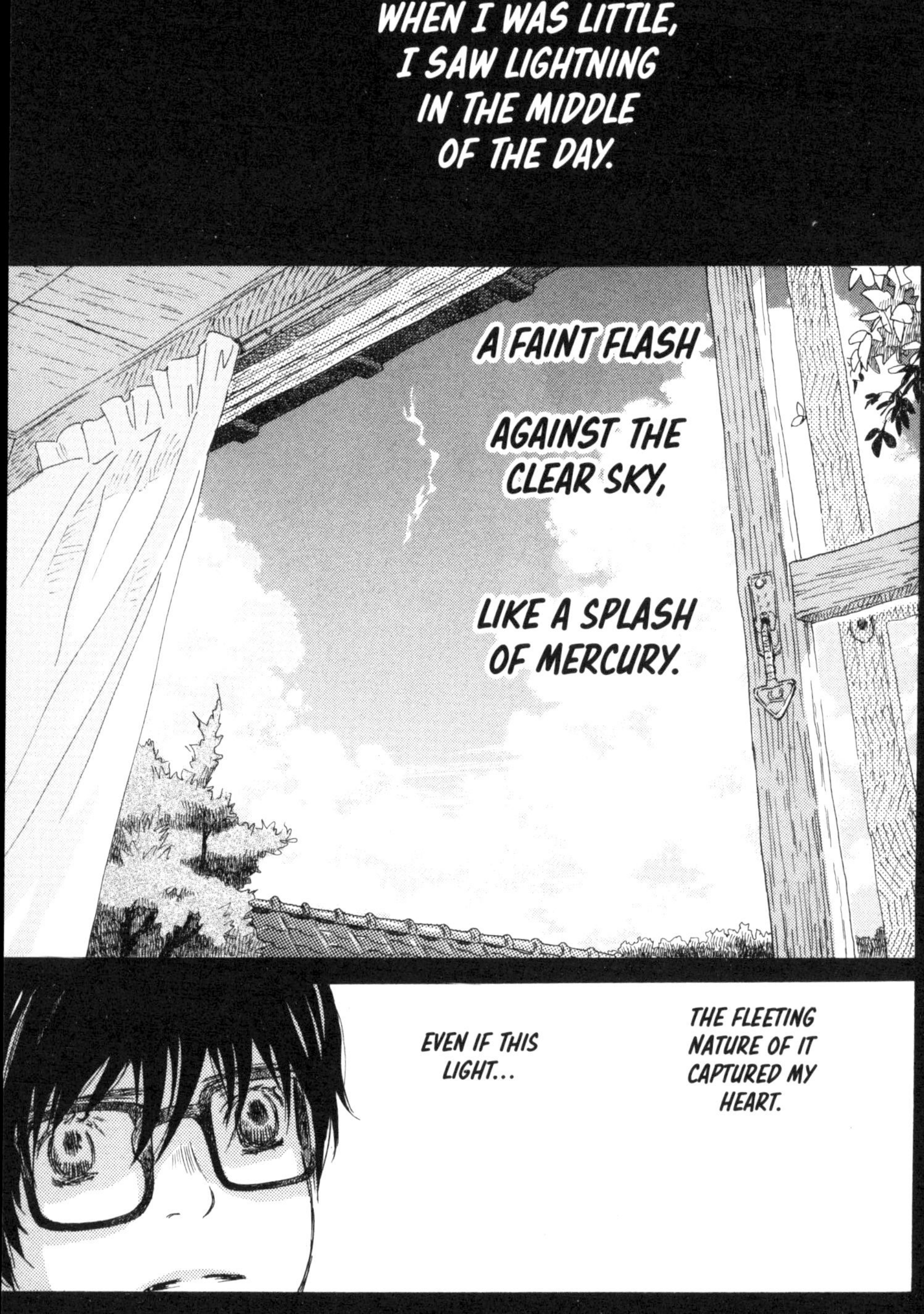
WHEN I WAS LITTLE, I SAW LIGHTNING IN THE MIDDLE OF THE DAY.
A FAINT FLASH
AGAINST THE CLEAR SKY,
LIKE A SPLASH OF MERCURY.
THE FLEETING NATURE OF IT CAPTURED MY HEART.
EVEN IF THIS LIGHT...

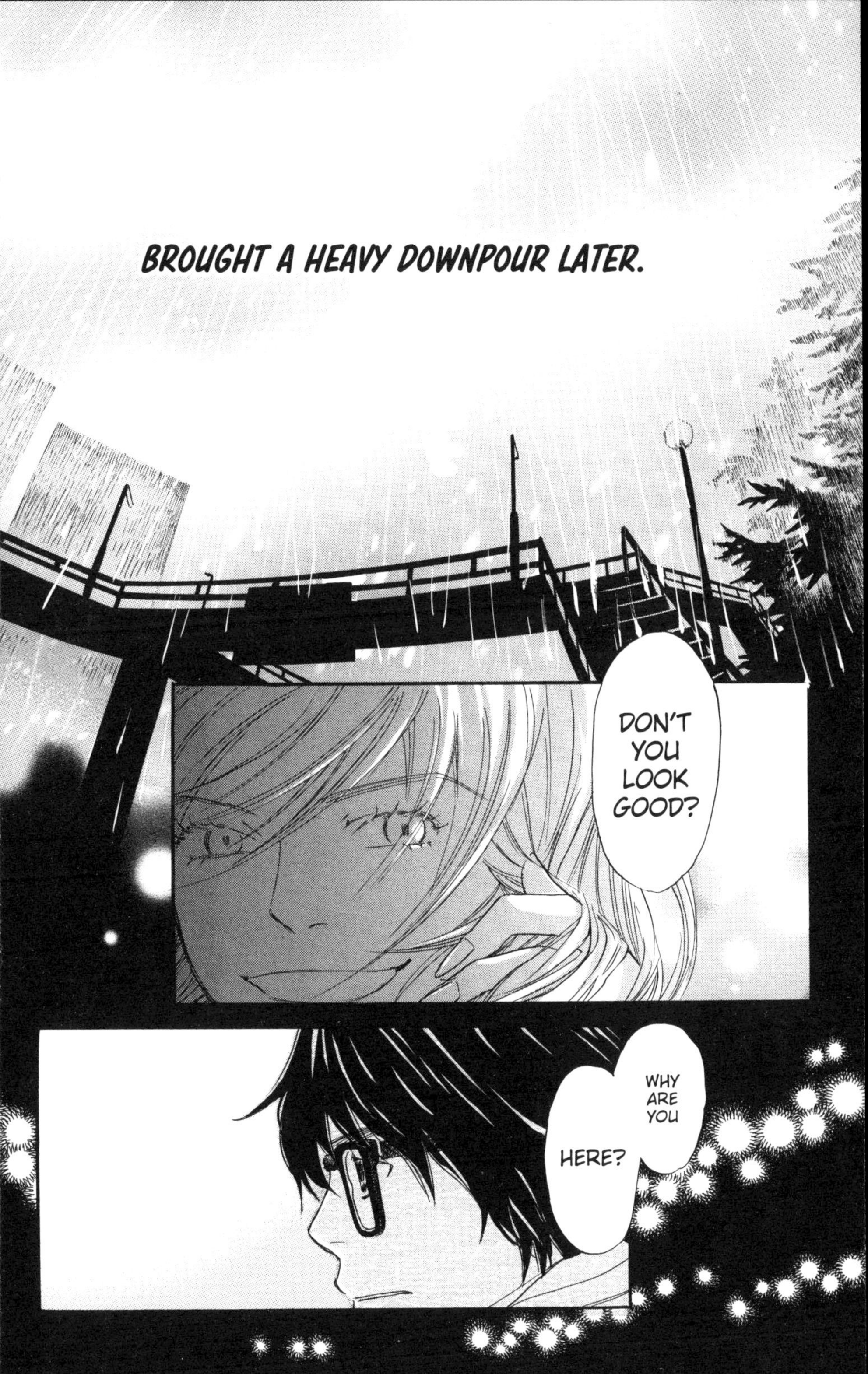
BROUGHT A HEAVY DOWNPOUR LATER.
DON'T YOU LOOK GOOD?
WHY ARE YOU
HERE?

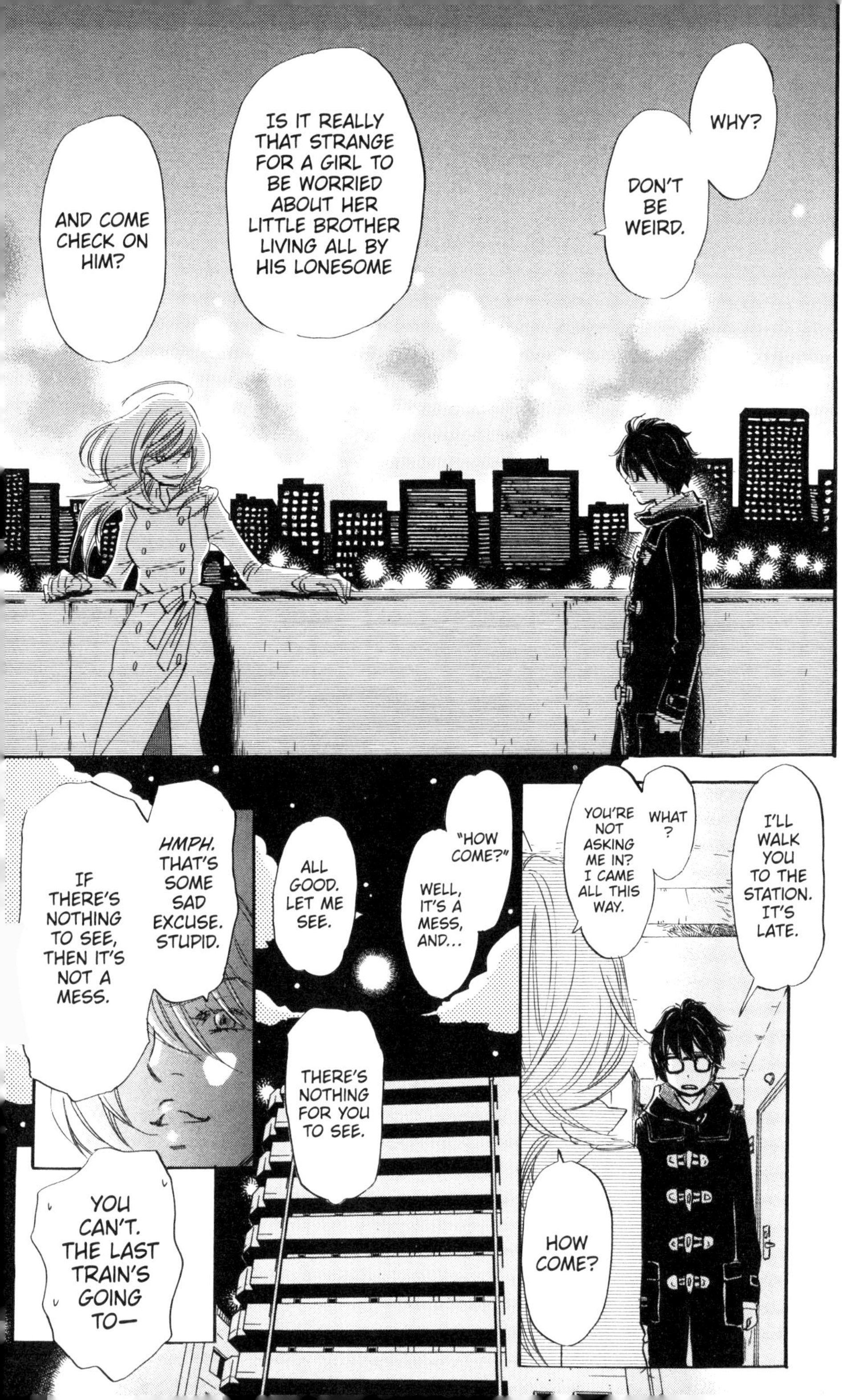
WHY?
DON'T BE WEIRD.
IS IT REALLY THAT STRANGE FOR A GIRL TO BE WORRIED ABOUT HER LITTLE BROTHER LIVING ALL BY HIS LONESOME
AND COME CHECK ON HIM?
I'LL WALK YOU TO THE STATION. IT'S LATE.
WHAT?
YOU'RE NOT ASKING ME IN? I CAME ALL THIS WAY.
HOW COME?
"HOW COME?"
WELL, IT'S A MESS, AND...
ALL GOOD. LET ME SEE.
THERE'S NOTHING FOR YOU TO SEE.
HMPH. THAT'S SOME SAD EXCUSE. STUPID.
IF THERE'S NOTHING TO SEE, THEN IT'S NOT A MESS.
YOU CAN'T. THE LAST TRAIN'S GOING TO—

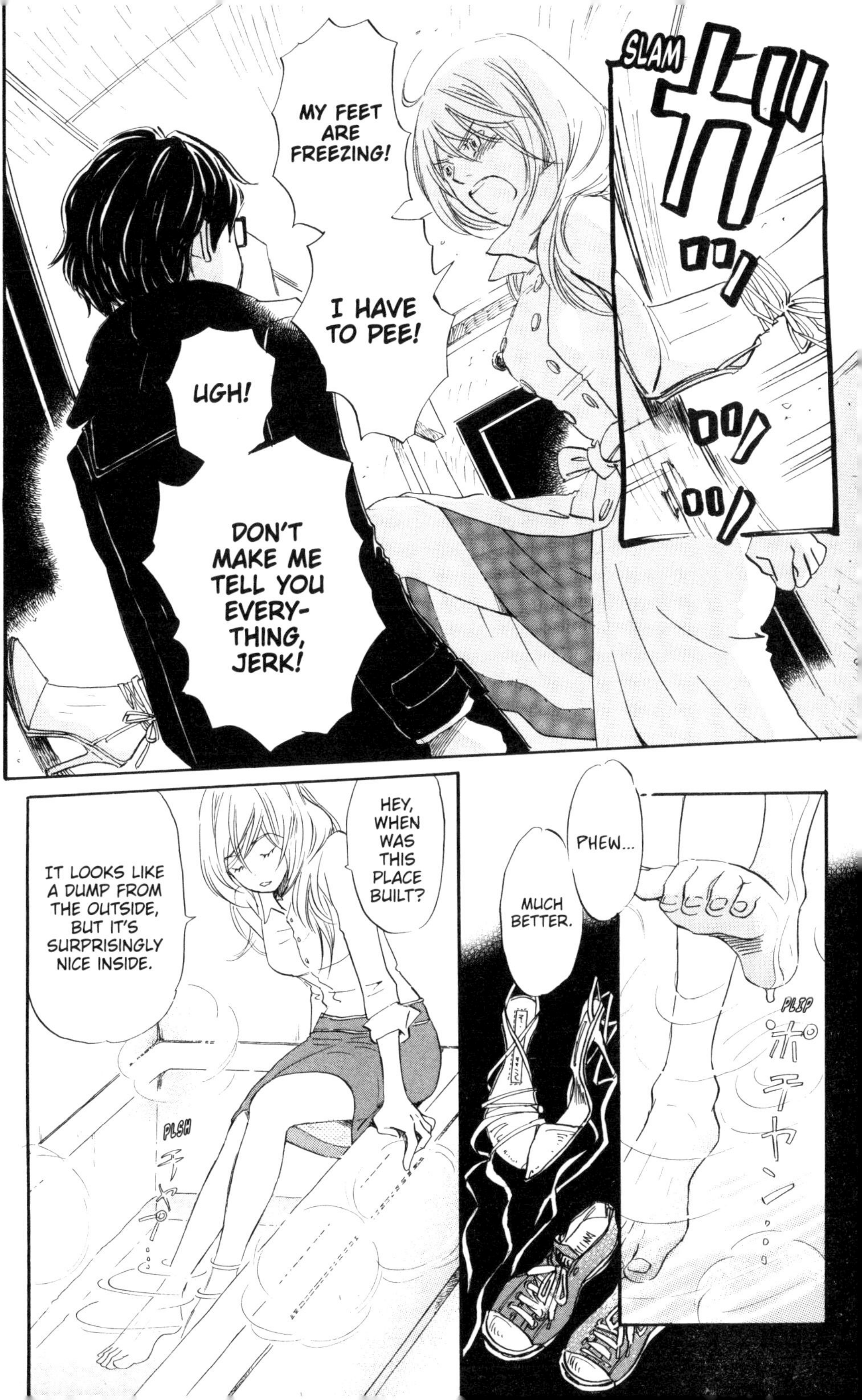
SLAM
ガ
MY FEET ARE FREEZING!
I HAVE TO PEE!
UGH!
DON'T MAKE ME TELL YOU EVERY-THING, JERK!
PHEW...
MUCH BETTER.
PLIP
ポチャン
HEY, WHEN WAS THIS PLACE BUILT?
IT LOOKS LIKE A DUMP FROM THE OUTSIDE, BUT IT'S SURPRISINGLY NICE INSIDE.
PLSH

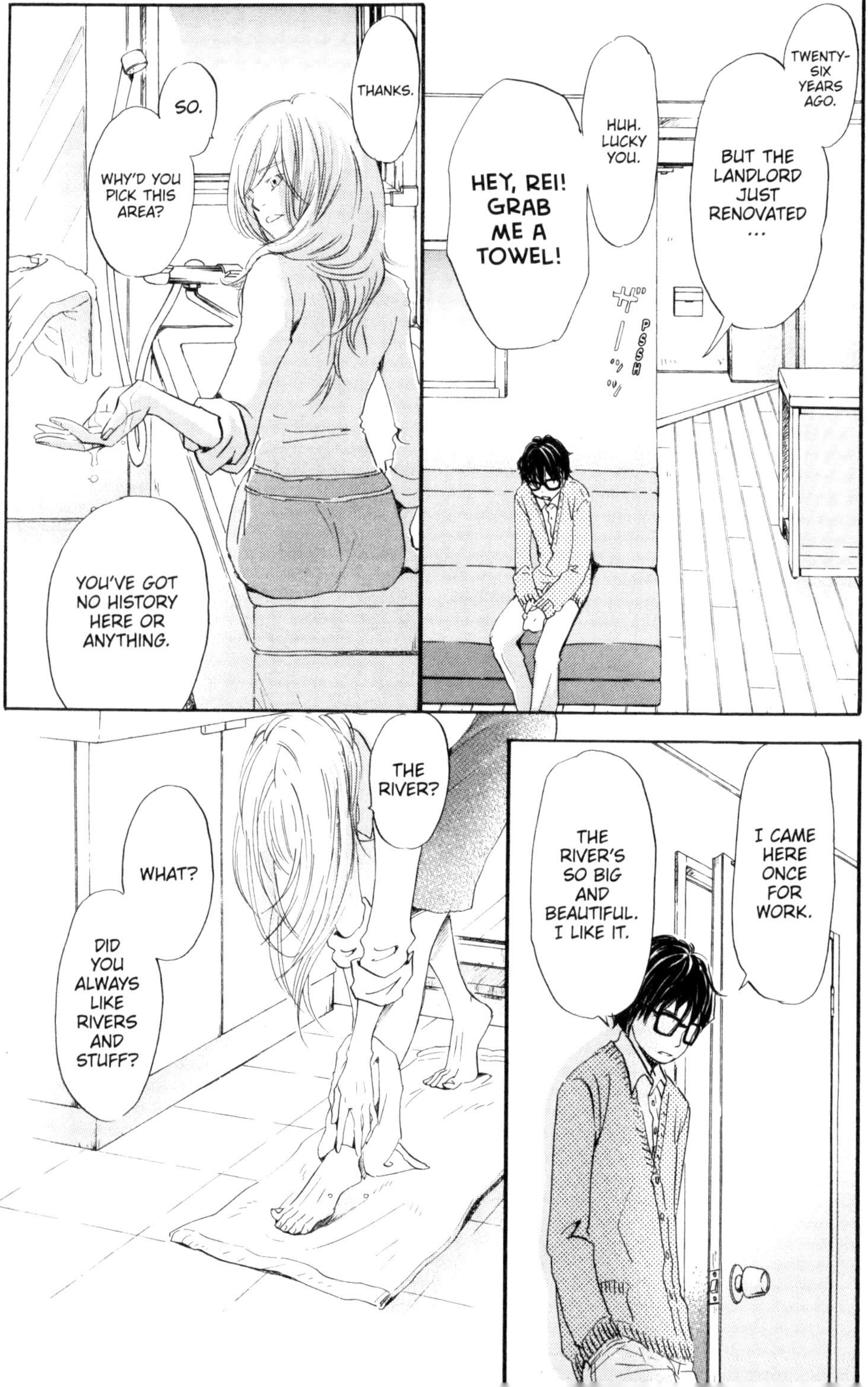
TWENTY-SIX YEARS AGO.
BUT THE LANDLORD JUST RENOVATED...
HUH. LUCKY YOU.
HEY, REI! GRAB ME A TOWEL!
PSSH
THANKS.
SO.
WHY'D YOU PICK THIS AREA?
YOU'VE GOT NO HISTORY HERE OR ANYTHING.
I CAME HERE ONCE FOR WORK.
THE RIVER'S SO BIG AND BEAUTIFUL. I LIKE IT.
THE RIVER?
WHAT?
DID YOU ALWAYS LIKE RIVERS AND STUFF?

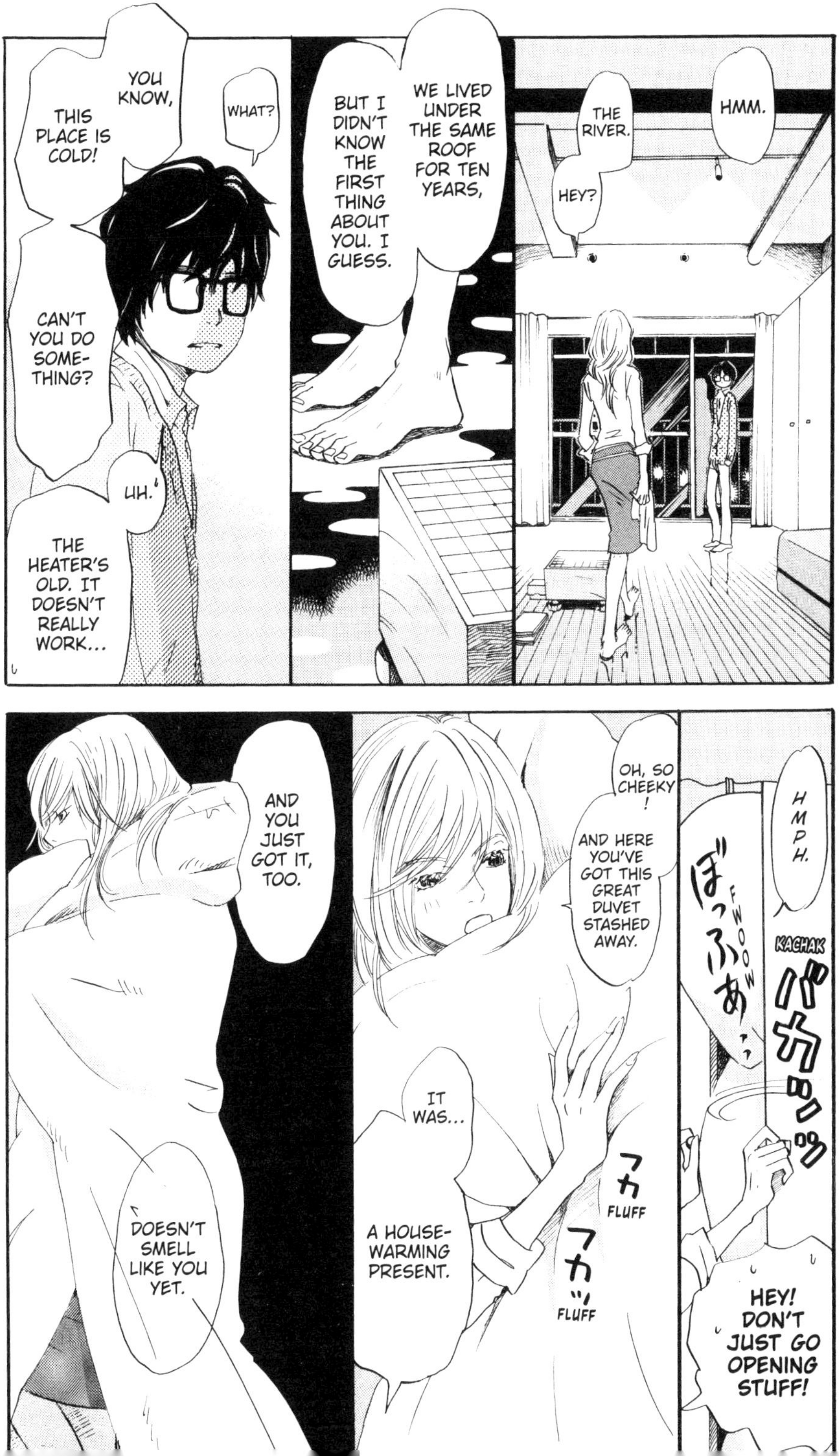
HMM.
THE RIVER.
HEY?
WE LIVED UNDER THE SAME ROOF FOR TEN YEARS,
BUT I DIDN'T KNOW THE FIRST THING ABOUT YOU. I GUESS.
WHAT?
YOU KNOW,
THIS PLACE IS COLD!
CAN'T YOU DO SOMETHING?
UH.
THE HEATER'S OLD. IT DOESN'T REALLY WORK...
HMPH.
ぼっふぁっ
FWOOW
KACHAK
パカッ
HEY! DON'T JUST GO OPENING STUFF!
OH, SO CHEEKY!
AND HERE YOU'VE GOT THIS GREAT DUVET STASHED AWAY.
IT WAS...
フカ
FLUFF
フカッ
FLUFF
A HOUSE-WARMING PRESENT.
AND YOU JUST GOT IT, TOO.
DOESN'T SMELL LIKE YOU YET.

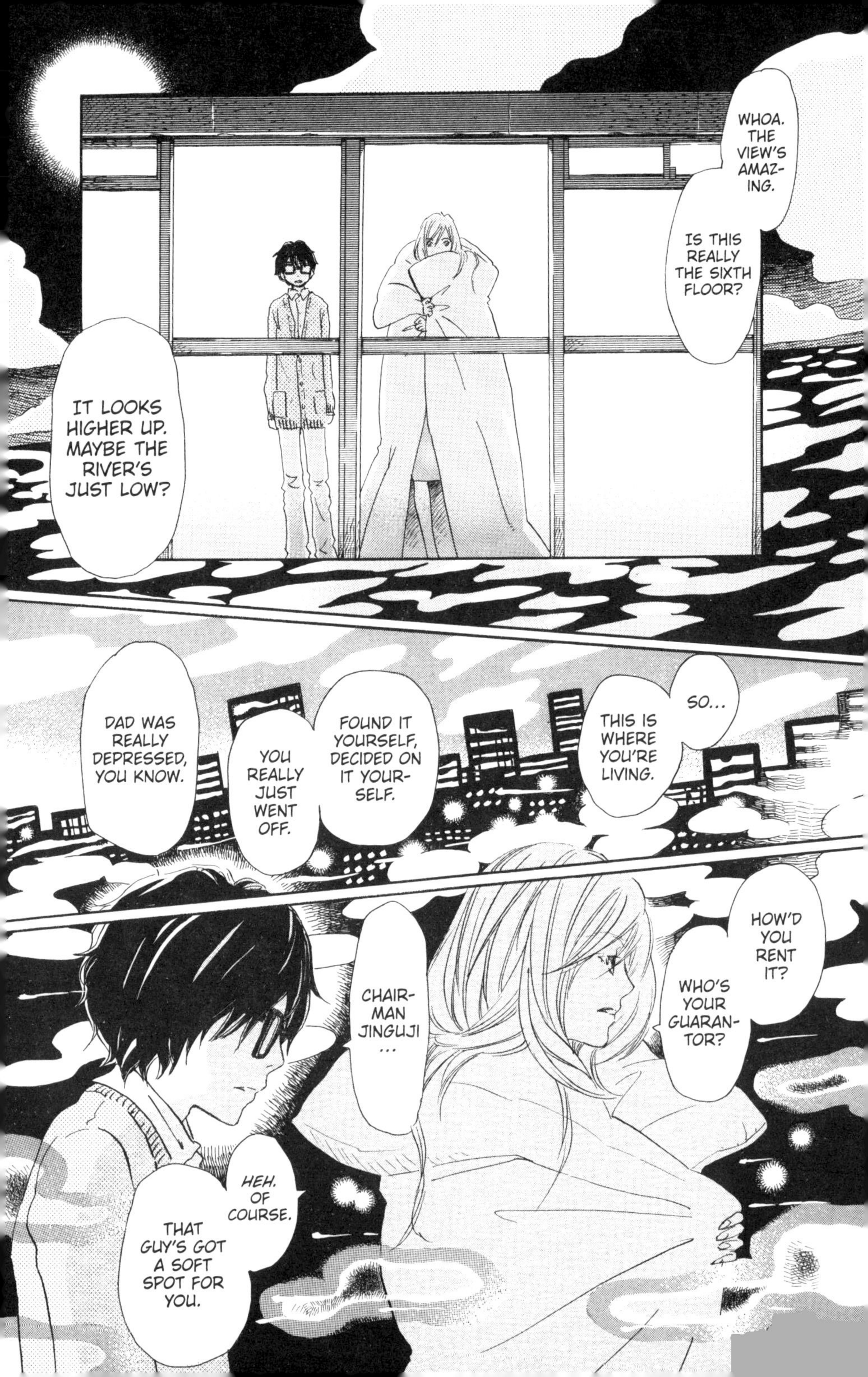
WHOA. THE VIEW'S AMAZ-ING.
IS THIS REALLY THE SIXTH FLOOR?
IT LOOKS HIGHER UP. MAYBE THE RIVER'S JUST LOW?
SO...
THIS IS WHERE YOU'RE LIVING.
FOUND IT YOURSELF, DECIDED ON IT YOUR-SELF.
YOU REALLY JUST WENT OFF.
DAD WAS REALLY DEPRESSED, YOU KNOW.
HOW'D YOU RENT IT?
WHO'S YOUR GUARAN-TOR?
CHAIR-MAN JINGUJI ...
HEH. OF COURSE.
THAT GUY'S GOT A SOFT SPOT FOR YOU.

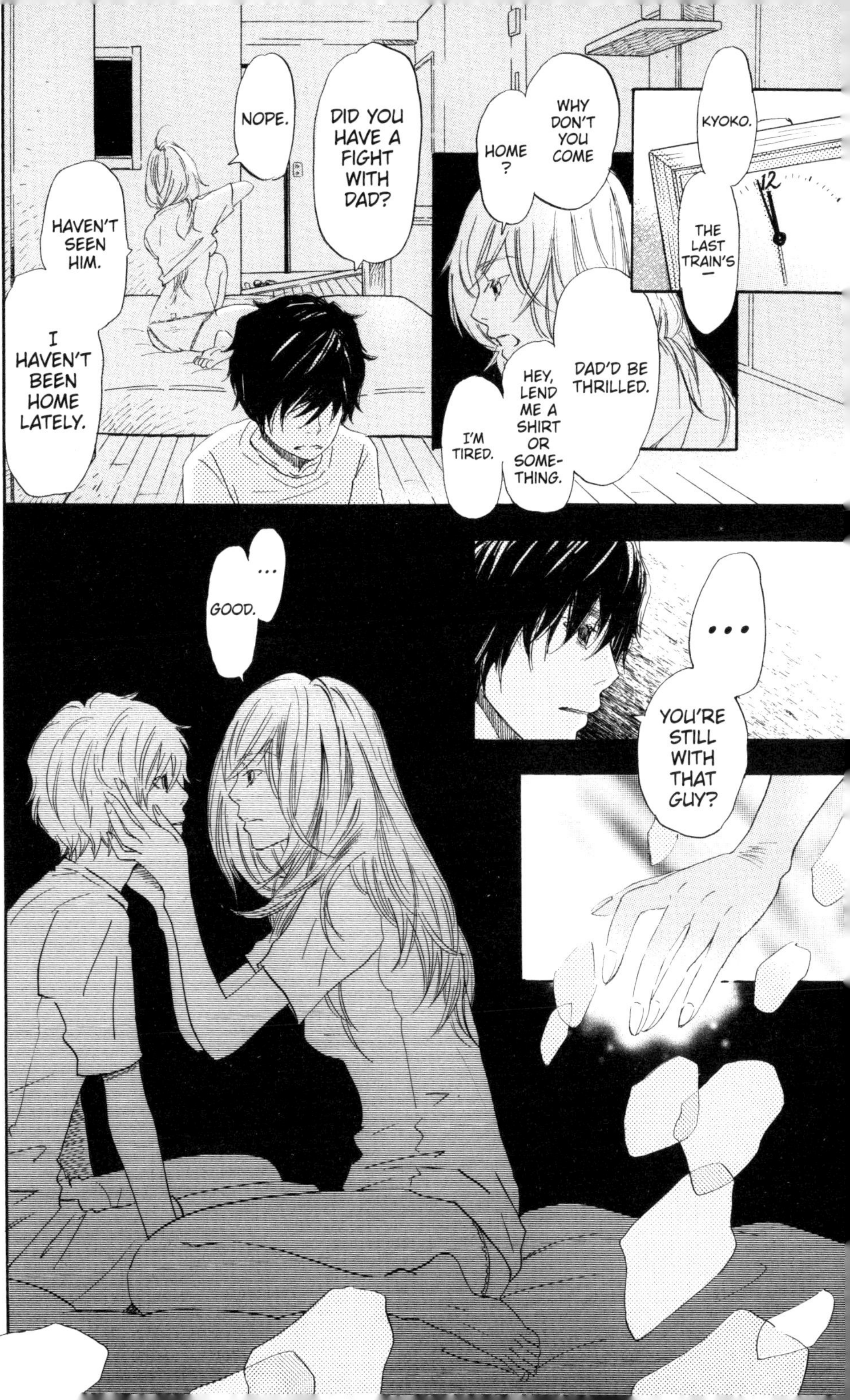
KYOKO.
THE LAST TRAIN'S —
WHY DON'T YOU COME HOME?
DAD'D BE THRILLED.
HEY, LEND ME A SHIRT OR SOME-THING.
I'M TIRED.
DID YOU HAVE A FIGHT WITH DAD?
NOPE.
HAVEN'T SEEN HIM.
I HAVEN'T BEEN HOME LATELY.
...
YOU'RE STILL WITH THAT GUY?
... GOOD.

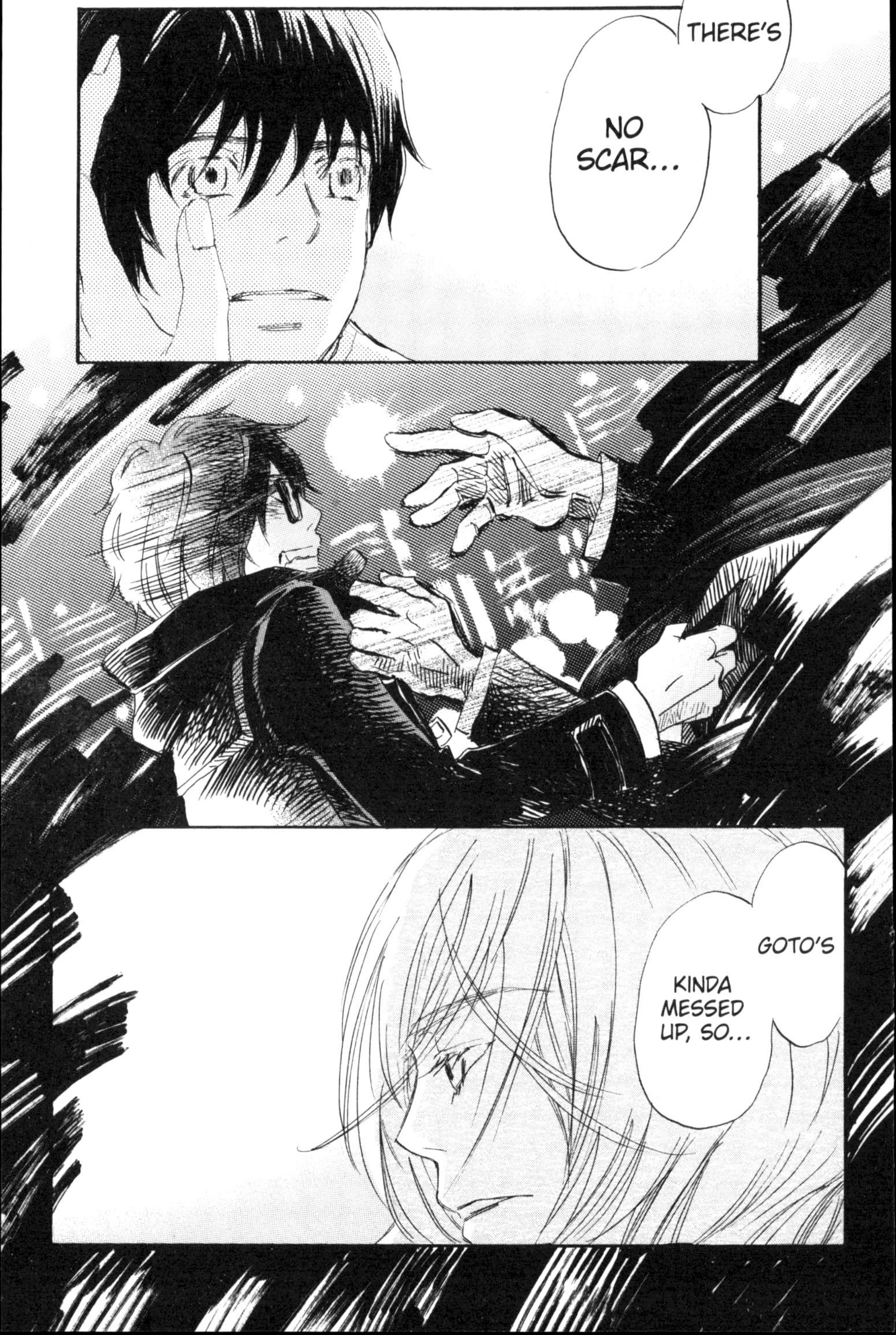
THERE'S
NO SCAR...
GOTO'S
KINDA MESSED UP, SO...

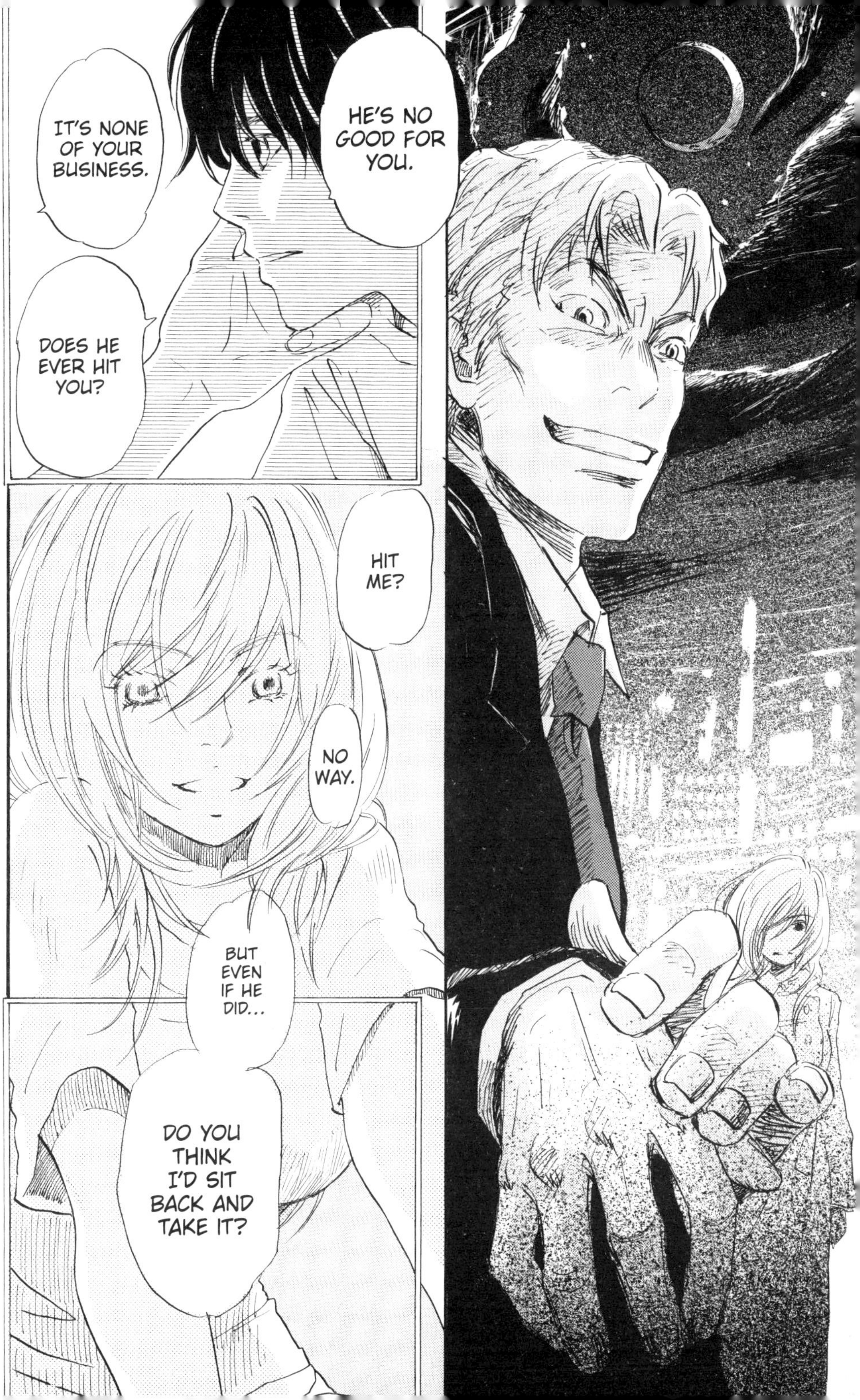
HE'S NO GOOD FOR YOU.
IT'S NONE OF YOUR BUSINESS.
DOES HE EVER HIT YOU?
HIT ME?
NO WAY.
BUT EVEN IF HE DID...
DO YOU THINK I'D SIT BACK AND TAKE IT?

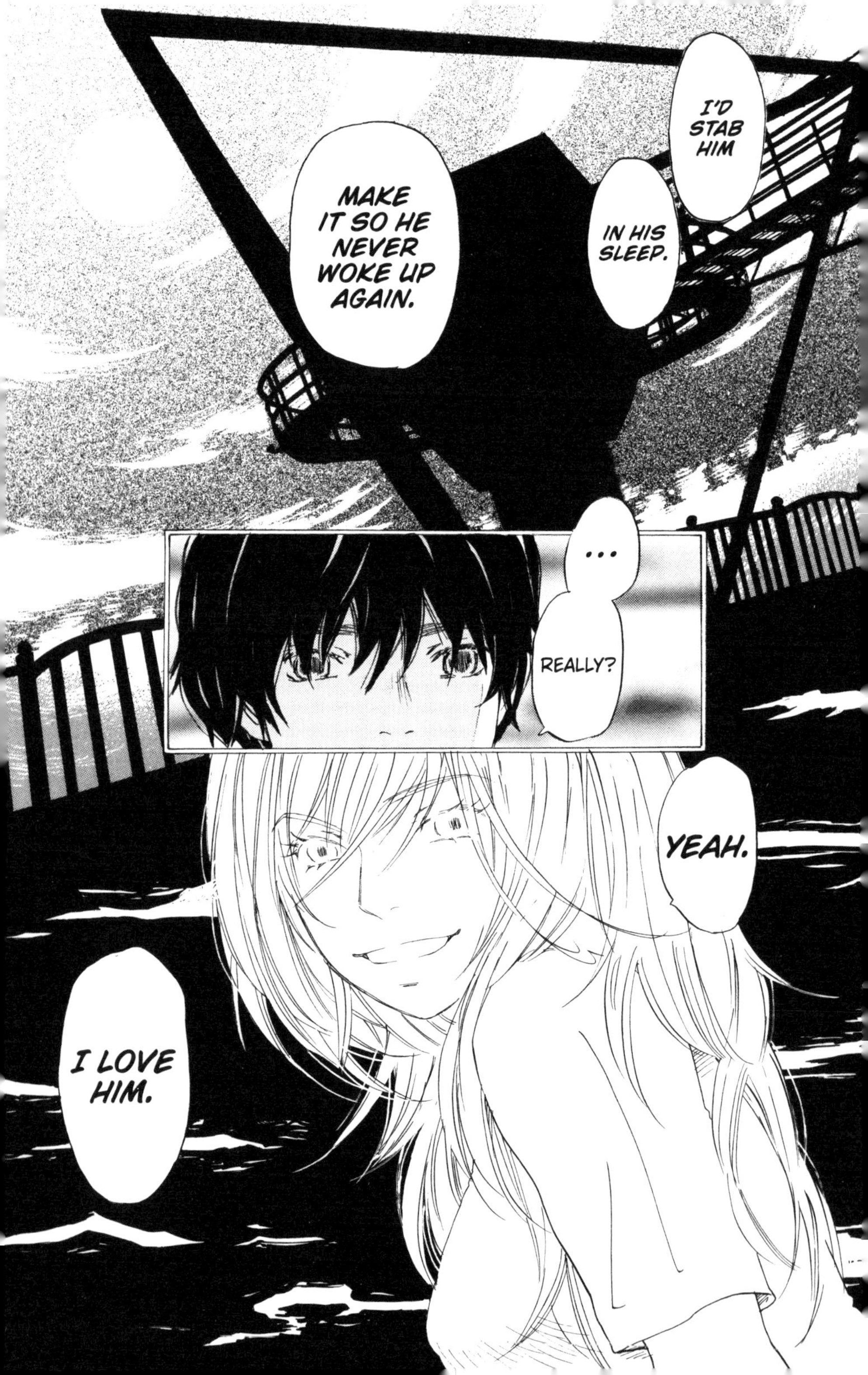

I'D STAB HIM
IN HIS SLEEP.
MAKE IT SO HE NEVER WOKE UP AGAIN.
...
REALLY?
YEAH.
I LOVE HIM.

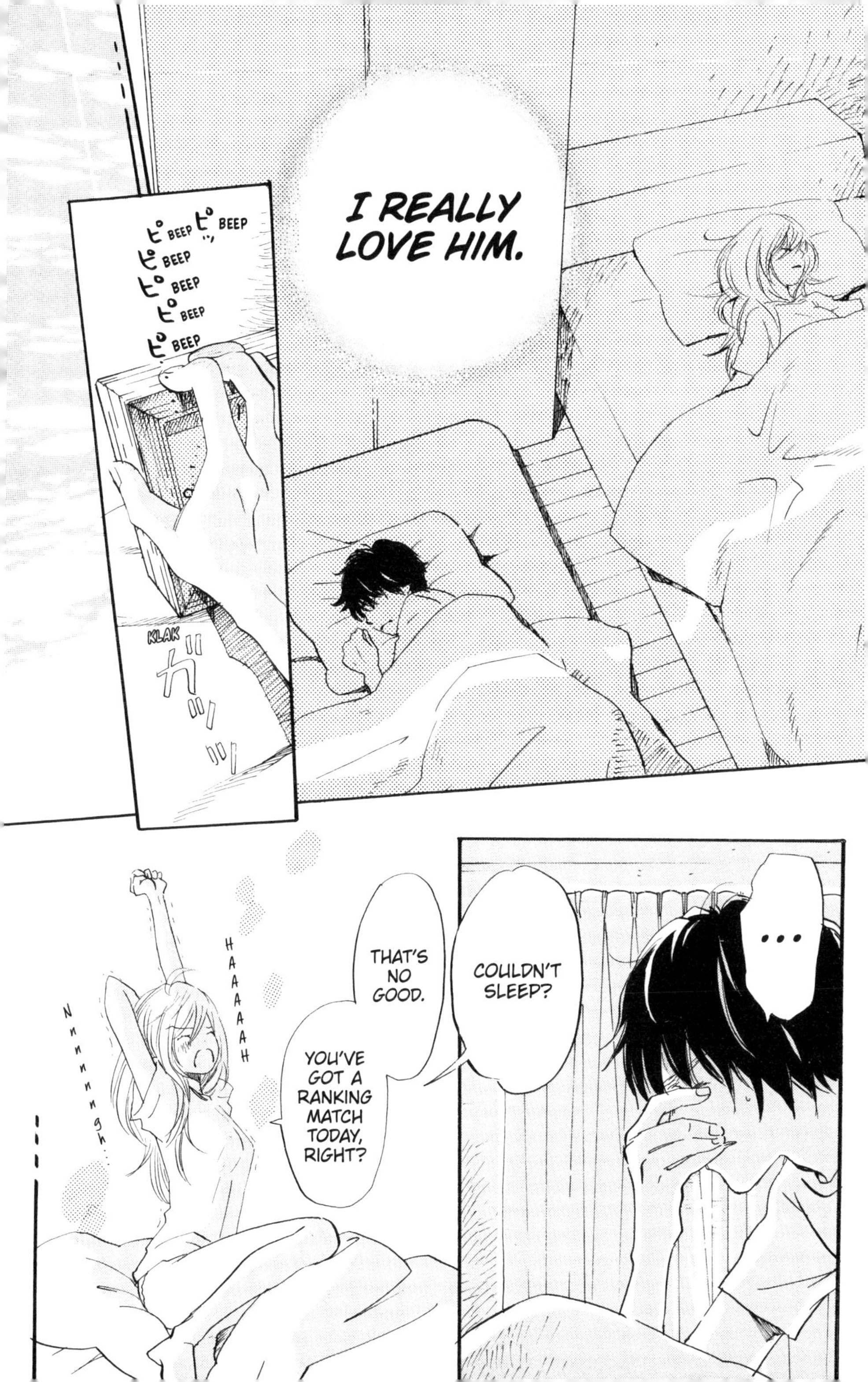
I REALLY LOVE HIM.
ピ BEEP ピッ BEEP
ピ BEEP
ピ BEEP
ピ BEEP
ピ BEEP
KLAK
ガッ
...
COULDN'T SLEEP?
THAT'S NO GOOD.
YOU'VE GOT A RANKING MATCH TODAY, RIGHT?
HAAAAAH
Nnnnnngh...
...

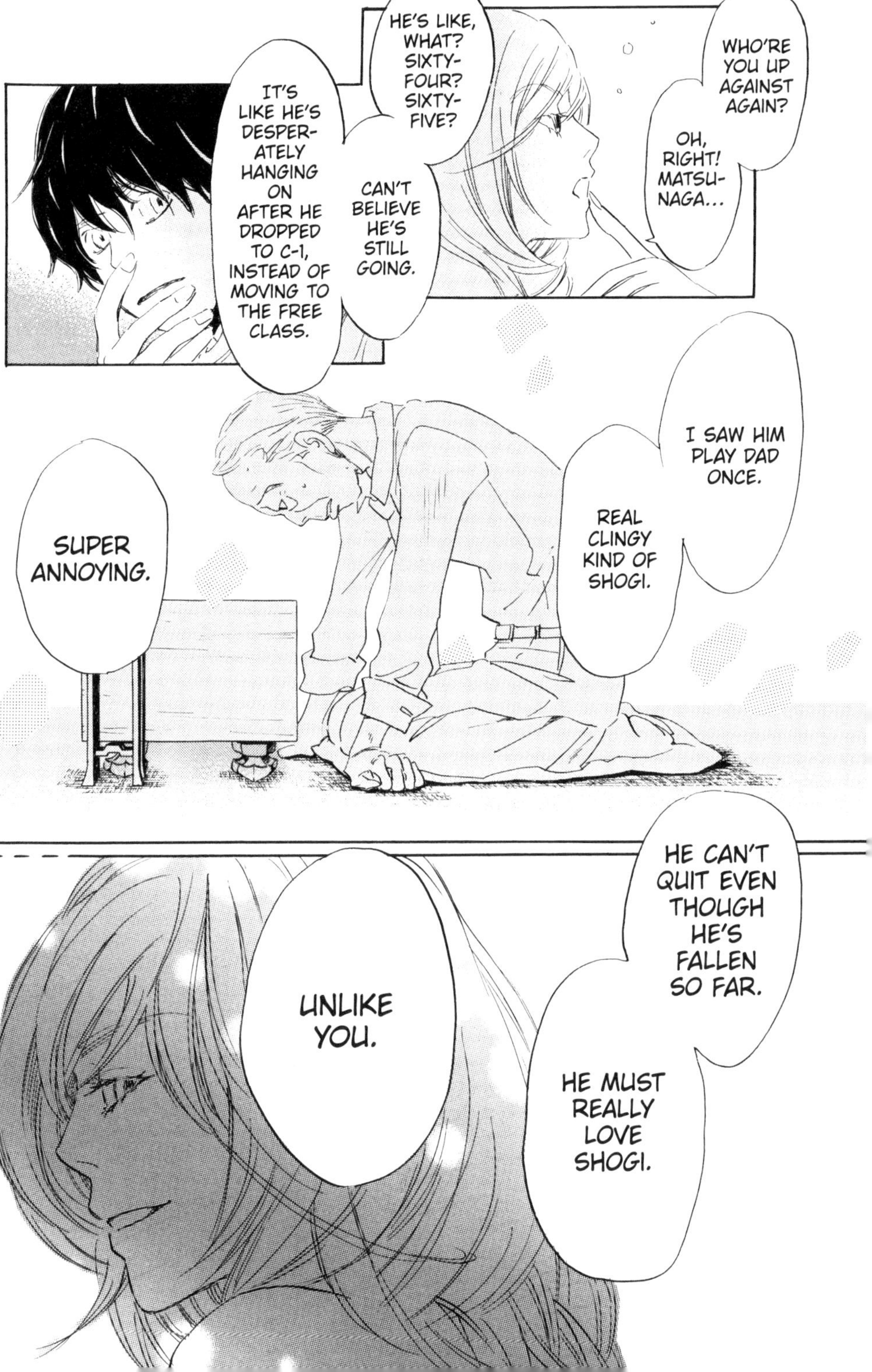
WHO'RE YOU UP AGAINST AGAIN?
OH, RIGHT! MATSUNAGA...
HE'S LIKE, WHAT? SIXTY-FOUR? SIXTY-FIVE?
CAN'T BELIEVE HE'S STILL GOING.
IT'S LIKE HE'S DESPERATELY HANGING ON AFTER HE DROPPED TO C-1, INSTEAD OF MOVING TO THE FREE CLASS.
I SAW HIM PLAY DAD ONCE.
REAL CLINGY KIND OF SHOGI.
SUPER ANNOYING.
HE CAN'T QUIT EVEN THOUGH HE'S FALLEN SO FAR.
HE MUST REALLY LOVE SHOGI.
UNLIKE YOU.

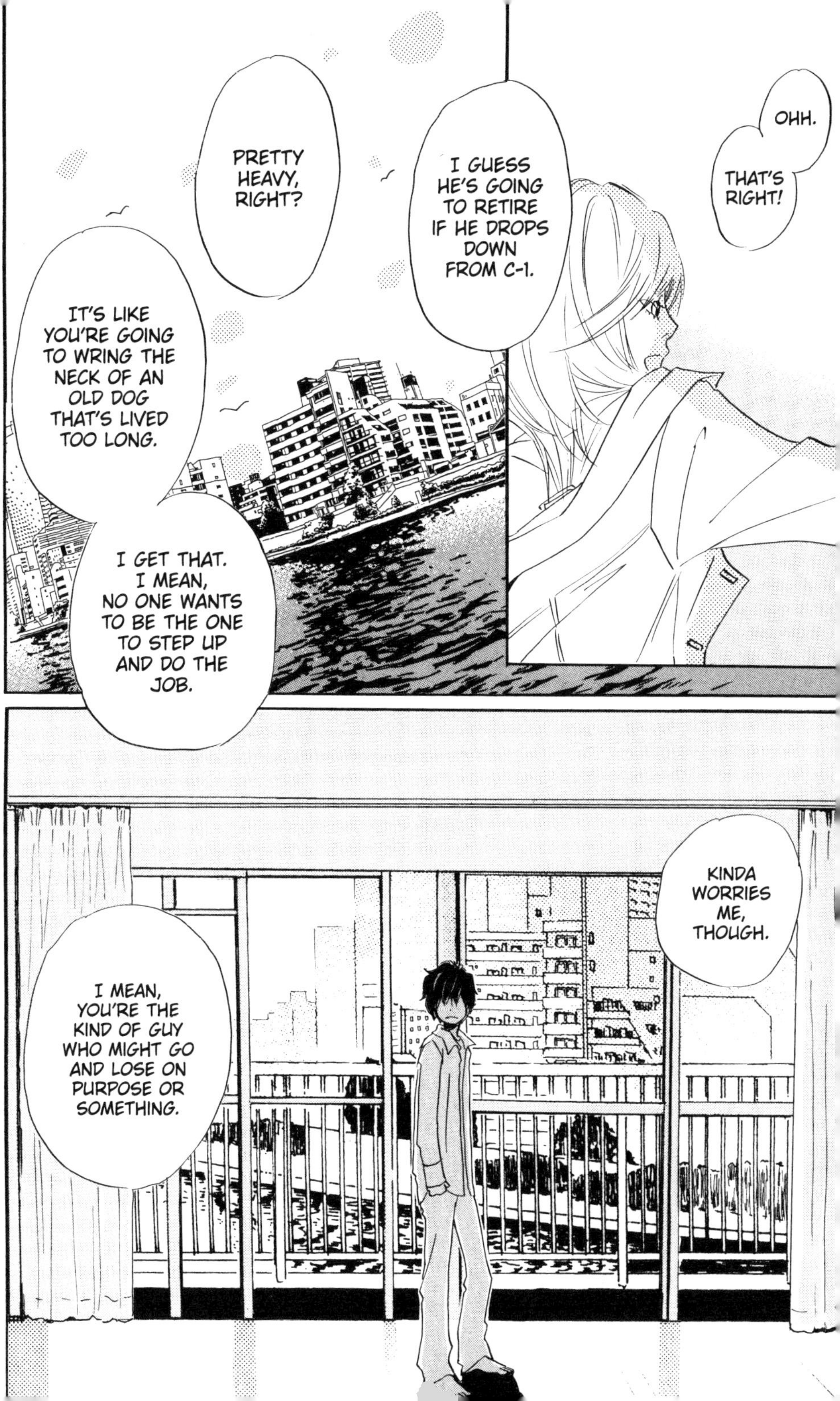
OHH.
THAT'S RIGHT!
I GUESS HE'S GOING TO RETIRE IF HE DROPS DOWN FROM C-1.
PRETTY HEAVY, RIGHT?
IT'S LIKE YOU'RE GOING TO WRING THE NECK OF AN OLD DOG THAT'S LIVED TOO LONG.
I GET THAT. I MEAN, NO ONE WANTS TO BE THE ONE TO STEP UP AND DO THE JOB.
KINDA WORRIES ME, THOUGH.
I MEAN, YOU'RE THE KIND OF GUY WHO MIGHT GO AND LOSE ON PURPOSE OR SOMETHING.

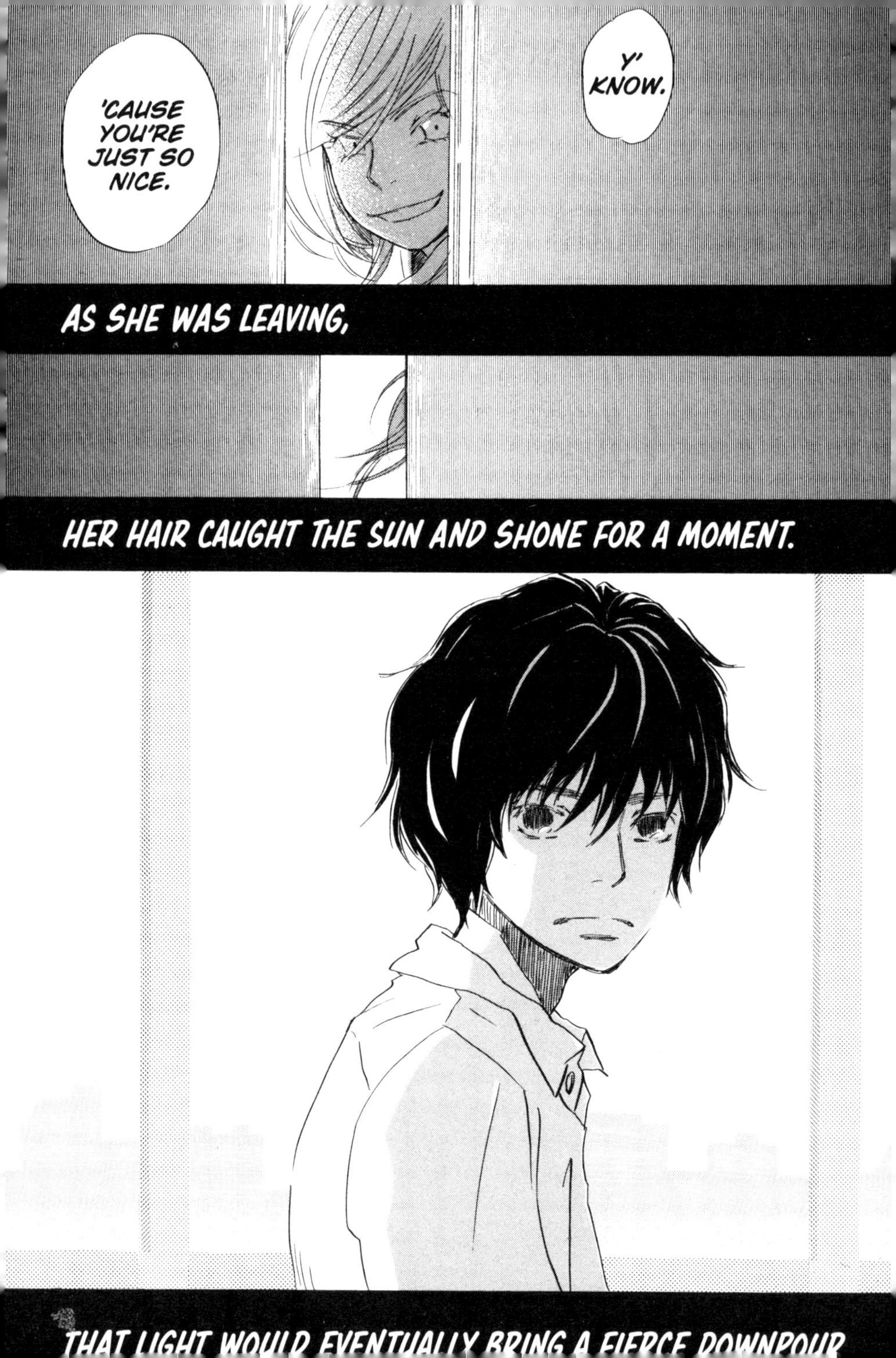
Y' KNOW.
'CAUSE YOU'RE JUST SO NICE.
AS SHE WAS LEAVING,
HER HAIR CAUGHT THE SUN AND SHONE FOR A MOMENT.
THAT LIGHT WOULD EVENTUALLY BRING A FIERCE DOWNPOUR

What Are Ranked Matches in the Life of a Pro Player?

For a professional shogi player, tournaments are all our lifeblood, but we make an extra effort for ranked matches. As the name implies, these are league tournaments that determine a player's ranking. The pinnacle is *Meijin*. Currently (2008), the reigning champion is Yoshiharu Habu. The *Meijin* rank is special, as it were. This champion does not play ranked matches.

The people in the A-class league tournament are the ones who determine the challenger to the *Meijin*. These ten players have nine league matches over the year, and the person who comes out on top goes on to the *Meijin* match against the champion. The two players at the bottom of the league ranking drop down to the class below. As in the diagram at right, the classes form a pyramid with A on top, followed by B-1, B-2, C-1, and C-2.

In the world of shogi, everything up to 3-*dan* is a training rank and are collectively referred to as the *Shoreikai*. This is a group of amateurs working toward turning pro at some point, something like the Makushita Division in sumo or the *zenza* in rakugo. Once you reach 4-*dan*, you become a recognized professional and are promoted into C-2 class. Meaning that although you might now be a professional player, you are starting from the very bottom of the professional pyramid. This is basically the same as society at large, and depending on your performance on the board, you can go up a rank or drop back down again.

Naturally, there are differences in salary and seeding with the ranked tournament classes. For instance, the NHK Cup discussed in the second column is seeded with players ranked B-1 and higher. The difference in salary is... Well, to put it roughly, each class is equivalent to about thirty percent. When you're promoted, your salary increases thirty percent over the previous year, and if you're demoted, it drops by that much.

The time control in league tournaments is a long six hours. With the two players, that's twelve hours. It's not unusual to start at ten in the morning and not finish until one the following morning. Obviously, in these matches, your opponent's standing is critical. When you'll advance as long as you win, that's called "jiriki," while it's "tariki" when even if you win, you need another player to lose in order to advance. Ranked matches start in June, with one every month after that until March. The players in that final match in March, with promotions (or demotions) on the line, become like lions, just as in the title of this manga.

Meijin
A
B-1
B-2
C-1
C-2
Shoreikai

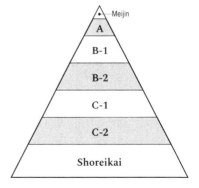

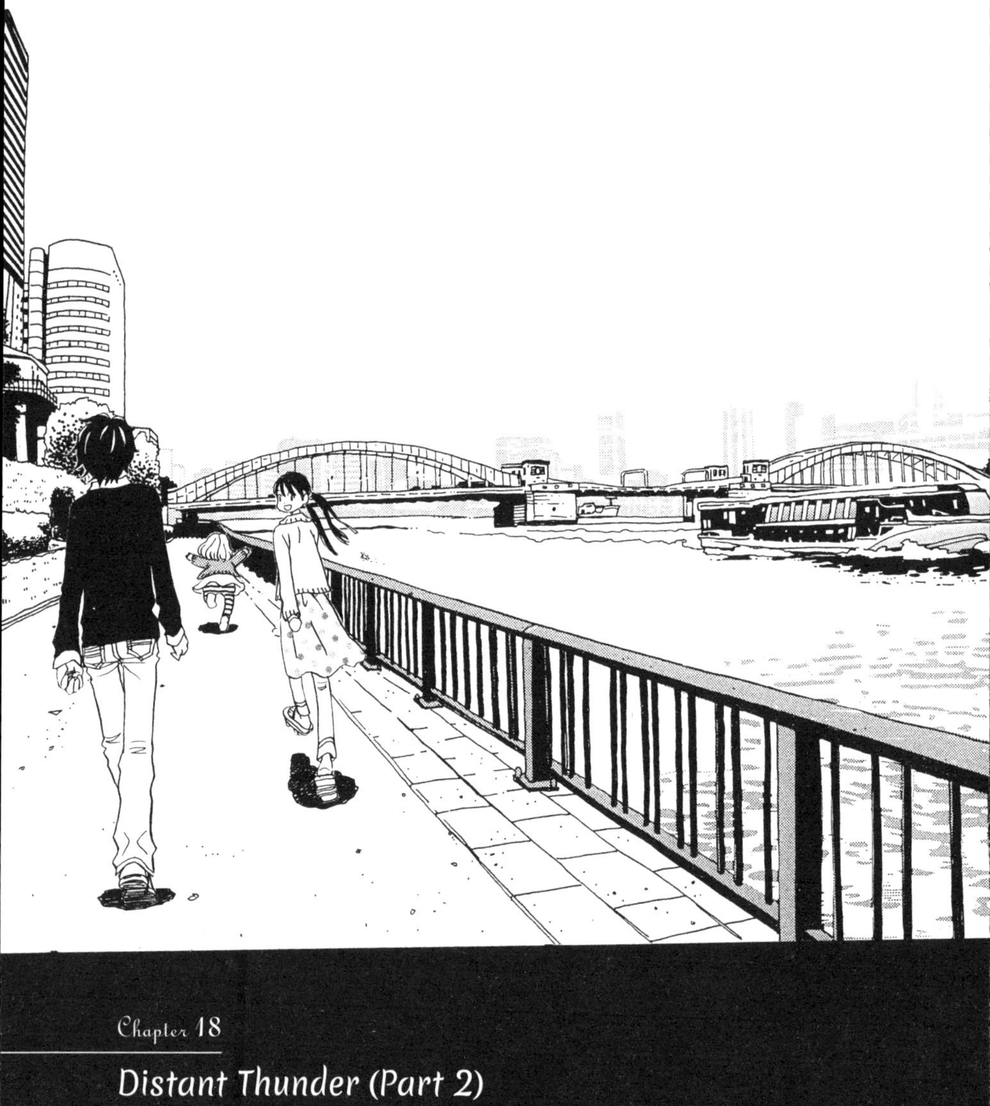

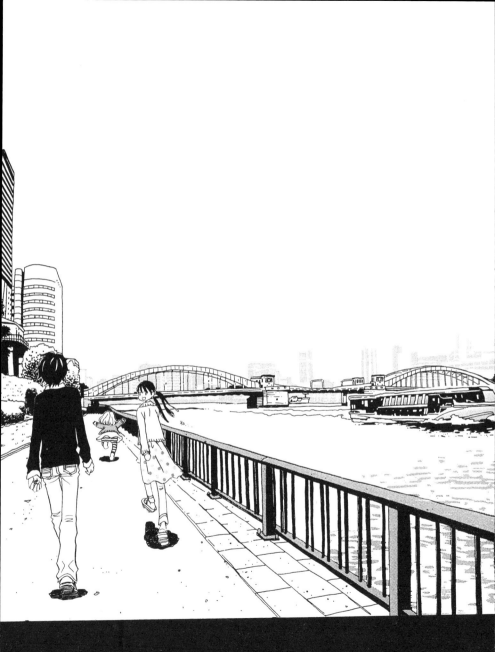

Chapter 18

Distant Thunder (Part 2)

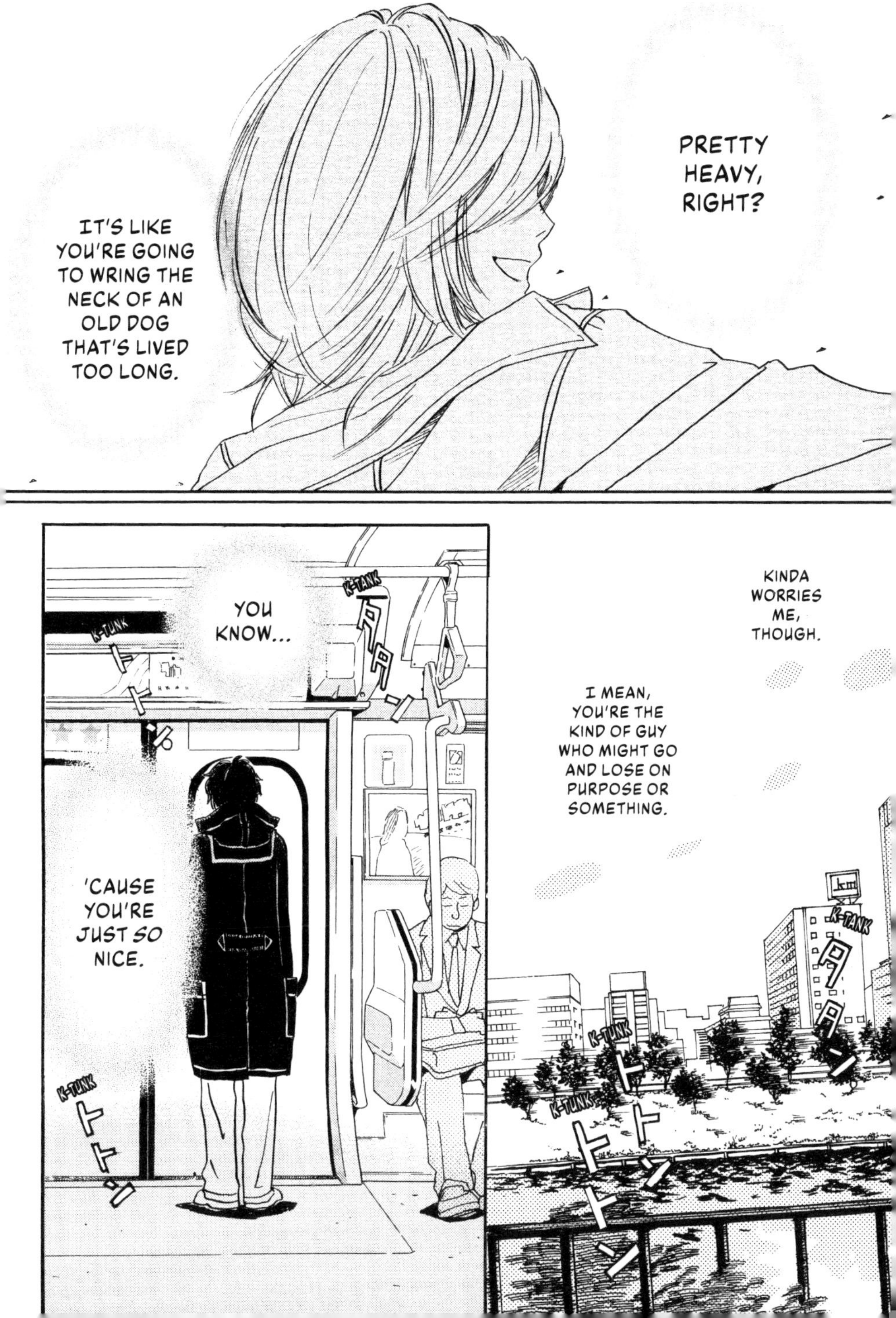
PRETTY HEAVY, RIGHT?
IT'S LIKE YOU'RE GOING TO WRING THE NECK OF AN OLD DOG THAT'S LIVED TOO LONG.
KINDA WORRIES ME, THOUGH.
I MEAN, YOU'RE THE KIND OF GUY WHO MIGHT GO AND LOSE ON PURPOSE OR SOMETHING.
K-TANK
K-TUNK
K-TUNKS
YOU KNOW...
K-TANK
K-TUNK
'CAUSE YOU'RE JUST *SO* NICE.
K-TUNK

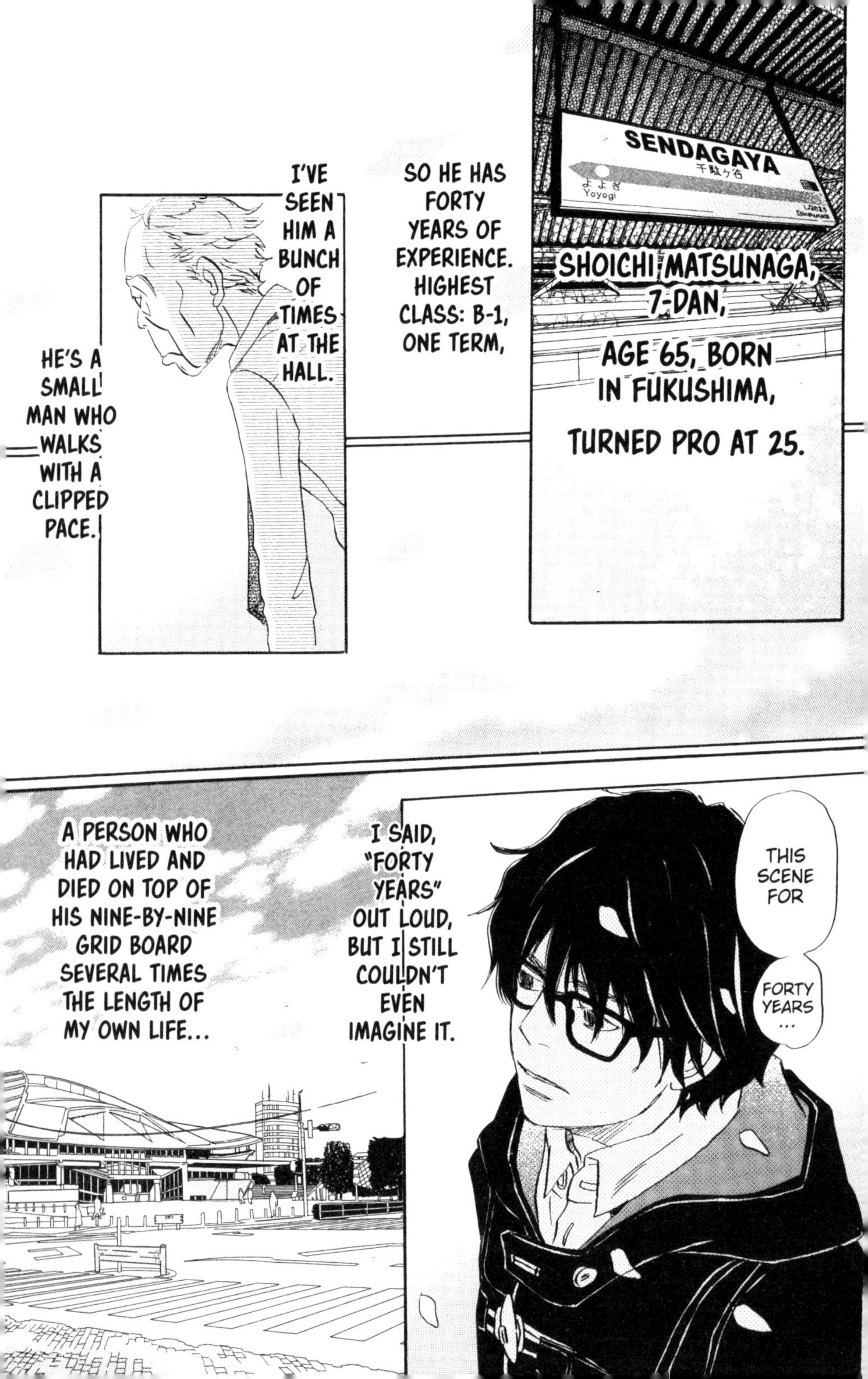
SENDAGAYA
千駄ケ谷
よよぎ
Yoyogi
SHOICHI MATSUNAGA, 7-DAN,
AGE 65, BORN IN FUKUSHIMA,
TURNED PRO AT 25.
SO HE HAS FORTY YEARS OF EXPERIENCE. HIGHEST CLASS: B-1, ONE TERM,
I'VE SEEN HIM A BUNCH OF TIMES AT THE HALL.
HE'S A SMALL MAN WHO WALKS WITH A CLIPPED PACE.
THIS SCENE FOR
FORTY YEARS ...
I SAID, "FORTY YEARS" OUT LOUD, BUT I STILL COULDN'T EVEN IMAGINE IT.
A PERSON WHO HAD LIVED AND DIED ON TOP OF HIS NINE-BY-NINE GRID BOARD SEVERAL TIMES THE LENGTH OF MY OWN LIFE...

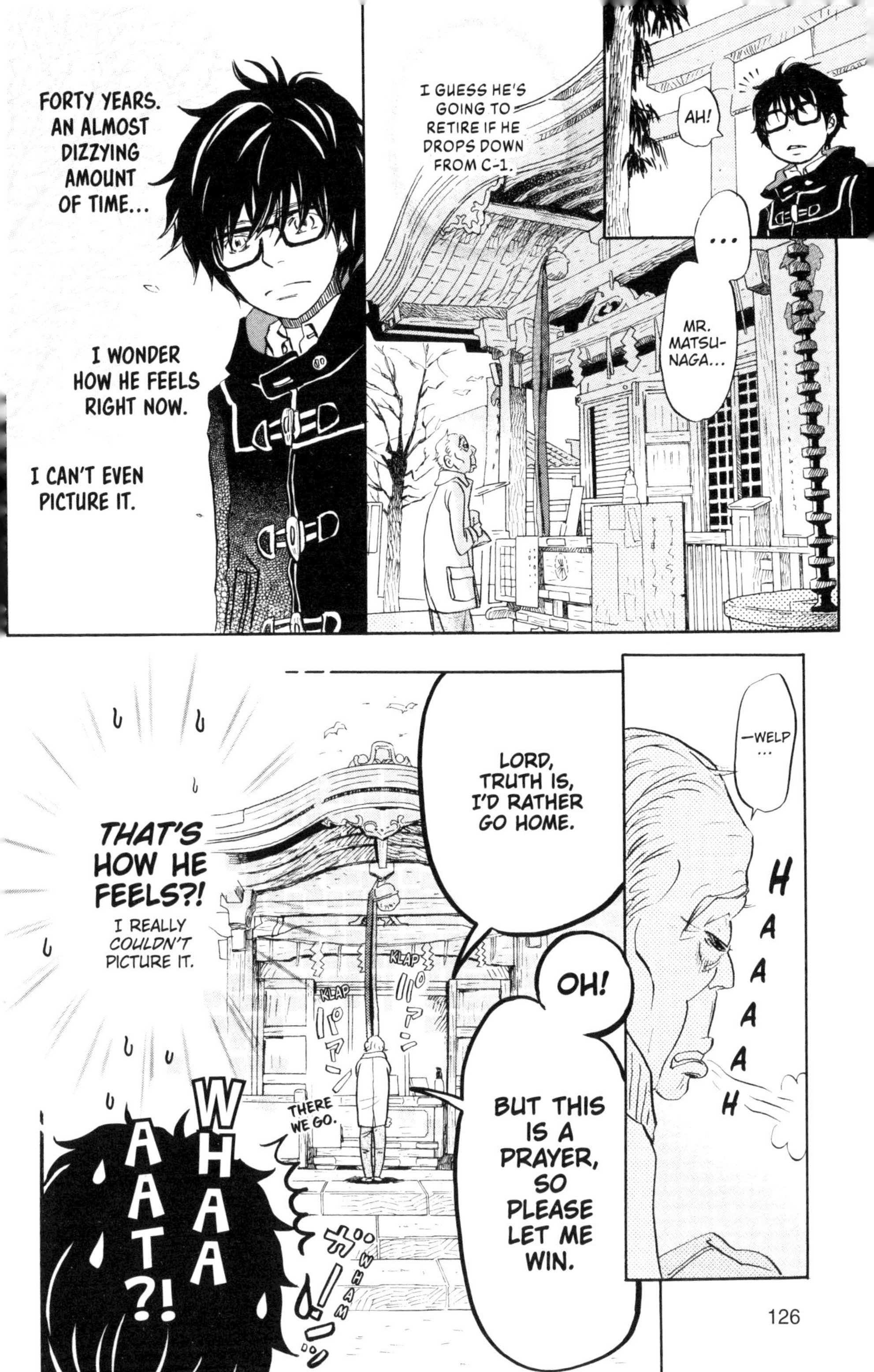
AH!
...
MR. MATSUNAGA...
I GUESS HE'S GOING TO RETIRE IF HE DROPS DOWN FROM C-1.
FORTY YEARS. AN ALMOST DIZZYING AMOUNT OF TIME...
I WONDER HOW HE FEELS RIGHT NOW.
I CAN'T EVEN PICTURE IT.
—WELP ...
HAAAAAH
LORD, TRUTH IS, I'D RATHER GO HOME.
OH!
BUT THIS IS A PRAYER, SO PLEASE LET ME WIN.
KLAP
KLAP
THERE WE GO.
WHAM
WHAAAAT?!
THAT'S HOW HE FEELS?!
I REALLY *COULDN'T* PICTURE IT.

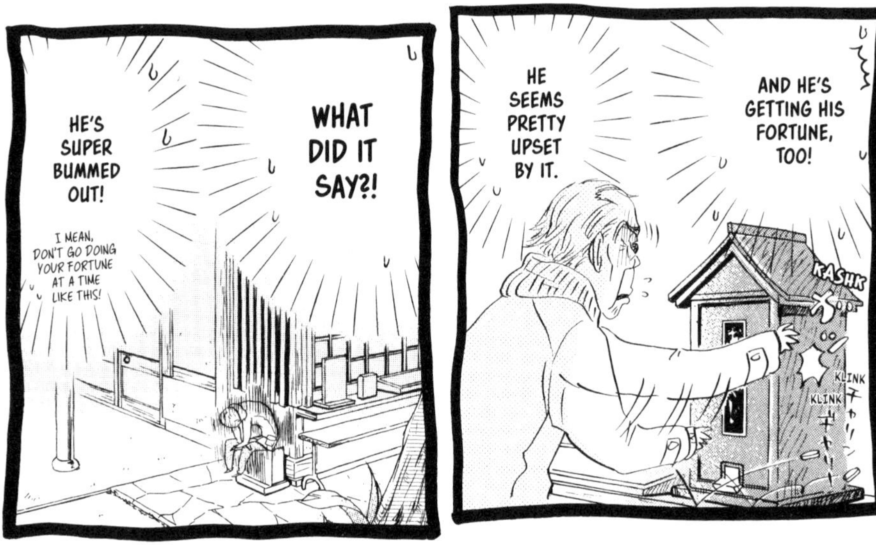
AND HE'S GETTING HIS FORTUNE, TOO!
HE SEEMS PRETTY UPSET BY IT.
KASHK
KLINK
KLINK
WHAT DID IT SAY?!
HE'S SUPER BUMMED OUT!
I MEAN, DON'T GO DOING YOUR FORTUNE AT A TIME LIKE THIS!

*Ordinary mind is the Way.

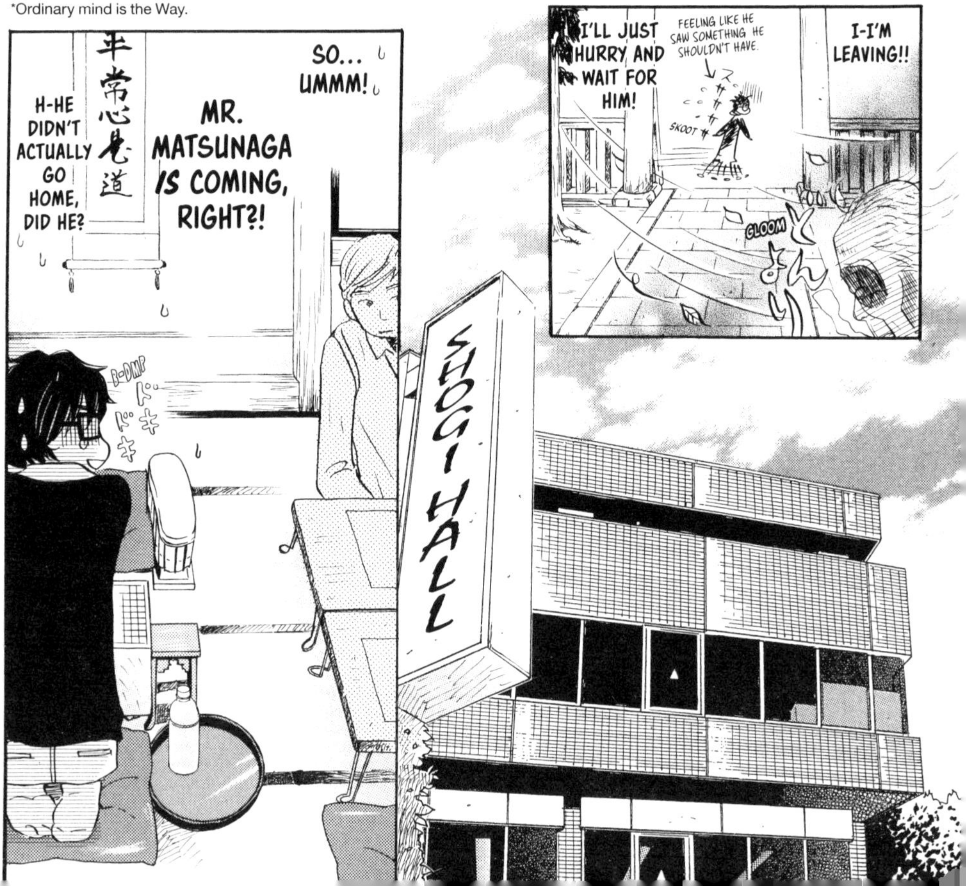
I-I'M LEAVING!!
FEELING LIKE HE SAW SOMETHING HE SHOULDN'T HAVE.
I'LL JUST HURRY AND WAIT FOR HIM!
SKOOT
GLOOM
SHOGI HALL
SO... UMMM!
MR. MATSUNAGA IS COMING, RIGHT?!
H-HE DIDN'T ACTUALLY GO HOME, DID HE?
B-DMP

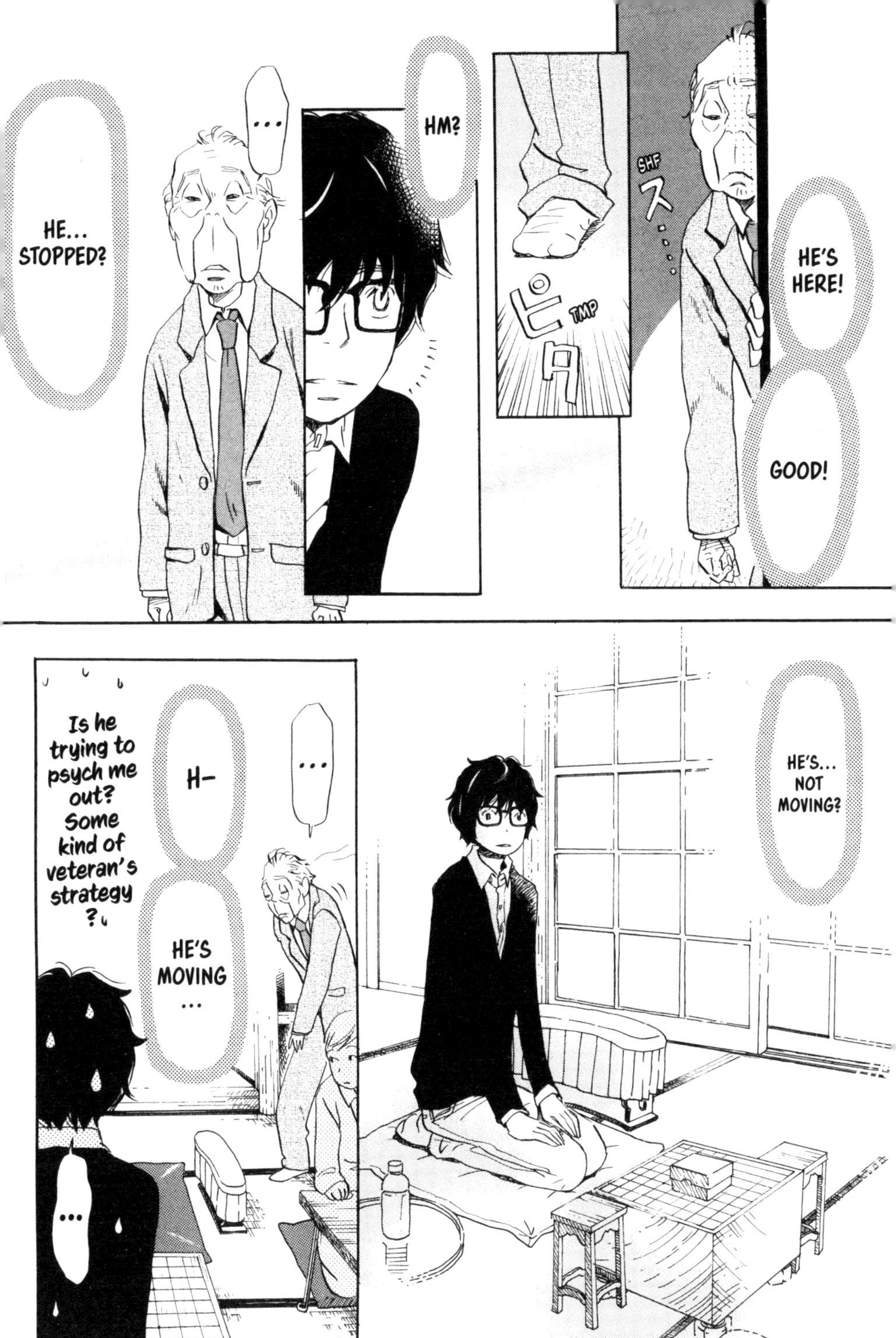
HE'S HERE!
GOOD!
SHF
ス
ピタ
TMP
HM?
...
HE... STOPPED?
HE'S... NOT MOVING?
...
H-
HE'S MOVING ...
Is he trying to psych me out? Some kind of veteran's strategy?
...

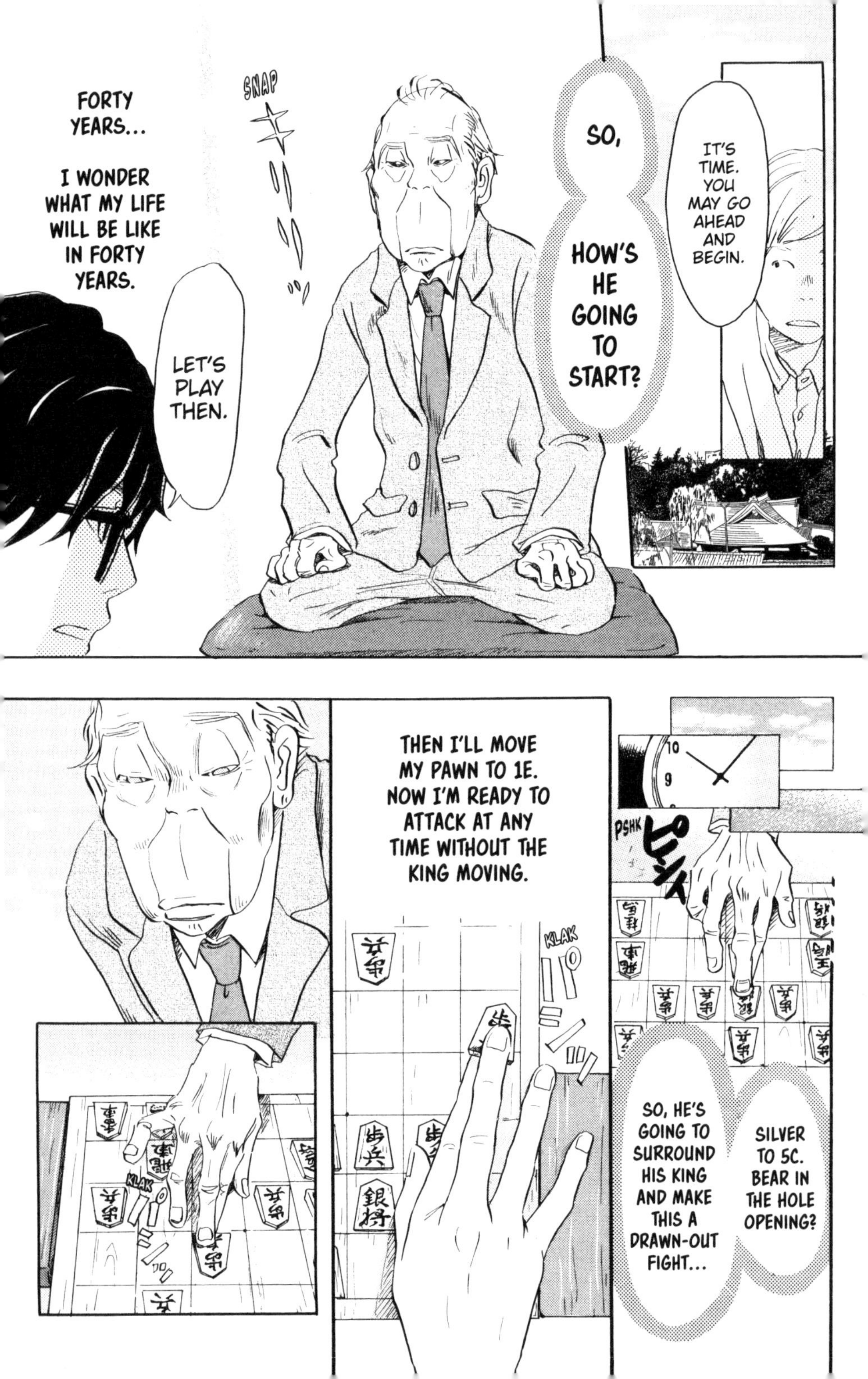
IT'S TIME. YOU MAY GO AHEAD AND BEGIN.
SO, HOW'S HE GOING TO START?
SNAP
LET'S PLAY THEN.
FORTY YEARS...
I WONDER WHAT MY LIFE WILL BE LIKE IN FORTY YEARS.
10
9
PSHK
SILVER TO 5C. BEAR IN THE HOLE OPENING?
SO, HE'S GOING TO SURROUND HIS KING AND MAKE THIS A DRAWN-OUT FIGHT...
THEN I'LL MOVE MY PAWN TO 1E. NOW I'M READY TO ATTACK AT ANY TIME WITHOUT THE KING MOVING.
KLAK
KLAK

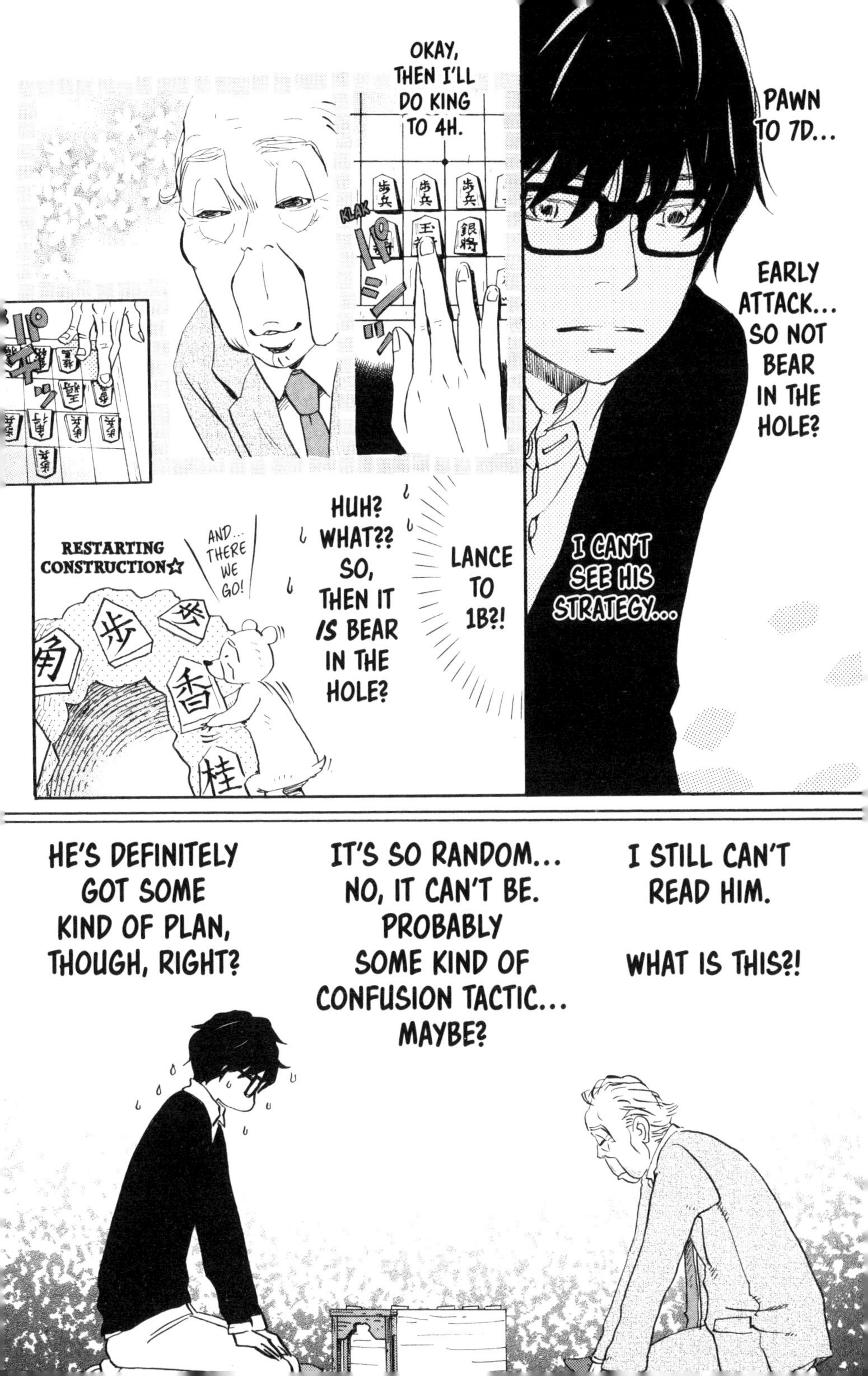
PAWN TO 7D...
EARLY ATTACK... SO NOT BEAR IN THE HOLE?
I CAN'T SEE HIS STRATEGY...
OKAY, THEN I'LL DO KING TO 4H.
KLAK
LANCE TO 1B?!
HUH? WHAT?? SO, THEN IT *IS* BEAR IN THE HOLE?
AND... THERE WE GO!
RESTARTING CONSTRUCTION☆
I STILL CAN'T READ HIM.
WHAT IS THIS?!
IT'S SO RANDOM... NO, IT CAN'T BE. PROBABLY SOME KIND OF CONFUSION TACTIC... MAYBE?
HE'S DEFINITELY GOT SOME KIND OF PLAN, THOUGH, RIGHT?

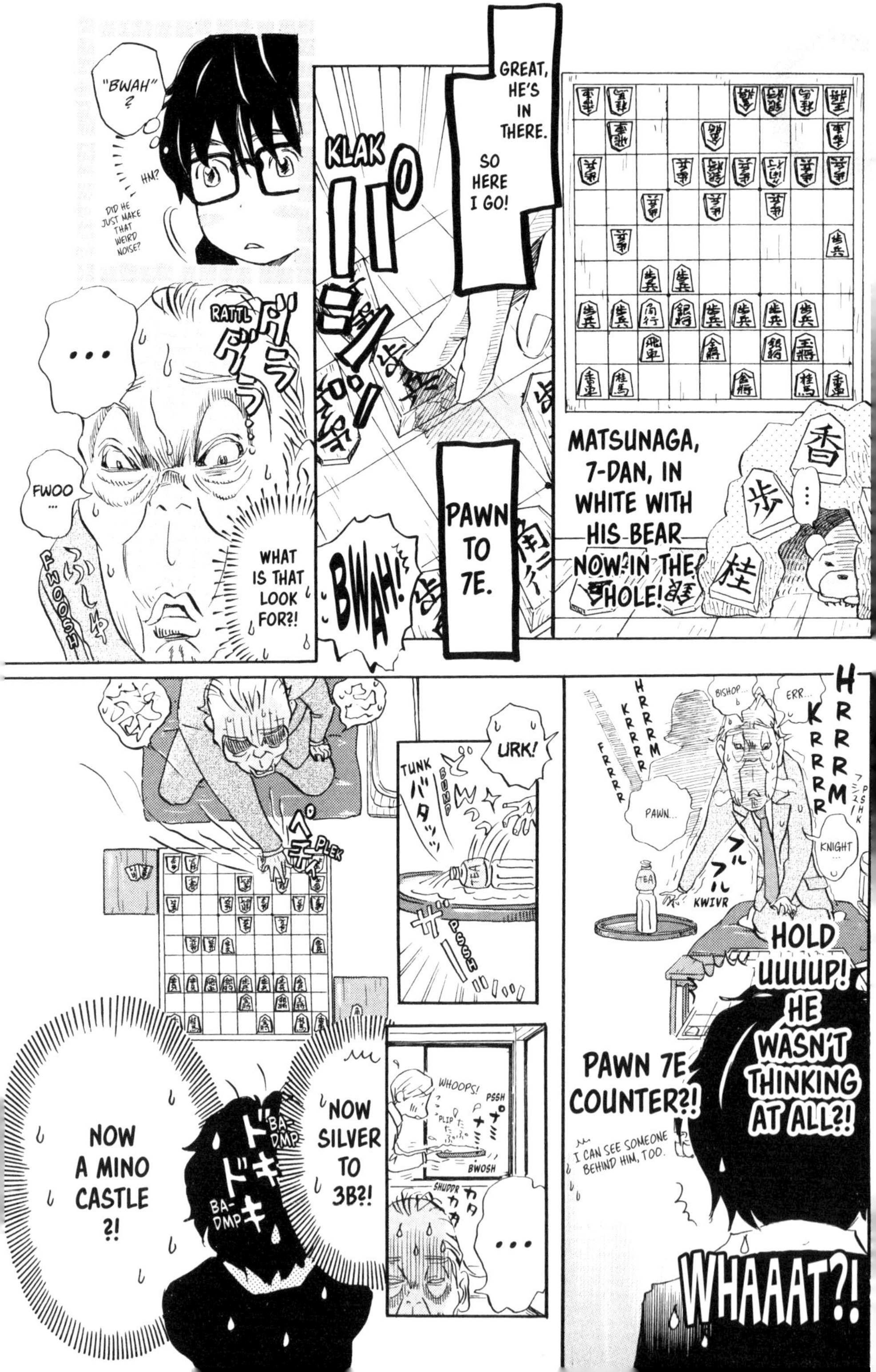
MATSUNAGA, 7-DAN, IN WHITE WITH HIS BEAR NOW IN THE HOLE!
...
GREAT, HE'S IN THERE.
SO HERE I GO!
KLAK
PAWN TO 7E.
BWAH!
"BWAH"?
HM?
DID HE JUST MAKE THAT WEIRD NOISE?
...
RATTL
FWOO ...
FWOOSH
WHAT IS THAT LOOK FOR?!
HRRRM
KRRRR
FRRRR
BISHOP...
ERR...
PAWN...
PSHK
KNIGHT ...
KWIVR
HOLD UUUUP! HE WASN'T THINKING AT ALL?!
PAWN 7E COUNTER?!
I CAN SEE SOMEONE BEHIND HIM, TOO.
WHAAAT?!
URK!
TUNK
BUMP
TEA
PSSH
WHOOPS!
PSSH
PLIP
BWOSH
SHUDDR
...
PLEK
NOW SILVER TO 3B?!
BA-DMP
BA-DMP
NOW A MINO CASTLE?!

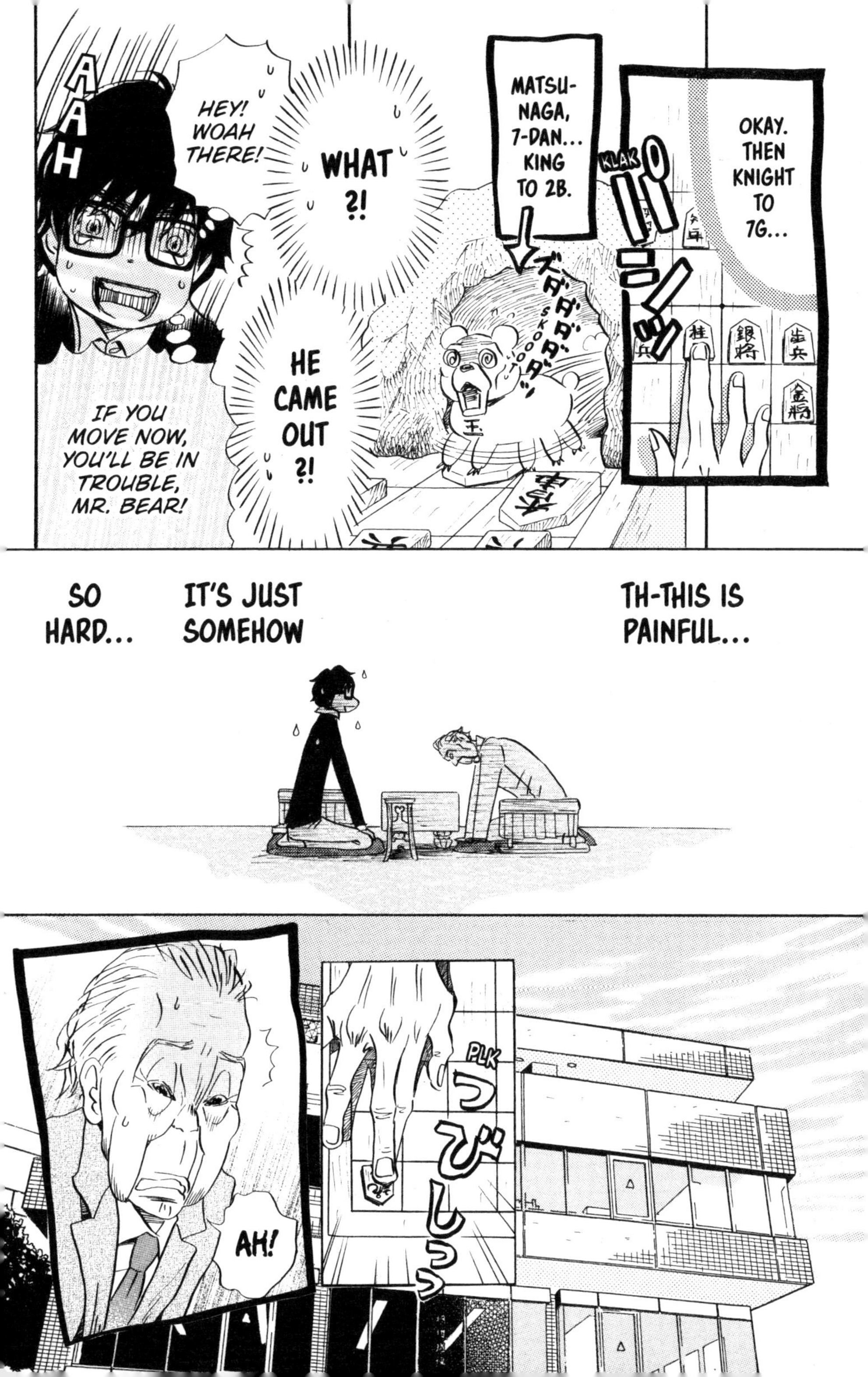

OKAY. THEN KNIGHT TO 7G...
KLAK
MATSU-NAGA, 7-DAN... KING TO 2B.
SKOOT
WHAT?!
HE CAME OUT?!
HEY! WOAH THERE!
AAAH
IF YOU MOVE NOW, YOU'LL BE IN TROUBLE, MR. BEAR!
TH-THIS IS PAINFUL...
IT'S JUST SOMEHOW
SO HARD...
PLK
AH!

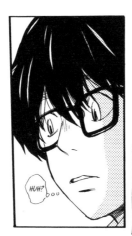

OH NO.
KWVR
KWVR
AUGH.
FORKING THE ROOK.
HUH?
TRUE...
BUT... IF I HIT THE BISHOP THERE,
Kiriyama / pieces in hand / Four pawns
Matsunaga / pieces in hand / Bishop, Lance, pawn
HE MATCHES IT AT 5E, KNIGHT TO 3F... WELL, EVEN IF IT IS SUSPICIOUS,
I'VE GOT THE UPPER HAND HERE—
O-
Oh no...
HUSH
If he hits my bishop,
HUSH
PEEK
A GLANCE?! HUH? WHAT? IS HE TRYING TO LURE ME INTO A TRAP? HE'S PLAYING ME?!
AND LIKE, HIS PERFORMANCE IS TERRIBLE!

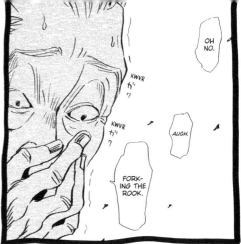

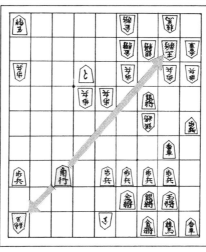

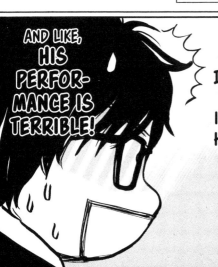

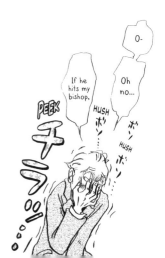

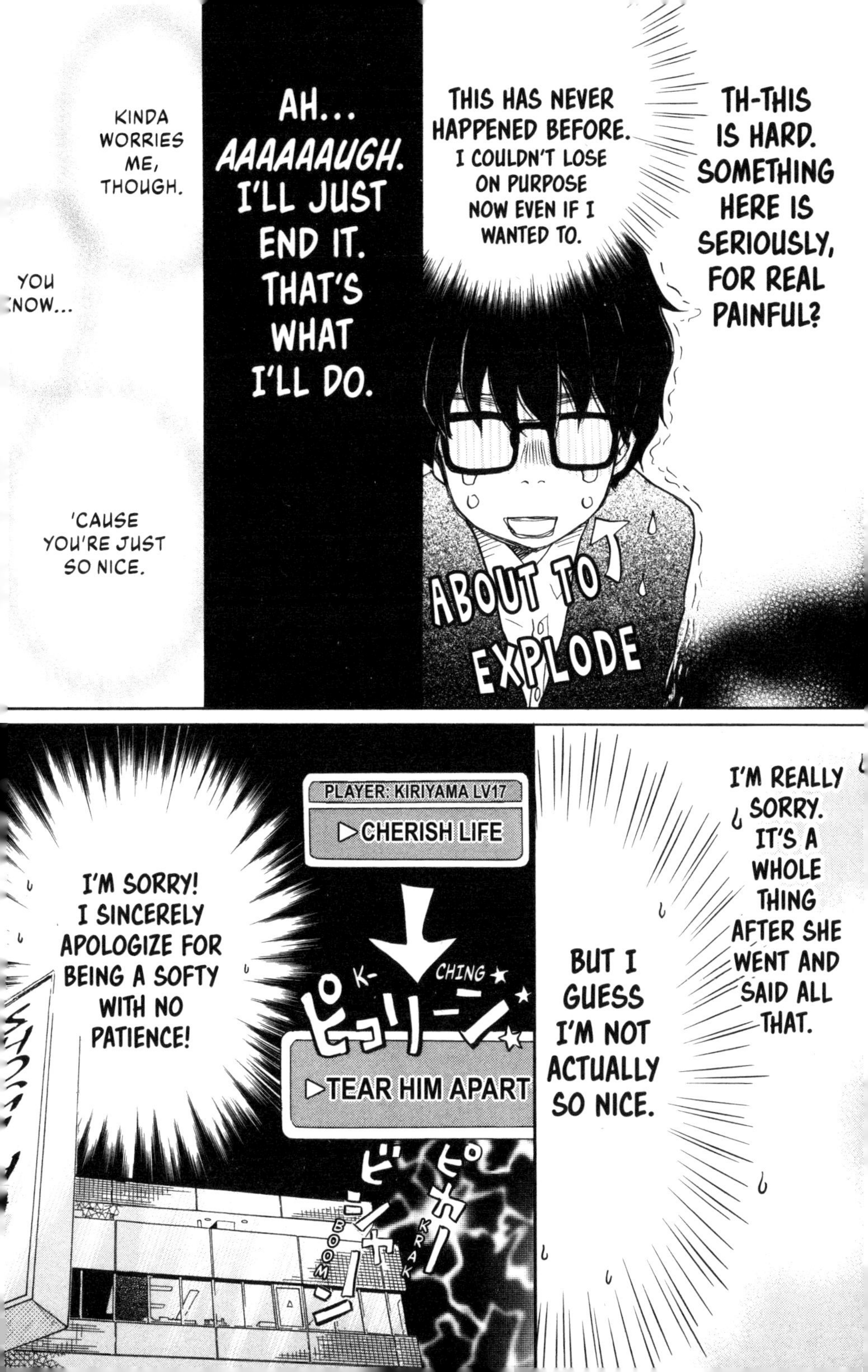
TH-THIS IS HARD. SOMETHING HERE IS SERIOUSLY, FOR REAL PAINFUL?
THIS HAS NEVER HAPPENED BEFORE. I COULDN'T LOSE ON PURPOSE NOW EVEN IF I WANTED TO.
ABOUT TO EXPLODE
AH... AAAAAAUGH. I'LL JUST END IT. THAT'S WHAT I'LL DO.
KINDA WORRIES ME, THOUGH.
YOU KNOW...
'CAUSE YOU'RE JUST SO NICE.
I'M REALLY SORRY. IT'S A WHOLE THING AFTER SHE WENT AND SAID ALL THAT.
BUT I GUESS I'M NOT ACTUALLY SO NICE.
PLAYER: KIRIYAMA LV17
▷CHERISH LIFE
K-CHING
ピコリーン
▷TEAR HIM APART
I'M SORRY! I SINCERELY APOLOGIZE FOR BEING A SOFTY WITH NO PATIENCE!
KRAK
BOOM

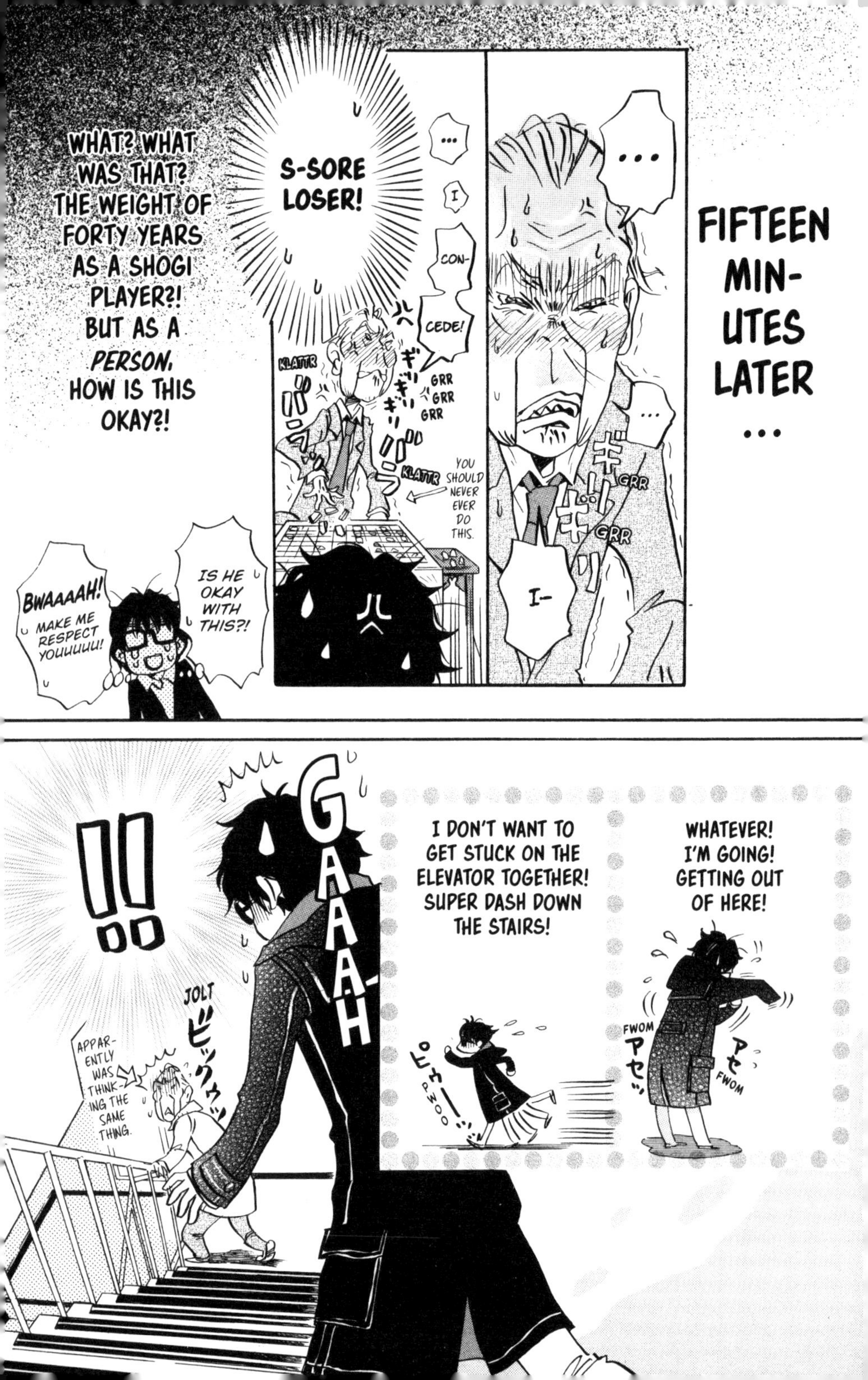
FIFTEEN MIN-UTES LATER...
...
...
GRR
GRR
I-
...
I
CON-
CEDE!
GRR GRR GRR
KLATTR
KLATTR
S-SORE LOSER!
YOU SHOULD NEVER EVER DO THIS.
WHAT? WHAT WAS THAT? THE WEIGHT OF FORTY YEARS AS A SHOGI PLAYER?! BUT AS A *PERSON*, HOW IS THIS OKAY?!
IS HE OKAY WITH THIS?!
BWAAAAH! MAKE ME RESPECT YOUUUUU!
WHATEVER! I'M GOING! GETTING OUT OF HERE!
FWOM
FWOM
I DON'T WANT TO GET STUCK ON THE ELEVATOR TOGETHER! SUPER DASH DOWN THE STAIRS!
PWOO
GAAAAH
!!
JOLT
APPARENTLY WAS THINKING THE SAME THING.

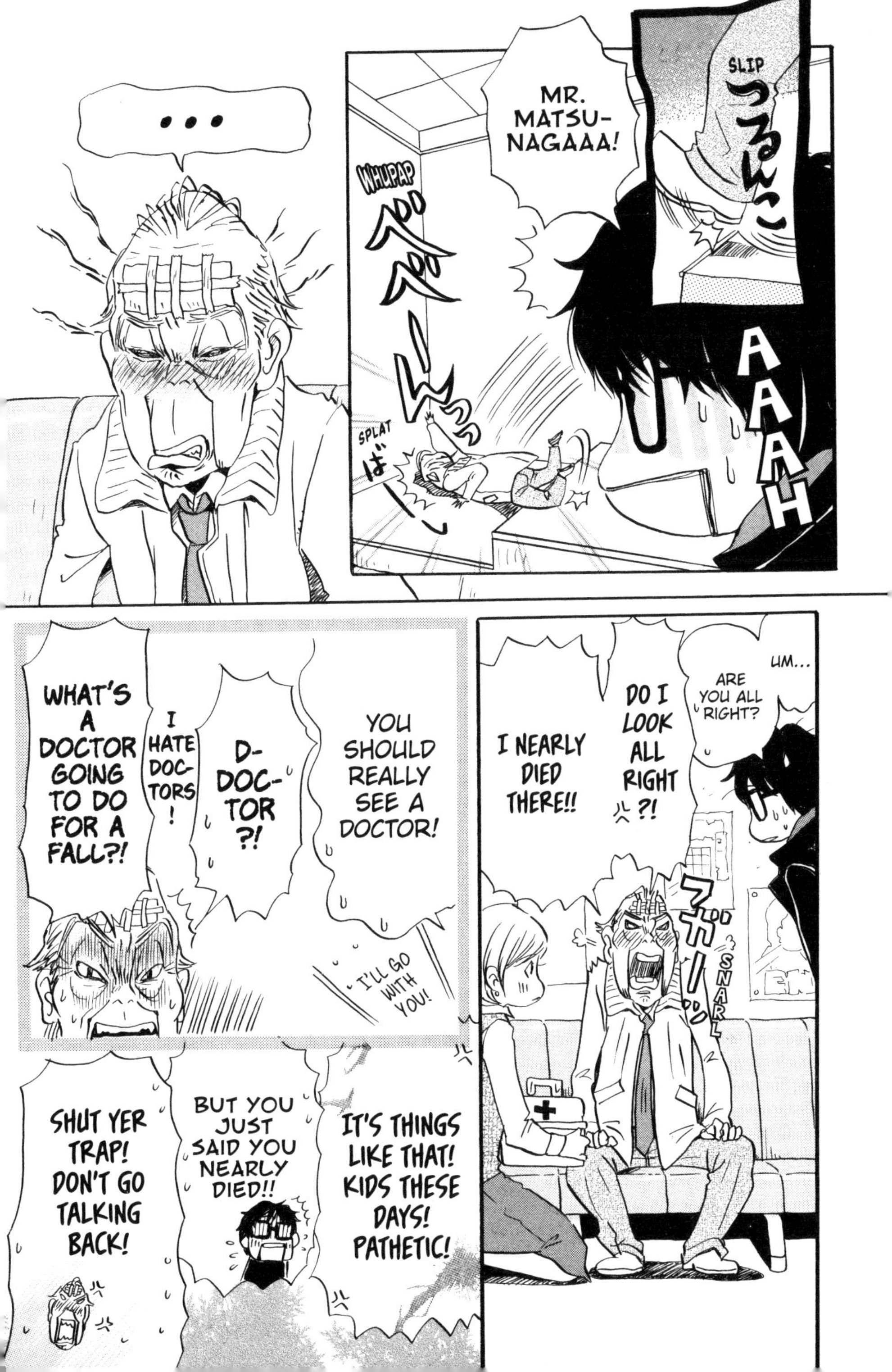

SLIP
つるんっ
MR. MATSU-NAGAAA!
AAAAH
WHUPAP
SPLAT
...
UM...
ARE YOU ALL RIGHT?
DO I LOOK ALL RIGHT?!
I NEARLY DIED THERE!!
SNARL
YOU SHOULD REALLY SEE A DOCTOR!
D-DOCTOR?!
I HATE DOCTORS!
WHAT'S A DOCTOR GOING TO DO FOR A FALL?!
I'LL GO WITH YOU!
IT'S THINGS LIKE THAT! KIDS THESE DAYS! PATHETIC!
BUT YOU JUST SAID YOU NEARLY DIED!!
SHUT YER TRAP! DON'T GO TALKING BACK!

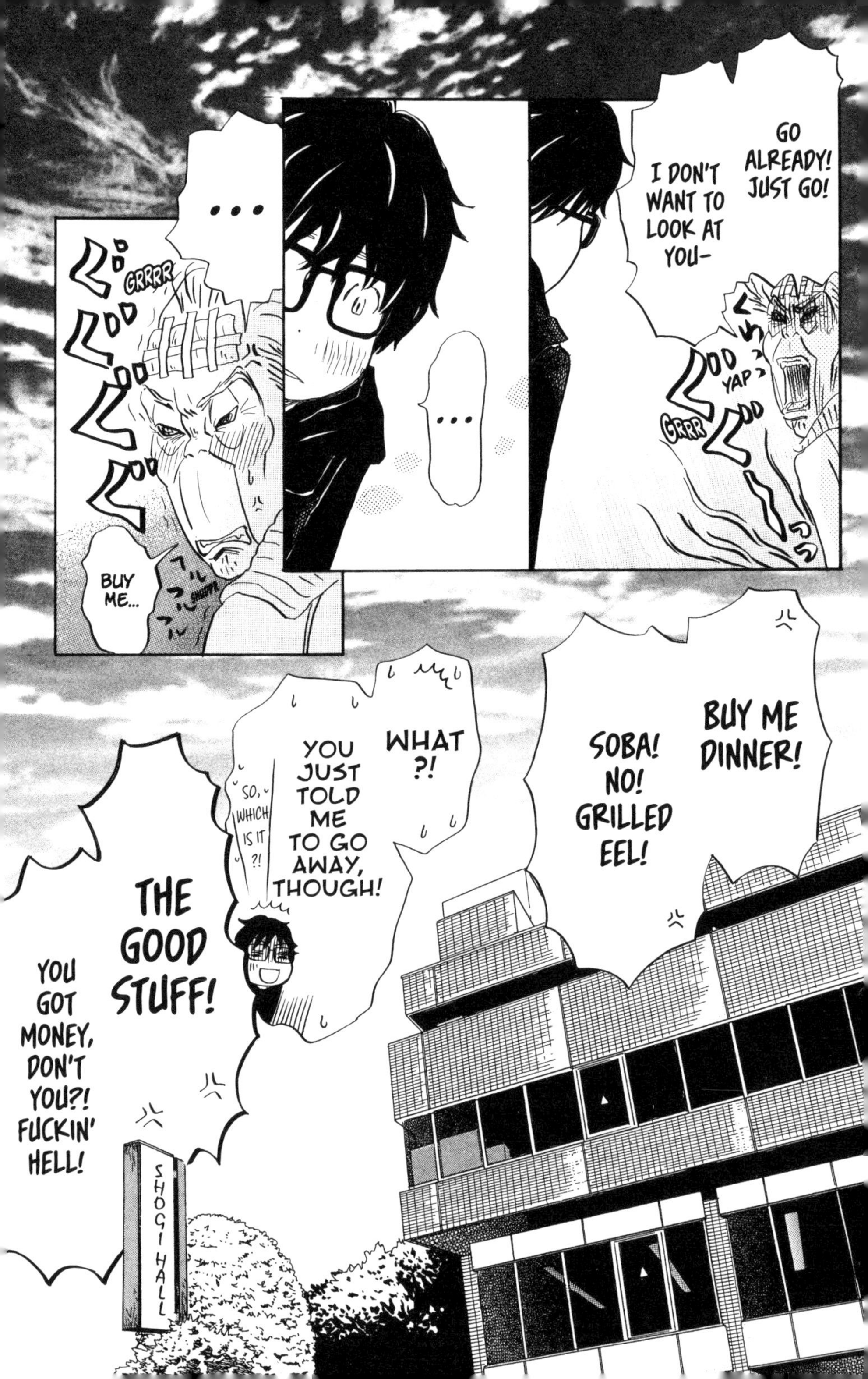
GO ALREADY! JUST GO!
I DON'T WANT TO LOOK AT YOU-
YAP
GRRR
...
...
GRRRR
BUY ME...
BUY ME DINNER!
SOBA! NO! GRILLED EEL!
WHAT?!
YOU JUST TOLD ME TO GO AWAY, THOUGH!
SO, WHICH IS IT?!
THE GOOD STUFF!
YOU GOT MONEY, DON'T YOU?! FUCKIN' HELL!
SHOGI HALL

Manabu Senzaki's Lion Shogi

by Manabu Senzaki

Bear in the Hole Isn't Just Annoying on the Board!

In *March*, there are a lot of match scenes. As the person who produces the boards, I take orders for this or that and try to come up with a board that suits the story before the final drawings are complete. As you'll know from reading the manga, I get all kinds of requests, but the most difficult one was Chapter 18, the match between Kiriyama and the old veteran, Matsunaga, 7-*dan*. This was the order: "Please make a sequence where the king goes into Bear in the Hole at 2b and then comes out right away again for some reason."

Hmm. After wrestling with this for a minute or two, I realized that this was no ordinary situation. My motto is "reality on the board beyond the picture on the page." Forced or extreme sequences are out of the question. I have this very fixed rule. (Eh heh!)

B-But the request was impossible. To have a king come out right away after going to the trouble of building the enclosure? I cradled my head in my hands and sank into thought.

Bear in the Hole is a move where you bring the king as quickly as possible to one of the four corners of the shogi board and bury the space around him with silver and gold generals. You see it most often in slow-paced openings (in endurance matches). This is a move the majority of professionals love. A particular feature to recommend it is that it makes it hard to check you. That's obvious just from looking at the pieces on the board. Professionals also hate being put into check, which is why they like Bear in the Hole. You can also have both players using this move as in the diagram above, for something called a Double Bear.

Now then, since this bear is so beloved, it first of all would not appear so soon. There's no reason. What's impossible is just impossible.

However, this was Umino asking. Personality-wise, she's quiet and agreeable, but when it comes to her work, she doesn't know the word "compromise." What I made for her then is the sequence in the story. I have to say I'm rather pleased with myself for coming up with something almost entirely natural in this difficult situation. With Bear in the Hole and the fascinating tale of Matsunaga attached to it, this chapter is one I'm particularly fond of.

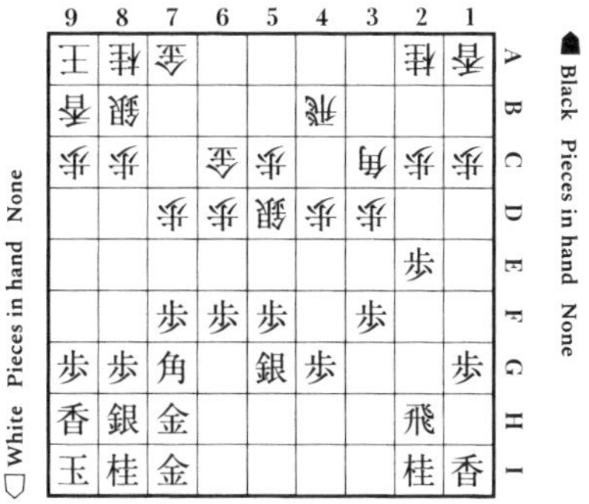
White Pieces in hand None
Black Pieces in hand None

Double Bear diagram

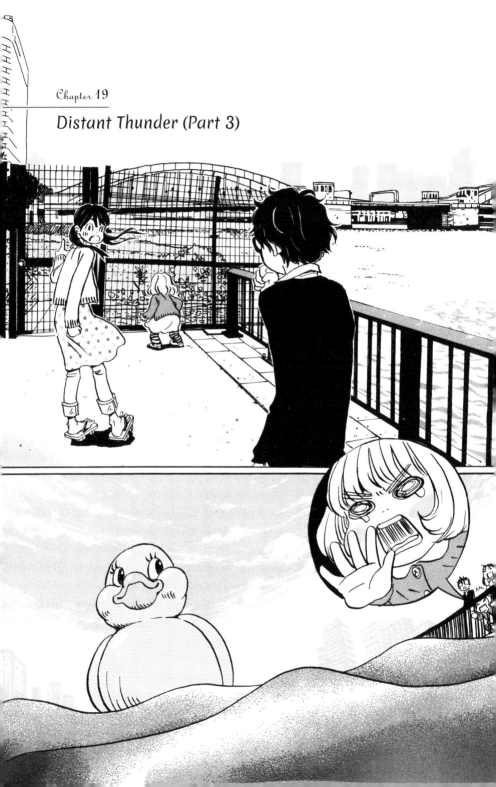

Chapter 19

Distant Thunder (Part 3)

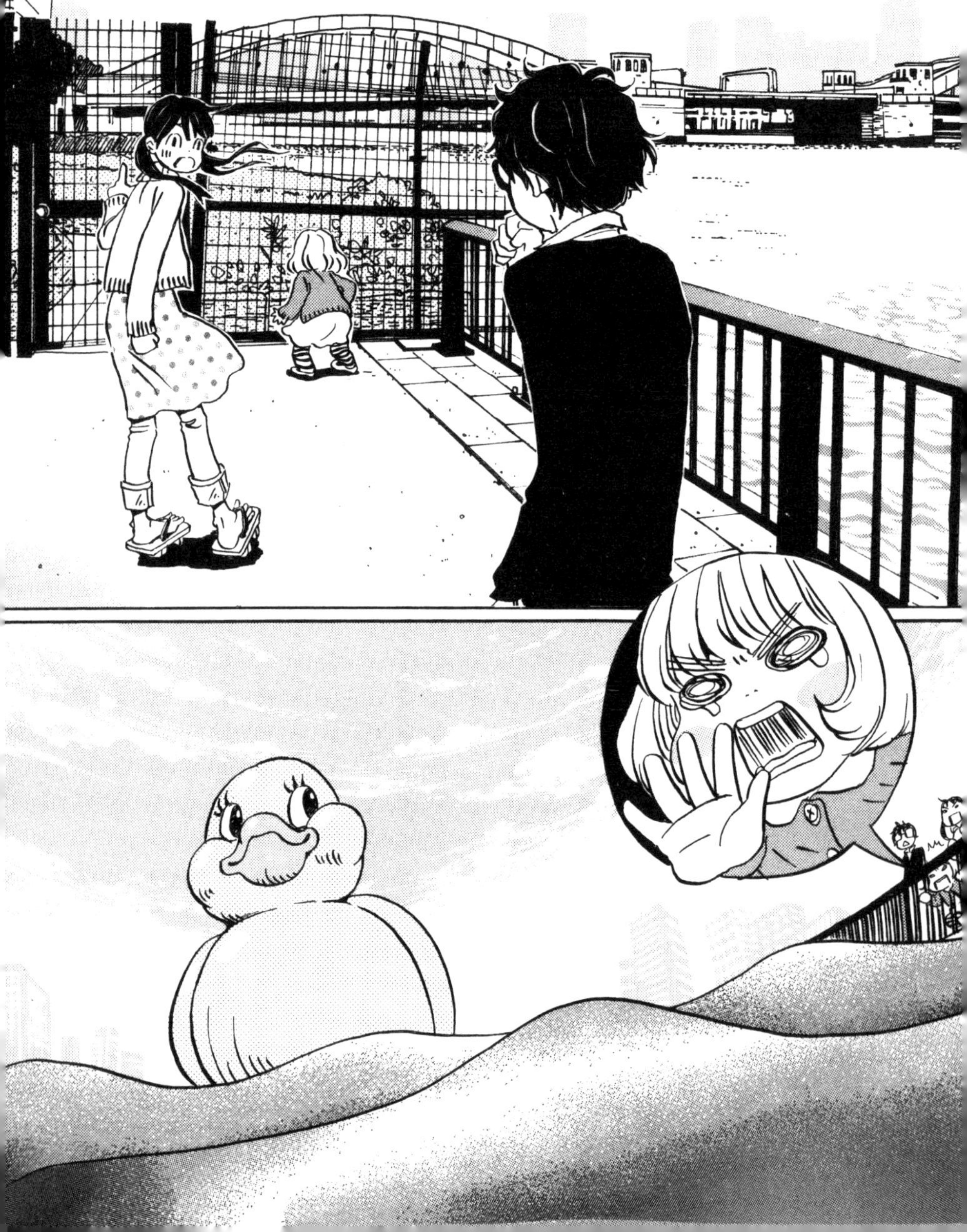

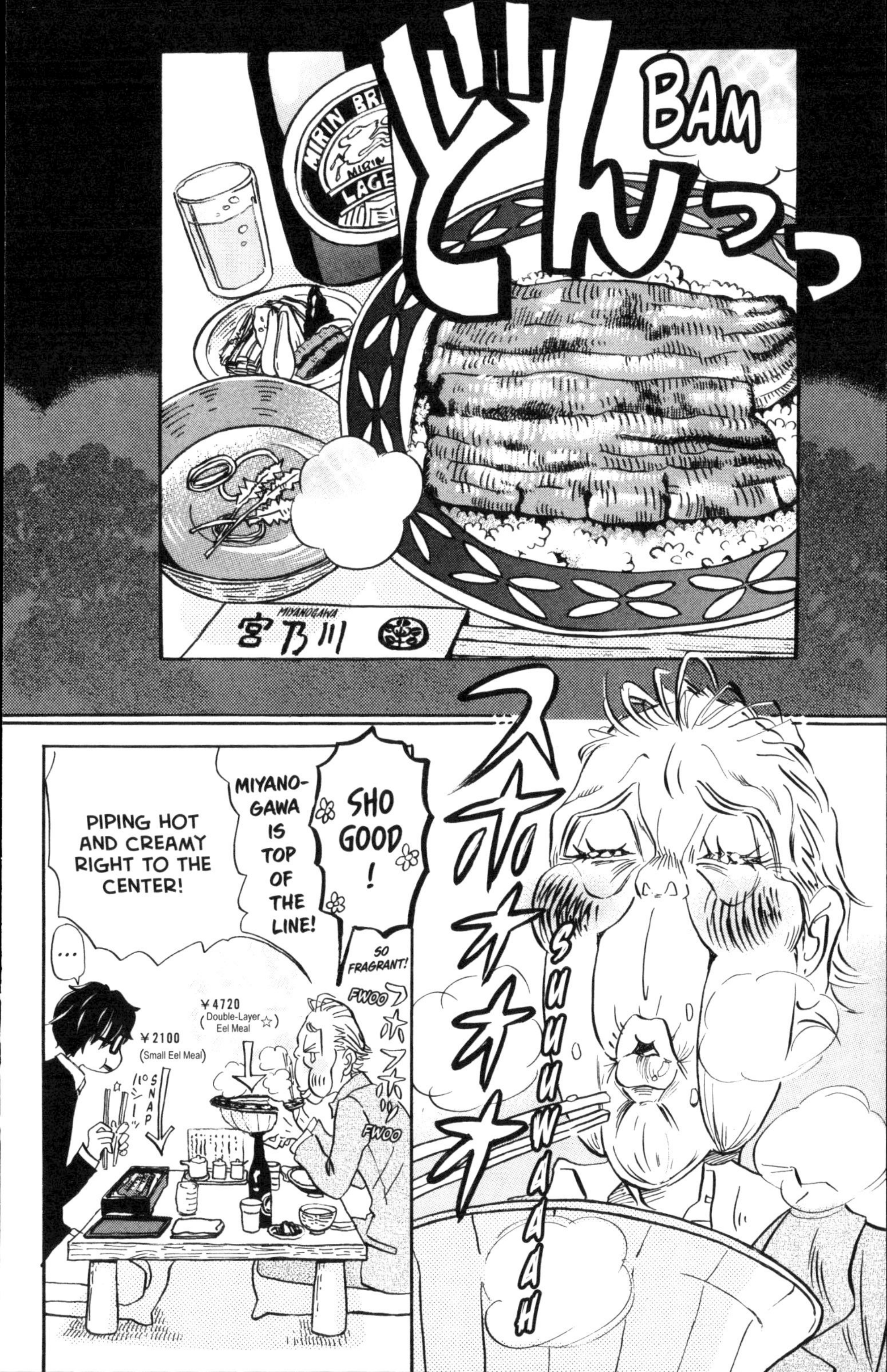
BAM
MIRIN
MIRIN
LAGE
MIYANOGAWA
宮乃川
SUUUWAAAAH
SHO GOOD!
MIYANO-GAWA IS TOP OF THE LINE!
PIPING HOT AND CREAMY RIGHT TO THE CENTER!
SO FRAGRANT!
FWOO
FWOO
¥4720 (Double-Layer Eel Meal☆)
...
¥2100 (Small Eel Meal)
SNAP

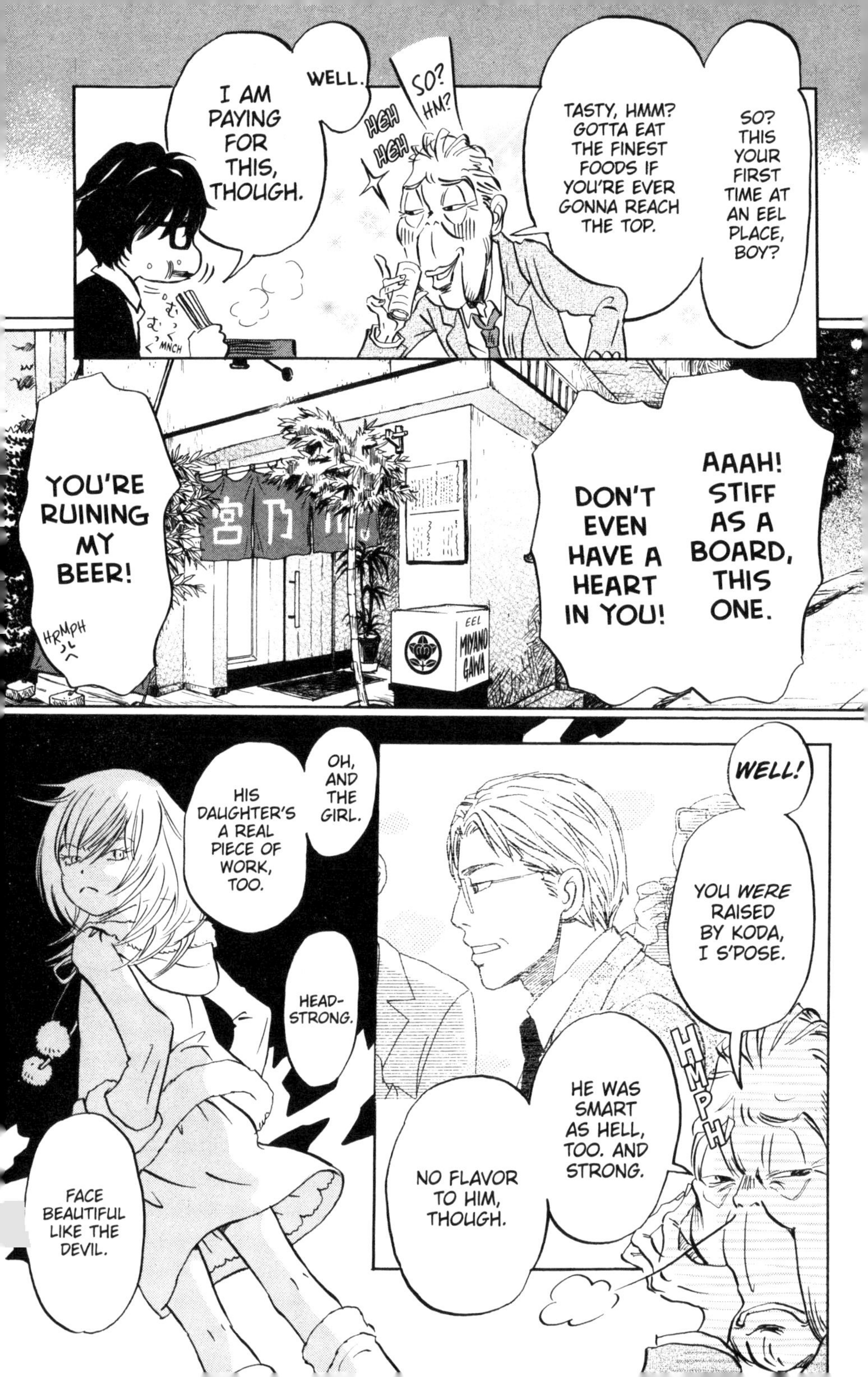
SO? THIS YOUR FIRST TIME AT AN EEL PLACE, BOY?
TASTY, HMM? GOTTA EAT THE FINEST FOODS IF YOU'RE EVER GONNA REACH THE TOP.
SO? HM?
HEH HEH
WELL.
I AM PAYING FOR THIS, THOUGH.
MNCH
AAAH! STIFF AS A BOARD, THIS ONE.
DON'T EVEN HAVE A HEART IN YOU!
宮乃川
EEL MIYANO GAWA
YOU'RE RUINING MY BEER!
HRMPH
WELL!
YOU WERE RAISED BY KODA, I S'POSE.
HMMPH
HE WAS SMART AS HELL, TOO. AND STRONG.
NO FLAVOR TO HIM, THOUGH.
OH, AND THE GIRL.
HIS DAUGHTER'S A REAL PIECE OF WORK, TOO.
HEAD-STRONG.
FACE BEAUTIFUL LIKE THE DEVIL.

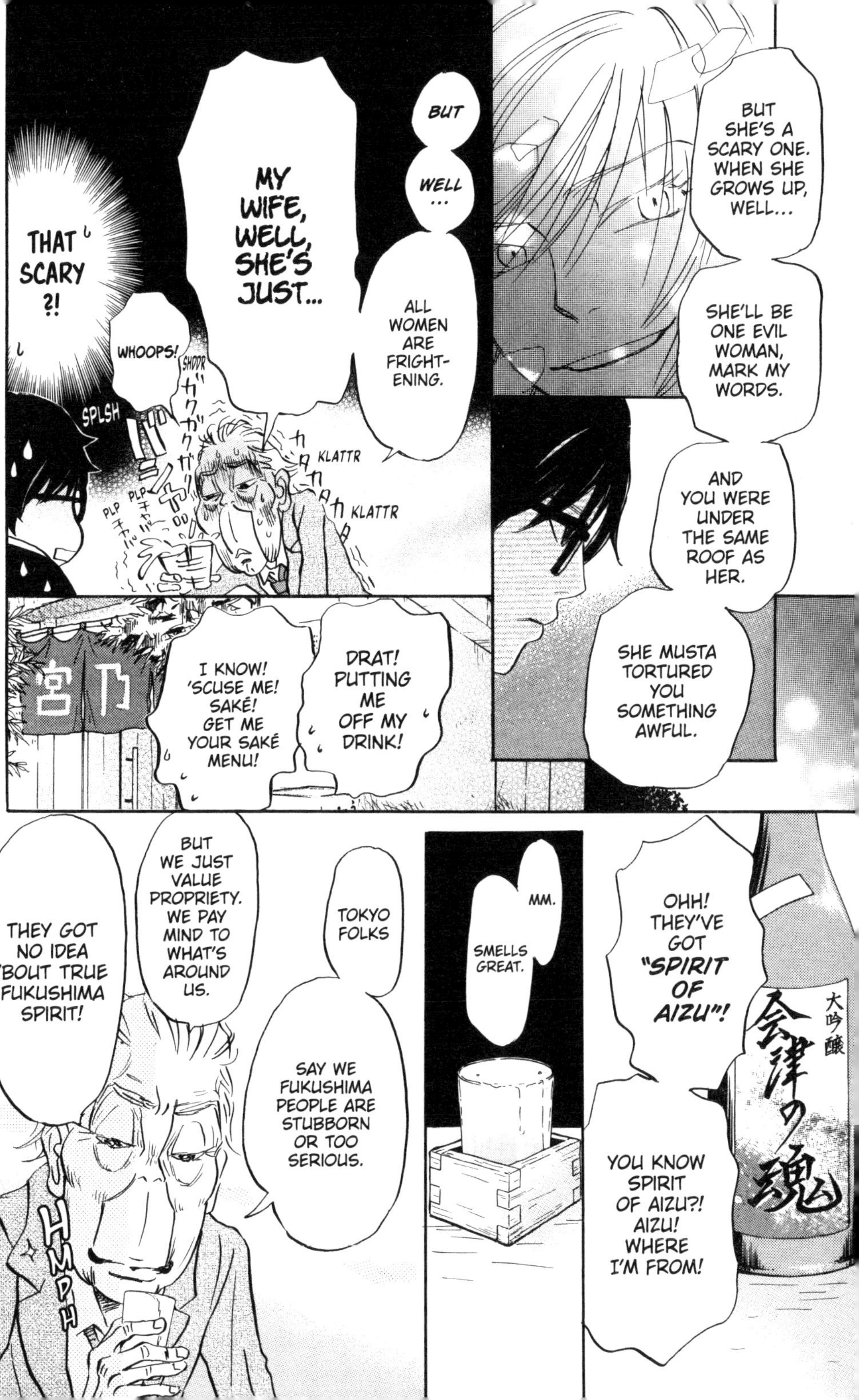
BUT SHE'S A SCARY ONE. WHEN SHE GROWS UP, WELL...
SHE'LL BE ONE EVIL WOMAN, MARK MY WORDS.
AND YOU WERE UNDER THE SAME ROOF AS HER.
SHE MUSTA TORTURED YOU SOMETHING AWFUL.
BUT
WELL...
ALL WOMEN ARE FRIGHT-ENING.
MY WIFE, WELL, SHE'S JUST...
THAT SCARY?!
KLATTR
KLATTR
SHDDR
WHOOPS!
SPLSH
PLP
PLP
DRAT! PUTTING ME OFF MY DRINK!
I KNOW! 'SCUSE ME! SAKÉ! GET ME YOUR SAKÉ MENU!
宮乃
OHH! THEY'VE GOT "SPIRIT OF AIZU"!
大吟醸
会津の魂
YOU KNOW SPIRIT OF AIZU?! AIZU! WHERE I'M FROM!
MM.
SMELLS GREAT.
TOKYO FOLKS
SAY WE FUKUSHIMA PEOPLE ARE STUBBORN OR TOO SERIOUS.
BUT WE JUST VALUE PROPRIETY. WE PAY MIND TO WHAT'S AROUND US.
THEY GOT NO IDEA 'BOUT TRUE FUKUSHIMA SPIRIT!
HMPH

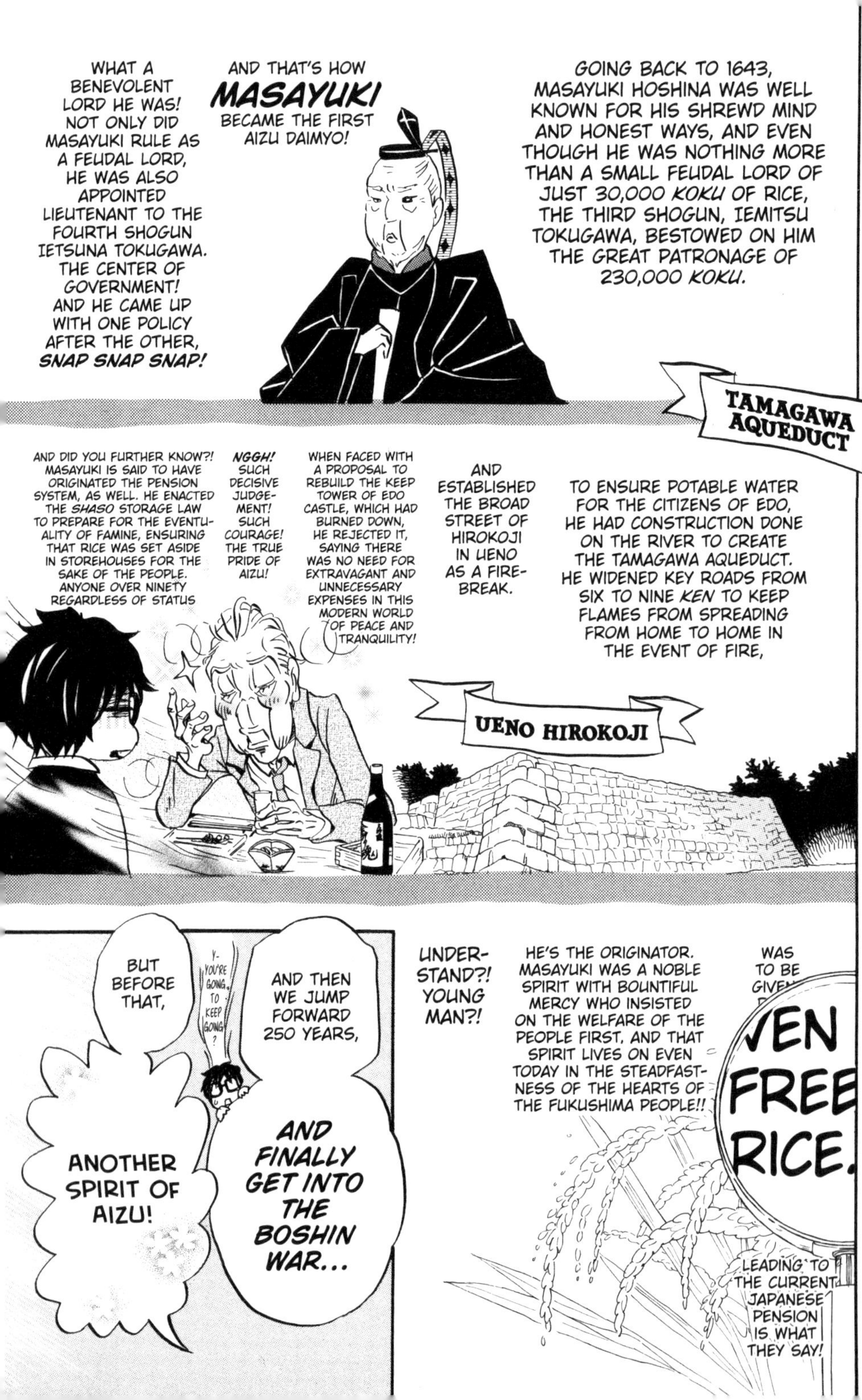
GOING BACK TO 1643, MASAYUKI HOSHINA WAS WELL KNOWN FOR HIS SHREWD MIND AND HONEST WAYS, AND EVEN THOUGH HE WAS NOTHING MORE THAN A SMALL FEUDAL LORD OF JUST 30,000 KOKU OF RICE, THE THIRD SHOGUN, IEMITSU TOKUGAWA, BESTOWED ON HIM THE GREAT PATRONAGE OF 230,000 KOKU.
AND THAT'S HOW MASAYUKI BECAME THE FIRST AIZU DAIMYO!
WHAT A BENEVOLENT LORD HE WAS! NOT ONLY DID MASAYUKI RULE AS A FEUDAL LORD, HE WAS ALSO APPOINTED LIEUTENANT TO THE FOURTH SHOGUN IETSUNA TOKUGAWA. THE CENTER OF GOVERNMENT! AND HE CAME UP WITH ONE POLICY AFTER THE OTHER, SNAP SNAP SNAP!
TAMAGAWA AQUEDUCT
TO ENSURE POTABLE WATER FOR THE CITIZENS OF EDO, HE HAD CONSTRUCTION DONE ON THE RIVER TO CREATE THE TAMAGAWA AQUEDUCT. HE WIDENED KEY ROADS FROM SIX TO NINE KEN TO KEEP FLAMES FROM SPREADING FROM HOME TO HOME IN THE EVENT OF FIRE,
AND ESTABLISHED THE BROAD STREET OF HIROKOJI IN UENO AS A FIRE-BREAK.
UENO HIROKOJI
WHEN FACED WITH A PROPOSAL TO REBUILD THE KEEP TOWER OF EDO CASTLE, WHICH HAD BURNED DOWN, HE REJECTED IT, SAYING THERE WAS NO NEED FOR EXTRAVAGANT AND UNNECESSARY EXPENSES IN THIS MODERN WORLD OF PEACE AND TRANQUILITY!
NGGH! SUCH DECISIVE JUDGEMENT! SUCH COURAGE! THE TRUE PRIDE OF AIZU!
AND DID YOU FURTHER KNOW?! MASAYUKI IS SAID TO HAVE ORIGINATED THE PENSION SYSTEM, AS WELL. HE ENACTED THE SHASO STORAGE LAW TO PREPARE FOR THE EVENTUALITY OF FAMINE, ENSURING THAT RICE WAS SET ASIDE IN STOREHOUSES FOR THE SAKE OF THE PEOPLE. ANYONE OVER NINETY REGARDLESS OF STATUS
WAS TO BE
FREE RICE.
LEADING TO THE CURRENT JAPANESE PENSION IS WHAT THEY SAY!
HE'S THE ORIGINATOR. MASAYUKI WAS A NOBLE SPIRIT WITH BOUNTIFUL MERCY WHO INSISTED ON THE WELFARE OF THE PEOPLE FIRST, AND THAT SPIRIT LIVES ON EVEN TODAY IN THE STEADFASTNESS OF THE HEARTS OF THE FUKUSHIMA PEOPLE!!
UNDERSTAND?! YOUNG MAN?!
AND THEN WE JUMP FORWARD 250 YEARS,
AND FINALLY GET INTO THE BOSHIN WAR...
Y-YOU'RE GOING TO KEEP GOING?
BUT BEFORE THAT,
ANOTHER SPIRIT OF AIZU!

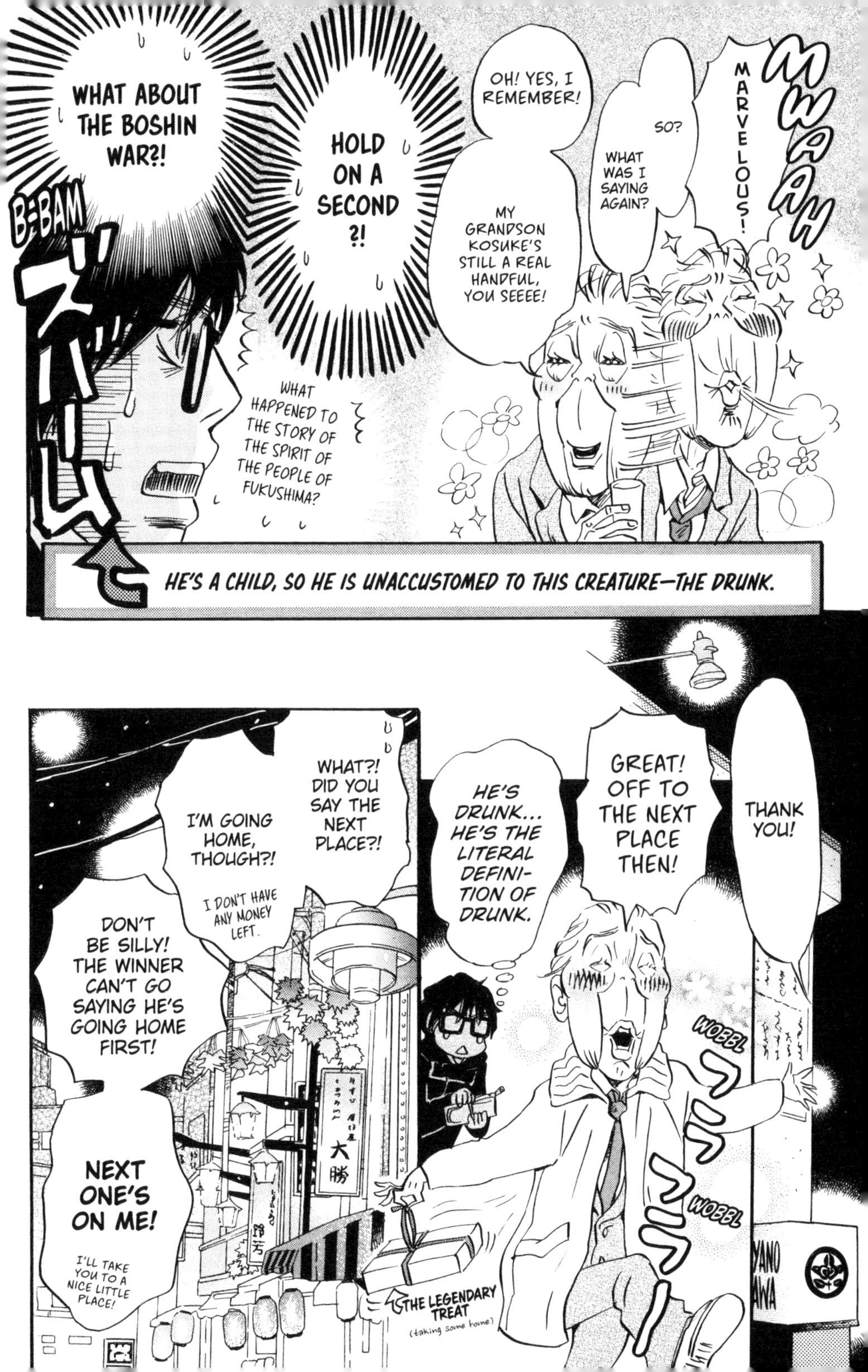
MWAAH
MARVELOUS!
SO?
WHAT WAS I SAYING AGAIN?
OH! YES, I REMEMBER!
MY GRANDSON KOSUKE'S STILL A REAL HANDFUL, YOU SEEEE!
HOLD ON A SECOND?!
WHAT ABOUT THE BOSHIN WAR?!
WHAT HAPPENED TO THE STORY OF THE SPIRIT OF THE PEOPLE OF FUKUSHIMA?
B-BAM
HE'S A CHILD, SO HE IS UNACCUSTOMED TO THIS CREATURE—THE DRUNK.
THANK YOU!
GREAT! OFF TO THE NEXT PLACE THEN!
HE'S DRUNK... HE'S THE LITERAL DEFINITION OF DRUNK.
WOBBL
WOBBL
THE LEGENDARY TREAT
(taking some home)
大勝
WHAT?! DID YOU SAY THE NEXT PLACE?!
I'M GOING HOME, THOUGH?!
I DON'T HAVE ANY MONEY LEFT.
DON'T BE SILLY! THE WINNER CAN'T GO SAYING HE'S GOING HOME FIRST!
NEXT ONE'S ON ME!
I'LL TAKE YOU TO A NICE LITTLE PLACE!

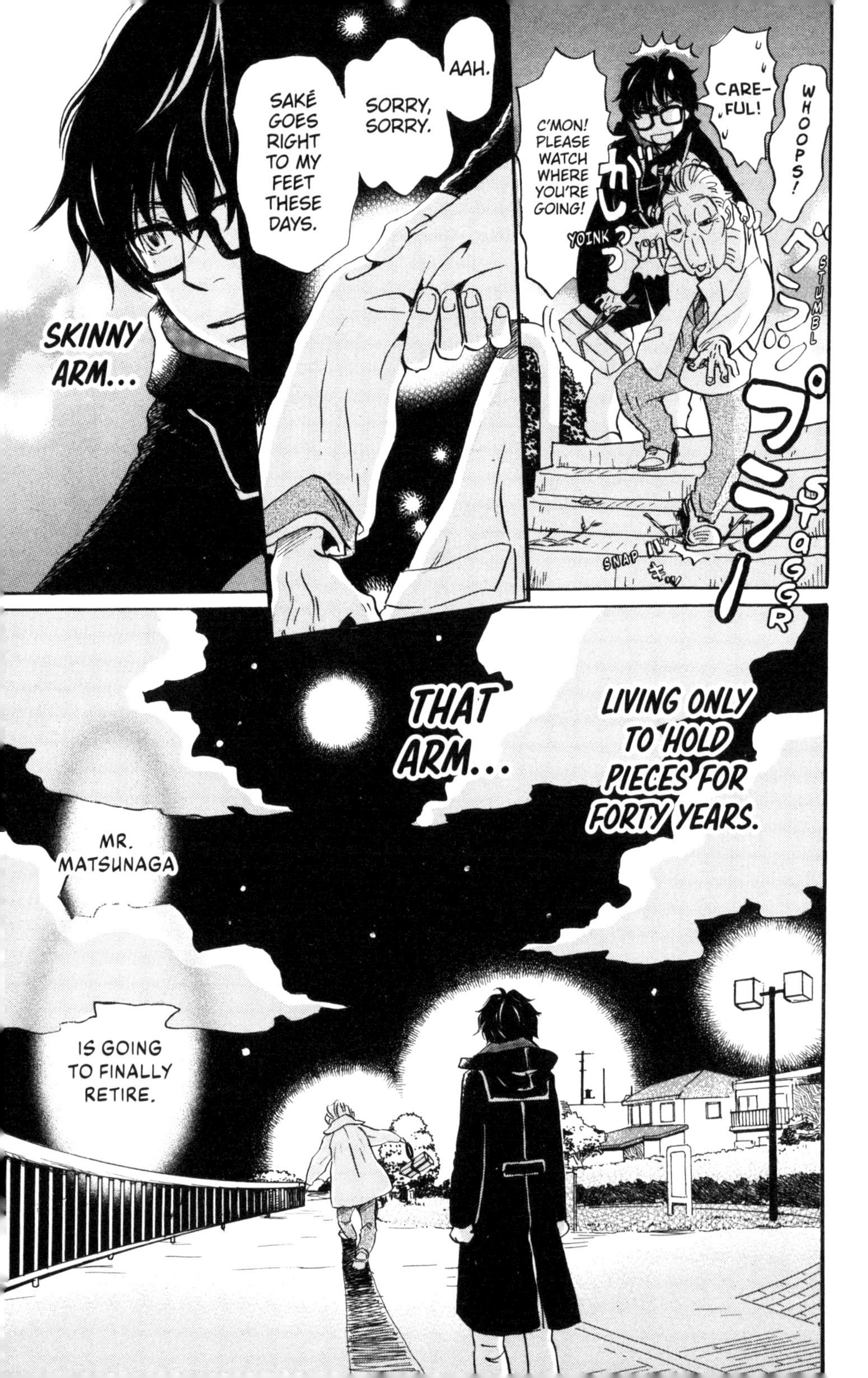
WHOOPS!
CARE-FUL!
C'MON! PLEASE WATCH WHERE YOU'RE GOING!
YOINK
STUMBL
STAGGR
SNAP
AAH.
SORRY, SORRY.
SAKÉ GOES RIGHT TO MY FEET THESE DAYS.
SKINNY ARM...
LIVING ONLY TO HOLD PIECES FOR FORTY YEARS.
THAT ARM...
MR. MATSUNAGA
IS GOING TO FINALLY RETIRE.

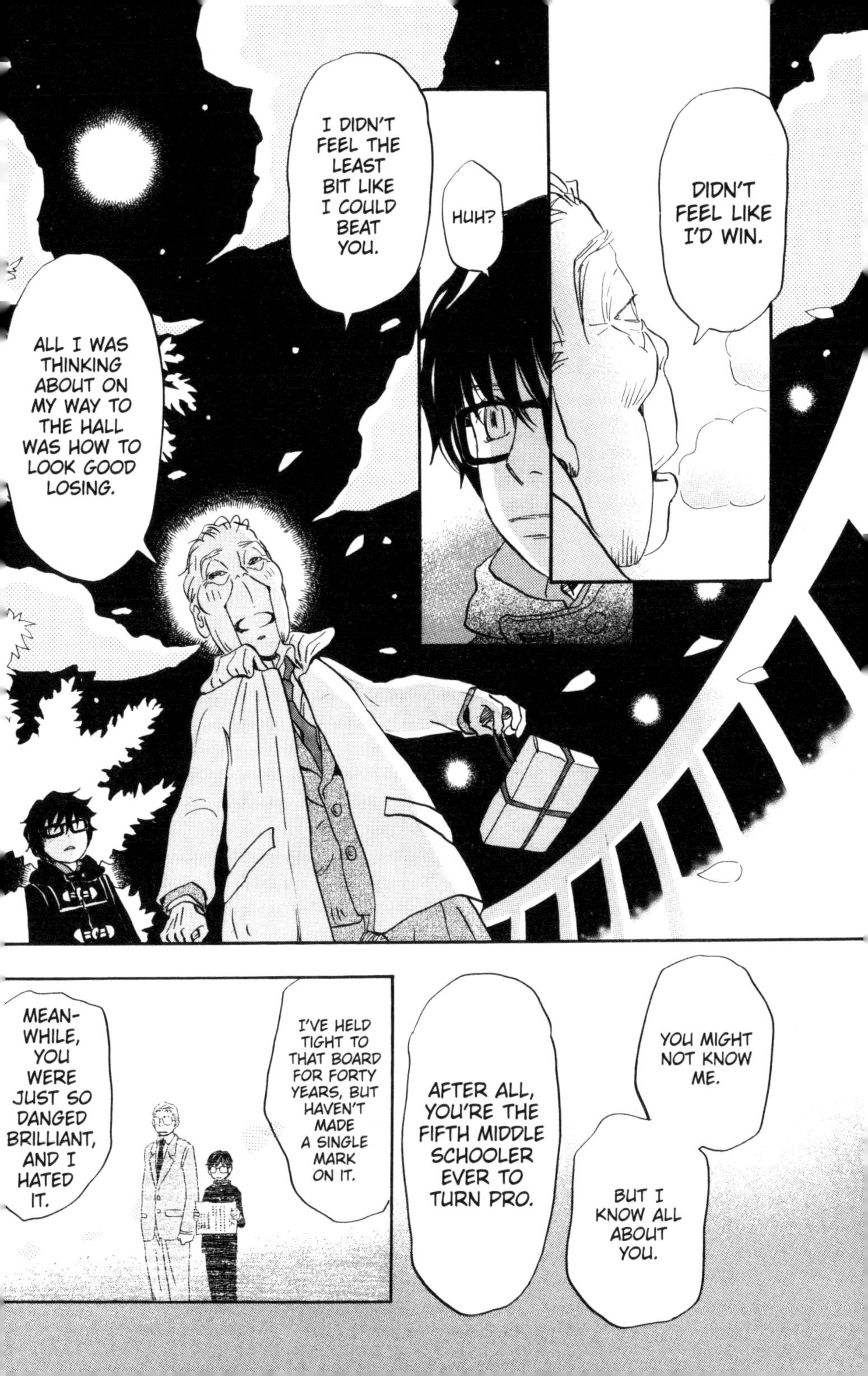
DIDN'T FEEL LIKE I'D WIN.
HUH?
I DIDN'T FEEL THE LEAST BIT LIKE I COULD BEAT YOU.
ALL I WAS THINKING ABOUT ON MY WAY TO THE HALL WAS HOW TO LOOK GOOD LOSING.
YOU MIGHT NOT KNOW ME.
BUT I KNOW ALL ABOUT YOU.
AFTER ALL, YOU'RE THE FIFTH MIDDLE SCHOOLER EVER TO TURN PRO.
I'VE HELD TIGHT TO THAT BOARD FOR FORTY YEARS, BUT HAVEN'T MADE A SINGLE MARK ON IT.
MEAN-WHILE, YOU WERE JUST SO DANGED BRILLIANT, AND I HATED IT.

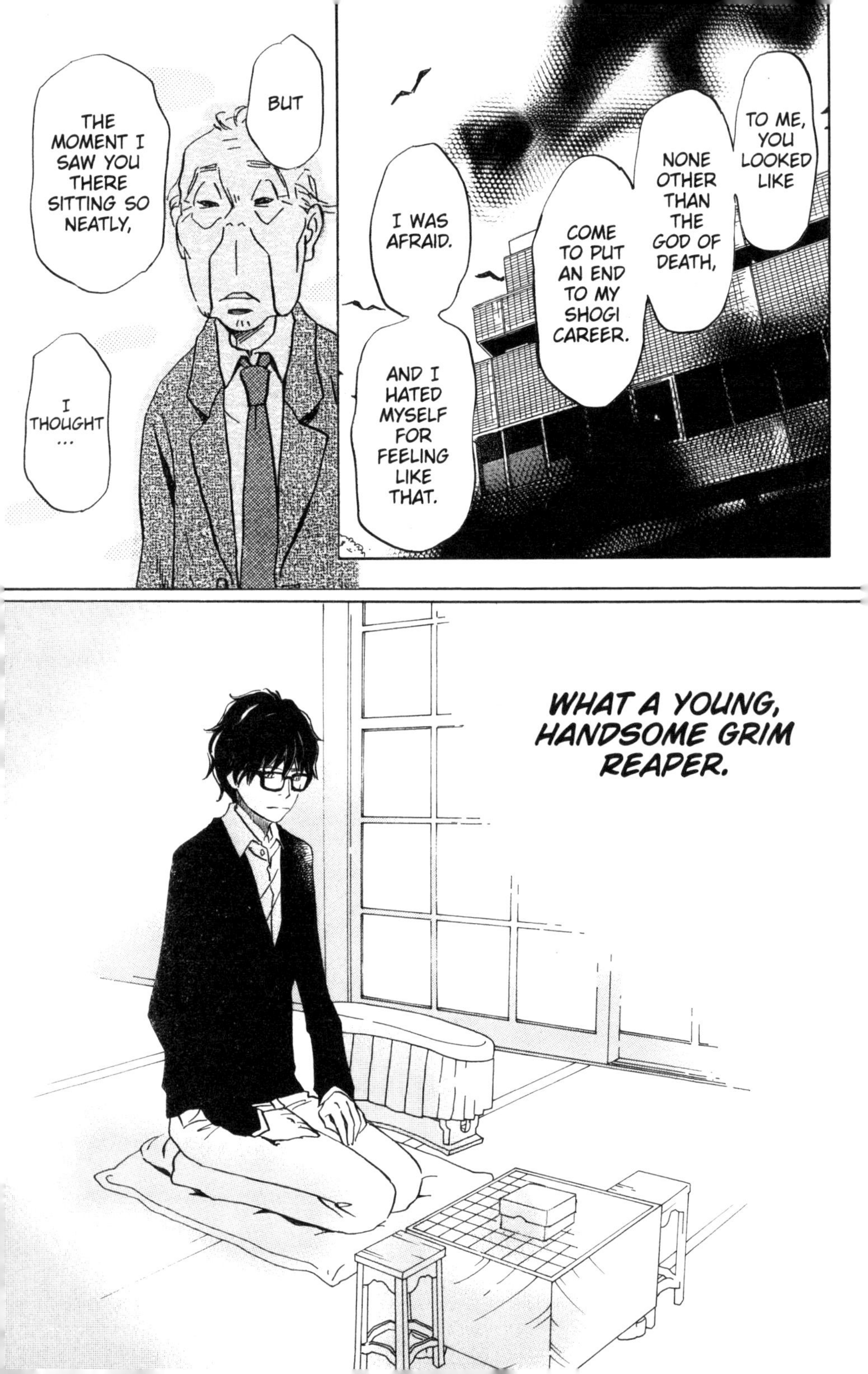
TO ME, YOU LOOKED LIKE
NONE OTHER THAN THE GOD OF DEATH,
COME TO PUT AN END TO MY SHOGI CAREER.
I WAS AFRAID.
AND I HATED MYSELF FOR FEELING LIKE THAT.
BUT
THE MOMENT I SAW YOU THERE SITTING SO NEATLY,
I THOUGHT ...
WHAT A YOUNG, HANDSOME GRIM REAPER.

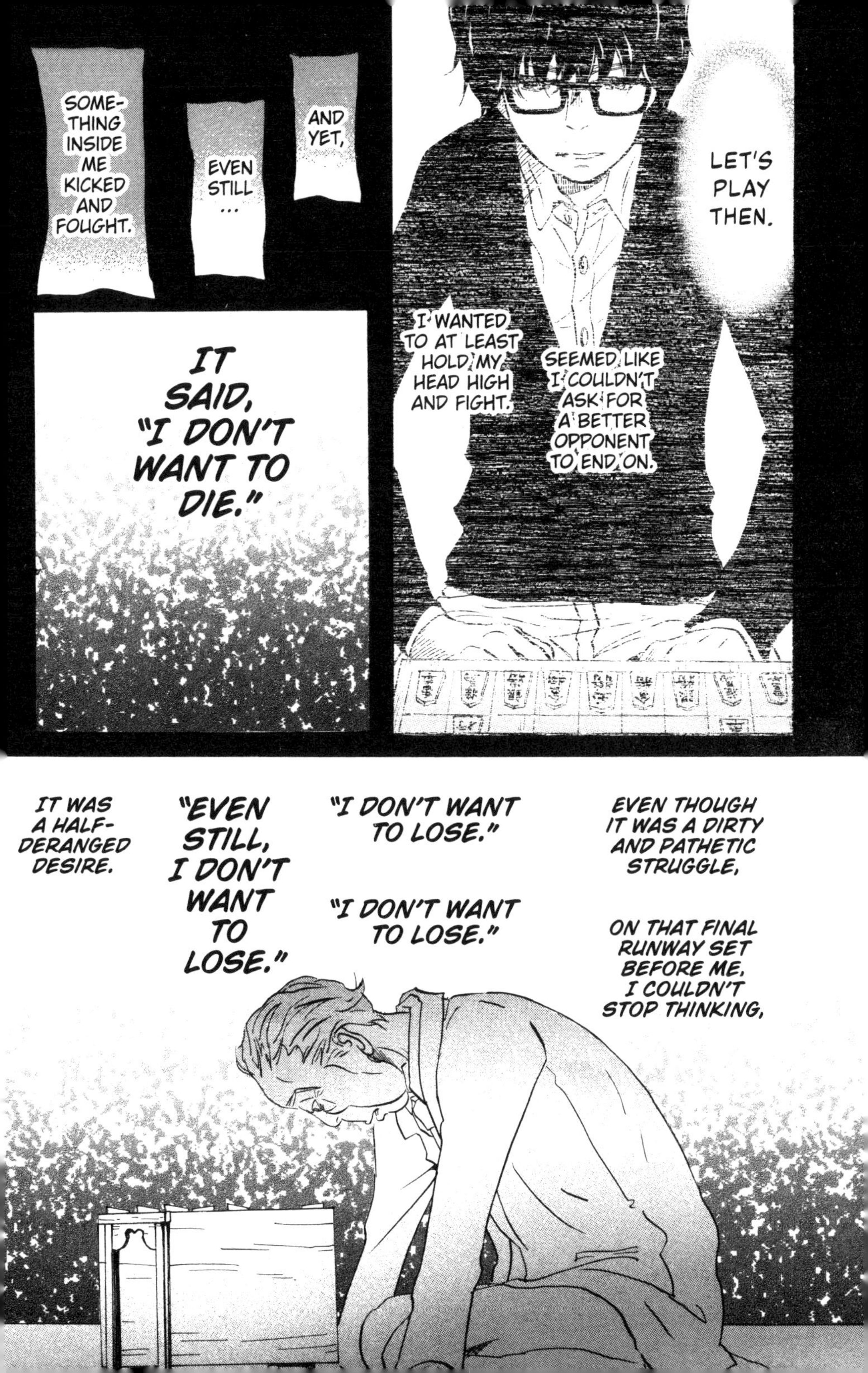
LET'S PLAY THEN.
SEEMED LIKE I COULDN'T ASK FOR A BETTER OPPONENT TO END ON.
I WANTED TO AT LEAST HOLD MY HEAD HIGH AND FIGHT.
AND YET,
EVEN STILL...
SOMETHING INSIDE ME KICKED AND FOUGHT.
IT SAID, "I DON'T WANT TO DIE."
EVEN THOUGH IT WAS A DIRTY AND PATHETIC STRUGGLE,
ON THAT FINAL RUNWAY SET BEFORE ME, I COULDN'T STOP THINKING,
"I DON'T WANT TO LOSE."
"I DON'T WANT TO LOSE."
"EVEN STILL, I DON'T WANT TO LOSE."
IT WAS A HALF-DERANGED DESIRE.

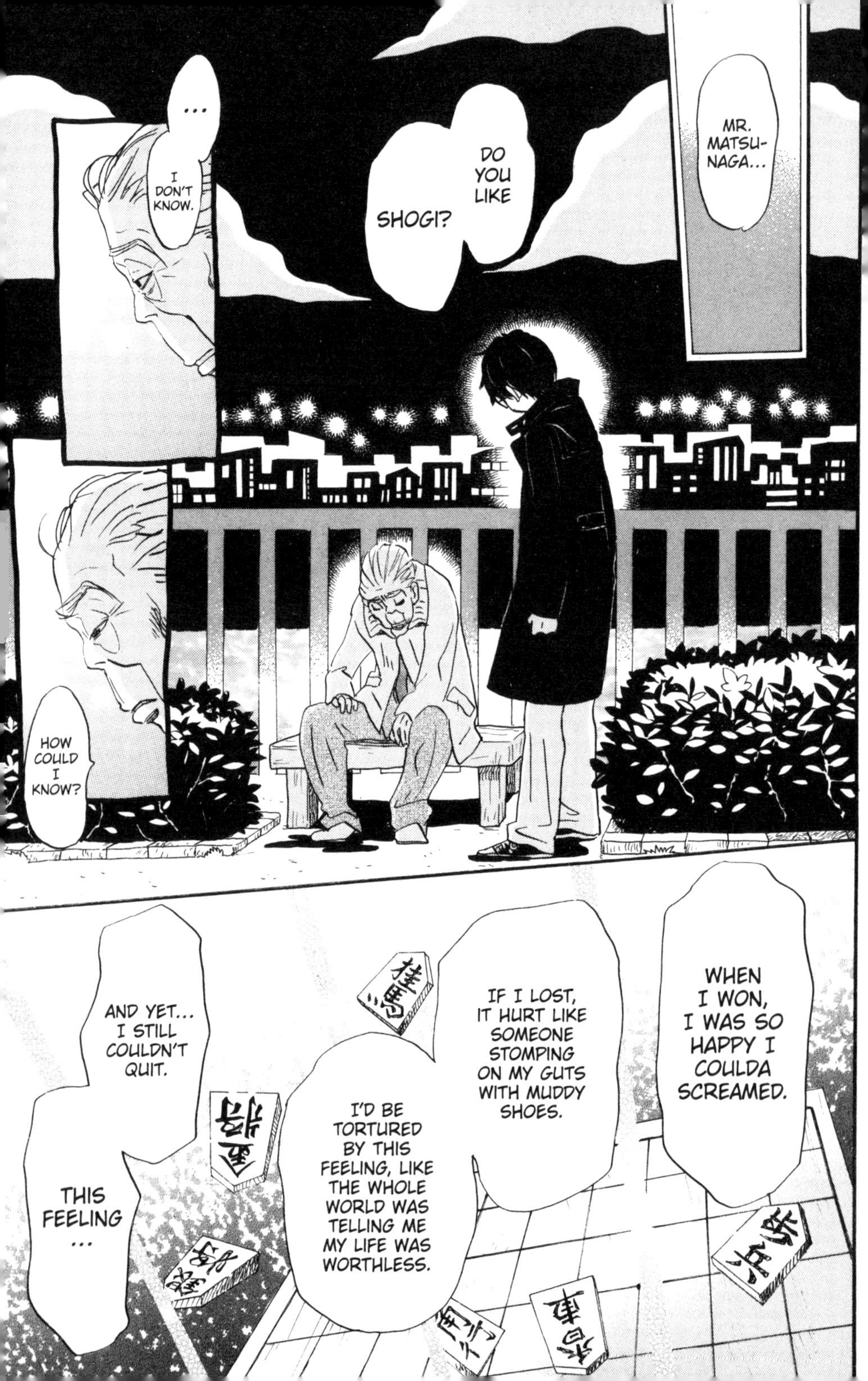
MR. MATSU-NAGA...
DO YOU LIKE SHOGI?
...
I DON'T KNOW.
HOW COULD I KNOW?
WHEN I WON, I WAS SO HAPPY I COULDA SCREAMED.
IF I LOST, IT HURT LIKE SOMEONE STOMPING ON MY GUTS WITH MUDDY SHOES.
I'D BE TORTURED BY THIS FEELING, LIKE THE WHOLE WORLD WAS TELLING ME MY LIFE WAS WORTHLESS.
AND YET... I STILL COULDN'T QUIT.
THIS FEELING ...

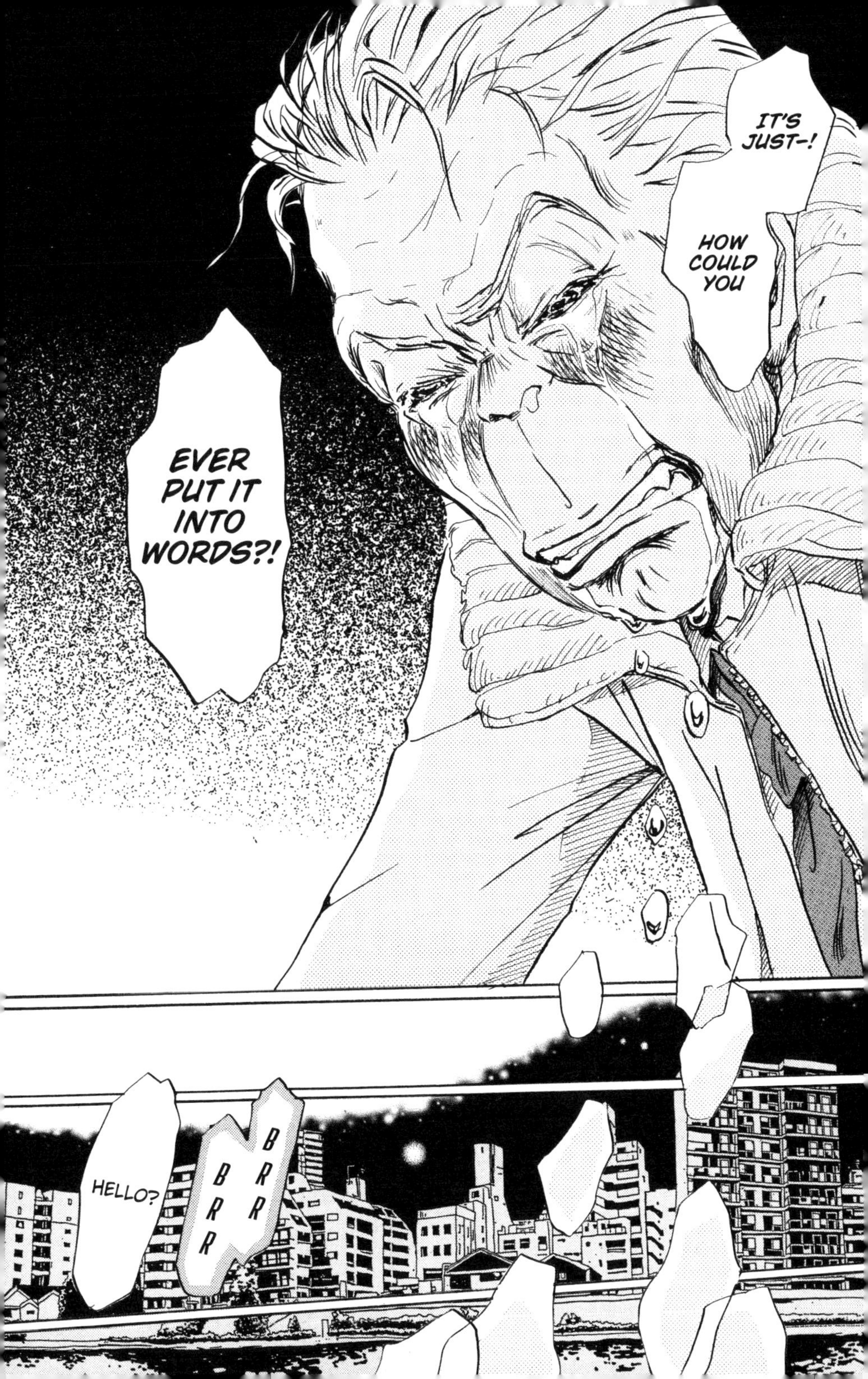
IT'S JUST-!
HOW COULD YOU
EVER PUT IT INTO WORDS?!
BRRR BRRR
HELLO?

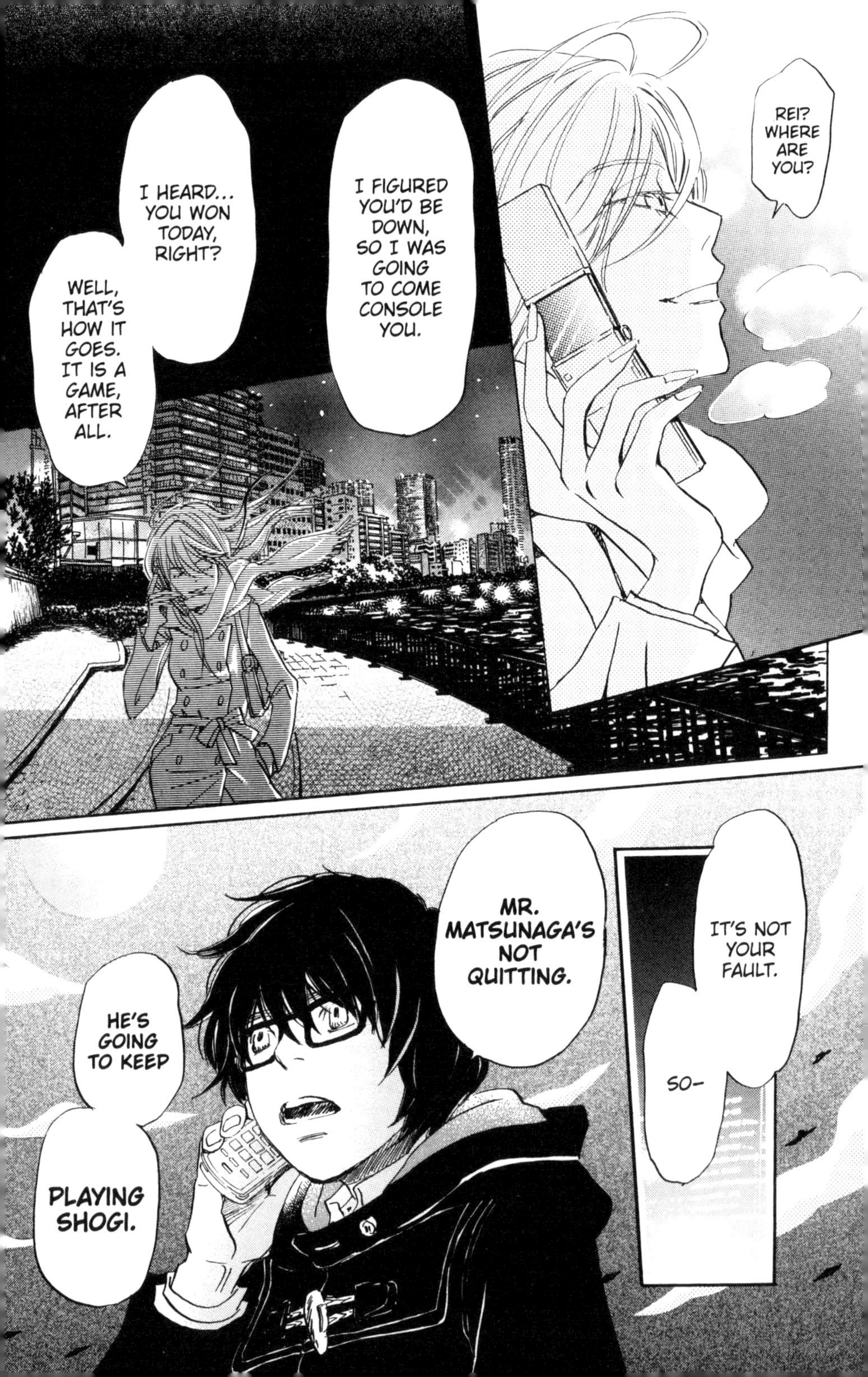
REI? WHERE ARE YOU?
I FIGURED YOU'D BE DOWN, SO I WAS GOING TO COME CONSOLE YOU.
I HEARD... YOU WON TODAY, RIGHT?
WELL, THAT'S HOW IT GOES. IT IS A GAME, AFTER ALL.
IT'S NOT YOUR FAULT.
SO–
MR. MATSUNAGA'S NOT QUITTING.
HE'S GOING TO KEEP
PLAYING SHOGI.

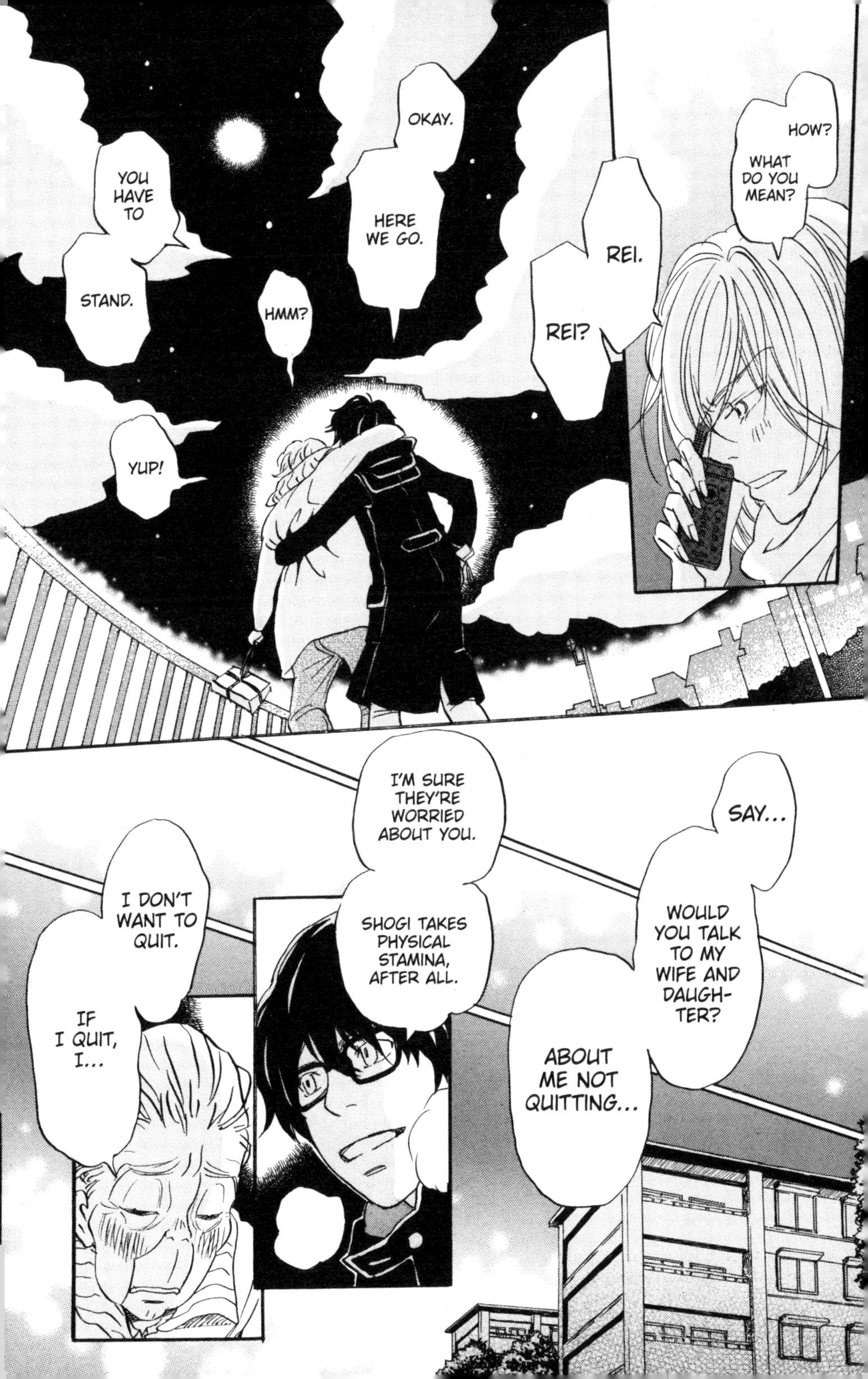
HOW?
WHAT DO YOU MEAN?
REI.
REI?
OKAY.
HERE WE GO.
HMM?
YOU HAVE TO
STAND.
YUP!
SAY...
WOULD YOU TALK TO MY WIFE AND DAUGH-TER?
ABOUT ME NOT QUITTING...
I'M SURE THEY'RE WORRIED ABOUT YOU.
SHOGI TAKES PHYSICAL STAMINA, AFTER ALL.
I DON'T WANT TO QUIT.
IF I QUIT, I...

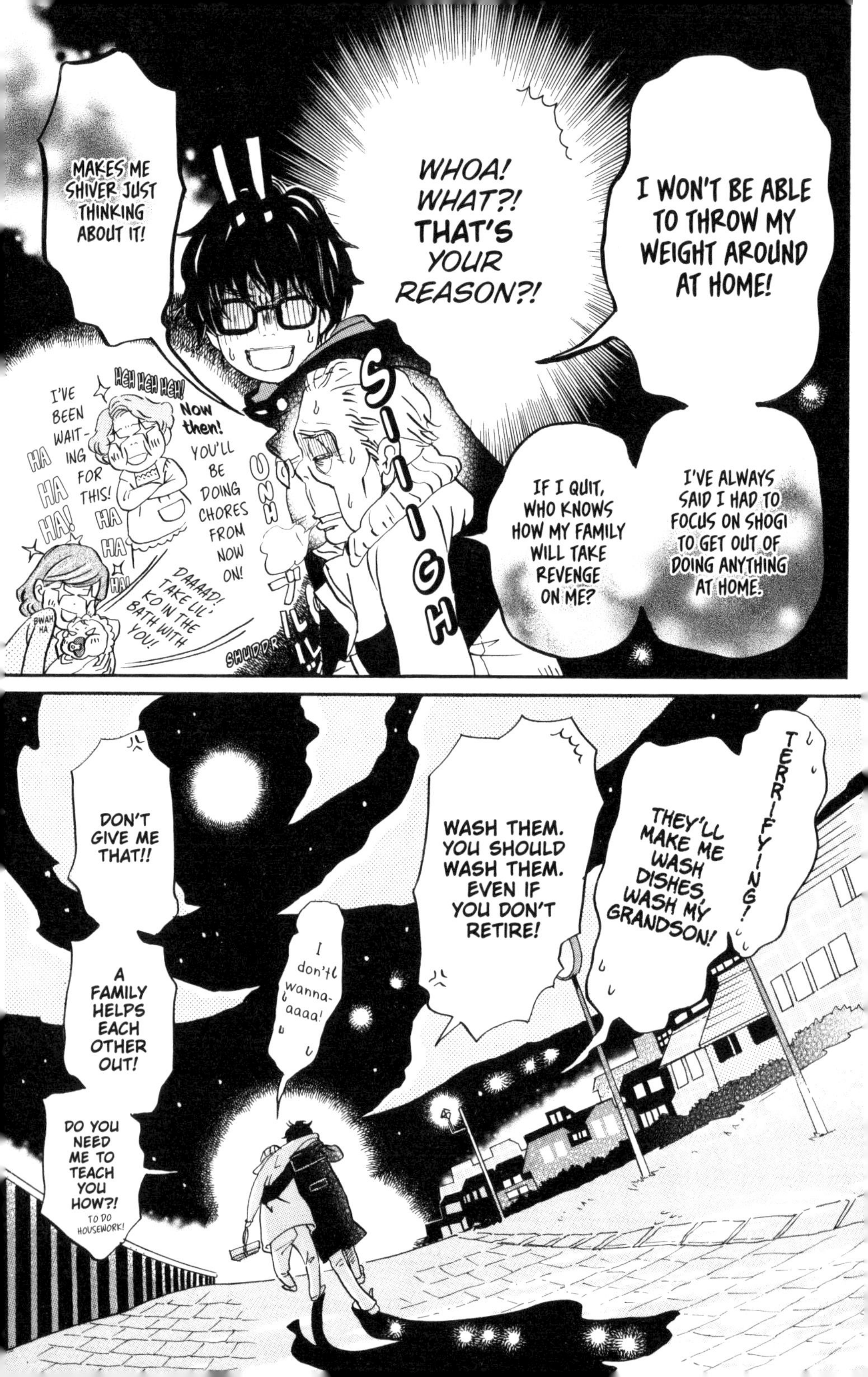
I WON'T BE ABLE TO THROW MY WEIGHT AROUND AT HOME!
I'VE ALWAYS SAID I HAD TO FOCUS ON SHOGI TO GET OUT OF DOING ANYTHING AT HOME.
IF I QUIT, WHO KNOWS HOW MY FAMILY WILL TAKE REVENGE ON ME?
WHOA! WHAT?! THAT'S YOUR REASON?!
SIIIIGH
MAKES ME SHIVER JUST THINKING ABOUT IT!
UNH
HEH HEH HEH!
Now then!
YOU'LL BE DOING CHORES FROM NOW ON!
I'VE BEEN WAIT-ING FOR THIS!
HA HA HA!
HA HA HA!
DAAAAD! TAKE LIL' KO IN THE BATH WITH YOU!
BWAH HA
SHUDDR
TERRIFYING!
THEY'LL MAKE ME WASH DISHES, WASH MY GRANDSON!
WASH THEM. YOU SHOULD WASH THEM. EVEN IF YOU DON'T RETIRE!
I don't wanna-aaaa!
DON'T GIVE ME THAT!!
A FAMILY HELPS EACH OTHER OUT!
DO YOU NEED ME TO TEACH YOU HOW?!
TO DO HOUSEWORK!

MS. **POCKET SKWERL**

CHARACTER FROM AN EDUCATIONAL SHOW
THAT HINA AND MOMO LIKE. SHE LIVES
IN THE POCKET OF THE WOMAN WHO
HOSTS THE SHOW.

March Comes In Like a Lion

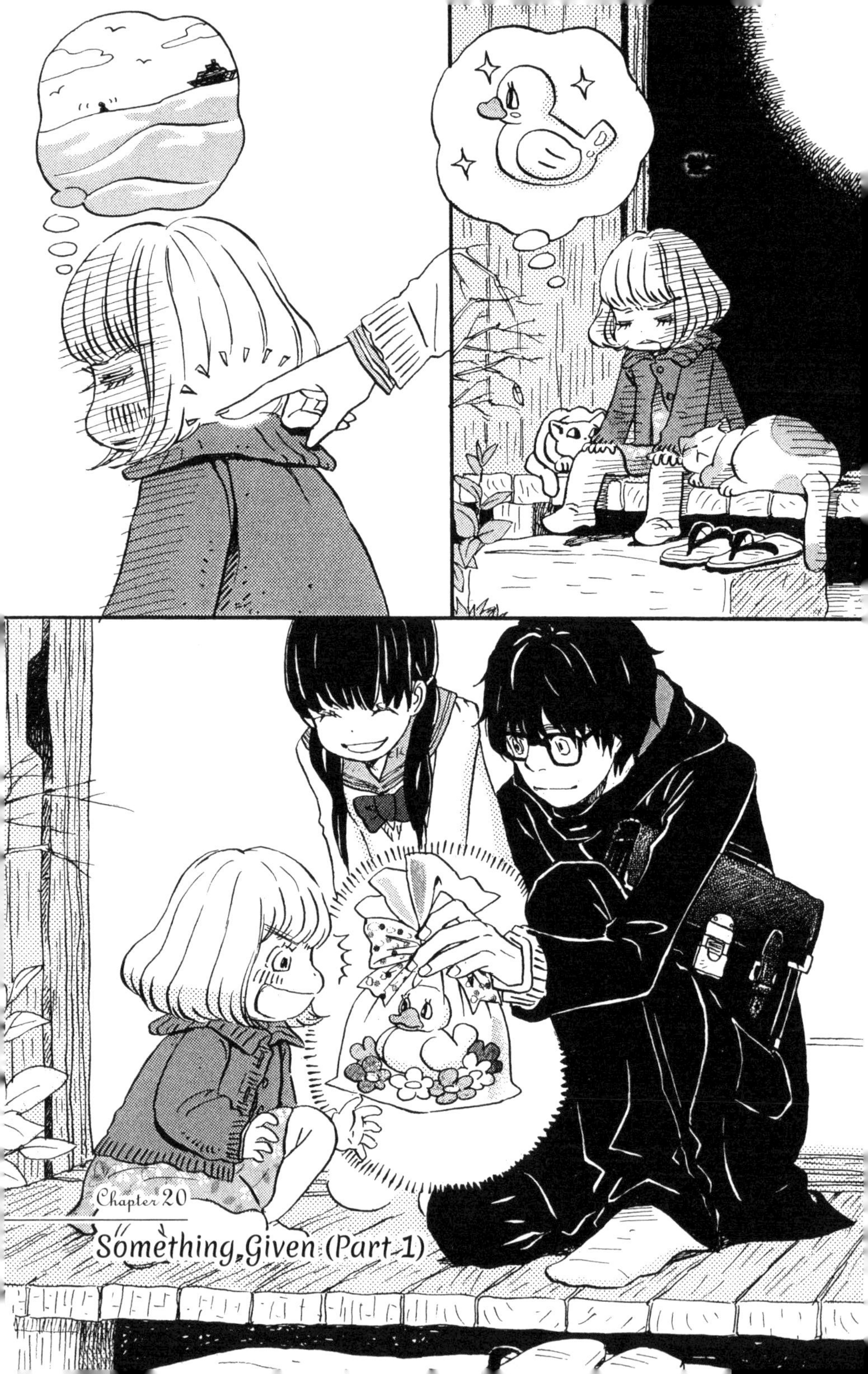
Chapter 20
Something Given (Part 1)

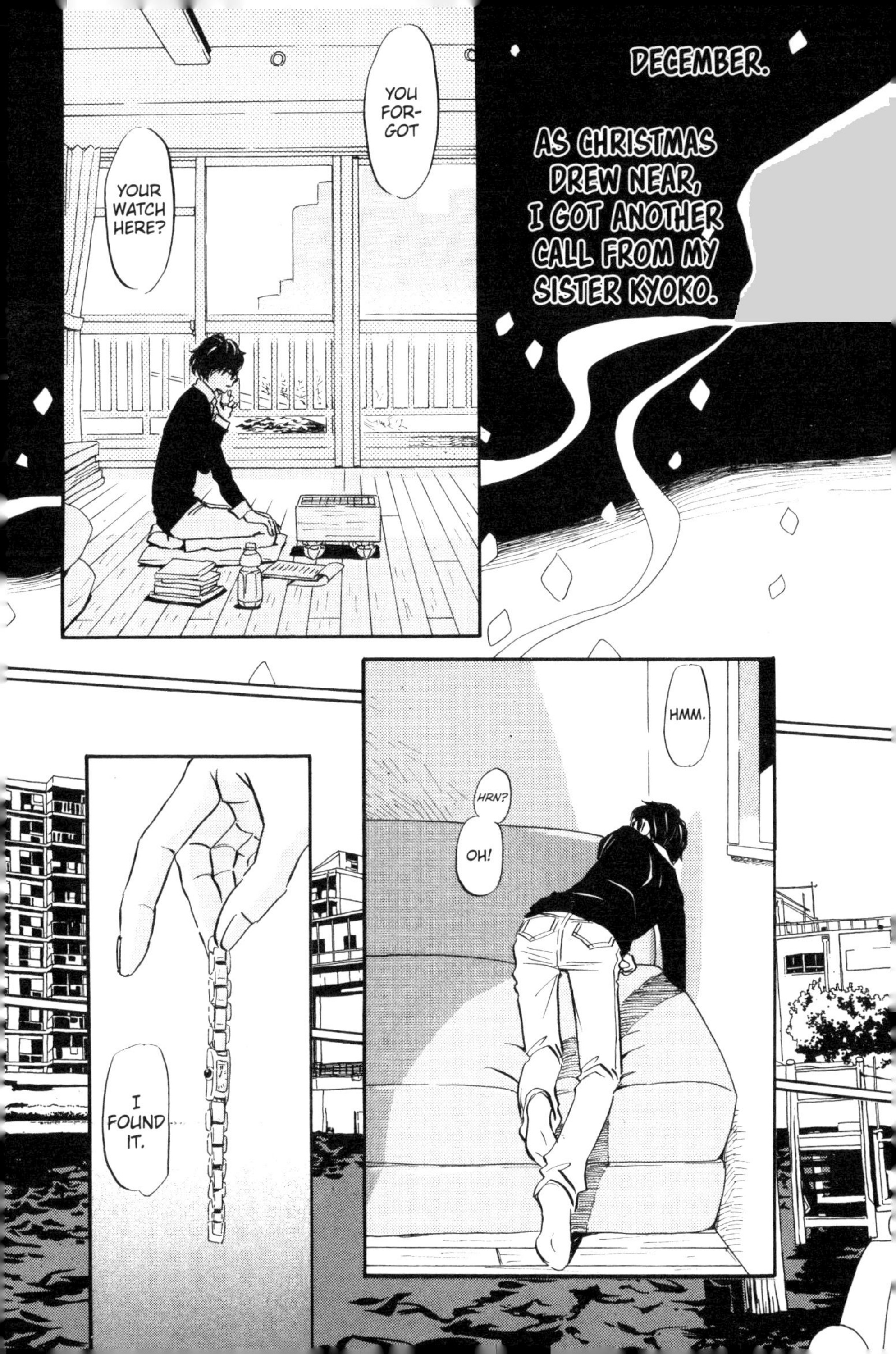
DECEMBER.
AS CHRISTMAS DREW NEAR, I GOT ANOTHER CALL FROM MY SISTER KYOKO.
YOU FOR-GOT
YOUR WATCH HERE?
HMM.
HRN?
OH!
I FOUND IT.

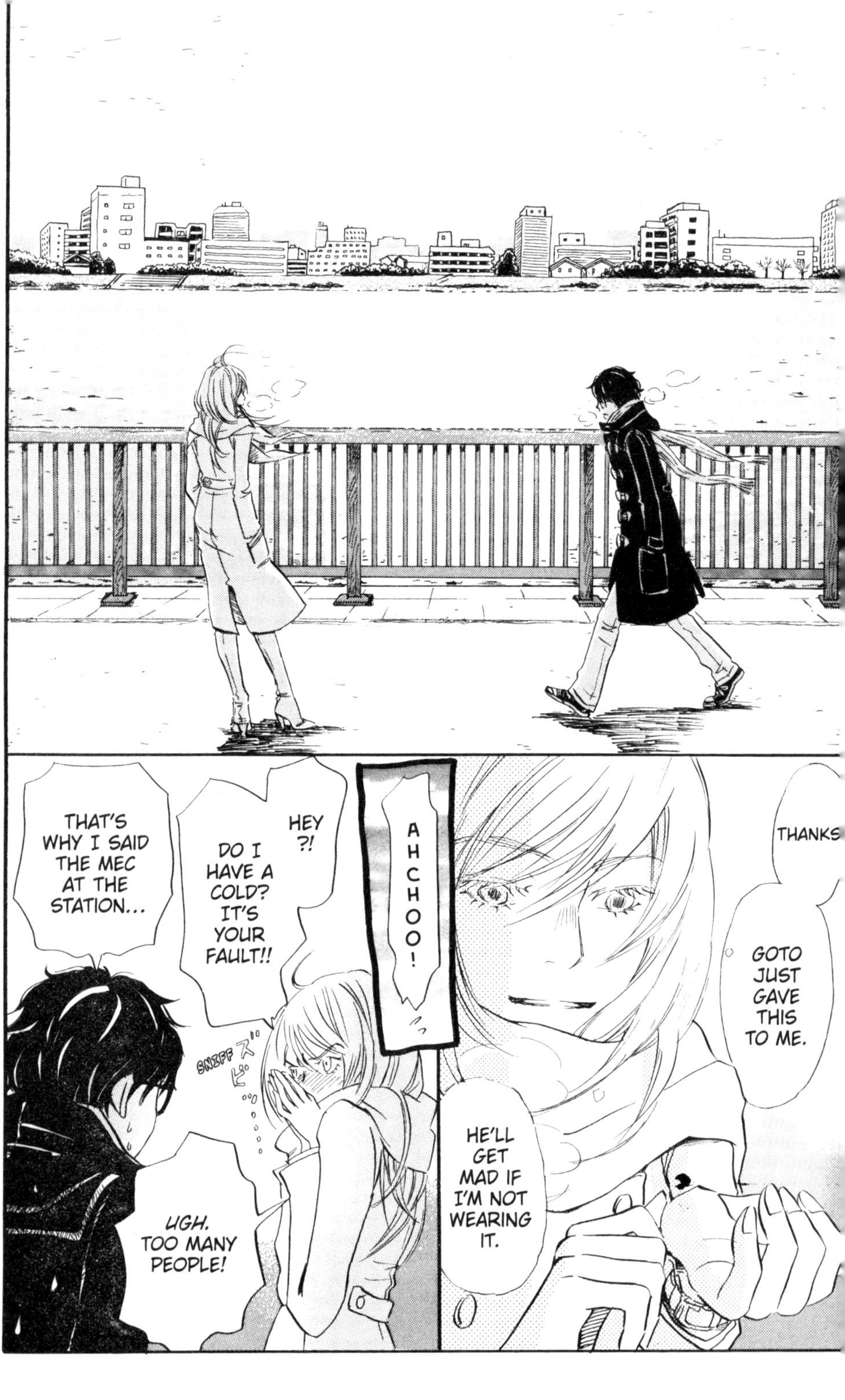
THANKS
GOTO JUST GAVE THIS TO ME.
HE'LL GET MAD IF I'M NOT WEARING IT.
AHCHOO!
HEY ?!
DO I HAVE A COLD? IT'S YOUR FAULT!!
THAT'S WHY I SAID THE MEC AT THE STATION...
SNIFF ズピ
UGH. TOO MANY PEOPLE!

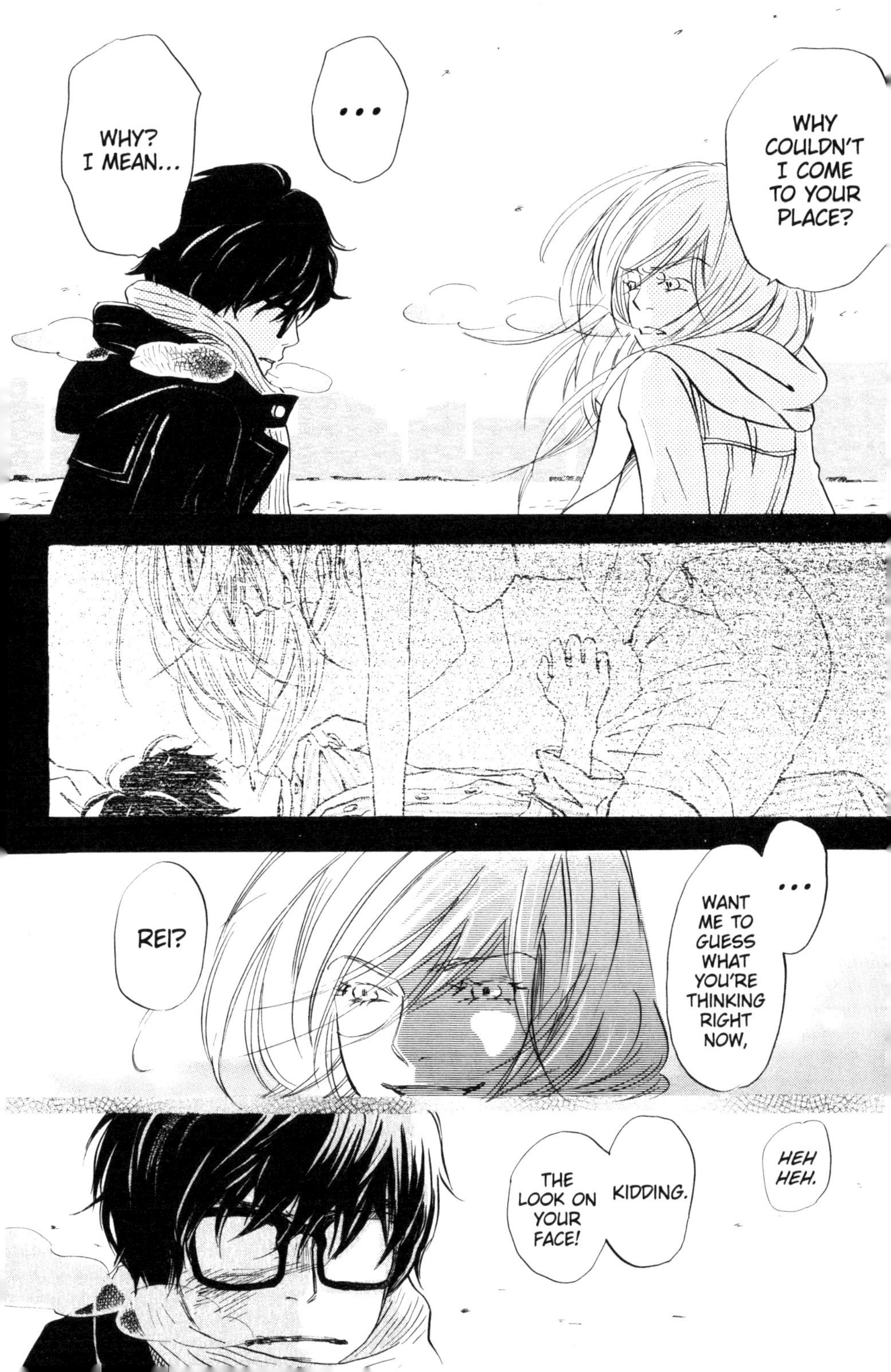
WHY COULDN'T I COME TO YOUR PLACE?
...
WHY? I MEAN...
...
WANT ME TO GUESS WHAT YOU'RE THINKING RIGHT NOW,
REI?
HEH HEH.
KIDDING.
THE LOOK ON YOUR FACE!

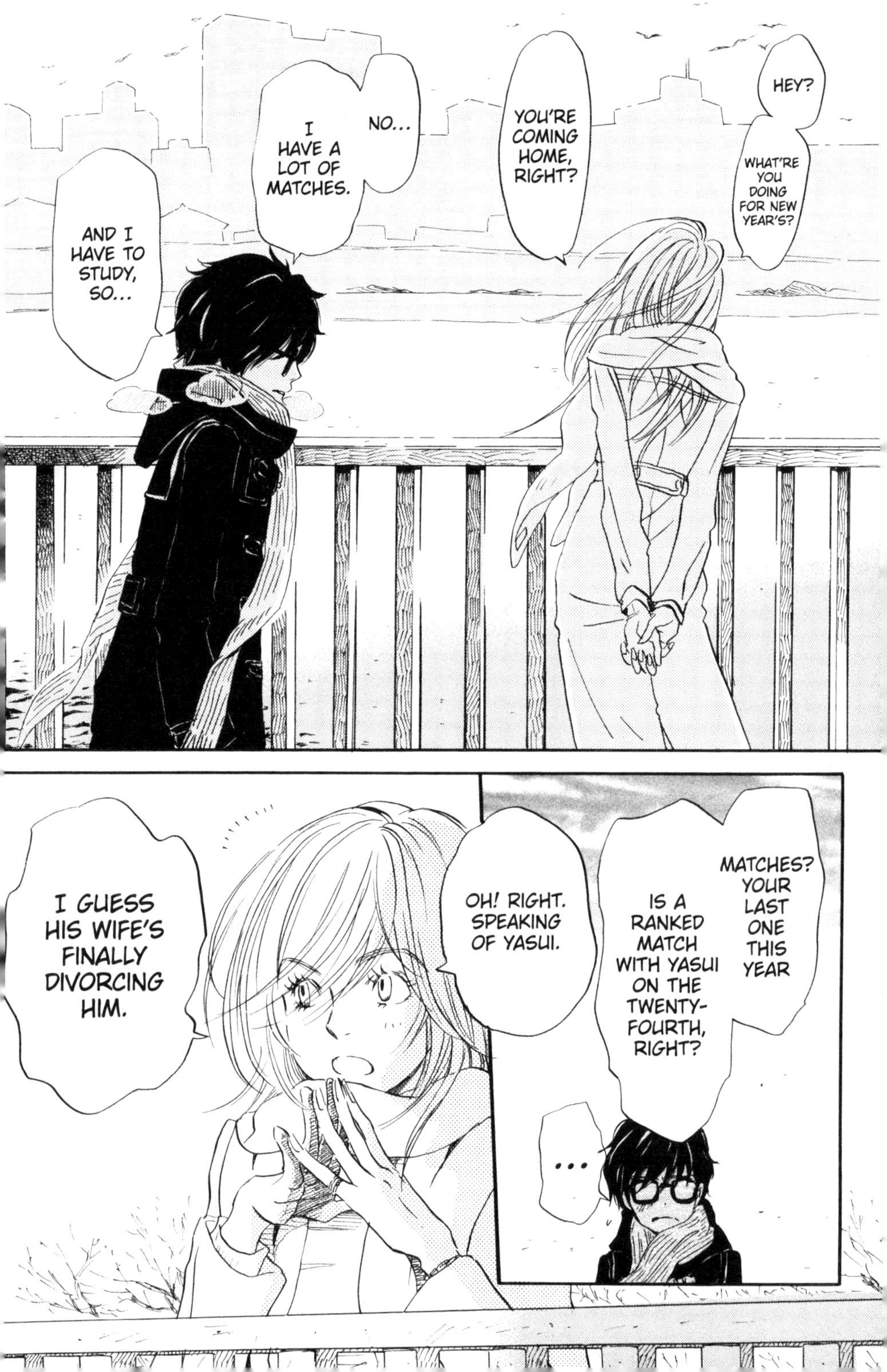
HEY?
WHAT'RE YOU DOING FOR NEW YEAR'S?
YOU'RE COMING HOME, RIGHT?
NO...
I HAVE A LOT OF MATCHES.
AND I HAVE TO STUDY, SO...
MATCHES? YOUR LAST ONE THIS YEAR
IS A RANKED MATCH WITH YASUI ON THE TWENTY-FOURTH, RIGHT?
...
OH! RIGHT. SPEAKING OF YASUI.
I GUESS HIS WIFE'S FINALLY DIVORCING HIM.

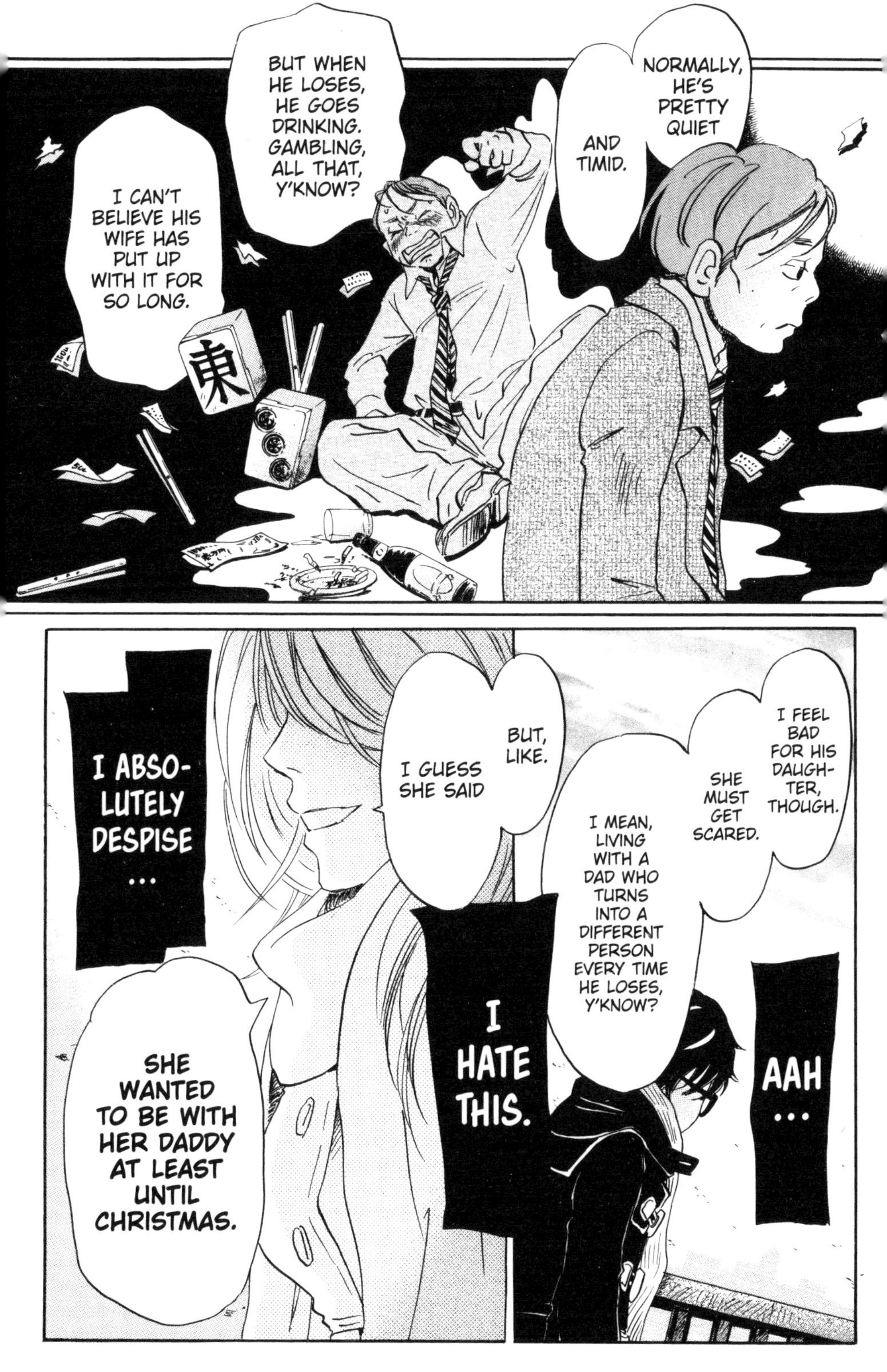
NORMALLY, HE'S PRETTY QUIET
AND TIMID.
BUT WHEN HE LOSES, HE GOES DRINKING. GAMBLING, ALL THAT, Y'KNOW?
I CAN'T BELIEVE HIS WIFE HAS PUT UP WITH IT FOR SO LONG.
I FEEL BAD FOR HIS DAUGHTER, THOUGH.
SHE MUST GET SCARED.
I MEAN, LIVING WITH A DAD WHO TURNS INTO A DIFFERENT PERSON EVERY TIME HE LOSES, Y'KNOW?
AAH...
I HATE THIS.
BUT, LIKE.
I GUESS SHE SAID
SHE WANTED TO BE WITH HER DADDY AT LEAST UNTIL CHRISTMAS.
I ABSO-LUTELY DESPISE...

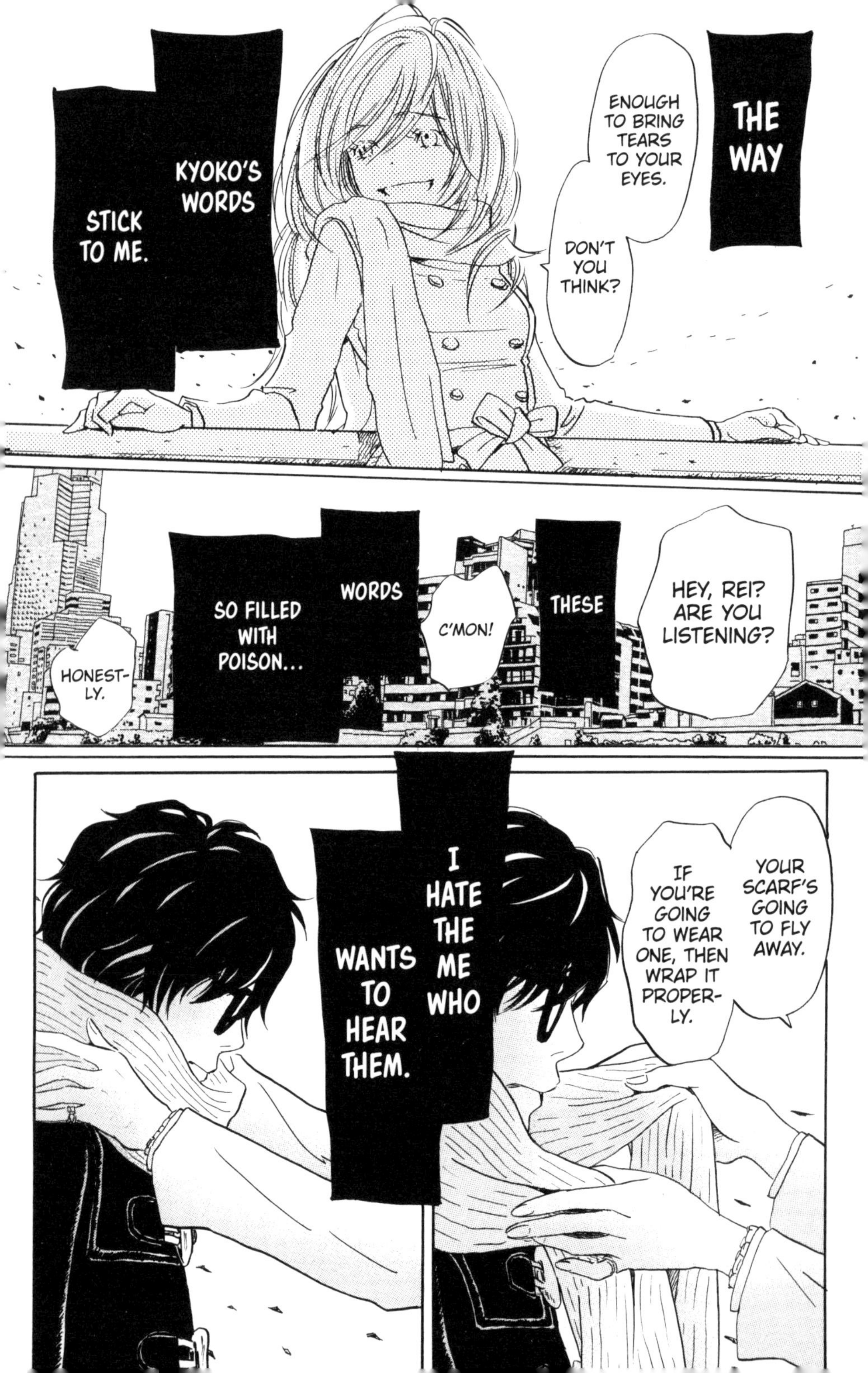
THE WAY
ENOUGH TO BRING TEARS TO YOUR EYES.
DON'T YOU THINK?
KYOKO'S WORDS
STICK TO ME.
HEY, REI? ARE YOU LISTENING?
THESE
C'MON!
WORDS
SO FILLED WITH POISON...
HONESTLY.
YOUR SCARF'S GOING TO FLY AWAY.
IF YOU'RE GOING TO WEAR ONE, THEN WRAP IT PROPERLY.
I HATE THE ME WHO
WANTS TO HEAR THEM.

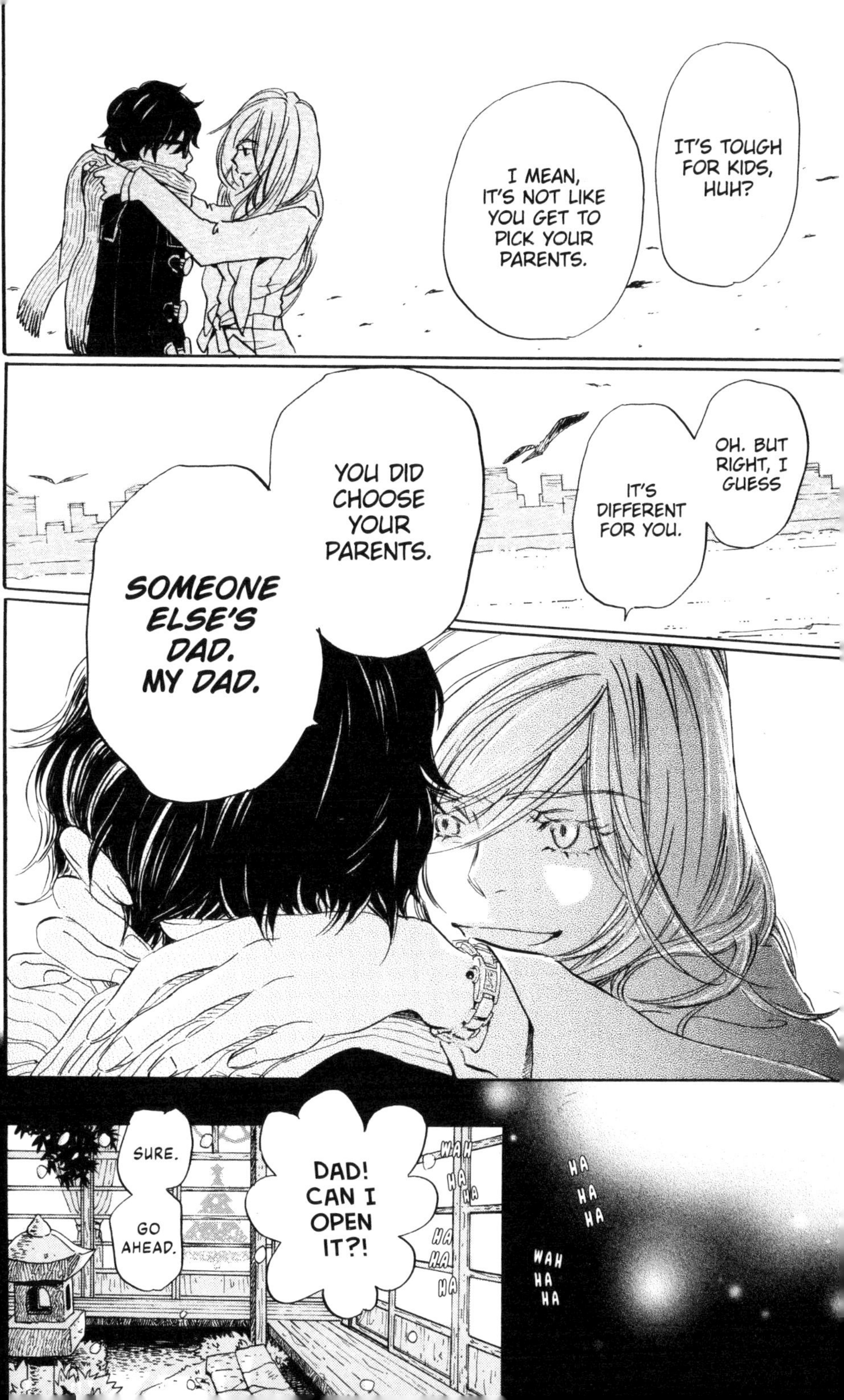
IT'S TOUGH FOR KIDS, HUH?
I MEAN, IT'S NOT LIKE YOU GET TO PICK YOUR PARENTS.
OH. BUT RIGHT, I GUESS
IT'S DIFFERENT FOR YOU.
YOU DID CHOOSE YOUR PARENTS.
SOMEONE ELSE'S DAD. MY DAD.
HA HA HA
WAH HA HA
WAH HA HA
DAD! CAN I OPEN IT?!
HA HA HA
SURE.
GO AHEAD.

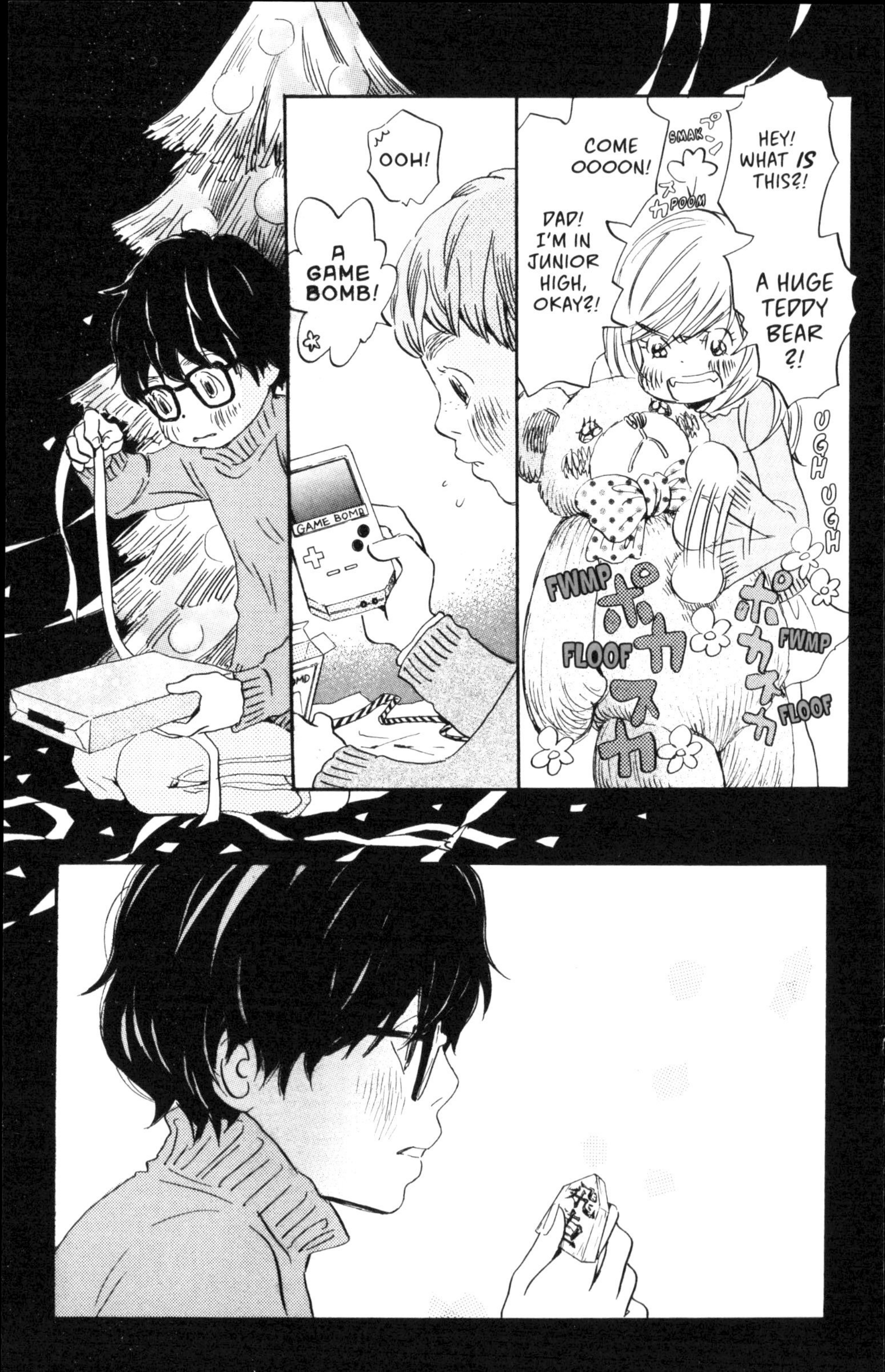
HEY! WHAT IS THIS?!
SMAK
POOM
COME OOOON!
A HUGE TEDDY BEAR ?!
DAD! I'M IN JUNIOR HIGH, OKAY?!
UGH UGH
FWMP
FLOOF
FWMP
FLOOF
OOH!
A GAME BOMB!
GAME BOMB

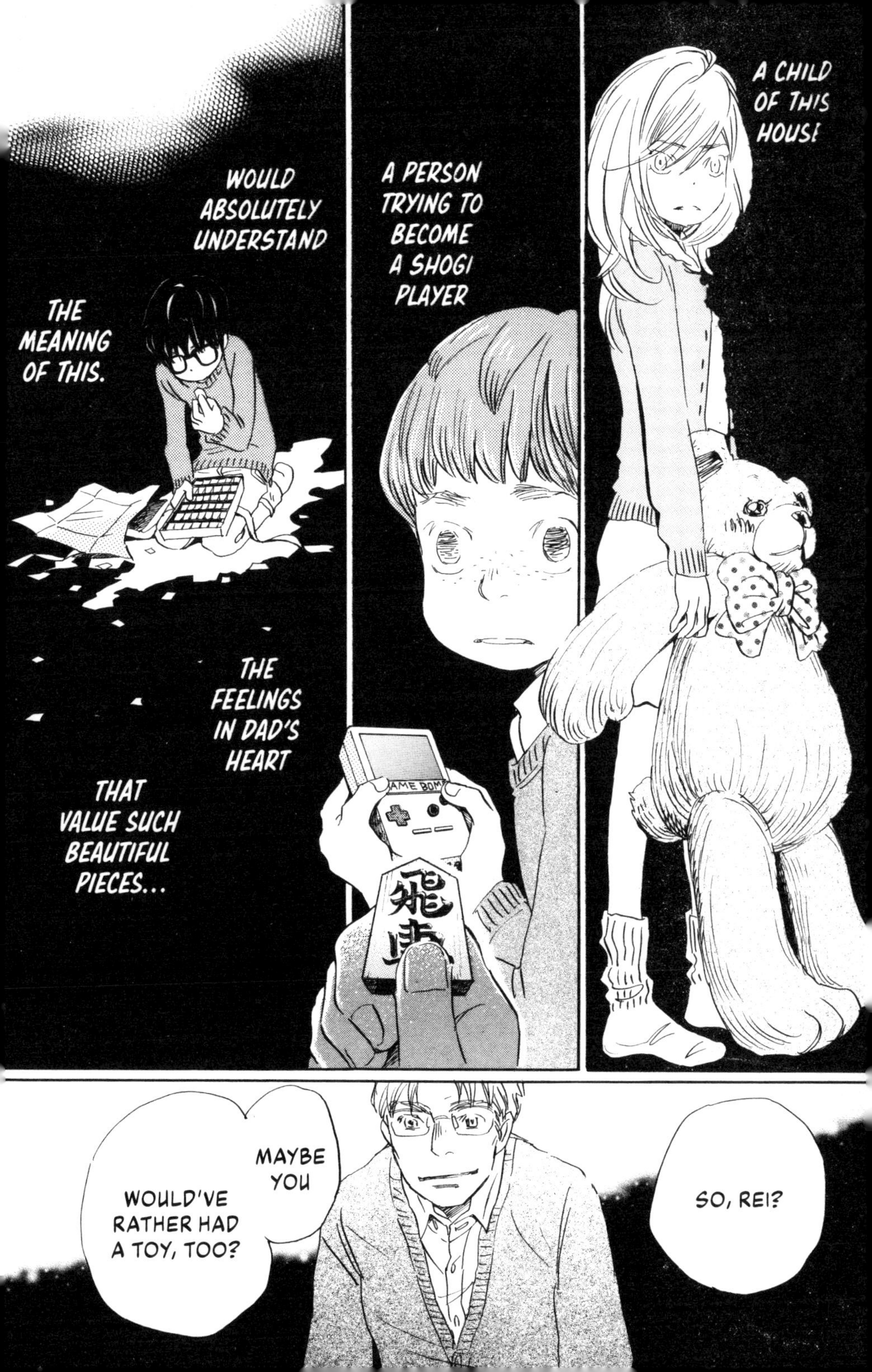
A CHILD OF THIS HOUSE
A PERSON TRYING TO BECOME A SHOGI PLAYER
WOULD ABSOLUTELY UNDERSTAND
THE MEANING OF THIS.
THE FEELINGS IN DAD'S HEART
THAT VALUE SUCH BEAUTIFUL PIECES...
SO, REI?
MAYBE YOU WOULD'VE RATHER HAD A TOY, TOO?

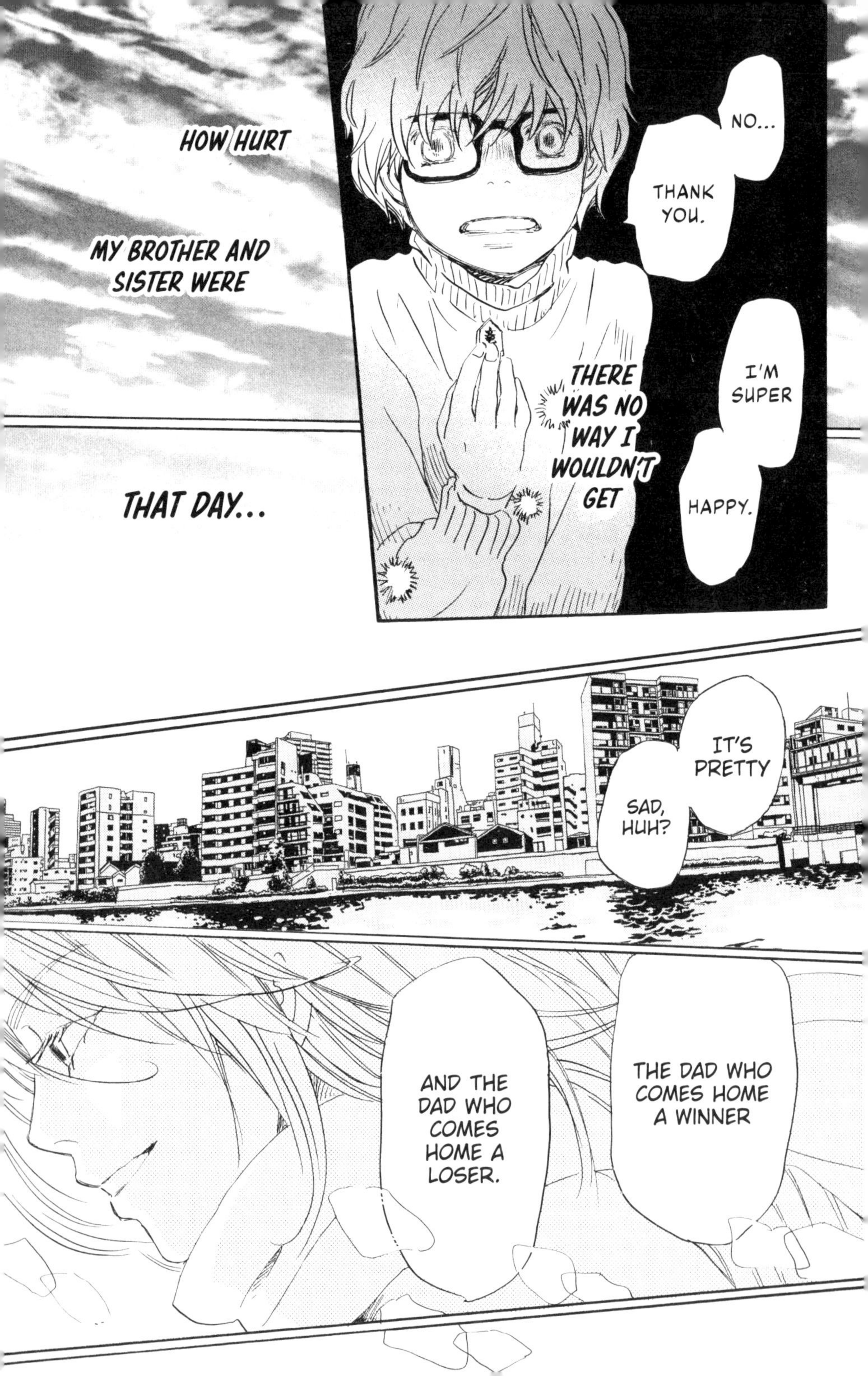
NO...
THANK YOU.
I'M SUPER
HAPPY.
THERE WAS NO WAY I WOULDN'T GET
HOW HURT
MY BROTHER AND SISTER WERE
THAT DAY...
IT'S PRETTY
SAD, HUH?
THE DAD WHO COMES HOME A WINNER
AND THE DAD WHO COMES HOME A LOSER.

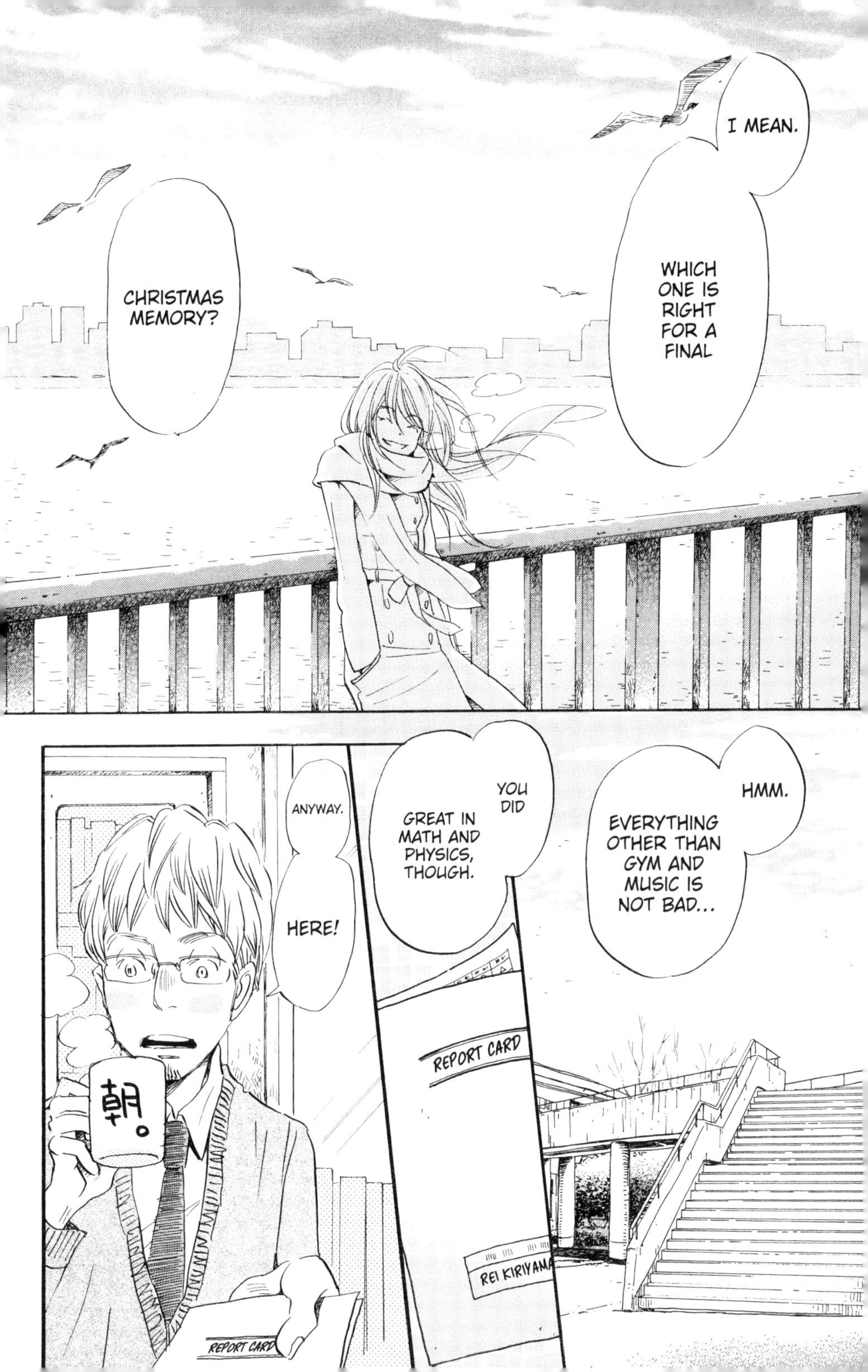
I MEAN.
WHICH ONE IS RIGHT FOR A FINAL
CHRISTMAS MEMORY?
HMM.
EVERYTHING OTHER THAN GYM AND MUSIC IS NOT BAD...
YOU DID GREAT IN MATH AND PHYSICS, THOUGH.
REPORT CARD
REI KIRIYAMA
ANYWAY.
HERE!
朝。
REPORT CARD

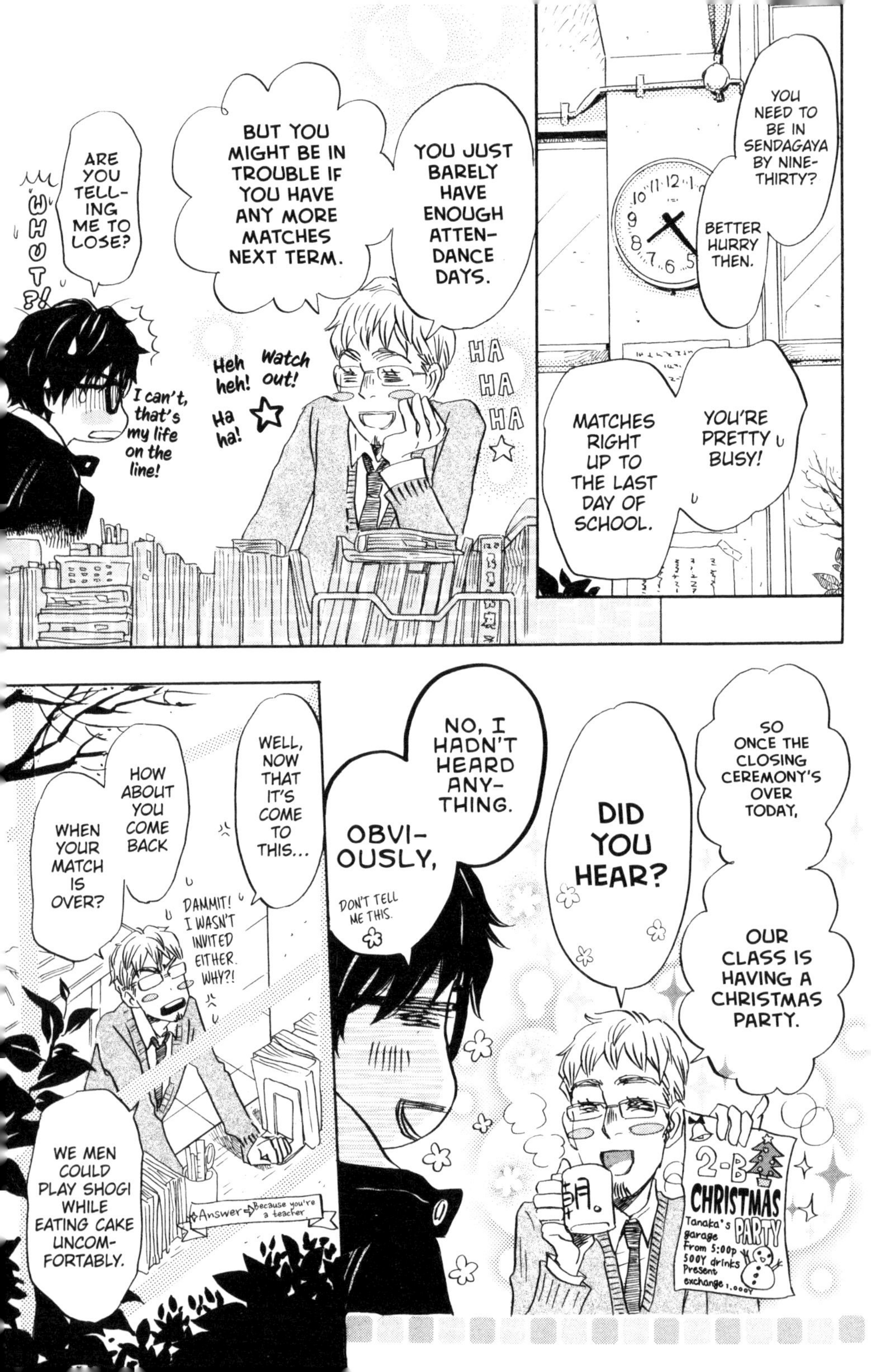
YOU NEED TO BE IN SENDAGAYA BY NINE-THIRTY?
BETTER HURRY THEN.
YOU'RE PRETTY BUSY!
MATCHES RIGHT UP TO THE LAST DAY OF SCHOOL.
YOU JUST BARELY HAVE ENOUGH ATTENDANCE DAYS.
BUT YOU MIGHT BE IN TROUBLE IF YOU HAVE ANY MORE MATCHES NEXT TERM.
HA HA HA
Watch out!
Heh heh!
Ha ha!
WHUT?!
ARE YOU TELLING ME TO LOSE?
I can't, that's my life on the line!
SO ONCE THE CLOSING CEREMONY'S OVER TODAY,
OUR CLASS IS HAVING A CHRISTMAS PARTY.
DID YOU HEAR?
2-B CHRISTMAS PARTY
Tanaka's garage
From 5:00p
500Y drinks
Present exchange 1,000Y
NO, I HADN'T HEARD ANYTHING.
OBVIOUSLY,
DON'T TELL ME THIS.
WELL, NOW THAT IT'S COME TO THIS...
HOW ABOUT YOU COME BACK
WHEN YOUR MATCH IS OVER?
DAMMIT! I WASN'T INVITED EITHER. WHY?!
WE MEN COULD PLAY SHOGI WHILE EATING CAKE UNCOMFORTABLY.
Answer ⇒ Because you're a teacher

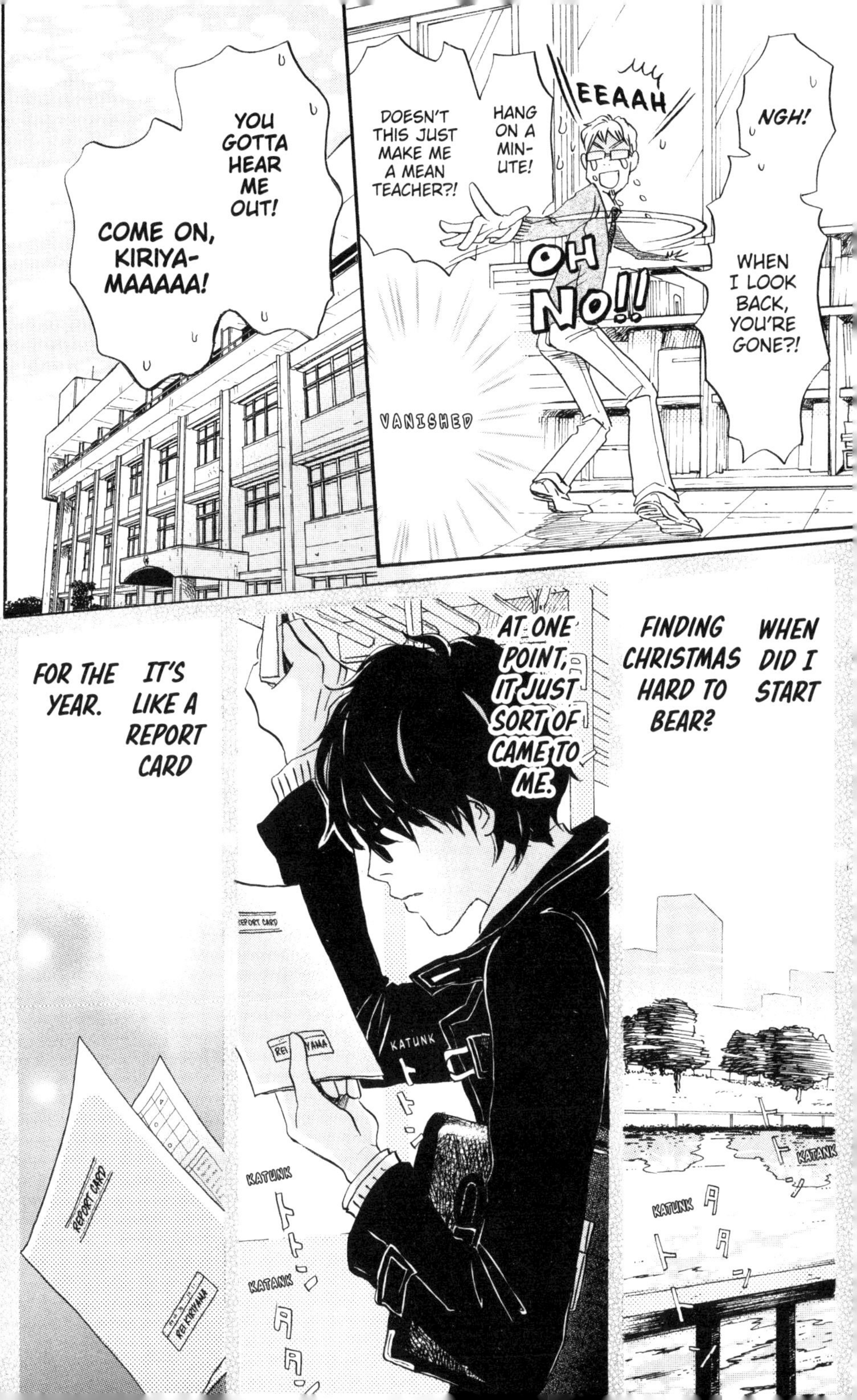
NGH!
WHEN I LOOK BACK, YOU'RE GONE?!
EEAAH
HANG ON A MIN-UTE!
DOESN'T THIS JUST MAKE ME A MEAN TEACHER?!
OH NO!!
VANISHED
YOU GOTTA HEAR ME OUT!
COME ON, KIRIYA-MAAAAA!
WHEN DID I START
FINDING CHRISTMAS HARD TO BEAR?
KATANK
KATUNK
AT ONE POINT, IT JUST SORT OF CAME TO ME.
REPORT CARD
KATUNK
KATUNK
KATANK
IT'S LIKE A REPORT CARD
FOR THE YEAR.
REPORT CARD
REI KIRIYAMA

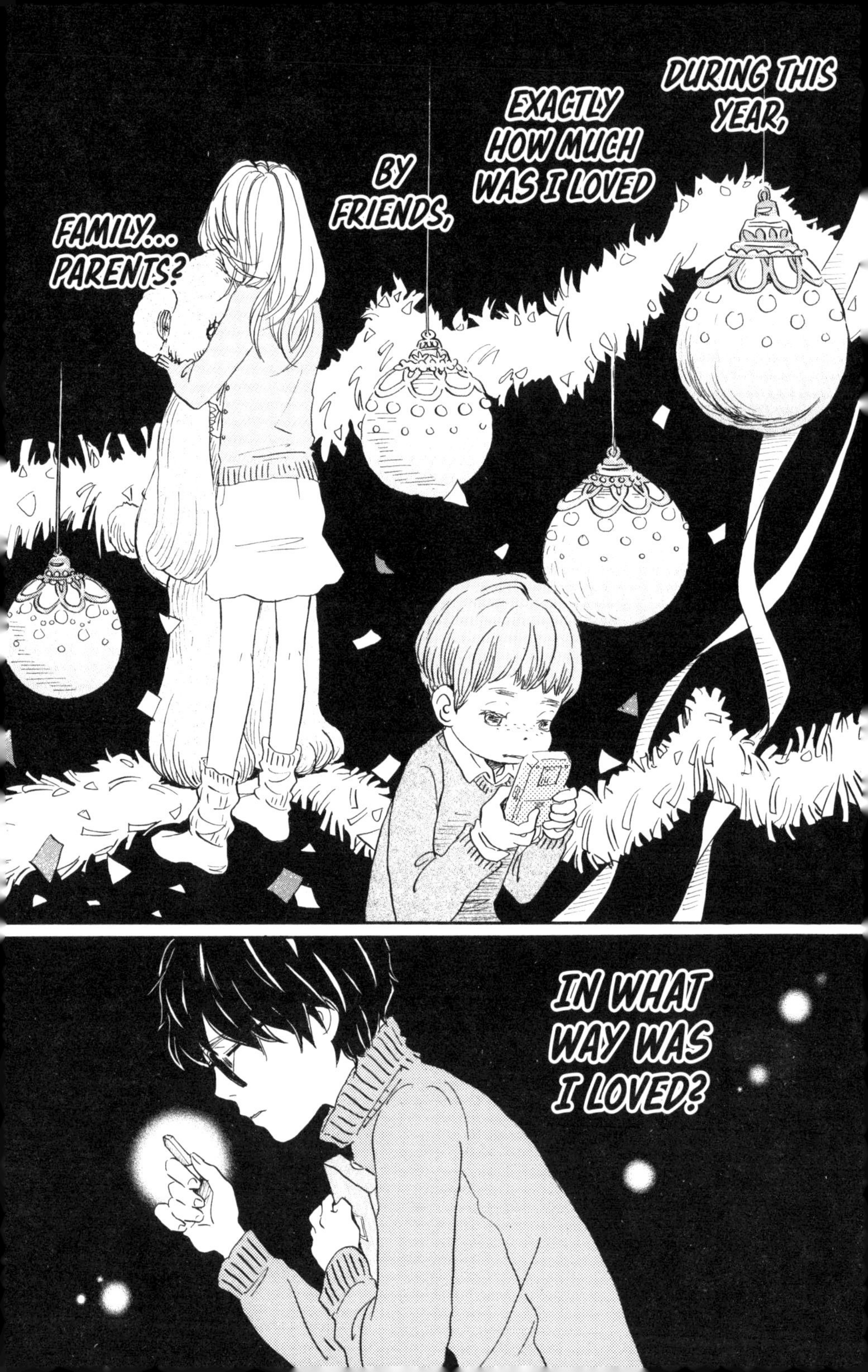
DURING THIS YEAR,
EXACTLY HOW MUCH WAS I LOVED
BY FRIENDS,
FAMILY... PARENTS?
IN WHAT WAY WAS I LOVED?

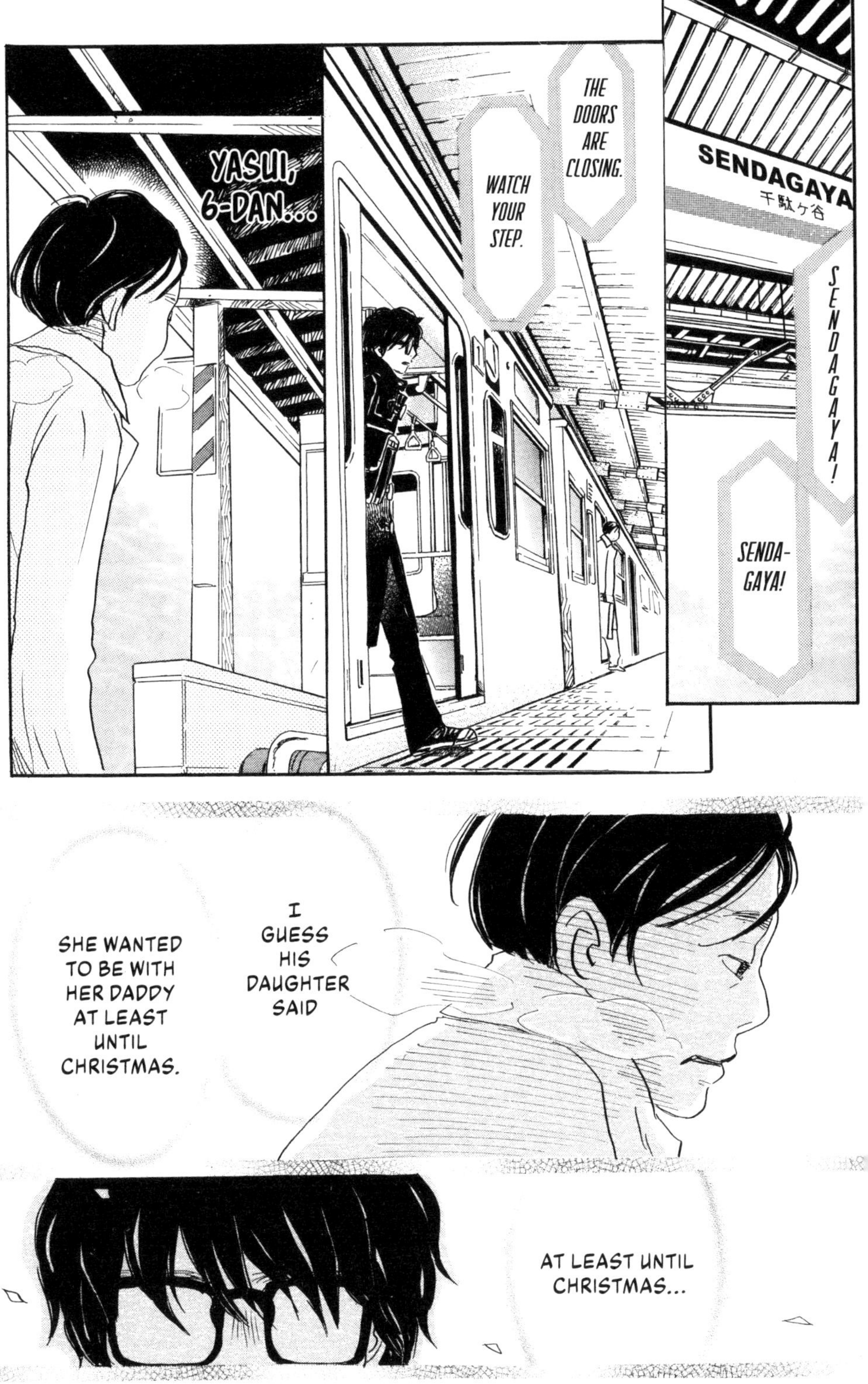
SENDAGAYA
千駄ケ谷
SENDAGAYA!
SENDA-GAYA!
THE DOORS ARE CLOSING.
WATCH YOUR STEP.
YASUI, 6-DAN...
I GUESS HIS DAUGHTER SAID
SHE WANTED TO BE WITH HER DADDY AT LEAST UNTIL CHRISTMAS.
AT LEAST UNTIL CHRISTMAS...

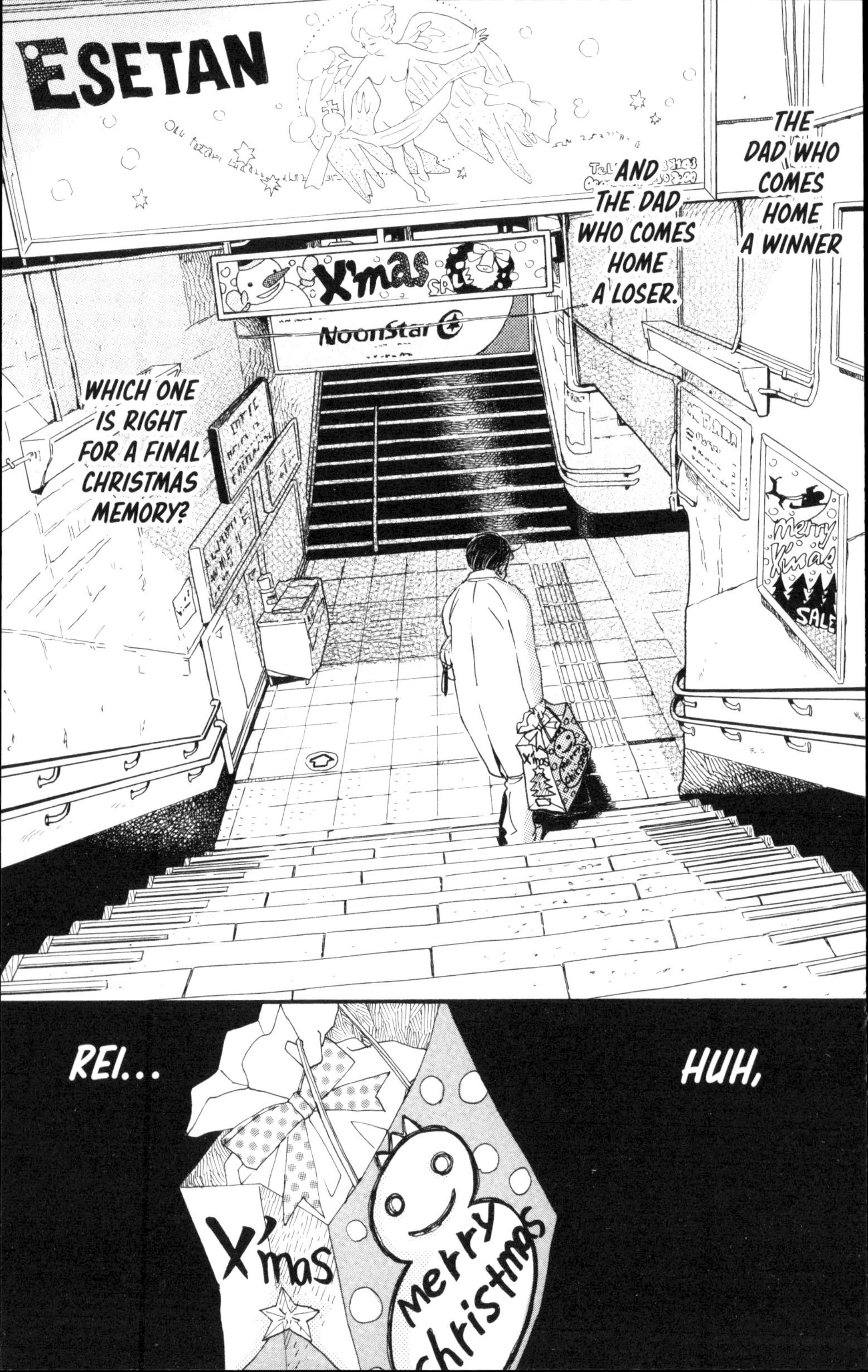
ESETAN
X'mas SALE
NoonStar
THE DAD WHO COMES HOME A WINNER
AND THE DAD WHO COMES HOME A LOSER.
WHICH ONE IS RIGHT FOR A FINAL CHRISTMAS MEMORY?
Merry X'mas SALE
X'mas
HUH,
REI...
X'mas
Merry Christmas

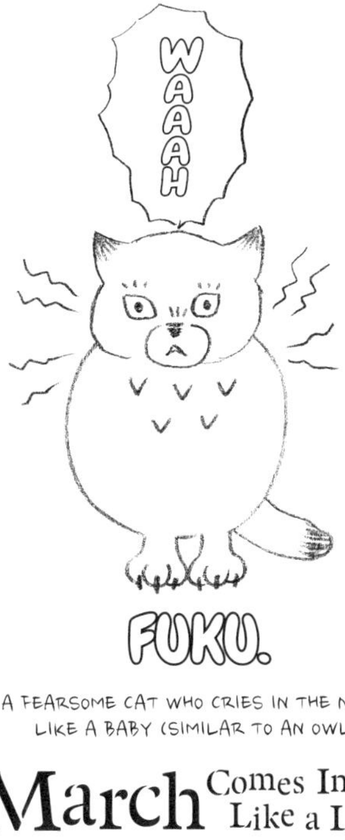
WAAAAH
FUKU.

A FEARSOME CAT WHO CRIES IN THE NIGHT LIKE A BABY (SIMILAR TO AN OWL)

March Comes In Like a Lion

Chapter 21

Something Given (Part 2)

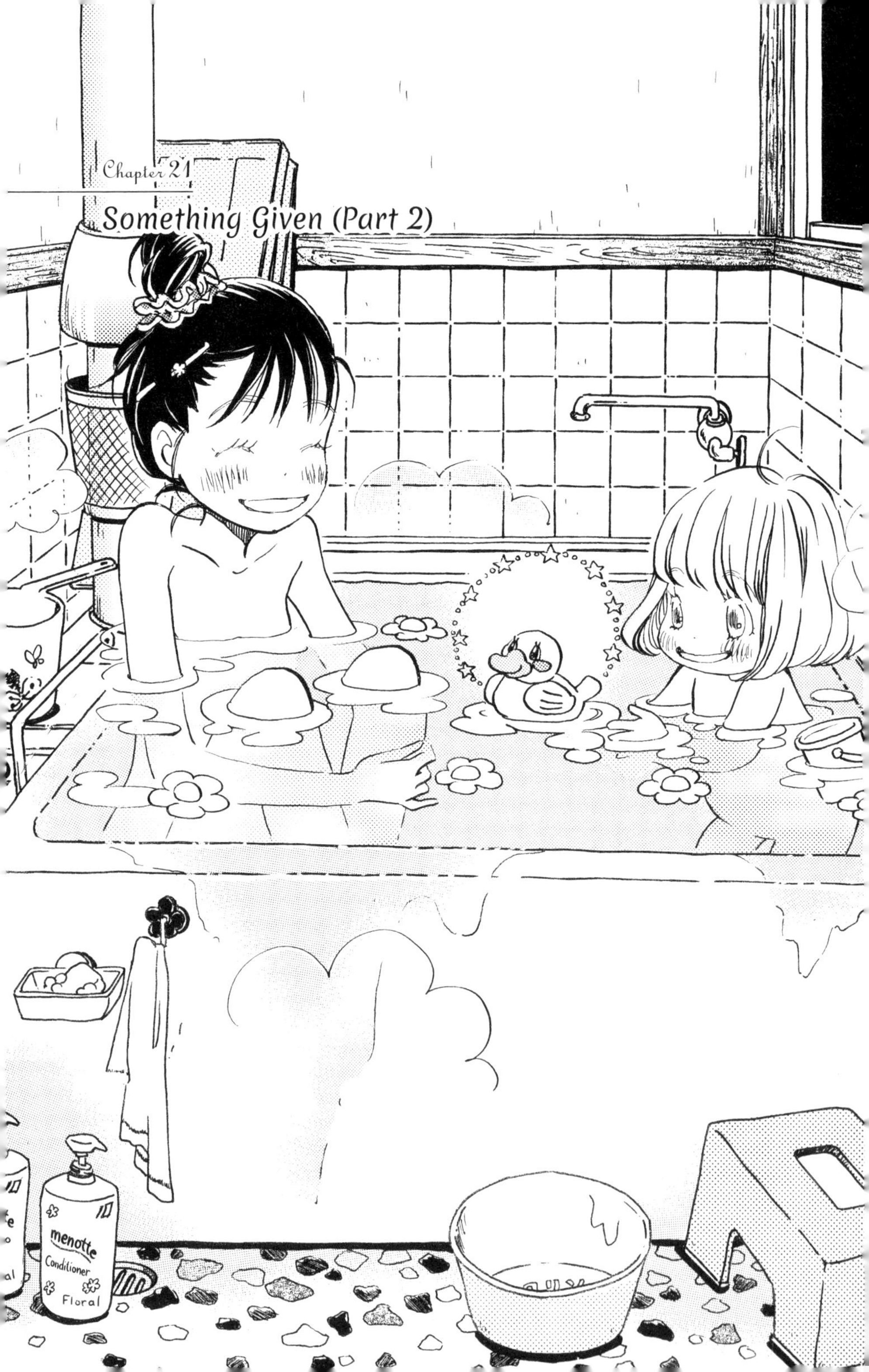
menotte
Conditioner
Floral

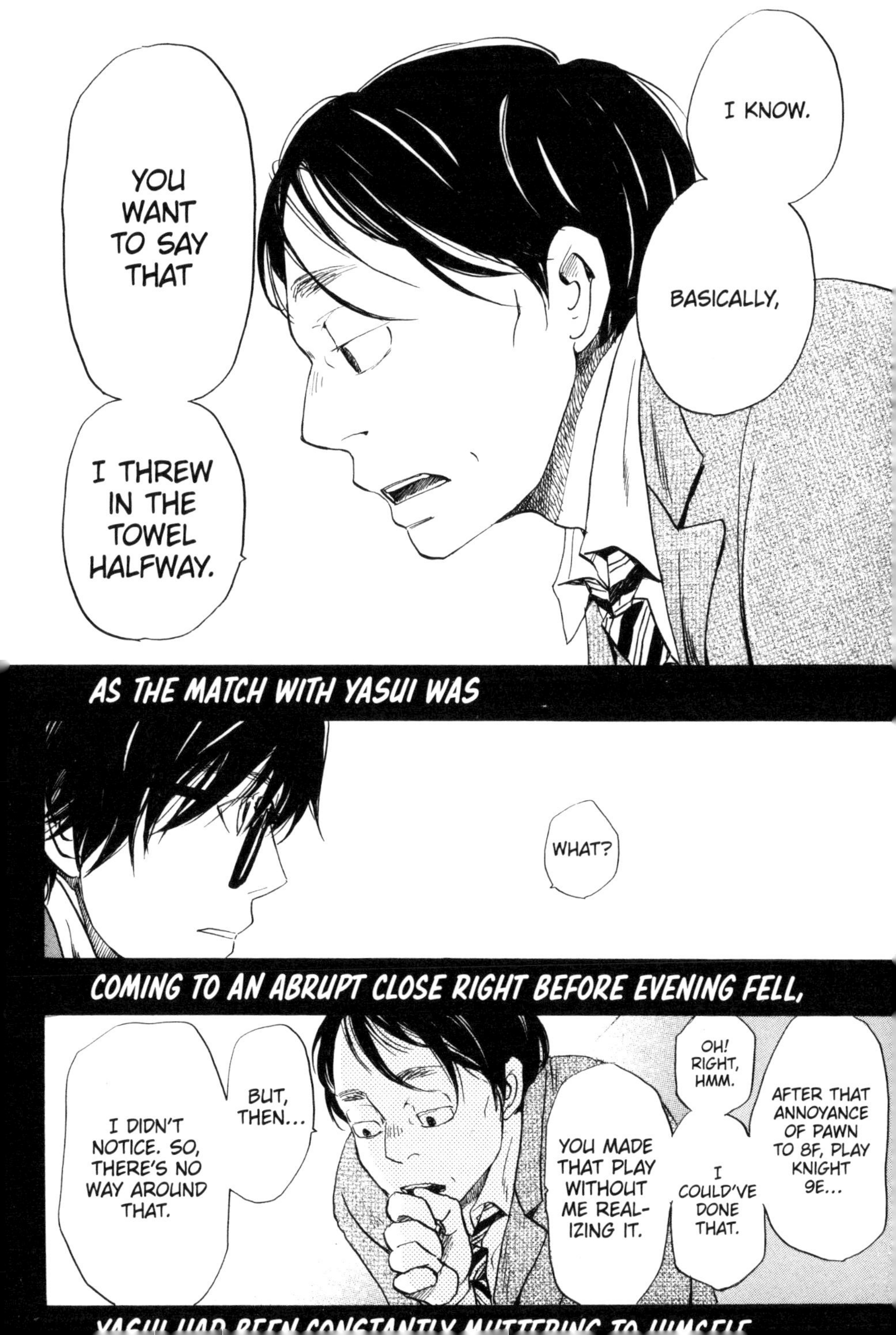
I KNOW.
BASICALLY,
YOU WANT TO SAY THAT
I THREW IN THE TOWEL HALFWAY.
AS THE MATCH WITH YASUI WAS
WHAT?
COMING TO AN ABRUPT CLOSE RIGHT BEFORE EVENING FELL,
AFTER THAT ANNOYANCE OF PAWN TO 8F, PLAY KNIGHT 9E...
OH! RIGHT, HMM.
I COULD'VE DONE THAT.
YOU MADE THAT PLAY WITHOUT ME REAL-IZING IT.
BUT, THEN...
I DIDN'T NOTICE. SO, THERE'S NO WAY AROUND THAT.

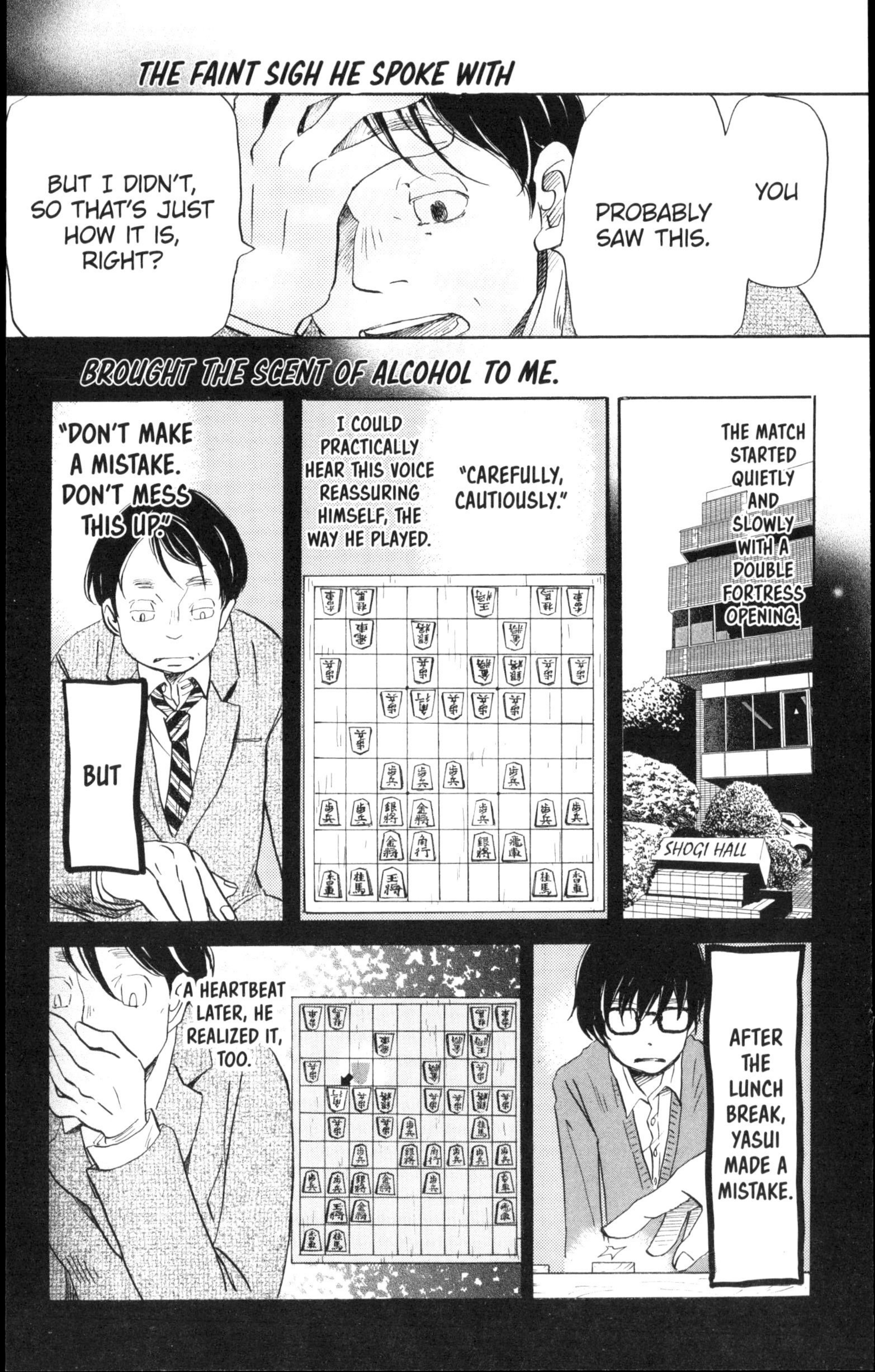
THE FAINT SIGH HE SPOKE WITH
YOU PROBABLY SAW THIS.
BUT I DIDN'T, SO THAT'S JUST HOW IT IS, RIGHT?
BROUGHT THE SCENT OF ALCOHOL TO ME.
THE MATCH STARTED QUIETLY AND SLOWLY WITH A DOUBLE FORTRESS OPENING.
SHOGI HALL
"CAREFULLY, CAUTIOUSLY."
I COULD PRACTICALLY HEAR THIS VOICE REASSURING HIMSELF, THE WAY HE PLAYED.
"DON'T MAKE A MISTAKE. DON'T MESS THIS UP."
BUT
AFTER THE LUNCH BREAK, YASUI MADE A MISTAKE.
A HEARTBEAT LATER, HE REALIZED IT, TOO.

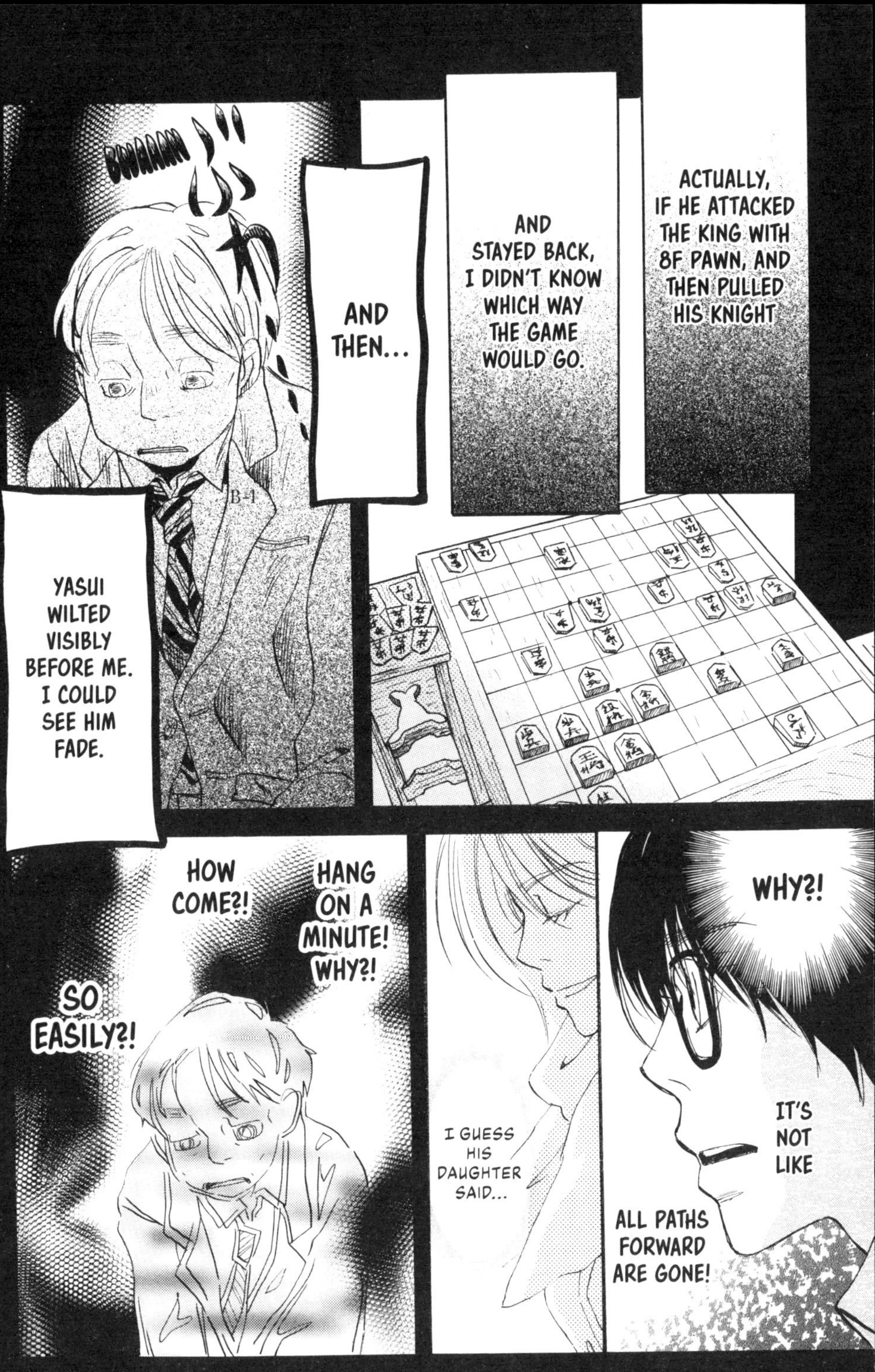
ACTUALLY, IF HE ATTACKED THE KING WITH 8F PAWN, AND THEN PULLED HIS KNIGHT
AND STAYED BACK, I DIDN'T KNOW WHICH WAY THE GAME WOULD GO.
AND THEN...
BWAAAM
YASUI WILTED VISIBLY BEFORE ME. I COULD SEE HIM FADE.
WHY?!
IT'S NOT LIKE
ALL PATHS FORWARD ARE GONE!
I GUESS HIS DAUGHTER SAID...
HANG ON A MINUTE! WHY?!
HOW COME?!
SO EASILY?!

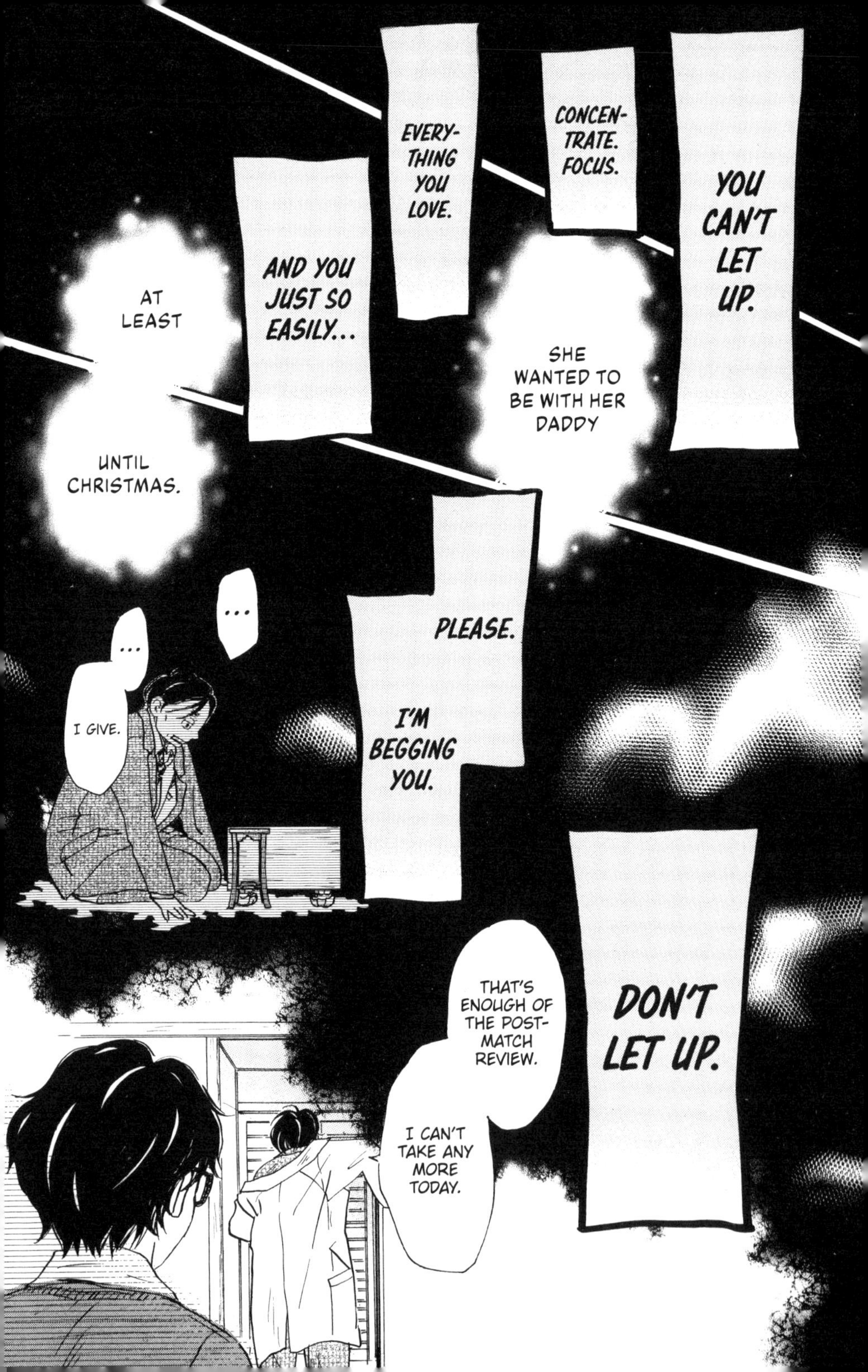
YOU CAN'T LET UP.
CONCEN-TRATE. FOCUS.
EVERY-THING YOU LOVE.
AND YOU JUST SO EASILY...
SHE WANTED TO BE WITH HER DADDY
AT LEAST
UNTIL CHRISTMAS.
PLEASE.
I'M BEGGING YOU.
...
...
I GIVE.
DON'T LET UP.
THAT'S ENOUGH OF THE POST-MATCH REVIEW.
I CAN'T TAKE ANY MORE TODAY.

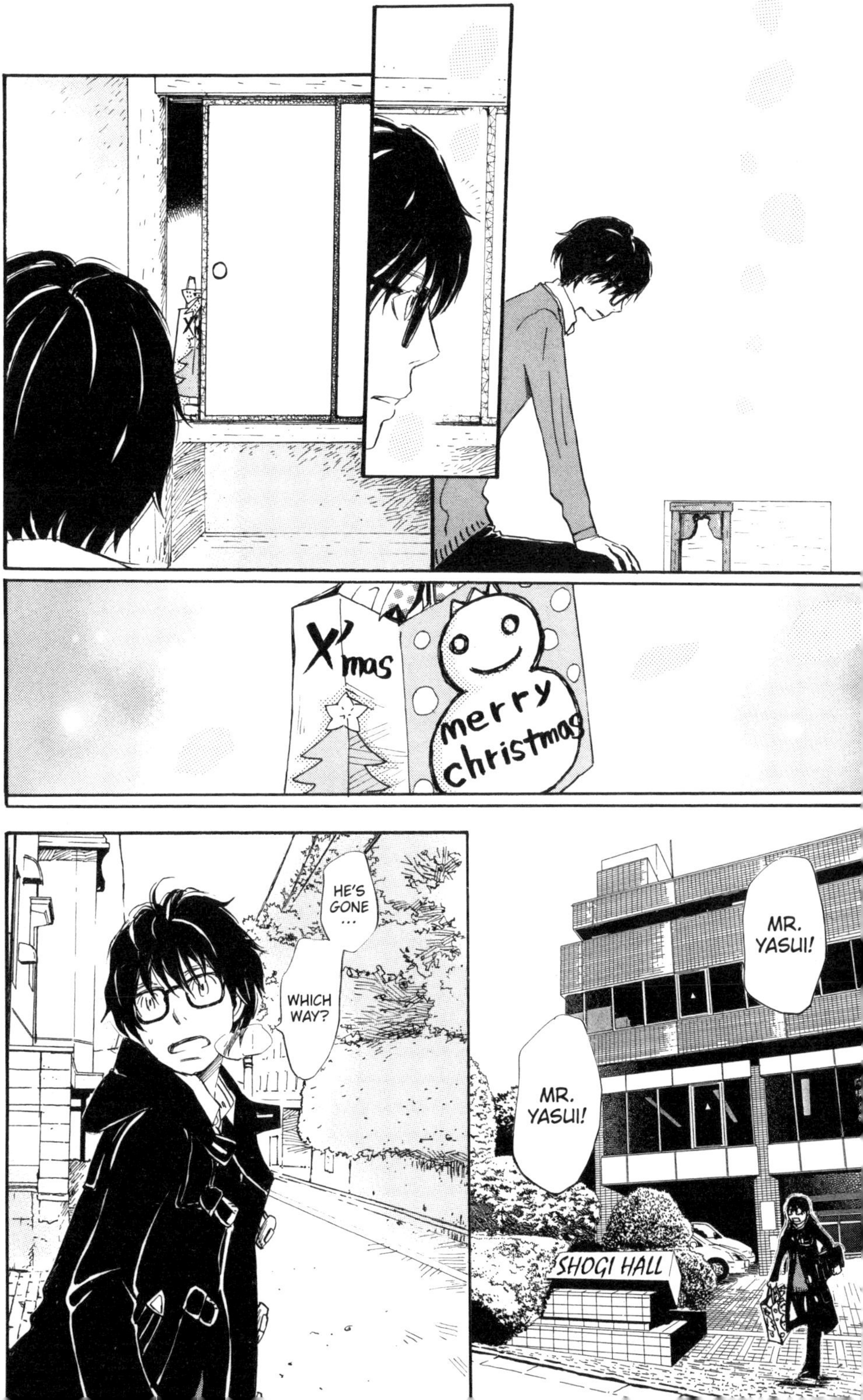
X'mas
merry christmas
MR. YASUI!
MR. YASUI!
SHOGI HALL
HE'S GONE ...
WHICH WAY?

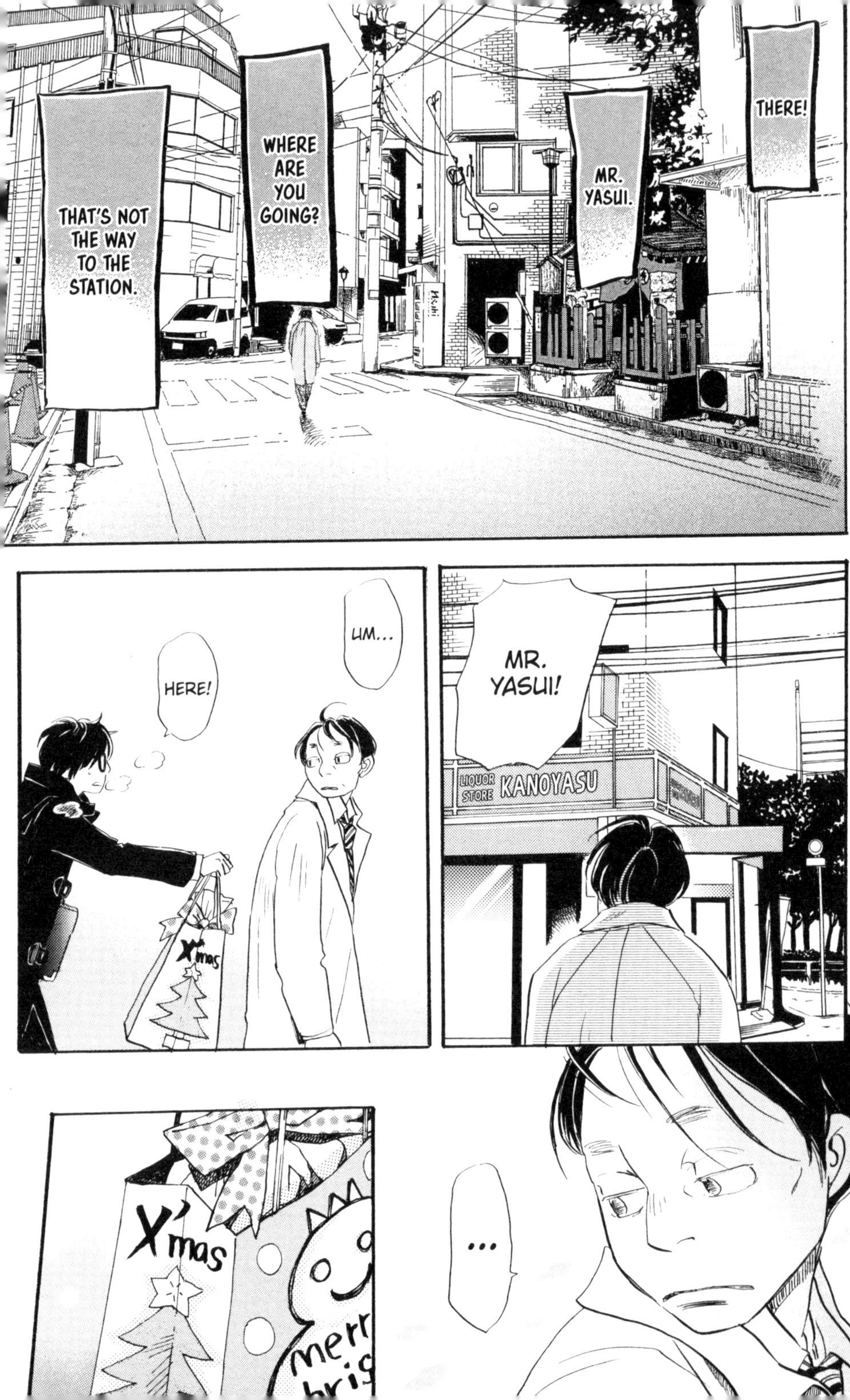
THERE!
MR. YASUI.
WHERE ARE YOU GOING?
THAT'S NOT THE WAY TO THE STATION.
MR. YASUI!
LIQUOR STORE KANOYASU
UM...
HERE!
X'mas
...
X'mas

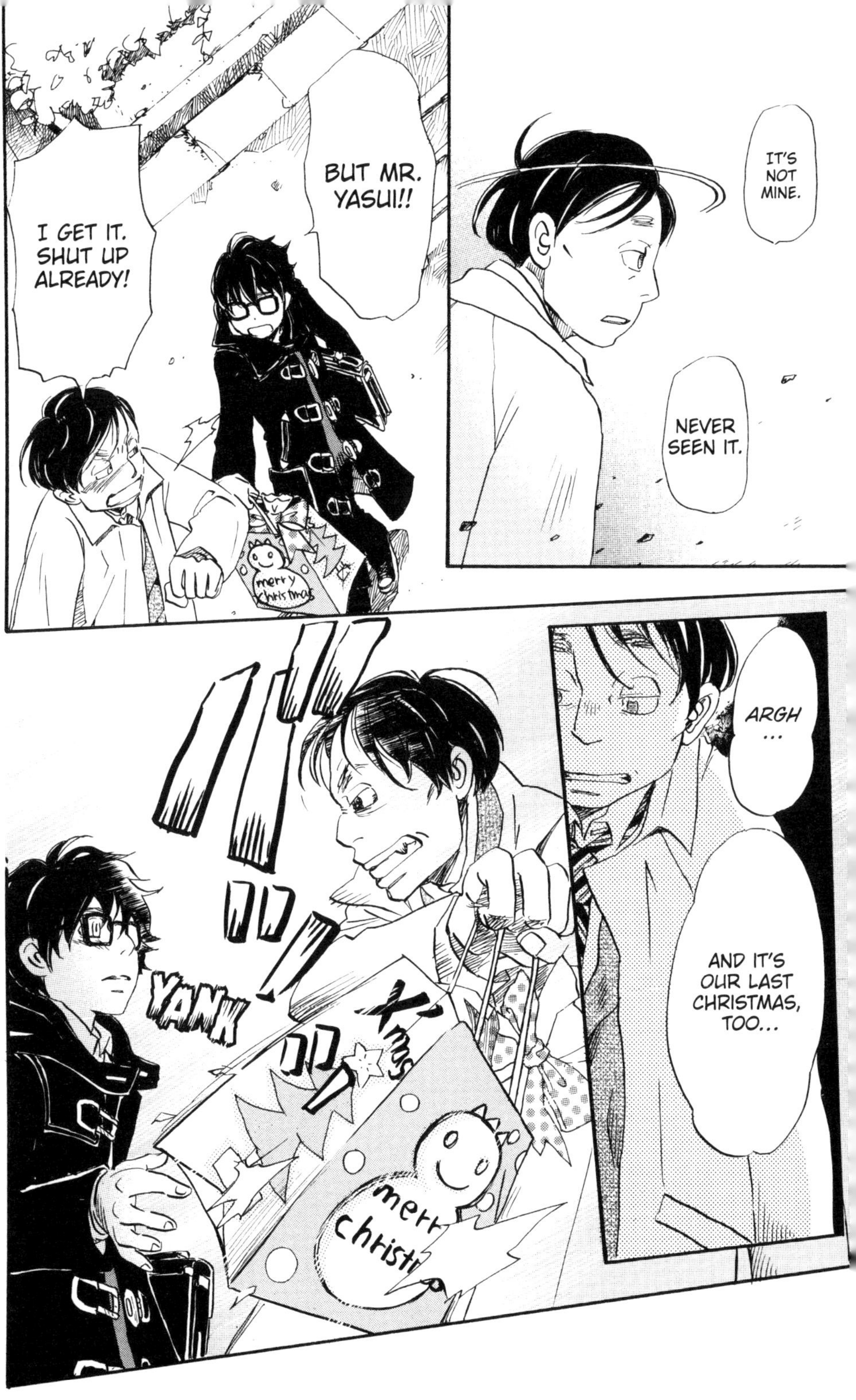
IT'S NOT MINE.
NEVER SEEN IT.
BUT MR. YASUI!!
I GET IT. SHUT UP ALREADY!
merry Christmas
ARGH...
AND IT'S OUR LAST CHRISTMAS, TOO...
YANK

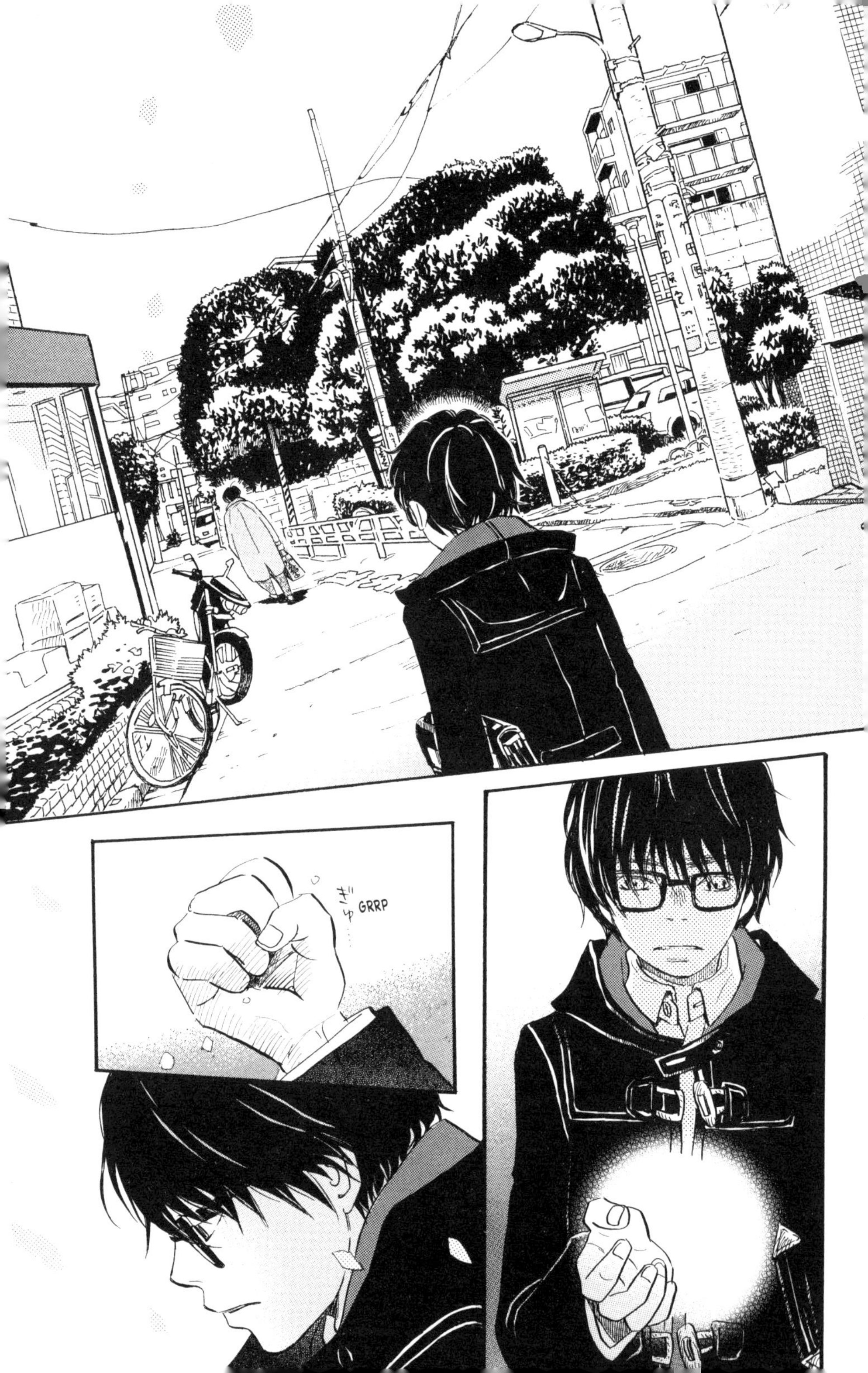
ぎゅ…
GRRP

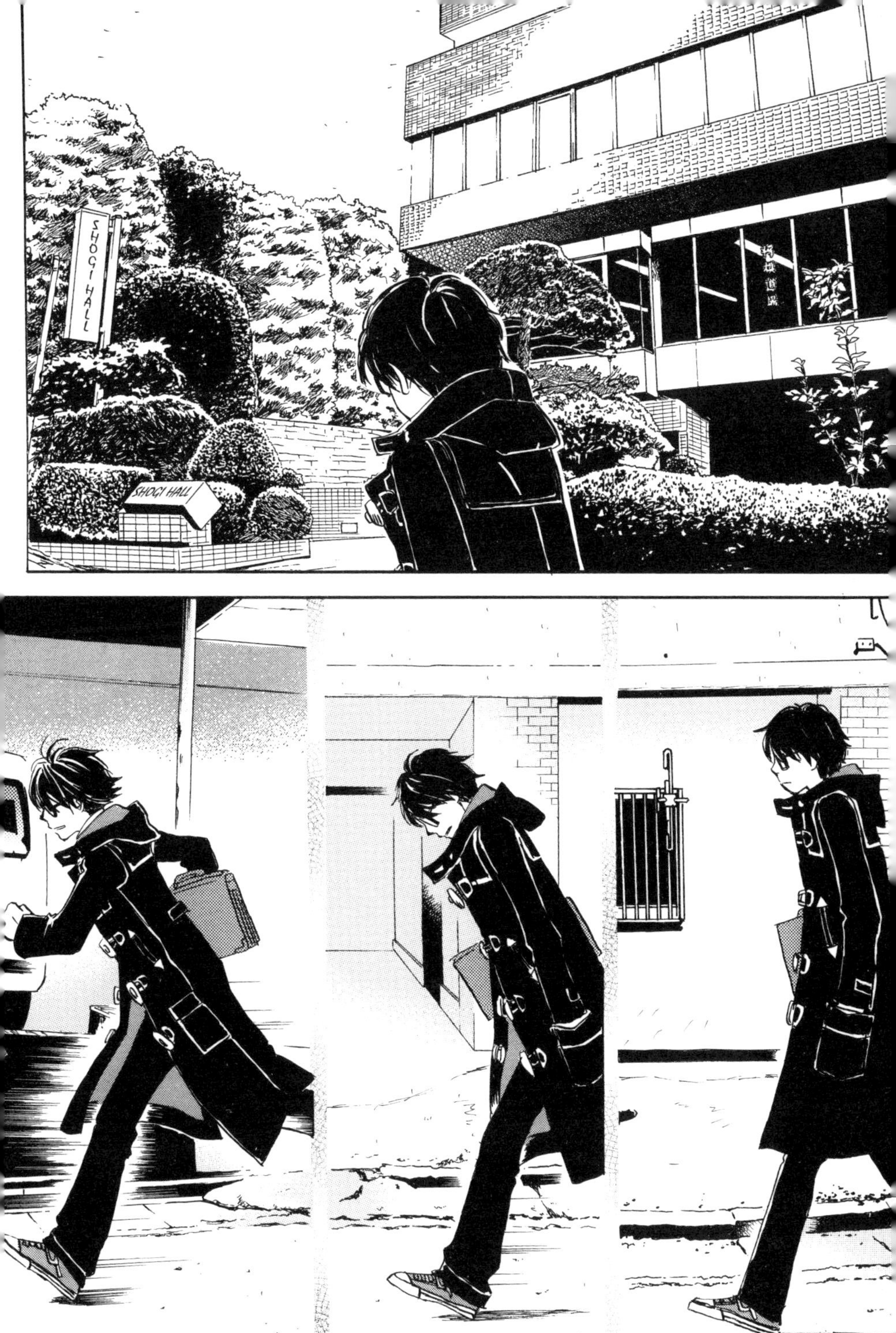
SHOGI HALL
SHOGI HALL

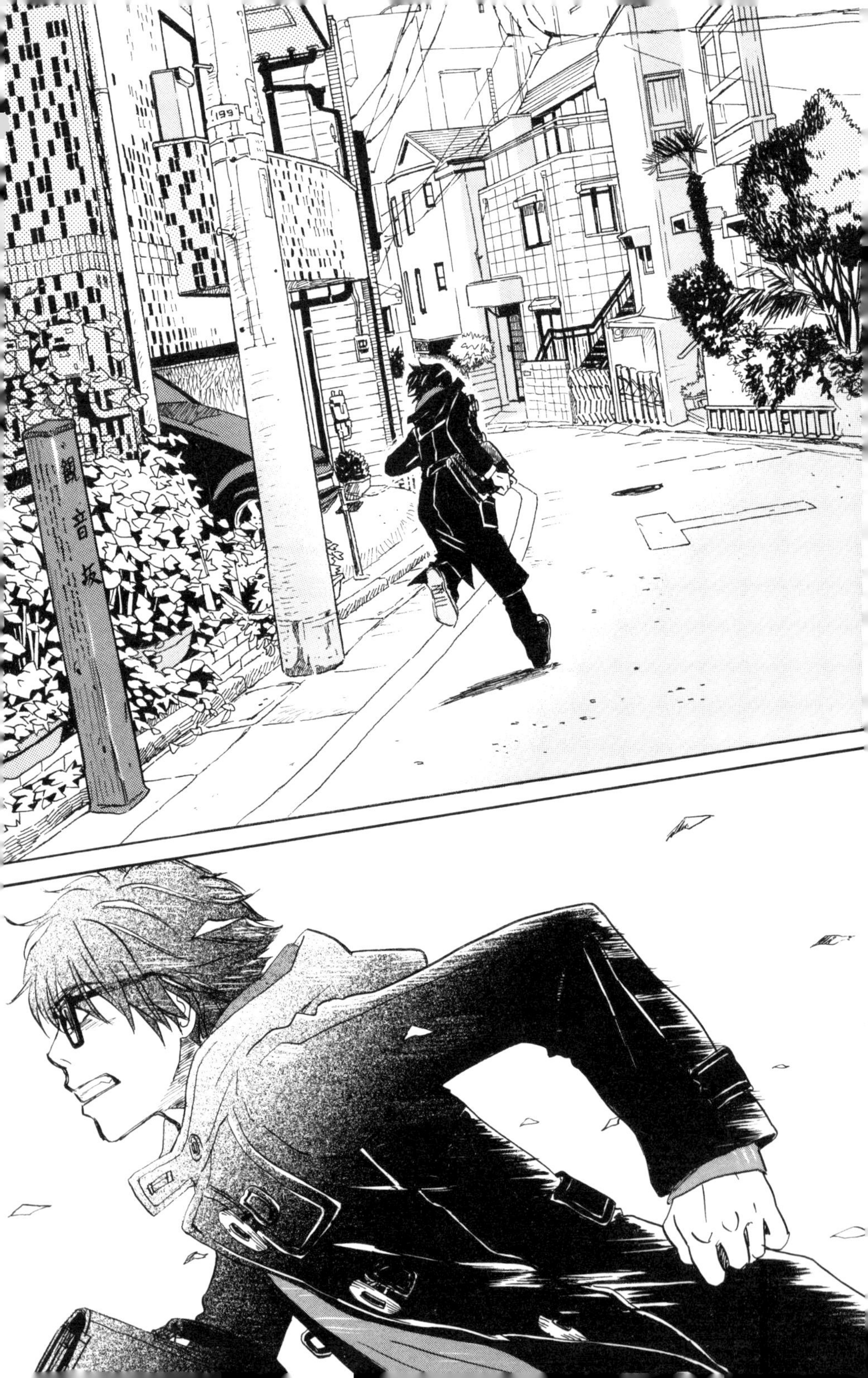
199
観音坂

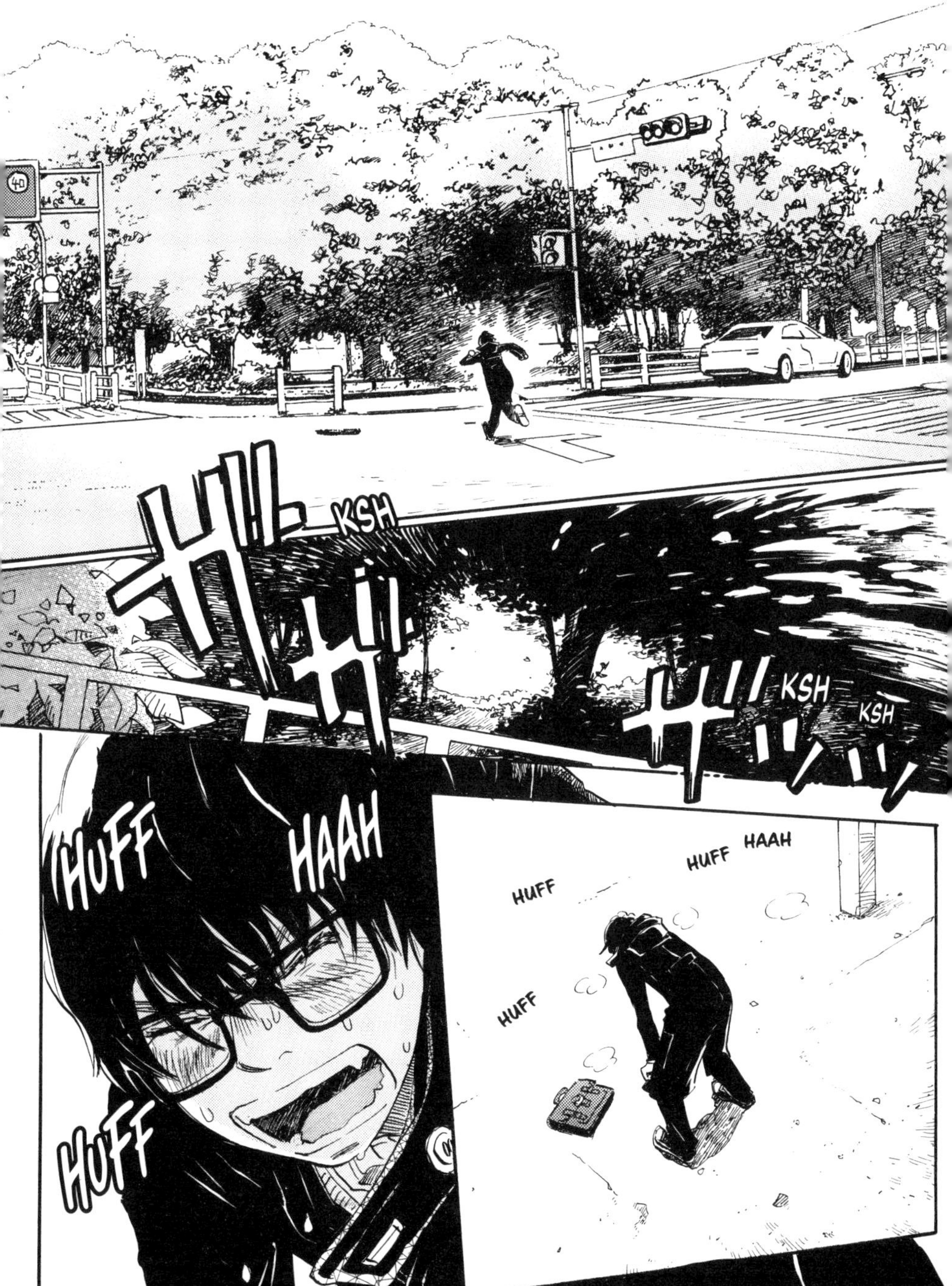
KSH
KSH
KSH
HUFF HAAH
HUFF
HUFF
HAAH
HUFF
HUFF

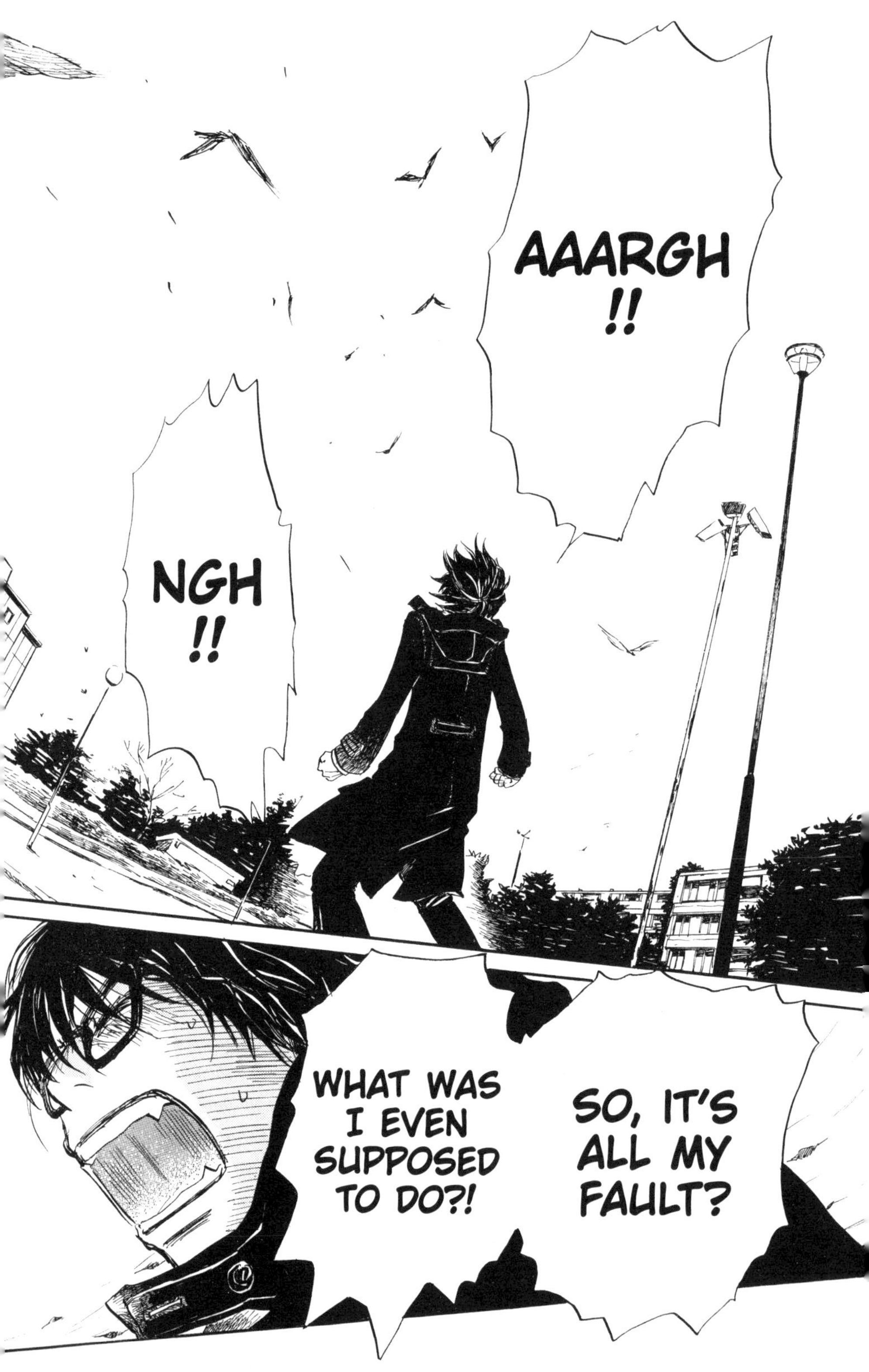
AAARGH!!
NGH!!
SO, IT'S ALL MY FAULT?
WHAT WAS I EVEN SUPPOSED TO DO?!

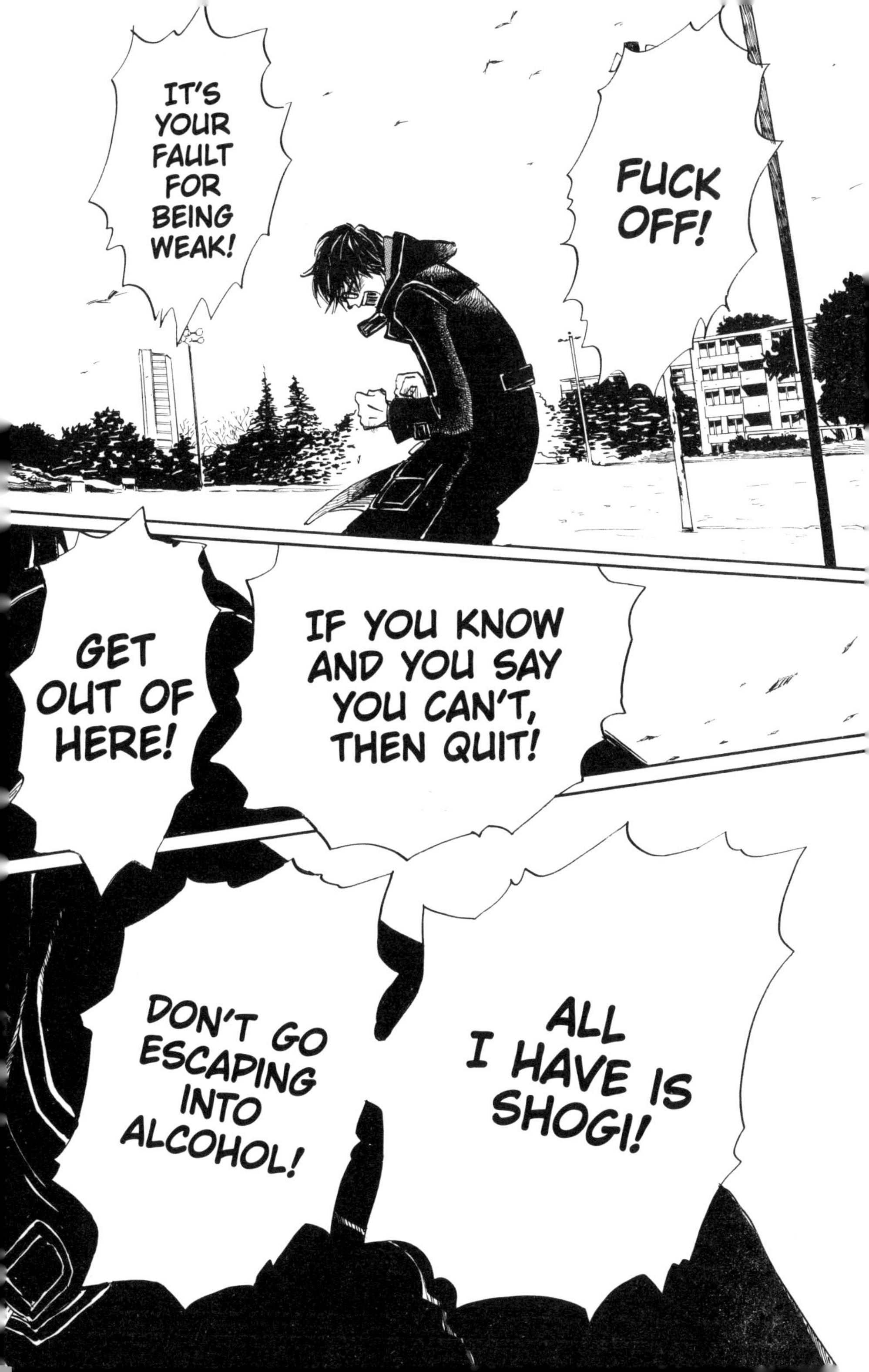
FUCK OFF!
IT'S YOUR FAULT FOR BEING WEAK!
IF YOU KNOW AND YOU SAY YOU CAN'T, THEN QUIT!
GET OUT OF HERE!
ALL I HAVE IS SHOGI!
DON'T GO ESCAPING INTO ALCOHOL!

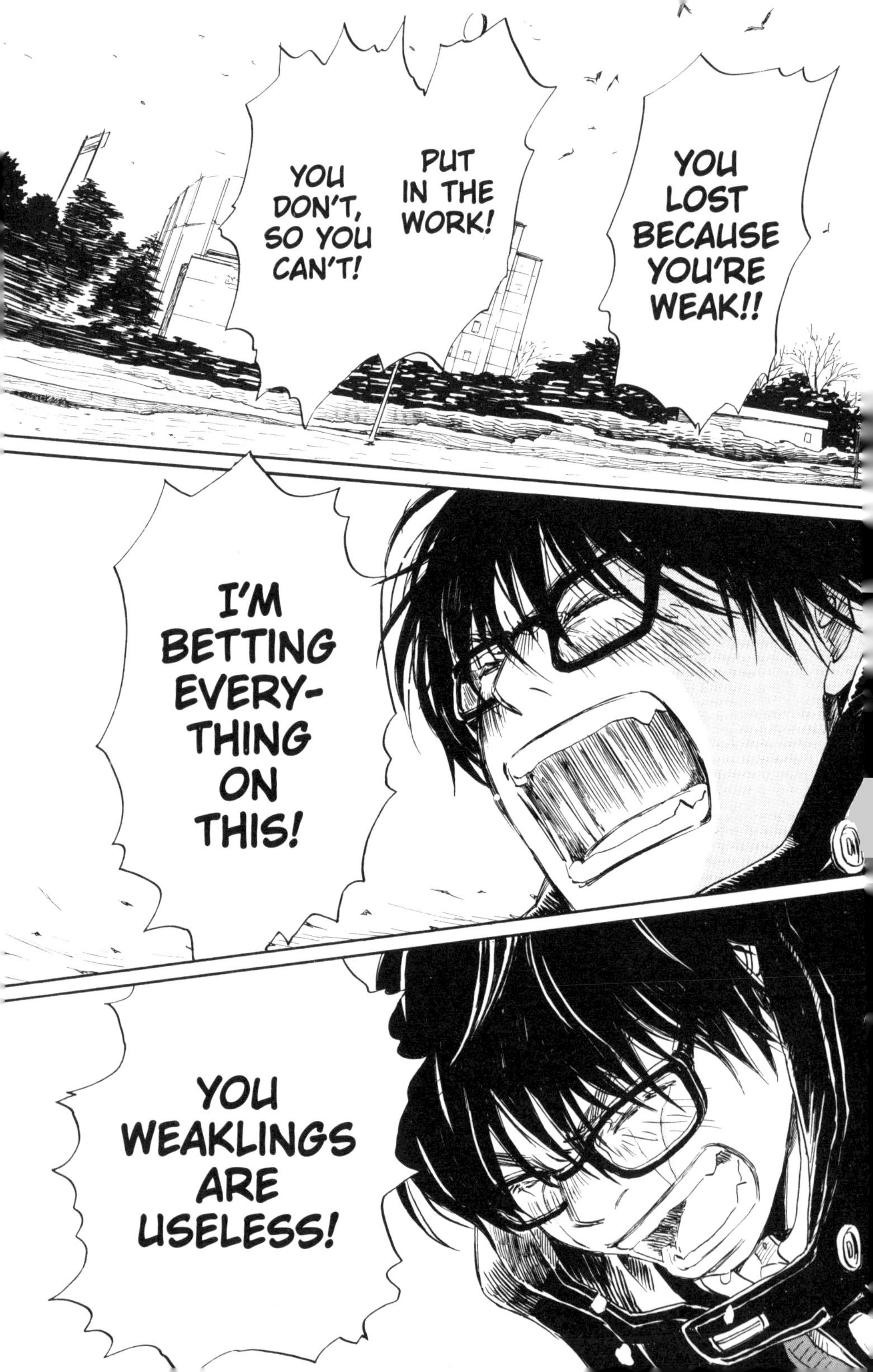
YOU LOST BECAUSE YOU'RE WEAK!!
PUT IN THE WORK!
YOU DON'T, SO YOU CAN'T!
I'M BETTING EVERY-THING ON THIS!
YOU WEAKLINGS ARE USELESS!

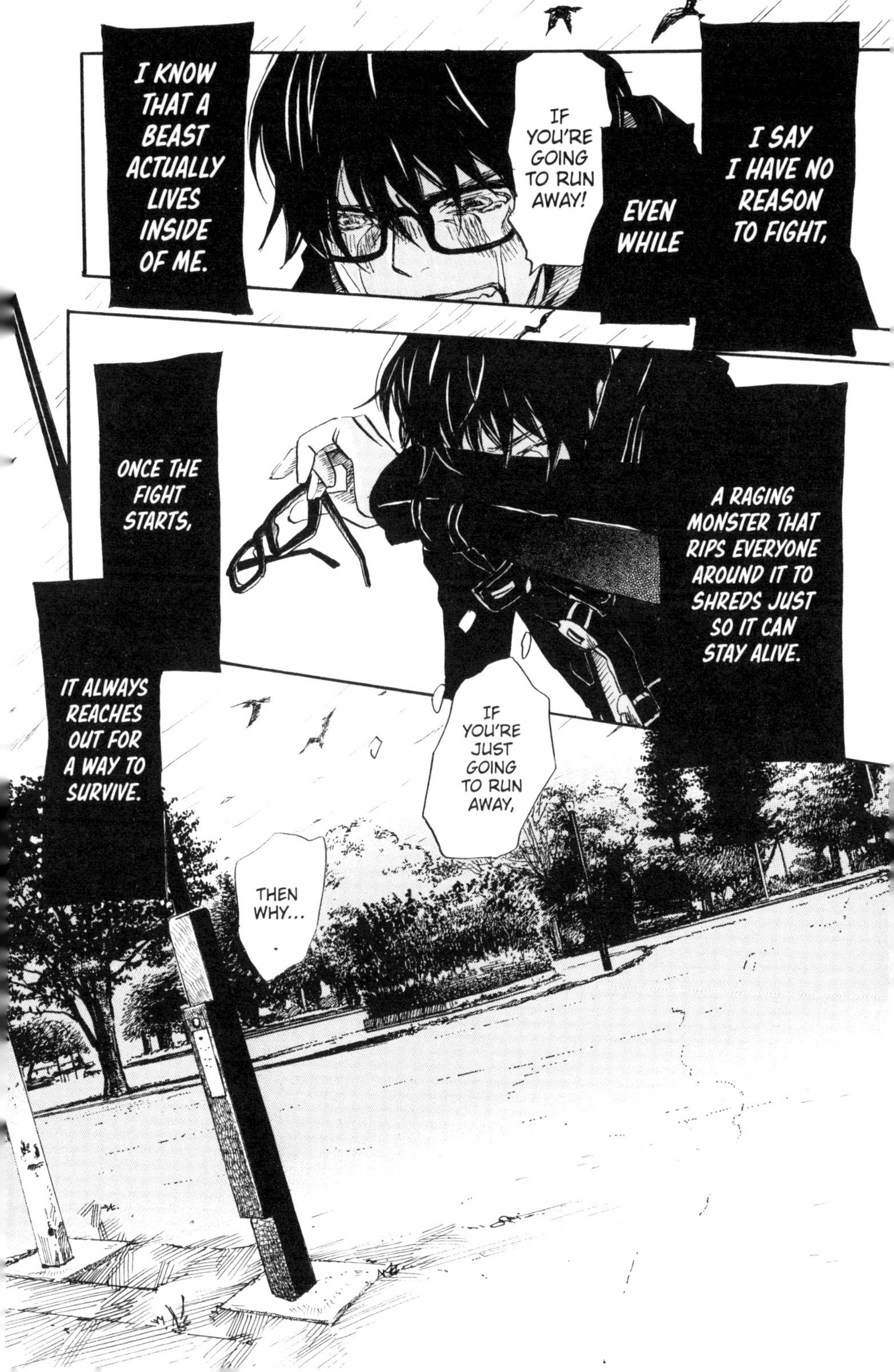
I SAY I HAVE NO REASON TO FIGHT,
EVEN WHILE
IF YOU'RE GOING TO RUN AWAY!
I KNOW THAT A BEAST ACTUALLY LIVES INSIDE OF ME.
A RAGING MONSTER THAT RIPS EVERYONE AROUND IT TO SHREDS JUST SO IT CAN STAY ALIVE.
ONCE THE FIGHT STARTS,
IT ALWAYS REACHES OUT FOR A WAY TO SURVIVE.
IF YOU'RE JUST GOING TO RUN AWAY,
THEN WHY...

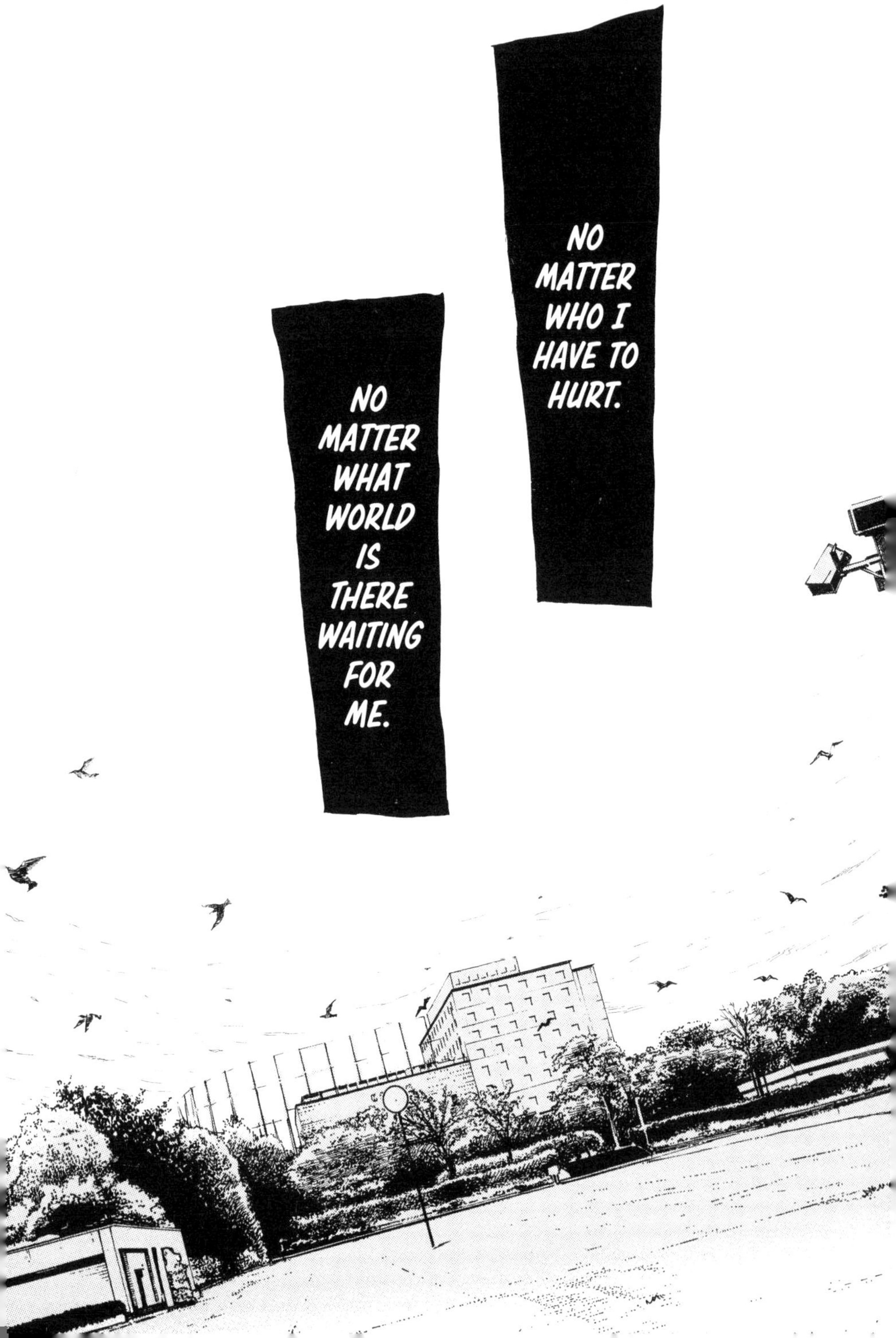
NO MATTER WHO I HAVE TO HURT.
NO MATTER WHAT WORLD IS THERE WAITING FOR ME.

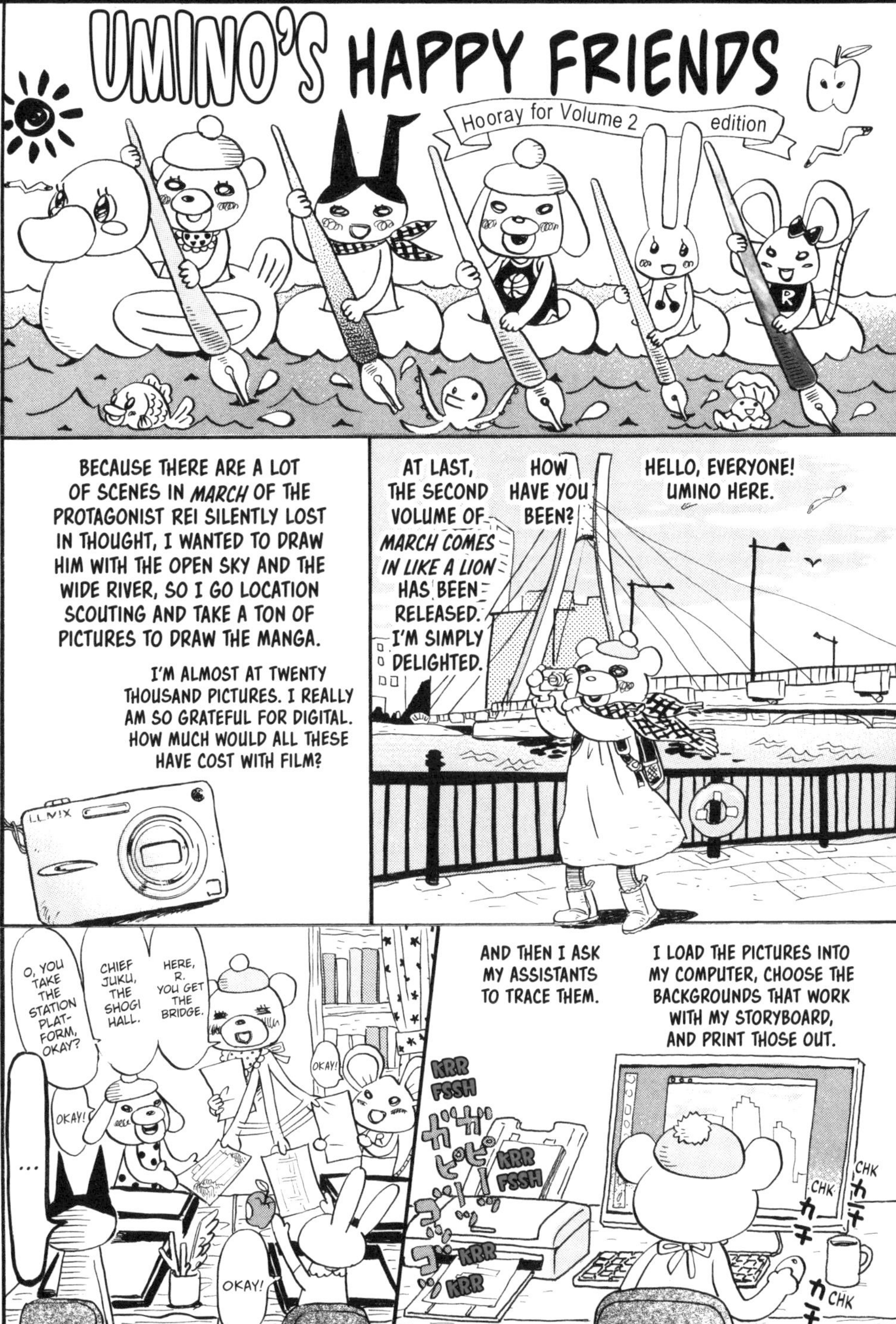
UMINO'S HAPPY FRIENDS
Hooray for Volume 2 edition
HELLO, EVERYONE! UMINO HERE.
HOW HAVE YOU BEEN?
AT LAST, THE SECOND VOLUME OF *MARCH COMES IN LIKE A LION* HAS BEEN RELEASED. I'M SIMPLY DELIGHTED.
BECAUSE THERE ARE A LOT OF SCENES IN *MARCH* OF THE PROTAGONIST REI SILENTLY LOST IN THOUGHT, I WANTED TO DRAW HIM WITH THE OPEN SKY AND THE WIDE RIVER, SO I GO LOCATION SCOUTING AND TAKE A TON OF PICTURES TO DRAW THE MANGA.
I'M ALMOST AT TWENTY THOUSAND PICTURES. I REALLY AM SO GRATEFUL FOR DIGITAL. HOW MUCH WOULD ALL THESE HAVE COST WITH FILM?
I LOAD THE PICTURES INTO MY COMPUTER, CHOOSE THE BACKGROUNDS THAT WORK WITH MY STORYBOARD, AND PRINT THOSE OUT.
CHK
CHK
CHK
KRR FSSH
KRR FSSH
KRR
KRR
AND THEN I ASK MY ASSISTANTS TO TRACE THEM.
HERE, R. YOU GET THE BRIDGE.
CHIEF JUKU, THE SHOGI HALL.
O, YOU TAKE THE STATION PLATFORM, OKAY?
OKAY!
OKAY!
...
OKAY!